ABOUT

Gerard Gleeson was born in Newcastle, Australia in 1964. For the past four years he has lived in Queensland with his wife. He currently works as a nurse. *Stalker* is his first novel.

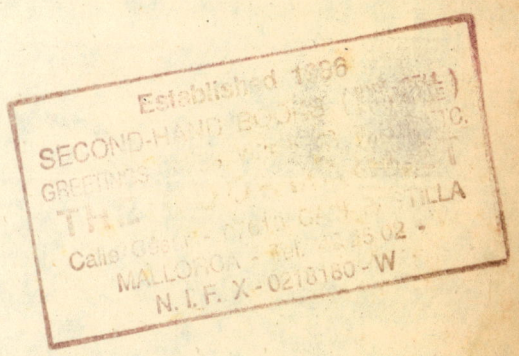

STALKER
GERARD GLEESON

HarperCollins*Publishers*

Dedicated to the memory of Glennis Rae Gleeson.

HarperCollins Publishers

25 Ryde Road, Pymble, Sydney, NSW 2073, Australia
31 View Road, Glenfield, Auckland 10, New Zealand
77–85 Fulham Palace Road, London W6 8JB, United Kingdom

First published in Australia in 1994
Reprinted in 1994 (twice)

Copyright © Gerard Gleeson, 1994

This book is copyright.
Apart from any fair dealing for the purposes of private study,
research, criticism or review, as permitted under the Copyright Act,
no part may be reproduced by any process without written
permission. Inquiries should be addressed to the publishers.

National Library of Australia
Cataloguing-in-Publication data:

Gleeson, Gerard.
 Stalker.
 ISBN 0 7322 5039 0.
 I. Title.

A823.3

Cover design by Darian Causby
Typeset by Midland Typesetters, Victoria
Printed in Australia by McPherson's Printing Group, Maryborough, Victoria

9 8 7 6 5 4 3
97 96 95 94

PROLOGUE

Jason Emery cursed his parents. Why the hell had they insisted on his joining them for their annual sojourn to the Gold Coast when they weren't going to allow him to enjoy any of its alluring night life? He sat and stared over the darkened roofs around him towards the lights of Surfers Paradise, sparkling with the promise of excitement.

The sound of his parents' laughter floated to him on the night breeze and he scowled. They were playing cards again, joined by their neighbours the Hewitts. Bloody cards. How did parents ever get to be so boring? He couldn't imagine any of them having been young, yearning for the start of their adult years as he did, longing for the delights that a place like Surfers promised.

He scrambled down from the wall and dropped with a muffled thud onto the sand below him. The tide was low in the canal and he knew he could follow the line of sand until he reached the jutting spit. From there he could look out across the water to Surfers — it looked as if it were floating, a giant ship ablaze with a thousand lights. If he closed his eyes he imagined he could hear the laughter, the sounds of music drifting across to where he sat as a spectator.

He stumbled on the darkened sand, almost sprawling into the black water before he regained his balance. What the hell was that? His first thought was that he had tripped on a piece of driftwood, left by the departing tide. He turned back, his curiosity aroused by a vague impression of softness, a feeling that there was something not quite right about it.

Jason bent to examine the object, but he couldn't make it out in the dark. He pulled back when his fingers touched warmth, puzzled by the disturbingly familiar texture. Steeling himself, he ventured a closer inspection, lifting the heavy object free of the sand.

His cry of horror was soundless, caught in his throat as if he were in his worst nightmare. He opened his hand and let the object fall with a thud, and his feet pounded the surface of the heavy sand as he fled towards the safety and protection of his parents. He couldn't erase the image of bloodied fingers silhouetted against the faint light from the distant street.

'Shit.' Errol Matthews turned his head. 'Over here.' He squinted as the bright glare of the spotlight swung in his direction. He took a deep, steadying breath, before he looked back at the desecrated remains of a human being. His years on the force were of no use to him in this situation; no training had prepared him for it.

The backyard of the ordinary suburban house was illuminated to a reality harsher than daylight. The gruesome remains were scattered throughout the garden. There had been no real attempt to conceal them.

'Jesus,' he heard the muttered blasphemy behind him. 'This torso's still warm!'

Matthews froze, jolted out of the numbing haze that had settled over his mind.

'All right, men, listen up,' he growled, and the four young constables quickly gathered around him. Matthews kept his voice low, alert to the presence of nearby residents hiding behind the safety of their own four walls. 'This fucker could still be around here somewhere. Bryson, Featherstone, you search this side of the street, Jackson and Elliot the other. Door to door. Keep knocking until it's answered, make sure you go through the houses. Half the street's probably awake by now anyway, so it shouldn't be too difficult. Keep together and watch each other's backs. Anything suspicious, wait for assistance. Got it?'

He glanced in turn at the nervous faces of the young cops, trying to instil some reassurance. 'I'll stay here and wait until the forensic boys arrive.' He wasn't sure which job he would prefer.

'We'd better kill those spots too.' The lights blinked off and darkness rushed in to reclaim the yard.

'And be careful,' he cautioned as the four officers moved away.

Matthews sat on the darkened porch, his own breath loud in his ears. Now he knew which job he would prefer, and it wasn't sitting here keeping a corpse company.

Mary Denyer's sleep had been disturbed by the sounds of the police sirens, and she was vaguely aware they had stopped nearby. The noises troubled her dreams so she tossed and turned restlessly, her house still stuffy from the heat of the day. She dared not leave any windows open, not at this time of the year when the Coast attracted all manner of vagrants to its warmth and tropically opulent atmosphere.

Only last week a house further down the street had been broken into, its contents pillaged. The vandals had made a clean getaway via the canal at the bottom of the garden, the police believing they had used a 'tinny', waiting until they had cleared the end of the canal before starting the boat's motor. God knows it would have been easy enough. Half the houses facing hers across the canal had been vacant for much of the winter, the rental demand not picking up again until the beginning of spring, when the promise of casual work brought the young people flocking.

She half wished she could do what many owners of the vacant houses had done — return to her native Victoria. Like thousands of others, she and her husband Frank had retired to the Gold Coast after years of coming up for holidays. It had seemed the ideal plan, the envy of many of her long-time friends in the bridge club back home. Then Frank had died, damn him, leaving her alone and friendless after only three months in their new canal front home.

She just hadn't been able to make any new friends, it was so hard at her age to get out and about. Frank had been the outgoing one. She missed him so much now. If only she could go back home to her old friends, but pride and lack of finances kept her bound to their 'dream home'. It had become a nightmare. All she had now was her garden, and even then she had to be inside by four to escape the marauding bites of the tiny midges. No, Surfers Paradise hadn't turned out to be paradise at all. Not for her, not for Frank.

The nights were the worst time.

Mary sighed. She wasn't going to get back to sleep unaided, she just knew it. She shrugged into her dressing gown from force of habit — at least the warmth was kind to her arthritis, unlike the crippling cold down home. She allowed herself a tired smile. There were some advantages to living here.

She turned her head sharply in the direction of the laundry, heart racing. She was certain she had heard a noise coming from the darkness there. She had always been worried about that laundry door with the window right beside it, but Frank had assured her that its concealed entry would fool any prospective thief. Besides, it faced the street, and she knew the main danger was from the direction of the canals. It was probably nothing. She was always imagining noises in the big empty house. She'd learnt to ignore them. Almost.

1.30 am. God, was that all? She couldn't possibly

start her day at this hour. They were long and empty enough as it was. A mogadon would do the trick she decided, reaching up to the top of the fridge.

A blur of movement jagged in the corner of her eye. Pill bottles crashed to the floor as she turned.

'No, oh God, no …' The scream never reached her lips as flashing, razor-sharp metal made contact with human flesh.

'I've had just about enough of this,' Barry Jackson complained. 'It's getting on for 2.30, the bastard must be miles away by now. Let's go back.'

'We'll just finish doing this side of this street, there's only a couple of houses to go. Then we can go back and report to Matthews.'

Jackson knocked heavily on the door of the second last house in the street.

'Sure is quiet around here.' He surveyed the neat street scene of manicured lawns and graceful poincianas, many of the houses hidden behind tall brick fences. 'Not exactly your high-crime area,' he commented, repeating the heavy knock on the door.

'We're giving ourselves a great name tonight, waking people up at this hour. Undoes all that PR work pretty quickly,' Elliot commented wryly.

'Doesn't worry me. We're awake, aren't we?' Jackson shrugged. Elliot rolled his eyes in the darkness.

'Come on, answer the door,' Jackson said impatiently.

'You reckon there's anyone home?'

'Who knows? Let's take a look.' He walked to the

nearest window, looking into what appeared to be a kitchen. He flicked on the powerful beam of the flashlight.

'Jesus.' Jackson swallowed hard against a wave of nausea, turning away from the window and pressing his back against the cold bricks. 'We've got another one.'

Blood was everywhere, coating the tiled kitchen floor thickly and already turning black. The police found pieces of the victim's body scattered throughout the house, marks on the walls indicating that the murderer had thrown them into rooms at random.

'We're dealing with some kind of fucking animal,' Errol Matthews said quietly, shaking his head. 'God, it never gets any easier.'

He put a comforting hand on Barry Jackson's shoulder. 'Listen, why don't you go outside and cordon off the yard? We don't want anyone walking in and trampling any possible clues.' Jackson nodded gratefully, relieved to get out of the house.

'Look out, here comes Hughes,' Elliot called from beside the window.

'Shit!' Matthews muttered. 'Just what we all needed.'

Detective Sergeant Warren Hughes did not appreciate being dragged out of his bed in the middle of the night for anything. He screwed up his nose as he entered the brightly lit house, the stench of blood and death not agreeing with the pizza he had eaten hours before as a late-night snack. He looked as though he had just woken up, as he wore a stained T-shirt tucked loosely into a too-small pair of trousers, the first things he had grabbed out of the wardrobe. He hadn't bothered to brush his hair.

'All right, what's going on here?' he demanded loudly, stepping quickly past the kitchen and into the relatively undisturbed lounge area.

'Looks like a murder, sir,' Elliot said from the doorway.

Hughes rounded on him, fixing him with a cold stare. He wasn't sure if the young uniform was being over-smart or just dumb. Probably dumb, Hughes decided.

'You in charge here?'

'No, sir,' Elliot said. 'He is.' He pointed over Hughes's shoulder and Hughes turned to follow the direction of his finger.

'Hughes,' Errol Matthews nodded.

'That's *Sergeant* Hughes. *Detective Sergeant* Hughes, and don't you forget it. Matthews.' Hughes's mood was not improved by the sight of Errol Matthews.

'Right, I'll take over now. What have you got?'

Matthews filled him in briefly, too much the professional to allow any feelings of personal animosity to interfere with his job.

'Why wasn't I called out earlier?' Hughes exploded.

'I radioed in as soon as we discovered the first body,' Matthews said quietly, keeping the anger out of his voice. 'When I called back half an hour later they said they still couldn't raise you, sir.'

'Oh. Well, I still should have been notified earlier. You might already have missed something vital.'

'Yes, sir,' Matthews agreed, tight-lipped.

'You'd better call for forensics, too,' Hughes said, surveying the mess with distaste.

'They're already around at the other scene,' said Matthews.

'On whose authority?' Hughes demanded.

'On mine, sir. Since I was the ranking officer and they were having difficulty getting onto you, I took it upon myself.'

'Right. Come through here with me, Matthews.' Hughes stepped outside, indicating with a fat finger that Matthews should follow him.

'Now listen to me, Constable,' he said.

'That's Senior Constable,' Matthews replied.

Hughes reddened.

'I couldn't give a fuck what your rank is, Matthews, do not, I repeat *do not* attempt to make me look like a fool. May I remind you that you are no longer in that poor excuse for a police force down south, and that up here I outrank you. Clear?

'Now, I know all about your little escapades down there. I've heard about the little games you played and I will have you know that I will not tolerate it. Got it, Mr Big Shot? Up here we follow procedures, we do things by the book. You've been on the job up here long enough to know that. Right? So just cut it with the smart-arsed shit and do your job.'

Matthews stared coldly into the perspiring face of his senior officer, barely controlling the anger that boiled inside him. This fat fuck wasn't a cop's bootlace. God only knew how he had managed to scramble his way to the position he held, but he'd be willing to bet it hadn't been earned by merit.

'Is that all, sir?'

'I'm warning you, Matthews,' Hughes cautioned. 'Don't cross me. Now, get your uniformed boys out of this house and let us get on with the real work before you fuck up any more clues.'

Errol Matthews was white-lipped with fury when he re-entered the house.

'Right, Elliot, Bryson, Featherstone — outside. Sergeant Hughes is concerned that we may be interfering with evidence in here.'

Elliot caught the look in Matthews's eye and made no comment.

'Arsehole,' he muttered once he was outside the door. Unless the murderer virtually gave himself up, he figured there was little chance of Hughes ever catching him.

It was after five in the morning and the first rays of dawn were streaking the sky with pink before Detective Sergeant Hughes allowed the five uniformed officers to leave the scene. None of them was particularly happy about standing idly by while the trail grew cold.

CHAPTER 1

Mervyn Breene exhaled loudly, blew out a lungful of stale air and replaced it with a lungful of bitter smoke. He felt restless, trapped within the confines of his small car as he had been for the past twelve hours, his thigh muscles jiggling with agitation.

He wound the window down and crisp morning air rushed in, chasing the cobwebs from his weary mind. So this was it, the fabulous Queensland Gold Coast. His gaze flicked idly over the myriad tall buildings that surrounded him, his curiosity dulled by the long overnight trip from his Rushcutters Bay home in Sydney. The traffic was already thick, although it flowed much more smoothly than the traffic in Sydney.

He was relieved to be out of that rat race, even if his respite was only a brief one. Irritated, he pushed thoughts of Sydney aside. It was the first day of a three-week holiday and already he was thinking about having to go back.

'Loosen up, Breene,' he cautioned himself. He

fumbled for another cigarette and lit it from the end of the butt in his mouth before he flicked it out the window and replaced it with the fresh one. His chest wheezed in protest and he frowned. Bloody cigarettes. They had become more than a prop and he hated the thought of being dependent on anything, especially something as destructive as cigarettes.

Not that they were the only destructive element in his life. He struggled under the weight of more than enough for one man, his job as a senior detective not the least of his burdens. Add alcohol, a less-than-satisfactory love life, not enough exercise and a shit load of stress and dissatisfaction, and that about summed it up.

He smiled sourly. All this was a bit too heavily weighted towards self-pity, a habit he could do without.

His attention was caught by the imposing bulk of a large sandstone coloured building shaped like a multi-tiered pyramid complete with a large moat-like lake and lush green gardens, the sign on the top proclaiming it as the Hotel Conrad, home of the famous Jupiter's Casino. He stored that away for future reference, somewhere to blow his holiday pay if nothing more substantial presented itself.

That line of thinking drew him irresistibly towards Sylvia. The thought that she was living up here had lurked in the back of his mind for much of the long night, though he would have preferred to deny it. What was it, six months since they had split up? It must have been at least three since he had even heard from her or made the effort of calling her himself.

Not that calling her would have done him any good, she probably didn't want to hear from him anyway.

The thought really did leave a sour taste in his mouth. Maybe, just maybe, he would get around to calling her while he was up here. For old times' sake.

Shit! He jumped at the sudden blaring of a horn close beside him. He had allowed the Fiat to drift across into the next lane, weariness and lack of attention dulling his reflexes. He returned the one-fingered salute to the irate BMW driver who pulled alongside him briefly, and turned his head, cutting off the stream of abuse directed at him by winding up his window. It was about time he got off the road, at least until the rush-hour traffic had exhausted its frenzy.

He pulled over and got out of the car, his bare feet enjoying the sensation of the sun-warmed bitumen. He stretched to his full height of six feet and ran his hands through his ruffled hair, aware as always of the ravages time was inflicting on his hairline. He grinned to himself, for once not caring about this, the smile smoothing away many of the fine lines on his careworn face. The sun's heat was already sufficiently intense to prickle at him through his light track pants and long-sleeved cotton shirt, its tail flapping in the wind, and he felt slightly out of place in his warm clothes. Even at this advanced stage of spring Sydney provided no competition for the tropical warmth of south-east Queensland. It had been damned cold when he left home last night.

He walked barefoot around to the side of the road where a green, grass-covered bank sloped gently down to the river. He sucked the warm air greedily into his lungs in a vain attempt to dispel the abuse of the long night as he surveyed the mansions across the expanse of water. Now, this was beautiful. There were even a couple of palm trees, their branches swaying gently in the slight breeze. Breene sank gratefully down onto the grass and rested his back against one, taking advantage of its coarse bark to stimulate his tired muscles.

That was better. He closed his eyes and drifted, allowed his mind to catch up with the twelve hundred or so kilometres that separated him from the pressures of his everyday life. None of that mattered now, not up here, not for the next three weeks. It was a luxury that he rarely afforded himself, time off, time out, but he sure as hell needed it.

He sat and watched as the morning grew, the sun sparkling on the wide blue water of the Nerang River busy with the activity of numerous pleasure craft. The mansions across the water looked like something from a still life painting, two and three storeys tall, immaculately lawned and gardened with barely a sign of life. Breene wondered idly how the hell anybody could afford to own one of them; they were certainly well beyond the reach of his modest salary. He shrugged mildly. Envy was not one of his vices.

By the time he stretched himself into a standing position the traffic on the road behind him had thinned visibly. Relieved, he got back into the Fiat and headed more or less in the direction of the beach in the hope of catching a glimpse of the surf, maybe even taking a stroll on the sand before he found his unit and slept away the remainder of the day.

The pedestrian traffic thickened dramatically as he entered the area signposted as Surfers Paradise. Breene had always thought it was an ambitious sort of a name, but it obviously had its attractions, judging by the crowds of tourists. He abandoned the Fiat in the nearest available parking spot and joined the throng.

He had never been up to the Gold Coast in all his thirty-eight years. In his mind it had taken on the proportions of a legend, a mythical mecca that spelt sun, surf and sand, big money, night life and beautiful women. He tried to suppress the childlike surge of excitement that swelled in his chest, exaggerated by a night deprived of sleep, but he knew he was smiling like an idiot. People were everywhere, dressed in every colour and style, mostly bright, mostly fluorescent, but he did not see anyone in track pants and a long-sleeved shirt. Not that he cared.

He rolled up his sleeves, exposing his Sydney tan to the warmth of the sun. He crossed the Cavill Avenue mall, the broad expanse of paving tiles crowded with people eating, laughing, holding hands. Shops on either side attracted tourists with gaudy signs, vying for their share of the dollar.

It was almost too much for the sleep-deprived Breene. He was beginning to feel a little dazed by it all. He was relieved when he crossed the road to find the blue Pacific stretching out before him and was tempted to strip down to his underpants and head for the surf, but it didn't seem to be quite the done thing, not on this beach. Nubile young bodies frolicked in the sun or were draped with studied casualness on brightly coloured towels. Japanese tourists were having a field day with their cameras as they threaded their way between the serious beachgoers, snapping off shots of 'Typical Australian beach life' to take home for the amazement of their friends and relatives. The whole scene had a carnival atmosphere, kites fluttering boldly in the breeze fifteen metres above the ground, a line of girls, plus a few men lined up outside a canvas pavilion where a berry-brown man dispensed suntan lotion from a spray gun.

Breene couldn't help smiling. He felt as if he had stepped into a postcard. He slipped his shirt off and rolled up the bottoms of his track pants. At least he could go for a walk along the shoreline — it didn't seem likely that anyone would even take any notice of him. He stepped onto the grainy white sand and winced in sudden pain as something sharp embedded itself in the soft underside of his foot.

'Shit!' he cursed, reaching to pluck the offending item from the sand. A bloody syringe. Just his luck. He was surprised to find it here, right in the middle of Surfers Paradise beach. It seemed decidedly out of place, a hidden menace lurking below the surface of the glamour, a trap for the unwary. He had never stepped on a used syringe on any of Sydney's beaches. Then again, he was more careful on the rare occasions when he walked on the beaches of Sydney, alert to such lurking dangers. He never even stepped onto the sand without some sort of protective footwear.

He definitely hadn't expected to find a syringe in the middle of paradise. It left a vaguely uneasy feeling in his gut, brought him back to earth. He should have expected it. Even here. He was glad he'd had his course of hep B shots, mandatory in the NSW police force and probably up here as well. Infection was one of the ever-present dangers in dealing with the public these days. He pushed the fear of more sinister diseases from his mind, trusting to the advice of experts that harmful bacteria died once they were exposed to the air.

He walked back to his car, pausing only to buy the morning paper, intending to head straight for his accommodation. He had a sudden desire for a good hot shower. And a nap. The headline caught his eye as he threw the paper onto the seat beside him.

TWO SLAIN IN SHOCK MURDERS
POLICE SEEK PUBLIC HELP

He ran his eye quickly over the lead paragraphs, crashing quickly back through his sleep-deprived euphoria.

'Yep,' he sighed. Even here. Paradise or not.

'So what have you come up with on the murders to this point, Hughes?'

'Bugger all so far,' Hughes admitted sourly. 'I've been busting my hump all night and come up without a fucking thing.'

Inspector Arthur Bryant eyed the detective with distaste. Hughes was about eight kilograms overweight and he wore his clothes sloppily, the tail of his shirt hung loose and dark perspiration stains were under his arms. His black hair was too long, the fringe hanging across his eyes so he had developed the irritating habit of flicking his head back after every few sentences. A small dark moustache clung to his upper lip. Thank God it wasn't obvious that he was a cop.

Bryant, on the other hand, wore his uniform with pride. His shirt was always meticulously ironed, with a couple of spares in the locker in his office for when the going got tough. His salt-and-pepper hair was cut military style and his steel-grey moustache was always trimmed and combed. Bryant was a career cop, nearing the end of his long service at the helm of the Surfers Paradise police station, his reward for loyalty.

At least, that was how it had been. This sort of shit was definitely not supposed to happen on his turf. Definitely not.

'I assume you've followed the correct procedures?'

'Of course.' Hughes bristled at the implied criticism.

'Such as?'

Hughes sighed and listed his actions.

'Searched the grounds for a weapon, got the forensic boys to go over both houses with a fine tooth comb, door to door questioning of the neighbours in the vicinity...'

'What about the canals? Have you got the divers in?'

'First thing this morning. There wasn't much point before that, was there?'

Bryant nodded stiffly.

'What about the door-to-door? I heard you called that off after the discovery of the second body. That was a risk.'

'Yeah, but the targets were obviously random, the second body was long cold and we had a neighbour who stated she heard a motorbike departing the scene at about the time of the second murder. We couldn't predict if or where he might strike again that night, so I thought it was useless to continue and risk upsetting more people than we already had.' In truth, Hughes couldn't have cared less about how many people he upset in the line of duty, but continuing was of no use. Any idiot could have seen that.

'And if he'd struck again? What then?'

Hughes shrugged.

'I don't see how the fuck we could have prevented it.'

Bryant bristled. Hughes was downright insubordinate, a smartarse whose record didn't give him the right to such cocky arrogance.

'All right, Hughes.' Bryant swallowed his anger. He had an impending lunch meeting with the mayor that he was not looking forward to. The mayor had been far from happy on the phone, and the fact that there was an election coming up meant even more pressure on the police to make him look good. Bloody hell. He needed a crazed murderer like he needed a hole in the head.

'What's your next step?'

'Continue the door-to-door,' Hughes shrugged. 'I'll go over and talk to the next-door neighbour, see if I can get her to come in and look at the mug books. Who knows, one of the faces may jog her memory. If she's settled down any — she was pretty shaken up last night.'

'Do what you can,' Bryant nodded. 'We have to bottle this one up fast, Hughes, real fast. A lot could be riding on it. Even a promotion for the right man.'

That got Hughes's attention. A promotion. A chance to hotfoot it further up the ranks, more money, more prestige, and more distance between himself and the action, getting his hands grubby on the street. A well-paid desk job with plenty of extra perks — that was his goal, not digging around at filthy murder sites seeing things that would make the sternest man's stomach turn. That wasn't why he had joined the force: it was for power, prestige, having men jump when he demanded something. That was what Warren Hughes wanted. Any way he could get it.

'So what do I tell the mayor?' Bryant muttered.

'Tell him we've got everything in hand, tell him we're following up on some substantial leads,' Hughes shrugged.

'Yeah,' Bryant sighed. Fuck this job, arse-kissing the mayor, attending social functions he had to pretend to enjoy. There was no real police work to do, nothing to get his teeth into. All he really wanted now was to get the hell out of the job, kiss the shit goodbye. He didn't get anything out of it any more.

'Use all the men you need, I don't care where you have to pull them from,' said Bryant, 'And keep me posted.'

'Of course.'

Hughes watched Bryant disappear into his office and scowled. What the fuck was he supposed to do now? They had stuff all, there didn't appear to be anything linking the two victims, apart from the fact that they were old ladies on their own. He reached for the phone and dialled Harris on the uniform desk.

'Get somebody to check out any organisations that cater to the elderly in the Broadbeach area — Meals on Wheels, nursing services — you know the rundown. Any links that turn up must be reported to me immediately. Is that clear?'

'Understood. I'll get somebody onto it straight away.'

'*Sir*,' Hughes insisted.

There was a brief pause.

'Sir,' Harris responded, and broke the connection.

Hughes smiled, enjoying the privileges his position gave him over other cops, even guys like Harris, who had been in the job for a good ten years longer than Hughes. The advantages of powerful friends, he mused. But that route wasn't quick enough, and it was vaguely unsatisfying. If he could crack this one…well, he could silence a few grumbles. Not that they bothered him.

He glanced at his watch. 11.30. He had better get his finger out and get over to see this woman, the neighbour. If she had seen anything, he'd get it out of her, one way or another.

'Come in Bryant,' Tex Ellicott, mayor of the Gold Coast City Council motioned him into the room.

Bryant's gut was tied into knots, the steadying shots of whisky he had slugged down before his meeting with the mayor playing havoc with his ulcer. 'I'm too old for this,' he thought fleetingly, and the thought surprised him because he realised it was true.

'Take a chair.' Ellicott motioned him graciously into the chair on the wrong side of the huge expanse of desk. 'Drink?' He moved to the well stocked bar, fixing himself a gin and tonic.

'No thanks,' Bryant declined, wishing the bastard would get on with it. These meaningless civilities grated on him.

'Well.' The mayor made eye contact for the first time after he had settled his bulk behind the safety of his desk. 'It looks like you've got yourself a bit of a problem, Bryant.'

Bryant made no reply. He wasn't even surprised that the problem had suddenly become his.

'So what are you doing about it?' said Ellicott.

'Everything we can. I've got every available man on the case checking the neighbours, combing the grounds, canals…'

'And?'

'It's early days yet, Tex.'

'*Early days?*' Ellicott exploded, slapping his meaty hand down on the shiny surface of his desk. '*Early days*? Do you realise what something like this does to a place like Surfers Paradise, Bryant? *Do* you? Apart from the fact that it blows our immediate tourism prospects right out the window, apart from the fact that business is already crippled by the recession — for Christ's sake, we're the tourism capital of Australia — do you realise what percentage of our population consists of the elderly, the retired?' He glared at Bryant, wiped his hand through his greased dark curls and pulled it away in disgust, reaching for his handkerchief to wipe the oil off.

Bryant held the mayor's stare but refrained from comment.

'Jesus!' Ellicott propelled his chair backwards and heaved himself up, then hunched forward towards Bryant. 'My fucking opponents are going to have a field day with this one. They've been going on in the papers for weeks about the rising crime rate, and now this. They'll fucking well crucify me, Bryant.' This was the heart of the matter. An election was coming up in six weeks, supposedly the last time Ellicott would stand for re-election after successfully winning three terms. He didn't want anything to upset his precious plans, especially not some lunatic butchering old women. How could he control the damage that would cause? All the PR work in the world couldn't override that one. Unless the problem was cleared up quickly and efficiently. Which, of course, landed the ball squarely in Bryant's court. His ulcer wouldn't get any better until this case had been laid to rest.

'I'm doing all I can,' he said quietly.

'It's not enough! Do you hear me? It's not

enough. Nothing you do will be sufficient until you catch this animal. Jesus, I can't believe this has happened. Not here. Not now.'

'Neither can I.'

Their eyes locked and held for a long moment. Ellicott was the one who dropped his gaze, his shoulders slumping.

'Who have you got heading up the case?' he asked, his voice weary.

'Detective Sergeant Hughes,' Bryant replied, tight-lipped. 'He was the detective on call out last night.'

'The Police Minister's cousin?'

'Yeah.'

Ellicott sighed heavily.

'We've got to get this bastard, Arthur. And we've got to do it soon.'

Bryant raised his eyebrows. So suddenly it was 'we'. 'Maybe I'll take you up on the offer of a drink now.' He rose from his chair and headed for the bar.

'Sure. Fix me one while you're at it.'

Hughes wasn't getting anywhere with Molly Kurts.

'Yes, Mrs Kurts, so you say you heard a motorcycle start up at about 1.30 am.'

'Yes, it woke me up. It was so loud, I've never heard anything like it. You can imagine how that startled me. And just when I was beginning to settle again, those young constables knocked on the door. Almost frightened a poor old lady to death.'

'I wish I could say the same for Mary Denyer,' Hughes sighed.

Molly Kurts pursed her lips.

'I imagine you think I'm a selfish old lady,' she said haughtily. Hughes made no reply.

'Well, old ladies need their sleep, you know. And I'm far from a well woman.'

Damn that Mary Denyer. She'd never liked the woman in the first place, not from the very moment she'd bought the house next door from Doris and Harry. They'd been such a nice couple, and at least they were Australians. Molly didn't hold with foreigners, never had. Not in her street.

'Did you catch a glimpse of the person on the bike?' asked Hughes. 'You say it was outside under the street light there. Surely you must have seen something?'

'It's hard to be sure,' Molly said, not liking this policeman one bit. He was rude and she could smell his body odour from where she sat. If he hadn't shown her his badge, she never would have believed he was a policeman.

'Was he tall, short, skinny, fat — anything at all, Mrs Kurts?'

'Well, he did have a lot of trouble starting the bike — such a loud noise in the dead of night…oh, dear.' 'Dead' wasn't the right choice of words at all. When she thought what the dreadful man had done, and right next door to her house, too! Poor old Wilf would have had a heart attack, if he hadn't already been dead. Such a dear old man, and she missed him so. He'd done his bit for the country, fought to keep it free of dirty foreigners.

A sudden thought occurred to her. 'Do you

know, I bet he was one of those filthy Japs. You can't trust them, the Japs. I should know. I heard the stories from my Wilf when he got back from the war. Ooh, the dreadful things they did.' She put her hand to her mouth.

'Why do you say that, Mrs Kurts?' Hughes sighed wearily. It had already been a long day, and it was far from over.

'Well, he just…well, you know, he had that look about him, and of course he was riding a motorcycle — they all seem to ride motorcycles, don't they, sergeant?'

'So you do remember something about his physical appearance?'

'Yes, now that I come to think of it. I'm sure I caught a glimpse of black hair, although of course he was wearing a helmet.' She gasped suddenly. 'Do you know, I'm sure that he looked in my direction, just for an instant. Yes, yes, he was definitely a Japanese.'

The more she thought about it, the more certain she became. You just couldn't trust them, they never should have let so many of them into the country. Not after everything Wilf and brave Australians like him had done to repel the invasion only forty years ago. She could almost feel the hatred that had burnt in those eyes.

'All right, Mrs Kurts. How about if you come down to the station and we'll have a look at some photos? Do you think you'd recognise the man if you saw him again?'

'Oh yes, I'm certain of it,' said Molly Kurts

eagerly. 'But I'll have to get my glasses if you want me to be looking at photos. My eyes aren't as good as they used to be, you know.'

'Were you wearing your glasses last night, Mrs Kurts?'

'Of course not, I don't wear them to bed, you know.'

Hughes sighed. He hoped this wouldn't take too long.

CHAPTER 2

The jarring ring of the telephone dragged Mervyn Breene from his slumber, banishing vaguely disturbing images of Sylvia from his mind. He reached for the phone, frowned when he couldn't find it in its usual place and then remembered he was on holidays.

'Hello?' He muttered.

'Merv? It's Jack. How the bloody hell are you?'

'Jack!' Breene struggled to sit up on the side of the bed, fighting the sluggishness of sleep from his brain. Jack Warner was an old buddy from the force, part of the reason for Breene's trip to the Gold Coast. At least, that was what he had convinced himself of.

'When did you get in?'

'About 8.30 or so, drove all night. What time is it now?'

'Two o'clock, buddy. Time you hauled your arse out of bed and came and had a drink with your old mate.'

'Jesus, Jack, that's about the last thing I feel like.'

'Come off it, Merv, don't say you've gone soft on me! Get a couple of beers under your belt, it will do you the world of good.'

Breene stared out the window through bleary eyes and blinked in the glare of the afternoon sun reflected on the surface of the rolling ocean. He had a faint headache, the product of his sleep deficit, and his throat was raw and parched. He knew Warner wasn't about to take 'no' for an answer, detected his friend's need to see him, and sighed.

'All right mate, give me half an hour to wake up. Where should I meet you?'

'Now, that depends on how well you know your way around.'

'I know the highway I came in on. So far that's about it.'

'Hmm.' There was a pause at the end of the line. 'No problem. You know the Cavill Avenue Mall? Right in the heart of Surfers?'

'I guess so. It's probably the one I walked through this morning.'

'Heaps of cafes, restaurants, all out on the sidewalk?'

'Yeah.'

'Go back to the corner there and I'll meet you in the bar — it's called the Birdwatchers' Bar.' He chuckled. 'You'll see why when you get there.'

'All right, Jack. See you in half an hour.'

What the hell, Breene thought as he dragged himself from his bed. He'd have plenty of time to catch up on his sleep later.

He stood under the hot shower, let the water needle into his skin and drive the remnants of an unsatisfying sleep from his brain. Jack Warner. It was three years since he'd seen him, three years since the corruption charges that had ended Jack's long and distinguished police career. Breene still bristled with anger when he thought of the charges, and of the bastards who had caused them to be laid. Jack Warner didn't have a corrupt bone in his body, couldn't have bent the rules if his own career had depended on it. And yet the charges had stuck, gone all the way to an official hearing, while Jack was stood down without pay. A great return for his years of dedicated service.

Problem was, Jack Warner was too rigid. He had stood on too many toes, knew too many secrets about men who had climbed the ranks around him. These men had a vested interest in seeing Jack shamed and discredited so their own skeletons could remain safe in their closets. And Jack had been the bunny.

Breene owed the man. Owed him more than he could ever hope to repay, owed him because Warner had taken him under his wing in his rookie days, when Breene had laboured under the huge chip on his own shoulder. Already a sergeant when Breene had joined, Warner had been a crusty, hard, no-nonsense bastard. Definitely not the man to cross. But Breene had chosen to lock horns with him, the nearest authority figure, the closest within reach for a raw recruit still wet behind the ears. He had never understood why Warner hadn't bounced him, and bounced him hard, but the fact was that he hadn't. He had gone out of his way to accommodate Breene, advised him, stood up for him, coaxed him out of his self-destructive anger and helped him to realise that he really did have what it took to make a good cop. To realise that that was what he wanted to be.

And when the time had come to return the favour, Breene had been found wanting; at least, that was how he saw it. He hadn't done enough, hadn't shouted down the accusers for fear of being tarnished with the same brush.

Breene lit a cigarette and sucked the bitter smoke in, let it mingle with the bitter memories, but they remained after the smoke was expelled.

To hell with it. He shrugged. It was all past history, forgotten, water under the bridge. But he couldn't let it go.

He still owed Jack Warner.

'All right!' Hughes faced the group of uniformed cops and felt the swell of his own power in his chest. These men were all here to do his bidding. This was his case, daunting as that may be, and he was ready to face the challenge. However this case turned out, it would be on his shoulders. And he badly wanted that promotion. These were the people who would give it to him, whether they liked it or not.

'Listen up. I'm sure everybody is familiar with the details of the case so far, you've all read the papers. For the time being that's about as much as we know.' He sighed and ran his hand through his lank hair, pushing it away from his forehead. 'We've got some fucking nut running around cutting up old ladies.'

A murmur ran through the room. Hughes let the men talk for a minute, allowing the gravity of the situation to sink in.

'Okay, shut up. Reports from the men who've been door-knocking the neighbourhood,' he demanded. He was damned tired and all he really wanted to do was go home.

'Sergeant Hughes, if you wouldn't mind, I could give a summary of the findings so far,' said Senior Constable Gordon. 'There hasn't been a hell of a lot, and I've spoken personally to all the men who were canvassing the area and taken the liberty of jotting down their findings for convenience sake.' Hughes scowled at Gordon, seeing his initiative as a challenge. But then again, Hughes didn't want this crap to go on any longer than necessary.

'All right,' he shrugged. 'I'll pull you up if there's anything I want clarified.'

'I've tried to narrow it down as much as possible, cut out various sightings of suspicious-looking characters in the area before 10 pm — at least for the time being.'

Hughes bristled. 'Explain your reasons, Senior?' he demanded.

'Well, sir, there were so many varied descriptions — the area is predominantly occupied by elderly people, mostly retired, and, well, they describe just about anybody as suspicious. If we tried to run on all of them to start with, we'd never get anywhere.'

'I think that's for me to decide,' Hughes barked.

'Of course, sir. I have a full list of names and addresses of people who reported such sightings. Frankly, sir, there were a lot of spooked old ladies, and you know how they are.'

'I want every lead tracked down, I want every description taken, with Identikit pictures where possible. Is that clear?'

'Yes sir.' Gordon kept his eyes on his notebook. Fucking fat prick. They'd be tied up for days, and none of the descriptions tallied. The first murder couldn't have happened until 11.30 at the earliest, so they could easily have narrowed down the alternatives, especially to start with.

'All right, carry on,' said Hughes.

'After 10 pm we had four separate sightings of suspicious-looking characters, but so far none of the people felt confident enough to go beyond a vague description. Two of them thought the person they saw was probably a woman, short and overweight, one described a tall thin man dressed in dark clothing. The other was a young male or female, the witness couldn't be sure, waiting on a street corner for about ten or fifteen minutes before being picked up by a car.'

'Are you following up on them?'

'Of course, sir,' Gordon replied. 'We also had a half dozen or so reports of residents hearing a motorcycle.'

'Anyone see it?' Hughes's interest quickened.

'No, sir, no reported sightings.'

'Keep onto that one, there may be something in it. Somebody must have seen it.'

Molly Kurts had proved worse than useless when he'd brought her in, poring over the mug books and muttering away to herself. All she really seemed to have been worried about was being woken up by a motorbike in the middle of the night.

He frowned, not bothering to acknowledge Gordon as he sat down. A bloody motorbike — without anything else, it really amounted to nothing.

A knock on the door interrupted his musing.

'Yes?'

'Y-y-you w-wanted to s-see me, s-sir?'

'Who the hell are you, man?' Hughes bellowed.

'P-p-Peter El-ellis, sir' the man replied, his face crimson. 'F-f-forensics.'

'Oh, right. Come in. Ellis, was it? We're ready for your report.' Hughes shook his head and wondered how anybody got on with living with such a bad speech impediment.

Ellis cleared his throat and shuffled a sheaf of papers nervously in front of him.

'All right, Ellis, whenever you're ready,' said Hughes.

With an effort, Ellis squared his shoulders and perched a pair of glasses on the bridge of his nose.

'First, b-b-both v-victims were murdered w-w-with the s-s-same weapon. The instrument used was a blade, approximately f-fifteen inches in length. The killing blow in both cases was to the neck, severing the spinal chord instantly. From this we would assume the culprit was either a man, or an unusually strong woman. Left-handed.'

Hughes listened to the growing confidence in the

man's voice with fascination. Ellis's stutter had almost disappeared.

'The dismemberment of the bodies was subsequent to their deaths. Neither operation was carried out with any precision.'

'Wait a minute, what do you mean by that?' demanded Hughes.

'Th-the b-bodies were b-b-butchered, sir. H-hacked to pieces. There was n-n-no evidence the attacker w-w-was experienced w-w-with such an operation.'

'And what do you surmise from that?'

'A-a-nger, sir. It w-would suggest that the attacker was in s-s-some s-sort of a frenzy.'

'All right. Go on.'

Ellis returned to his written report with obvious relief. He began to detail the individual wounds, how the blows had been dealt. The facts washed over Hughes — they were of little import, as far as he was concerned. The two old women were dead.

'Any evidence of sexual deviance, interference?'

'N-no, sir' Ellis blushed. 'No-none whatsoever. No s-semen, n-no evidence that the…c-c-cavities had been in-interfered with.'

Hughes nodded and Ellis continued. Hughes watched him, fascinated. There was barely a trace of his stutter while he was on safe ground, on his own territory. But as soon as Hughes or one of the others asked him a question it came back with renewed force. He couldn't help wondering why.

Ellis wasn't a bad-looking bloke, about medium

height, solid build, his glasses hiding bright blue eyes below a shock of black hair. Hughes found himself wondering what made somebody like him tick. The debilitating stammer was obviously related to some sort of confidence problem.

'Thank you, Ellis,' Hughes said at the end of the report. 'Any further questions?'

Nobody said anything. The room was filled with an embarrassed silence.

'All right, get your arses out there and find me this bastard. I want his balls pronto. Ellis, just a minute, I'd like a word with you.'

Ellis waited nervously while the rest of the men filed out of the room.

'Sit down.' Hughes motioned to a chair across the table. He'd done a bit of psychology at university, and this Ellis character fascinated him. 'Unusual case, wouldn't you say?'

'Y-yes sir, n-no doubt ab-about th-that.'

'Any guesses about motive?'

'N-no, s-sir,' Ellis shrugged. 'H-h-ow do you ex-explain something like this?'

'Hmm. I agree.' Hughes held Ellis's gaze, ignored his discomfort. 'And you say the wounds were inflicted as if the attacker was angry? "In a frenzy," I think you said.'

'Y-y-yes, sir. It w-w-ould appear so.'

'Ever seen a case like this one before, Ellis?'

'N-no, sir. N-not in my time.' He was visibly relaxing, on safe ground.

'Been here long, Ellis?'

'Ab-about s-six m-months, sir.' The question had

thrown him badly. Hughes watched his face redden with detached interest.

'And what made you choose forensics?'

'I d-d-don't know, s-sir.' Ellis stared over Hughes' head, refusing to meet his eyes. It looked as if he would rather be anywhere else than here.

'Allright, Ellis. Thanks for the report. Interesting.' Hughes stroked his chin. Obviously personal questions caused an increase in his stuttering. Hugely self-conscious perhaps?

'Is th-that all then, s-sir?'

'Yes, yes, thank you Ellis. You've been a great help.' Hughes smiled warmly. Ellis nodded, his eyes resting briefly on Hughes before he made a hasty exit.

'Hmm. Very interesting,' Hughes thought. He wondered whether he could worm his way into Ellis' confidence, see if the stuttering decreased at all. Just as an experiment. It might be amusing.

He dragged his mind back to more immediate problems, glanced at his watch and shrugged. He couldn't do anymore today; it was time he went home. After all, he'd been at work since two that morning. Not a bad day's work, Warren, he congratulated himself. The fact that he was making little to no headway was of no concern to him. What more could he do? He was only human after all, and this was only a job.

Breene and Warner had already drunk more than was good for them, but Warner seemed hellbent on drinking until he dropped.

'So how are you going, Jack? How are you really going?' Breene asked, when they had consumed enough beer to allow them to cut through the bullshit. Warner looked bloody awful — the last three years obviously hadn't been kind to him. He looked more like fifty-seven than forty-seven, his face haggard and lined. His hair, formerly dark brown, had gone completely grey.

'I'm getting by,' Warner shrugged. He looked out the window, avoiding Breene's eyes. 'Things are a lot harder than I thought they'd be, Merv. A lot harder.'

'What about the PI game? Do they keep you busy?'

Warner snorted in derision.

'Jealous husbands keeping an eye on their wives, insurance fraud. It's a laugh a minute. Real challenge.' He rolled his eyes and downed the rest of his beer. 'How about if we get down to some serious drinking? I've just about had a gutful of this shit. Feel up to a bourbon? J.D.?'

'Sure,' Breene shrugged. 'Why not?' Might as well do the job properly.

'You know' Warner stared contemplatively into the depths of his drink. 'I've got a lot to be grateful to the police force for.'

'Oh?'

'Yeah,' Warner nodded. 'Gave me some of the best years of my working life, I made plenty of good friends. And if it wasn't for the money I got from the super fund I'd be fucked by now. At least it was enough to set myself up here, own my house and still leave some over to get by on. Although that's not gonna last forever.'

Breene didn't interrupt or bother to share his thoughts. The police force had shafted the poor bastard, even if he had been cleared by the tribunal. Anybody else would have asked for his old job back, but not Jack Warner. Pride dictated his course of action, but it didn't look like pride was doing him any good now. Breene shook his head. So much for sticking to the moral high ground. He wondered if the good guys ever really did come out on top, or if that was the stuff of fairy tales.

He downed his drink and shrugged off the feeling of melancholy that hovered over him like a dark cloud. Plenty of time for that when he was alone.

'Bottoms up, Jack.' He downed his drink in one shot. 'Another?'

'Of course,' Warner smiled.

Breene smiled back. Fuck being serious.

The cloud that had hovered over him broke the moment he entered the unit where he was staying. He stared out over the brooding sea, the last faint traces of daylight scattered on its surface, and sighed heavily. He was familiar with the dull ache, had tried unsuccessfully to drown it with alcohol on more than a few occasions during the past months.

Sylvia. He had been able to suppress thoughts of her while he was with Warner, but he knew they were there, lurking. He snatched up the phone and punched in the number before he had time to reconsider, stood holding the receiver with sweaty hands and a knot in his gut.

'Sylvia?'

'Merv? Is that you?' She recognised his voice instantly.

'I'm on holidays. Up here.' He heard the slur in his own voice. Bad idea.

'And you're drunk,' she said flatly.

'Yeah. I've been out for a few drinks with Jack. Just thought I'd give you a call.'

'How nice of you. Pity you couldn't manage it sober.' There was ice in her tone.

'Yeah, well.' He felt a slide in his gut. 'Do you think we might be able to see each other, while I'm up here, I mean?'

'Maybe.' She was non-committal. 'I'm pretty snowed under with work at the moment.'

He could imagine her, surrounded by the clutter of paints and silk screens, probably wearing one of those loose cotton men's shirts with the sleeves rolled up. Jesus. Talk about torturing yourself.

'I'd like to see you, Sylvia.'

'We'll see, okay? I've got to go. Bye.' She cut the connection.

Breene stared at the receiver beeping in his hand, and slowly replaced it in its cradle. Fuck it. He tore the whisky bottle out of the paper bag and poured himself a healthy slug, flicked the TV on for company and slumped into the lounge. He passed out before he was halfway through his drink.

'Where have you been, Jack?' Pam Warner heard the shrillness of her own voice and regretted it. She knew it would only get him going, but she was getting damned sick of his attitude.

'What does it matter where I've been, woman? It's none of your damned business.'

Amanda Warner got up from the lounge chair and headed for her room.

'Drunk again,' she muttered quietly as she walked past the kitchen door where her parents were squared off against each other.

'You see?' Warner said, pointing in the direction of his daughter's room. 'You see what an attitude you're giving my daughter? She hasn't got any respect for me any more.'

'I'm not bloody surprised, and it's got nothing to do with me. You're the one who comes home pissed every night, acting like a drunken fool. What do you expect?'

'What? What do you mean I come home pissed every night? I work damned hard, don't you bloodywell forget that. So what if I have a few drinks at the end of the day?'

'It's hardly the end of the day, Jack. I've been home since two this afternoon and you were out then. By the look of you, you'd been at it for some time before that.'

'I went to see my old mate Merv. Is there something wrong with that?'

'Mervyn Breene? You didn't even tell me he was up here.'

'No, because I couldn't stand the thought of how you'd carry on about it.'

'Well, I certainly would have had a good reason

to. Just look at you. I wouldn't mind if you went on like this now and then, but it's every night. What's wrong with you, Jack? What the *hell's* wrong with you? Isn't coming home to your family enough for you any more?'

Warner stared at her belligerently. He knew that part of what Pam was saying was true, but he wasn't going to admit it. He was so bloody angry every time he walked through the door. He hated all the fighting. He hated himself for it. But that only seemed to make matters worse.

'Listen to me!' He shook his finger at his wife. 'If you don't stop riding me, there's going to be trouble.'

'Threatening me now, are you, Jack? Well, that's very brave of you, isn't it. Don't you get enough of that on the streets?'

'You can't talk to me like that. I don't even know where the hell *you* are half the time, so don't go putting the shit on me. I won't stand for it!' he bellowed.

'That's fine, Jack, that's just fine,' Pam said quietly, close to tears but not about to let him know it. 'Your dinner's in the oven. I hope you enjoy it.' She turned and walked away and Warner heard the bedroom door close firmly.

'Damn you!' he yelled. Another night on the fucking lounge. He shook his head wearily and reached for a beer.

Amanda sat on her bed and stared out of the window into the darkness, listening to the uneasy calm that settled over the house after her parents had stopped fighting. She turned on the radio by her bed to drown out the sounds of her mother's muffled sobs. She was sick of their fighting.

Breene woke late in the night and stared bleary-eyed at the TV screen, which featured an old black-and-white John Wayne movie. It brought a smile to his lips. He got up and turned it off, wincing at the throbbing in his head and the dryness of his throat. He stared out the window at the moonlit streets below, the territory of the restless and the fun seekers. This place never slept. It was kind of comforting to look down and see the street life, the cars winding through the brightly lit fairyland of street lights and shopfronts.

Somewhere he heard the tinkle of shattering glass, followed by the piercing shriek of an alarm. It broke the spell, and Breene crawled into the big double bed. He had to put a pillow over his head to block out the sound.

He lay on his bed in the sanctuary of his bedroom, successfully blocking out the sounds his mother made in the next room. He smiled to himself, satisfied.

Last night had gone smoothly, though he had difficulty remembering much of the detail. He remembered the terror on their faces and the blood. So much of it. He felt ritually cleansed, free of his mother now.

And he knew that it had begun. He had taken the first steps to assure his ascendancy. Finally. He closed his eyes, revelling in the silence, and slept.

CHAPTER 3

Michael Finch was hunched over the table, the muscles of his back and shoulders tense with concentration. The bright fluorescent lights flooded the stainless steel bench, glinting on the array of surgical instruments he had laid out in precise order. He smiled at the sight of them, his white teeth flashing in the dark tangle of his woolly beard.

He loved the feeling of power as he stood over the inert body stretched out before him. He was the key to its final secrets, the last contact between this world and the one beyond. On his shoulders rested the unravelling of the final mysteries that life, extinguished before its time, had to offer.

The dog had been lying on the side of the busy highway, gasping its final agonised breaths as he hauled it into the back of his four-wheel-drive. He had soon put an end to its desperate struggles for life, watching in fascination as the spurting jet of bright red blood ceased to pulse from the ruptured neck cavity.

It was a big dog, a red setter, he thought as he surveyed his handiwork. It lay spreadeagled on the bench, its limbs pinned outwards so that its ribcage and soft underbelly were exposed.

Finch shaved the matted hair from the underbelly, working down the body with smooth, sure sweeps of the scalpel blade, his strokes revealing the soft pink skin protecting the vital organs below. He ran his fingers caressingly over the smooth tracks the scalpel had cleared, delighting in the still-taut skin, the heat of life not quite dissipated. He hadn't nicked the skin once. Not that he expected any less of himself. He thought of this as his craft, a skill to be practised and honed. It was his duty, his purpose, not merely his job.

He made his initial incision along the breastbone, the skin and flesh and sinew parting magically beneath his sure hand. He halted at the base of the sternum, taking up the crude saw to part the bones of the ribcage. He nodded, noting that several of the ribs had been fractured, piercing both the right lung and the chambers of the heart. Little wonder there had been so much blood at the time of impact. He could never have altered the damage inflicted. Laying down the saw he reached for a long-bladed scalpel, its edge wickedly sharp.

His stroke was deceptively gentle, the pressure of his index finger sufficient to part the flesh and the muscle. Just enough pressure, not too much.

A foul odour filled the room as he punctured a loop of the large intestine.

'Fuck!' He cursed in fury. 'Fuck fuck fuck fuck!'

He reached below the bench and pulled out a large meat cleaver, its edge honed to a bitter sharpness, and hacked viciously at the ruined corpse, severing the hindquarters with a single blow, consumed with blind rage.

Eventually, his breathing stilled, the blind rage passed. He blinked his eyes owlishly, relaxed the tension from his bunched shoulders and surveyed the ruin around him. His hands and his white coat were splattered with blood, the antiseptically clean surfaces of the lab defiled. That wouldn't do, it would not do at all. Panicked, he rushed to change his jacket and wash his hands.

Amanda Warner looked around for a receptionist of some kind, curious that the desk had been left unattended. She had rung through beforehand, checked to ensure that her visit to the forensic laboratories would be okay. She'd followed the directions the man had given her, gone to the rear entrance of the police building and entered the unmarked door, descending the steps into the starkly illuminated corridor. She rubbed her hands over her arms, chilled by the cool temperature of the labs. She convinced herself that her feeling cold had nothing to do with the empty expanse of corridor, the apparent absence of life in the stark clinical setting.

'Excuse me,' she called as a white-coated man strode briskly from a doorway down the corridor. He paused mid-stride and turned to meet her gaze.

'Y-y-es? C-c-can I h-help you?'

She was momentarily embarrassed for the young

man, but he was far enough away for her to cover her reaction before he noticed.

'I was supposed to meet somebody here to show me through the labs. I'm Mandy Warner. I rang through earlier, and the man said it would be all right.'

'Oh?' Peter Ellis frowned as he walked towards her. 'I d-don't know wh-wh-where the man on the d-desk has g-gone.' He couldn't help noticing the fresh beauty of the young girl, her sun-golden hair radiant in the stark glow of the fluorescent lights, her face alive with health and vitality. It was quite a contrast to what he was used to down here in the labs, buried beneath the bustle of the busy city police station.

'W-well,' he said as he looked into the warm depths of her nut-brown eyes and saw the hesitant plea in her smile. 'I g-g-uess I c-could sh-show you around. If y-y-you would l-l-like me to?'

'That would be great. I'd really appreciate it.' Amanda smiled warmly, wanting to put him at his ease. His eyes were so blue she wondered if he was wearing contact lenses, but of course he wasn't — his metal-rimmed glasses were perched on his nose. He was sort of attractive in a scholarly, intellectual way. His black hair was the perfect foil to his fair skin and blue eyes. She could just imagine him lost in his work, completely devoted to his science.

Ellis realised she was staring at him and felt the flush of red creeping up his neck.

'C-c-come on, we-we'll st-start up here.' He swallowed, forced himself to slow down his words. 'I'll show you my lab,' he pronounced carefully.

'That would be nice,' she smiled.

'It's d-down this w-way.'

A door burst open and a burly, darkly bearded man burst through it, almost knocking into the two of them.

'What the…' His face was mottled red with rage, his hand straying to the blood-spattered front of his lab coat. His eyes followed Ellis's glance and he drew in a sharp breath when he saw Mandy. She shrunk back, frightened by Finch's appearance.

'I-I…' Finch silenced Ellis with a glance, took a long searching look at Mandy and abruptly turned and re-entered the room from which he'd emerged.

Mandy let out her breath, unaware that she'd been holding it.

'He w-works here, too,' Ellis said quietly. 'C-c-come on, my l-l-lab's this way.' He turned and hurried down the corridor. Mandy took a deep breath, unable to dispel the memory of Finch's face as she raced to keep up with Peter Ellis.

Breene had been awake since the sun came up, watched as the new day cast its first pink feelers over the edge of the ocean and then creep cautiously up until the sun burst over the horizon and brazenly climbed into the sky. His thoughts had never strayed far from Sylvia. He had been stupid to ring her last night when he was drunk. He waited until nine, debating whether he should ring her back, all the while knowing he would. His trip to the Gold Coast would be wasted if he didn't at least give it his best shot.

He dialled the number, surprised to find himself breathing shallowly, his heart beating quickly in his tight chest.

'Hello,' came her voice. 'This is Sylvia. I'm not in right now, but if you'd care…' Fucking answering machine. He hung on, clung to the tenuous link that connected him to her.

'Sylvia, it's Merv again,' he said heavily after the tone. 'I wanted to…'

'Merv?' Her voice cut in on him. 'It's me.'

'Oh.' Now what did he say? The lines he had rehearsed all morning had vanished, leaving him bare, exposed. 'Sylvia, I…look, I'm sorry about last night.'

She made no comment and Breene frowned. The least she could do was make things a bit easier for him.

'I guess I needed the courage, you know, after so long. I mean, what's it been, a couple of months?'

'Twelve weeks.' It sounded as if she had been counting.

'Yeah.' Breene sighed heavily and an uncomfortable silence grew between them.

'So how have you been?' he asked lamely.

'So-so. Busy — there's a lot to do, setting up again.' Her living area doubled as a studio and office. 'I guess I'm getting there. How about you?'

'You know, same old stuff, really. Nothing much has changed.' Jesus, they sounded like a couple of casual acquaintances. Maybe she had changed, didn't want to have anything more to do with him. She sure wasn't giving him any come-ons.

'Listen Sylvia, I really would like to see you. Catch up, have a talk.' He paused, had to screw himself up before he admitted, 'I miss you.'

'Jesus, Merv, it's been three months since you even called.'

'And you lost my phone number?' He couldn't keep the edge from his tone. 'Look, I'd like to see you. If you don't want to see me, you just let me know.' He waited, angry for showing his hand, angry at her for making him. He should have stayed at bloody work filling his mind with the endless tasks that choked his days.

'Okay,' she said quietly.

'What? Okay what?'

'Okay, I'd like to see you, too.'

'Great.' He couldn't keep the smile from his voice. 'That's *great*. When?'

'Well...how about tomorrow? For lunch maybe?'

'Sure, sounds good to me.' Now that the meeting was arranged he began to have misgivings. Already.

'Okay. Call me later, sometime this evening, and we'll work out where and when,' she said casually, her voice light.

'Sure. Well, I'll talk to you then.'

'Okay. Bye.'

'Bye.' Breen was surprised by the anger that swept up within him. 'I miss you, goddamn it, I miss you,' he thought. He stared at the bleating receiver in his hand and slowly replaced it. How long did it take? When did the pain stop?

Why the hell was he bothering anyway? What was it that made her any different?

Fuck it. He never should have rung in the first place. He stalked over to the window and leaned out over the sill, staring gloomily at the heaving ocean. His eyes drifted back, towards the shore, across the sand. The people on the footpath below looked like dolls. It was a hell of a long way down and he wondered what it would feel like, how long it would take.

Fuck that too. Not over a damned woman, any damned woman. He wrenched himself away from the window, away from the chasm that seemed to suck at his body. Christ, why did it have to be so difficult? The unit was suddenly too small, stifling him. He hurried out the door. He knew Sylvia would still be there to haunt him when he returned, but if he went about things properly he would barely notice.

He was surprised at the number of patrons in the bar at this hour of the morning.

'Double scotch, please.' That should do the trick. At least partly.

GOLD COAST ELDERLY LOCK
THEMSELVES INTO "PARADISE".
Police baffled, no new leads

Hughes scowled as he scanned the story. Bryant was going to love this. He pushed the paper away from him and leaned back in his chair, brushed his hair out of his eyes. So far all the investigations had amounted to nothing. No leads, no clues, no apparent motive. All he had was a motorbike and a vague description from an old lady with poor eyesight.

And a killer who used a long blade and was crazy enough to dismember two old ladies in their homes.

Christ, it was every cop's nightmare. Random murder. There was nothing in the procedural manual to help him here because people were supposed to act in a certain manner, were supposed to conform to a certain pattern of behaviour. They were supposed to follow the rules, even when they committed a crime. Passion, revenge, lust, envy — normal human behaviour. Underline 'normal'. Hughes knew that wasn't what he was dealing with, not this time.

'Hughes, my office.' He was jolted from his reverie. He hadn't even seen Arthur Bryant approaching. He got slowly to his feet and sauntered in the direction of the glassed-in cubbyhole that served as his superior's office. Warren Hughes scowled. He didn't think he should have to take orders from anybody, least of all some washed-up old man treading water until he could retire.

Still, he supposed he would have to play the game. Sighing, he knocked on the door.

'In,' Bryant snapped. He was in no mood for games, not today. The mayor had already been on the phone this morning, disturbing Bryant's breakfast and upsetting his wife. He wasn't going to get any peace until this mess was cleared up, and he knew that could take quite some time. He glanced up as Hughes entered, irritated as always by the man's barely concealed arrogance. He wondered where the hell they were getting them from these days. Bloody college boys.

'Okay, Hughes,' he said wearily. 'What have you got for me?'

Hughes waited until he had settled himself in his chair before he answered.

'So far we've come up with stuff all, chief. It would appear that there are no links between the two victims, either of a social or welfare nature. No Meals on Wheels, nursing services, clubs, etcetera etcetera. We've drawn a blank with the neighbours, except for three reports of a motorcycle in the area around the time of the second killing.'

'Description?'

'Nope. They only heard it, no sightings. We're looking into sightings of suspicious-looking people seen in the area on the night, but none of them are too hopeful so far.'

Bryant swivelled in his chair and stared out the window. He had tried to explain the difficulties of tracking down a killer of this nature, no obvious motive, victims apparently chosen at random, but the mayor hadn't been interested. Bryant had stopped short of telling him that the two old ladies probably wouldn't be the last victims, that the killer was most likely deranged, and almost definitely working outside the realms of logic.

Christ, Bryant thought, why couldn't this have happened six months from now when he'd be retired? And why so close to an election?

He turned back to face Hughes.

'So what's the next move?'

'I have no idea,' Hughes admitted. 'Keep looking for a link, cast the net wider to friends, associates. I can't see any other way of catching the bastard.'

The two men eyed each other across the desk, their biggest fear unspoken. Maybe there weren't any links. Maybe they were dealing with a serial killer.

'All right, let's go to the public.' Bryant sighed. 'I don't see that we've got any alternative.'

Hughes started to protest at such an obvious admission that they didn't have a thing on the killer, but Bryant was right. They had no alternative. They had to admit they didn't have a clue, that they were stumbling around in the dark. And both of them knew that it was only a matter of time before he struck again.

She scrubbed at the bloodstains, frowned because her son had been careless enough to get so much blood on his clothes. Wasn't he worried about the risk of AIDS? He should have known better, there was enough about it in the papers these days. Sighing, she threw them in the wash with extra bleach. That should get rid of the stains.

Jack Warner woke late, sensed the yawning emptiness of the house as he sat up and stretched, his clothes twisted and crumpled from another night on the lounge. He stared moodily over the waters of the canal, remembering last night's fight, and the one before, and all the other fights in the weeks and months before that.

He got up from the lounge and wandered aimlessly within the confines of the house, his house, picking up an object here, touching a photo, opening cupboards and drawers. He had no idea what the hell he was looking for, knew he wouldn't find it in the house, knew he had lost it long ago.

Was it only three years? He found it hard to believe, to think that three years ago he had still been a cop, still working hard at a job he loved, a job to which he had dedicated the past twenty years of his life. A wave of bitterness engulfed him at the memory of what had happened, the shame of the inquiry, the rage that it could happen to him, that he was able to be trapped, the helpless victim of a set-up.

Christ, it was still all there, hidden away in the dark recesses of his memory where it brewed with silent malevolence, robbing him of any joy he might take in life.

He shook his head. What joy *was* there in his life? A struggling private eye snooping into other people's lives, nothing to get his teeth into, no pride in his 'profession'. He hated the whole stinking mess. And if it hadn't been for his superannuation he would be on the bones of his arse. At least he still had some of it left, though it was dwindling fast.

That was why Pam had gone and got herself a job. Warner punched at the air, gritted his teeth in anger. God damn her, God damn the necessity for her to go out to work. He sure as hell wasn't making enough to provide for them. And then what the fuck happened when he reached retiring age? What then?

He was a failure. A washed-up forty-seven-year-old failure who couldn't even provide for his family, whose only usefulness had been wrenched from him.

And he couldn't even be grateful that Pam could get a good job, earning enough to make ends meet. He couldn't reach out to her and tell her he loved her, not now, not any more. He didn't have the right. Instead he slunk around and got drunk, avoided her whenever he could, fought with her when he couldn't. And hated himself, more than anything else he hated himself. Seeing his old mate Merv had brought it all back, reopened the wounds, reminded him that the old Jack had existed, maybe he still did exist somewhere down in Sydney. In memory, if nothing else.

A funeral for a friend.

He laughed bitterly, might even have cried in self-pity but he wouldn't cry. A man didn't cry, not according to Jack Warner. A man got on with his life, dealt with his own problems, kept them inside. And if he couldn't deal with them he'd failed the test.

Well, he had failed.

He left the house and headed for the pub. It was the only answer he could find.

CHAPTER 4

Hughes had called the press conference for 2 pm. He preened himself nervously, knowing that the TV cameras would be trained on him. He wanted to make a good impression.

He flicked his hair back as he stepped onto the podium, noise erupting as a dozen reporters shouted their questions at once. He was taken aback to see so many, and he cursed Bryant for backing out at the last moment and leaving him holding the reins. He knew what that was all about — if they didn't get on top of things fast, it would be Hughes's face people remembered. Well, that worked both ways, too — when they did get the bastard, Hughes would be right in there to take the credit.

If they did.

He took his seat calmly, continuing to ignore the tumult of questions while he shuffled his papers, secretly enjoying the popping of the flashes, being the centre of attention. He held his hand up for silence and faced them, forcing his face to appear calm.

'Ladies and gentlemen, I have a statement I would like to read. You may ask questions after that, but I warn you my time is limited.' He cleared his throat and glanced down at the statement he had prepared.

'We are appealing for any assistance the public may be able to give to us in relation to the grisly slaying of two elderly ladies in their homes on the night of November 8. Our investigations to this point indicate that the person we are seeking was possibly riding a motorcycle on the night of the crimes. The perpetrator, either a man or a particularly strong woman, may or may not be of Japanese extraction. We believe that the individual would have had a considerable amount of blood on his or her person. Anyone who saw anything that may pertain to this case between the hours of 11 pm and 2 am on the night of the slayings is strongly urged to contact the police with all haste. All statements will, of course, be treated with absolute confidentiality. Thank you.'

There was a brief silence.

'Do you mean to say you haven't got anything on the killer at all?' Hughes faced the woman who posed the question. He could hardly avoid it — the rest of them were waiting for an answer.

'We are following several leads.'

'Such as?' A man at the back called out.

'Well, I'm not at liberty to say at this point…'

'Oh come on, do you really expect us to believe that?'

'Ladies and gentleman, please…'

His voice was drowned out by an avalanche of questions. Momentarily thrown, Hughes looked from one face to another, saw anger and fear, tried to decipher the questions that were being thrown at him.

'Have we got a serial killer on our hands?'
Silence.
'At this point, we have no idea. It appears obvious that the killer is mentally disturbed...'
'A psychopath?'
'It's impossible for me to say.'
'So you really have no idea?'
'We're following several...'
'Do you think he could strike again?'
'Are the residents of the Gold Coast safe?
'What are the police doing to protect the citizens?'
'Ladies and gentlemen,' Hughes shouted to make himself heard above them. 'I can answer only one question at a time.' This was definitely getting out of control.
'How many extra police have you got on the case?'
'Every available man is being used. We...'
'What are your credentials? How are you in charge?'
'Have you ever dealt with anything like this before?'

Hughes reddened in anger. How dare they question his competence?

'Thank you,' he shouted, rising from the chair. 'I'm out of time.' He stalked from the stage, a storm of questions trailing him. Fucking reporters, he cursed, seething. Who the hell did they think they were?

'Isn't it true that you only got where you are because you're the cousin of the Minister for Police?' That one voice cut through the others. Her voice again, the bitch in the front row. Hughes shot her a look of pure hatred before he stepped through the door and slammed it behind him.

Celia Thompson of the *Gold Coast Herald* smiled. In her time she had dealt with bigger fish than Detective Sergeant Hughes and won. Signalling to her photographer, she hurried away from the stage, the story already forming in her mind. Sergeant Hughes definitely wasn't going to like it.

Michael Finch waited until nightfall before he slid the body drawer open. He turned his head away, not willing to witness the evidence of his failure again. He hastily shoved the dismembered remains into a thick black plastic bag, knotting the top and absolving himself of any fault in the matter. He should have resisted the chance finding, should have listened to the voice of caution. His subjects were usually chosen with much more care.

He hoisted the bag onto his shoulder, grunting under the weight, grateful for the strength of his upper body. Nobody was about at this late hour, but he checked the darkened corridor to make sure before slipping quietly out through the back entrance and climbing the stairs into the deserted carpark.

Now it was only a short drive through the quiet backstreets, avoiding the glare of the bustling night-life that the tourist strip spawned. He came to a halt just short of the bridge and turned off the lights, leaving the engine running as he slid down the dark bank. A heave of his powerful shoulders sent the heavy bag far out over the water, where it landed with a splash.

He smiled in the darkness, wiping his hands on his trousers as the cold water washed away all traces of his failure.

In the quiet hour preceding dawn Ted Lambert let his little tinny drift with the current of the dark waters of the Nerang River, trailing his set lines behind it. He sat back and sighed, rolling himself a thick cigarette with practised hands and sucking the biting smoke deeply into his lungs. The air had a cold nip to it at this hour, even here on the Gold Coast, and he hunched forward cupping his hands around the cigarette. Not that Ted was bothered by a bit of cold. His lined face creased into a grin as he remembered working on the Snowy River Dam Project. Now, *that* was cold.

He must have drifted off, though whether he was sleeping or lost in his memories he couldn't have said. The light was growing in the sky, casting a pink blush on the walls of the tall unit blocks that lined the beach. Down on the river the gloom seemed to thicken, the faint stirrings of the day not penetrating the night that still clung to the water.

One of the lines clattered against the metal of the boat and his heartbeat quickened as he reached for it.

'Damn,' he muttered, his experienced fingers recognising a snag. The line had caught on something on the river bottom. He tugged at it, trying to pull it free, but it was stuck fast. Reaching back, Ted Lambert pushed the starter and coaxed the reluctant engine into life. He quickly pulled the other lines in and headed back upriver to find the source of the snag.

It was bloody heavy, whatever it was. The hook had stuck fast and he was about to cut it loose when he felt the snag shift. He manoeuvred his little boat directly over the spot and hauled on the line, straining to pull it free. There was a good thick trace on it, and he was reluctant to let it go if salvage was at all possible.

It took him a good ten minutes to inch the object into the boat and he had to catch his breath before he could examine the contents of the black plastic bag.

'Jesus,' he cursed weakly, the gruesome contents spilling from the slit he'd made with his knife. 'Sick bastards.' He turned his head and spat into the water, his mouth suddenly bitter with the taste of bile.

'A what?' Bryant snapped.

'A dog sir, red setter by the looks of it. It was dismembered, sir.' Hughes still felt nauseated by the memory. He had owned a red setter as a boy.

'Christ!' Bryant jerked himself up from behind his desk. 'A dog. You'd better keep the lid on this one, Hughes, for all our sakes. If any word of this is leaked to the press we'll be in for a shitload of trouble.' He turned and stared out the window. His ulcer burned in his stomach.

'They dragged it out of the river this morning, snagged on a fisherman's line.'

'Any idea of how long it had been in there?'

'Not yet — I haven't had a chance to check with forensics. I wanted you to know as soon as possible.'

Bryant's weary gaze rested briefly on Hughes's face, but couldn't read the expression there.

'Okay, Hughes,' he nodded. 'Thank you.'

'Still, it seems fairly obvious that it's the same person, wouldn't you think?'

'I bloody well hope so. We don't want two crazy bastards running around cutting up bodies, even animals. But you can't discount the possibility of a copycat.'

'Or maybe the guy's practising. Maybe we've just dug up one of his dry runs before he graduated to the real thing.'

'God only knows, Hughes, God only knows. I only hope we can keep this dog thing under wraps. You know what the public's like, it's odds on that there would be more outrage over this than there was over those two poor old ladies.' He sighed. 'I'd hate to have the mayor find out, he's giving me enough heat as it is.'

'Do you want me to talk to him? Maybe I could snow him a bit, take some pressure off your shoulders.' Hughes kept the sudden surge of hope carefully bottled. If he could get the mayor on his side, a promotion higher up the ranks would be that much easier. A couple of words in the right places…

'No, I'll deal with that,' Bryant said, tight-lipped. He wasn't totally blind to Warren Hughes's ambitions. 'You get on with things, check with forensics.' Nobody was going to start treading on his toes, tempting though it might have been to offload some of the bullshit that went with this job. Why anybody would want to step into the administrative side of the game he had no idea. It wasn't policing, not as far as he was concerned, but it was the price you paid for promotion.

'That's all sergeant,' he said, dismissing Hughes. The man was an arsehole and he'd hate to see what he'd be like when he had moved a few rungs further up the ladder, but that wasn't Bryant's problem. He'd be well out of it by then.

Breene was nervous, more nervous than he should have been. Sure, it was a while since he'd seen Sylvia, and sure he'd done a hell of a lot of thinking about her, but couldn't he try to act a little bit cool? It was only lunch, after all.

Who was he fooling? It was a hell of a lot more than a simple lunch. After all, he had travelled a thousand kilometres to get here, to make the effort of seeing her. And to catch up with Jack Warner, of course. It hadn't all been for Sylvia.

Funny thing about it was that six months ago he'd been only too happy to free himself of Sylvia, to shake off the shackles of their relationship and be 'free' again. The whole thing had been his idea, his response to Sylvia's desire for more 'commitment' from him.

Commitment. He shuddered at the very sound of the word and all its connotations. Commitment, like his parents perhaps? His old man had been so committed to his mother that even after she left him, even after she'd walked out, leaving him to bring up their eight-year-old son on his own, all he could do was blame himself. She'd done no wrong in his eyes, even though she never even bothered to take advantage of her access visits, never came near Breene or his father once she'd started her 'new life'. That's when the old man had started his affair with the bottle, withdrawn from life, withdrawn from his young son. He'd been dead inside long before cancer caught up with him at the age of fifty.

That's what commitment meant to Merv Breene.

So what the hell was he doing now? Chasing Sylvia halfway around the country, desperate to see her. He had never intended to allow anybody to get inside his defences, to allow anybody to mean too much to him. It was a lesson he had learned as a kid, reinforced by his years on the force. And yet he had been a willing participant when Sylvia came along. Dived right in and only just managed to save himself at the last moment. Or so he'd thought. The problem was that he just couldn't shake her, not even when he hadn't contacted her for three whole months. And he'd struggled to hold out for that long, had managed only by immersing himself in his work.

So now here he was, facing the same dilemma, fighting the same battles he had fought six months ago. Trying to keep her out of his life, and losing.

Jesus, why did it have to be so damned difficult?

He looked at his watch. Still an hour to go before

he went to meet her. He stared out at the ocean, tried to soothe himself by watching the roll and heave of the swell. Maybe a coffee and a cigarette. Definitely a cigarette.

Hughes descended the stairs to the forensic labs, still smarting from Bryant's curt dismissal. A time would come when he wouldn't have to take that sort of shit from anybody. Maybe sooner than anybody imagined. He needed to crack this one, make a big hero of himself. A case like this could do it, he knew it could. Maybe even another murder wouldn't hurt, just to up the stakes a bit, put the fear of God into the elderly population just that bit more. Not that he wanted another murder to occur, but it could be to his advantage. It might at least give him a few clues to follow, the murderer might slip up next time. He could only hope.

He caught sight of Ellis in the corridor and remembered the reason for his visit. He shook his head in disgust — how could anybody do that to a poor, defenceless dog? The very thought of it made him angry.

'Ellis,' he snapped, his tone sharper than he intended.

Peter Ellis was startled by the sound of his voice in the silent laboratories.

'Y-y-yes?'

'Sorry,' Hughes forced a smile onto his face. 'I didn't mean to startle you.' He remembered his earlier resolve to try to strike up a friendship with Ellis. Just as an experiment.

'I'm interested to hear your findings on the corpse of that canine that came in this morning.'

'I-I-I've got my n-notes in the l-l-lab. J-j-just through here.' He indicated with his arm. 'D-d-d-did you want to review my f-f-findings now or l-l-later?'

'Now's as good a time as any,' Hughes shrugged. He followed Ellis into the stark lab, its stainless steel benches glowing in the flood of fluorescent lighting. He was vaguely disturbed by his interest in Ellis, but shrugged it off as curiosity about the man.

'Well, is it the same man?' he asked when confronted by the steady blue gaze of Ellis' eyes.

'I'm n-n-not sure. It m-m-may not be.'

'What? You must be joking.'

'W-well, th-there are certain d-differences, if y-you'll allow me to el-el-elaborate.'

'Okay, I'm all ears.'

Ellis consulted his notes.

'The c-c-cause of d-death appears to have been f-f-from an impact with a h-h-heavy object — in this case I'd as-assume it was an automobile.'

'What?'

'Th-th-the an-animal sustained injuries c-consistent with h-h-having been h-hit by a c-c-car, sir.'

'But what about the rest of it? How'd he get all cut up like he was? I've never seen a car do anything like that,' Hughes said sarcastically.

'If y-y-you'd j-just let me fin-fin-finish?' Ellis said, a flush of irritation in his cheeks.

'Sure, go ahead. I'm sorry, I'm under a bit of pressure.' Hughes remembered how badly Ellis had been thrown by questions the day before and resolved to make no further comment until he was finished.

'All right. As I s-said, the animal was a v-victim of a r-road accident. Impact occurred on the r-right side of the body, f-fracturing several ribs which punctured the lower lobe of the right lung and pierced the right atrium. The an-animal would have b-bled to death, s-s-sir.'

'Go on.'

Ellis explained the subsequent incisions that had been made, commenting on the obviously experienced hand of the technician who had made them.

'And then he just hacked the body to pieces?' interrupted Hughes.

'Y-y-yes sir, he has s-s-struck the b-b-body several times. I g-guess you c-could only d-describe his b-blows as frenzied.'

'Like the two old ladies?'

'Y-y-yes, sir.'

'Call me Warren,' Hughes offered with a smile.

Ellis flushed red.

'So tell me, Ellis — Peter, isn't it?'

Ellis nodded.

'So tell me, Peter, why don't you believe it to be the same person?'

'W-w-well,' Ellis avoided Hughes's stare. 'F-for one th-thing, the s-s-surgical n-nature of the in-in-incisions.'

'Maybe he was practising? You said the earlier jobs had been butchery. Maybe our killer is trying to refine his skills?'

'I suppose it's p-p-possible.'

'But you're not convinced?'

'He's used a sh-shorter-bladed weapon to d-dismember the b-body, s-sir.'

'So maybe he's got a collection? There's nothing to say the guy isn't some sort of a knife freak.'

Ellis didn't comment.

'So, Peter, is there any concrete evidence that we're actually dealing with a separate perpetrator, or are we just relying on your instincts? Because so far all the explanations I've offered are plausible, are they not?'

'Y-y-yes, s-sir, they're p-plausible.'

'Okay. We'll assume that it's the same nut. Thank you, Peter. You've been very helpful.' He winked, his smile genuine this time. 'Say, maybe we should get together for a drink some time, see if we can't put our heads together and come up with something on this case. What do you think?'

'I d-d-don't kn-kn-know, s-s-sir,' said Ellis.

'I'd appreciate it. Just so I could bounce my ideas off someone with a bit of intelligence. What do you say?'

'All right, I s-suppose,' Ellis shrugged.

'You live alone, Pete?'

'N-no, s-s-sir.' Ellis coloured.

'All right, Pete.' Hughes was strangely disappointed to think that Ellis had somebody at home. He guessed it was just because he lived alone himself and thought he had found a kindred spirit. 'See you later, then.'

Ellis watched as Warren Hughes departed and frowned when he'd gone through the door. What the hell was the cop after? Then he dismissed the question of Warren Hughes for the time being. He looked at the clock, saw that it was time for lunch and hurried to get out of the labs. He felt oppressed by them today, sensed the lingering presence of death around him more than usual.

It must have been because of her. Amanda. Mandy. He hadn't been able to get her out of his mind, not since he first saw her. He knew he was crazy, knew she couldn't possibly fall for him. But then again, maybe…?

He shrugged, propelled himself up the stairs and into the open air, welcoming the warm kiss of the sunshine on his skin. He joined the crowd on the footpath, glad to be jostling elbows with humanity, with life. He became very preoccupied with death sometimes, it rested on him like a weight, and especially now. The memory of the two old ladies was still very fresh in his mind.

He looked up at the blue sky, the clouds soaring far above the heads of the skyscrapers, and smiled. No matter how much man strove to train and restrain nature, in the big picture of things he made little difference to the heartbeat and purpose of the cosmos. It was a comforting thought.

Lost in his thoughts, he almost collided with the brooding hulk of Michael Finch, halted in front of a shop window and staring in with his menacing stare. Ellis stepped back, his apology forming on his lips, but Finch just glared at him before he turned and stormed away. Ellis watched after him, but was distracted by movement in the window.

Mandy. He couldn't believe his good fortune. He smiled broadly. He'd actually found her. She smiled back at him, started to mouth something when her attention was arrested by a customer in the shop. She turned and waved before hurrying off to serve.

Peter Ellis watched her go, his spirits soaring. Surely destiny had played a role in his seeing her again. And finding where she worked.

Then a dark cloud crossed his horizon. What had Michael Finch been staring at with such menace? He frowned. He'd have to keep an eye on Finch.

CHAPTER 5

She was even more beautiful than Breene remembered, her dark hair tinged with gold from the sun, her skin a shade darker. His chest felt tight. Why had he ever decided he wanted to see her again? Why did he feel as if he had no choice? Maybe there was still time to walk away, turn his back on her before he became engulfed in the magic of the woman again.

It was too late; she had seen him. Her smile was warm, showed off her even teeth, the whites of her eyes startling against the deep chocolate brown of her pupils. Breene knew those eyes only too well, had spent hours immersed in their warm depths.

God, stop it, he cautioned himself. He was in danger of acting like a fool, declaring his undying love for her in the middle of the lunchtime crowd of diners. Get a hold on yourself, man!

Sylvia watched him saunter over to her, casual as ever, his gaze sweeping the other diners with his usual cool. Cocky bastard, she thought, questioning the wisdom of meeting him again, even for lunch.

'Hi!' He flashed her a smile and she melted.

'You're late.'

'You're looking well.' He ignored the comment as he settled his frame into the fragile-looking chair.

'You, too.'

Secretly she thought he'd lost weight and the wrinkles around his eyes were deeper. Probably working too bloody hard, as per usual for him. He barely had time for anything but work. She was surprised he had even taken the time for a vacation.

An uncomfortable silence grew between them, broken when the waiter came to take their order.

'So.' Breene met her eyes. 'How are you enjoying living up here? Everything going according to plan?'

'Oh, you know how it is, setting up in a new area, getting used to a new place. It's hard, and it's… lonely. Sometimes.' Damn. She hadn't meant to say that, hadn't wanted to make any admissions, any concessions.

'I know what you mean.' Breene looked away, struggling to cope with the pain that flickered briefly in her eyes. He wanted to reach out and touch her, hold her hand, sweep the hair out of her eyes, but he restrained himself. There was a wall between them, a wall of his making, and he didn't know how to climb over it. He hadn't even decided that he wanted to.

'And how are things going with you? Any new developments?' she asked, her defences back in place.

Breene told her about his work, the endless little nothings that had made up his life over the preceding months, all the while cursing at the necessity for small talk when what he readlly wanted was to tell her how he missed her, how he'd come all this way because he wasn't sure he'd done the right thing, made the right choice. But any admission would be letting her back into his life, and the fear that she might reject the opportunity loomed large in his mind.

So they sat and talked about things of little consequence, each waiting for the other to step across the barrier, and fearing the repercussions. It was 3 pm before either had realised how quickly the time sped by between them.

'Well.' Their glances met briefly and fell away.

'I suppose I'd better be going. I've still got a pile of work to do at home.' Sylvia dreaded the thought of returning to the empty unit, the afternoon filled with thoughts of Breene, wondering about the significance of this statement, the way his eyes had lingered on her before looking away as if he was on the brink of saying something and then changed his mind.

'Yeah, me too. I told Jack I'd give him a ring this afternoon. He wanted to go over a few things with me,' Breene lied.

What a shitty way to end their lunch date, he thought. There had been a million things he'd wanted to tell her. He had come more than a thousand kilometres to see her, for Christ's sake. But the gap was too wide to cross, his need for self-preservation overriding his need for her.

'Listen, I'm up here for three weeks. I'd really like

to see you again.' Her face lit up. 'I've missed talking to you.' He'd blurted that one out before he'd had time to stop himself.

'Yeah. Me too.' She looked away before he read too much in her eyes. 'Look, I have to go. Give me a call, we'll do it again.'

'Sure.' His fingers brushed her arm. 'I will.'

'Okay, bye.' She pecked him quickly on the cheek, caught a hint of his aftershave — her favourite — and pulled away.

'Bye.' His voice was husky, powerful memories aroused by the soft touch of her lips. They touched hands briefly, avoiding each other's eyes, and then each went their own way.

'Shit.' Sylvia cursed under her breath.

'Fuck.' Breene shook his head angrily, caught a final glimpse of her before she rounded the corner. That hadn't worked out the way he'd intended. Not at all. The thought that he'd see her again before he left was only vaguely satisfying. Maybe he wouldn't even bother.

SLASH KILLER STRIKES AGAIN
DISMEMBERED DOG IN RIVER

Celia Thompson scanned the story for the evening edition of the *Gold Coast Herald* with satisfaction. She'd had difficulty persuading Charlie Stuart to keep the front page free without disclosing the meat of the story, but she knew he'd be satisfied once he saw this. It would put her back on top of the heap again. It had been a long time coming, but she knew she'd claw her way back eventually. All she had needed was the dedication. And the right tips, of course.

She was curious about the tip-off on this one — an insider at the forensic lab who 'thought the public should know'. What the hell, she'd take a tip from wherever she could get it. And the fact that it was going to put more heat on Warren Hughes, Detective Sergeant Warren Hughes, was a bonus. Maybe the fat bastard didn't remember her, but she sure as hell remembered him. He had caused her a shit load of trouble when he busted her for possession — one measly foil of pot. He could easily have let her off, nobody really gave a damn about pot any more anyway, but no, not Warren Hughes. Constable Hughes he'd been in those days. Even the judge had treated the charge as the minor misdemeanour that it was, but her then editor had been looking for any excuse to bust her down from her position as an investigative reporter, with the independence and the expense account that went with it. Bastard.

Well, it had been a long time coming, but she had clawed her way back, and now that she'd made it she wouldn't let go without a fight. And then it was payback time.

Mandy Warner was in a good mood by the end of the day. She was enjoying her job at the jean shop now they had asked her to work full time over her holiday period. At last she felt things were working out for her. School was over and she was looking forward to starting her real studies at university next year, but before then she had a lot of living to do. She stared out the window at the still-bright afternoon — it would be hours yet before the sun went down and she finished work in twenty minutes.

On an impulse she picked up the phone and dialled Jake's number.

'Jake?'

'Mandy. Hi, how's it goin'?'

'Will you pick me up after work? I thought we could go for a walk along the beach or something, and then maybe I could make dinner for you?'

'Sounds good to me, babe. I'll be in it.'

Mandy smiled. Jake was a hopeless cook.

'I'll wait for you out the front at five-thirty.'

'I'll be there. Bye.'

Now she wouldn't have to face the prospect of going home, at least not for a while. She never knew what to expect, but the mood had been decidedly chilly of late. She wished her father would do something about his problems besides trying to drink them away, but she didn't have much say in the matter. Her parents barely seemed to notice that she was growing up.

Not that things had always been that way, but Mandy almost preferred not to remember the way things had been. It all seemed too long ago.

Jake was sitting on the bonnet of his car when she came outside and he jumped off the moment he saw her. He tried to maintain his cool, but he couldn't restrain the affection he felt for her.

'Hey, babe.'

'Hi, Jake,' she smiled and went readily into his

arms. It always made her feel good to know that he loved her. Special.

'So what's the story? You've changed your mind and decided to move in with me, right?' he said, half joking.

Mandy laughed.

'Not quite.' He couldn't hide his disappointment. 'But you never know your luck.' She smiled up into his sparkling green eyes. That was as good as he was going to get. They had been through all this before and Mandy had explained her reasons for not wanting to move in with him. Apart from anything else, she thought she was much too young. Her refusals never stopped Jake from asking.

Maybe she would change her mind, but she had a lot of things to do with her life, and she wasn't about to jump into such a momentous decision without really thinking about it.

'Let's roll,' Jake said. 'The daylight's wasting.'

'Yeah, let's go.' For the time being she was just happy to be with him.

Neither of them noticed the motorbike that followed them all the way back to the block of units in Main Beach where Jake lived. Even if they had seen it, they would have made nothing of it.

The beach was beautiful, the long stretches of sand golden in the afternoon sun. It still had enough strength in it to hold off the chill of the sea breeze and Jake decided to go for a swim. Mandy sat and watched him, delighting in the coolness, digging her toes in the damp sand to work out the aches from a day on her feet. It was too late in the afternoon for her to be getting her long blonde hair wet, especially when Jake had no hair drier in his unit. Besides, she was happier to relax in the surroundings, soothed by the constant crash of the waves, the calling of the seagulls. It was the best place she knew of to lose herself, forget about her problems and worries. None of them mattered here. She lay back on the sand cradling her head in her hands and stared up at the deep blue sky. This was the life. This was all she needed.

She must have drifted off because the next thing she knew Jake was standing over her, dripping salty water onto her bare stomach.

'Hey!' She grabbed a handful of sand and threw it at him but he ducked aside and ran out of reach, taunting her. Mandy was up in a flash, ready to take the challenge. Jake grinned before he turned and sped off up the beach with Mandy in hot pursuit, her long brown legs almost outmatching him.

'Wait,' he gasped, laughing when she had almost caught up to him. 'Wait on.' He sidestepped suddenly and grabbed her as she passed, wrestling her to the ground. They were both out of breath from laughing and covered in sand by the time they got back to their feet.

'Just look at me!' Mandy cried in mock dismay.

'Nothing that a good shower won't fix,' Jake grinned mischievously.

'So that's what this was all about!' Mandy laughed. 'Are you trying to take advantage of me?' She stood with her hands on her hips.

'Yes.'

'Oh.'

They both laughed.

'Come on, let's go and see what you've got in your fridge that's good enough to cook,' she said. 'I'm starving.'

'Right,' Jake agreed. He held out his hand and she took it, sharing his smile.

Maybe she did love him. She just didn't know how she was supposed to find out.

He had been deeply disturbed when he saw her in the arms of another, but then she was still unaware of what awaited her. Events were already moving, had been set in motion with the ritual cleansing that had rid him of the influence of his mother. Her hold on him had been strong, had surprisingly required the deaths of two old ladies instead of one, but that was a small price to pay for what was to come. Even he had only a small inkling of his eventual purpose, but he rested sure in the knowledge that all would be revealed.

He sniffed at the waft of cooking smells from the kitchen and wrinkled his nose. Damned cabbage again. His mother had no imagination when it came to cooking.

Warren Hughes was furious when he saw the headlines in the evening paper. Celia Thompson — he knew that had to be the bitch he'd seen at the press conference. He punched the number of the *Herald* and waited while the phone buzzed in his ear.

'*Gold Coast Herald.*'

'I want to speak to Celia Thompson,' he demanded.

'Who may I say is calling, please?'

'It's Detective Sergeant Warren Hughes.'

'Celia Thompson.' Her nasal voice was full of smug confidence, irritating him further.

'Where the hell did you get your story?' he demanded.

'I'm sorry, who is this?'

'You know damned well who it is.'

'Sergeant Hughes?' She was enjoying this.

'Detective Sergeant,' he growled, rising to the bait.

'I'm sorry, sergeant, but much as I'd like to help you I'm afraid I can't reveal my sources. You know how it is,' she said with mock sincerity.

'Where do you get off, printing crap like that? It's bloody irresponsible.'

'You mean it isn't true?'

Hughes glowered at the phone, wished he had the bitch right there in front of him.

'Sergeant?'

'I've no comment to make on that.'

'Did you wish to add something further, something for the morning edition perhaps? I'm sure we could find room somewhere amongst the news.' This was sweet revenge, and there was more to come.

Hughes struggled to find a response, his mind clouded with anger. Smart-arsed reporters.

'The police are well on top of this case,' he said, tight-lipped. 'We're following several promising leads.' He cut the connection before she could reply, knowing he had come off second best.

'Hughes!' He jumped when Bryant shouted his name. Just what he needed at the end of a long day.

'Yes sir?'

'Get your fat arse into my office pronto.'

Hughes' face reddened and he bit back his retort. He had to crack this one and get that fucking promotion.

'Jesus, Hughes, how the hell did this get into the papers? I thought I warned you about that this morning.'

'I have no idea, sir. Obviously there's a leak somewhere.'

'That's just not good enough, man. A leak somewhere? You should have plugged all the leaks. This never should have got out.'

'But, sir...'

'Shut up.' Both men knew plugging the leaks was just about impossible, but Bryant had to have somebody to take his anger out on. Tex Ellicott had been on the phone for half an hour promising Bryant that his balls would be on the line if this maniac struck again. The man just wouldn't listen to sense, couldn't see past his own future in the next election. Bryant had been livid, but he knew the mayor could make his last six months very uncomfortable if he chose to.

'Find that bloody leak and plug it!' Bryant sank wearily into his chair. He almost wished he could retire early, drop this mess in somebody else's lap, but it wasn't exactly the way he had envisaged the end of his police career. He looked up at Hughes and couldn't even maintain his anger.

'All right, Warren, we'll let the matter drop for now.'

Hughes physically relaxed the tension from his shoulders, but he didn't drop his guard. He didn't trust Bryant, he knew the man didn't like him.

'What new developments have you come up with?' Bryant asked abruptly. 'Nothing? What about the press conference?'

'Not one thing that we can pursue with any confidence sir, not a bloody thing,' said Hughes.

'You can't be serious, man. There must be something.'

'Sure. We got plenty of calls from every weirdo and crackpot in the city, plus a helping hand from all the amateur sleuths, but none of it was on track. I've got some men checking out a few minor possibilities, but I'm telling you there's nothing to get excited about.'

Bryant sighed, scratched his head through the stubble of his crew cut. He reached for his top drawer.

'Drink, Warren?' He poured himself a generous slug of whisky, holding the bottle up quizzically to Hughes.

Hughes looked at his watch and shrugged.

'Sure, why not? It's after hours.'

'We could both do our balls on this one, you know that,' Bryant said after the first fire of the liquor had burnt its way into his gut. 'It's make or break.'

Hughes eyed him steadily and made no comment. He was going to protect his balls, no matter what.

Breene had been restless all afternoon, his agitation lessened only minutely by a long walk on the beach in the evening. He stood and stared out over the water nursing his drink, but even alcohol offered no solution tonight. Hating himself for his weakness, he picked up the phone and dialled her number.

'Sylvia?'

'Merv. What's up?' Her own afternoon hadn't exactly been a barrel of laughs.

'I just thought I'd see how you were going.'

'I'm fine.'

'Oh.' It had been a stupid idea to call her.

'I enjoyed lunch. It was good to see you again.'

'That's good,' he smiled. Maybe it hadn't been such a stupid idea after all. 'So when can we do it again? Or maybe dinner this time?'

There was a pause at the other end.

'I don't think so, Merv.'

'What? Why not?'

'Look, I don't see any point in torturing ourselves. I mean, it was nice to see you, but I've got a life to get on with. It's been damned hard to live with the ghosts of the past six months, Merv, but I think I'm finally starting to have a life again. I need time, Merv, and seeing you just started everything up again.'

'But Sylvia, that's why I came up here. I'm not altogether sure that I made the right choices six months ago. I've been doing a lot of thinking about things, about you and me, and, well, I could do a hell of a lot worse.'

'How flattering.'

'Okay, that didn't come out the way I wanted it to. I enjoyed seeing you today. I mean, really enjoyed it. Maybe we never should have broken up.'

'Yeah, maybe. But we did, and now I've moved on, Merv. I'm not prepared to give up everything I've fought to achieve in the past six months, not now, not for you.'

'Jesus Christ, Sylvia, I've come a thousand kilometres just to see you. I really want to work things out, I really want to make things work again between us.'

He listened to the silence that grew on the other end of the line and cursed himself for his weakness. It had happened anyway, despite all his efforts to remain an island, to avoid commitment. And he'd been too stupid to recognise it.

'Well?'

Sylvia sighed. 'Look, Merv, I love you. You know that, or you bloody well should. No matter how hard I try, that isn't going to change, not for a long time.'

Breene could feel himself smiling.

'But if you're serious, if you really mean what you said about us, then you're going to have to be prepared to make some changes, too. I'm not giving up the ground I've made.'

Breene's grin was slipping.

'So what do you mean?'

'Could you give up being a cop?' It was her turn to listen to the silence.

'That's just bloody unreasonable, Sylvia, and you know it. What the hell else am I any good for besides being a cop?' She was just playing with him. 'You know I couldn't give up my job.'

'Not even for me? Not when you say our relationship is so important?'

'That's bullshit, Sylvia, and you know it. You get what you see, that's it. Like it or leave it.'

'Then I'll bloody well leave it. You expect me to drop everything that I've worked for and come running just because you think you made a mistake? And what about the next time you decide you've made a mistake? What happens to me then? I'm stuck, stranded again, have to make another fresh start. I haven't got another fresh start in me, Merv. Not now. It's just too bloody hard.'

'So that's it then, is it? That's your answer?' His fingers were tight on the receiver, his breathing ragged.

'That's my answer Merv. It has to be,' she said in a small voice, part of her hoping he'd give some ground.

'Well that's fine with me,' he growled. 'You're not blackmailing me into anything, I can survive just fine.'

'Good. So can I.'

'Goodbye.'

'Bye.' She stared at the dead line in her hand and crushed the faint stirring of hope that had risen unexpectedly in her chest when he rang. Sighing, she surveyed the chaos of her unit. She had a lot of work to do, and there was no time like the present.

'Damn you, woman,' Breene snarled. He swept the phone from the table and it crashed into the wall, the receiver bleeping loudly in the silence of the unit. He grabbed his jacket and stalked from the unit, slamming the door behind him with a satisfying thud. *Women.*

It was later than she had intended to return home, but the evening with Jake had been so pleasant that she didn't want it to end. Besides, she was old enough now to be doing as she pleased, and her mum and dad would have to learn to accept the fact.

'I'll walk you to the door,' Jake offered when they came to a stop outside the dark house. 'It looks as if everyone is asleep.'

'Yeah,' Mandy whispered, hoping he was right. 'Just be quiet, all right?'

'Sure,' Jake grinned, his teeth flashing white in the gloom. Mandy stifled a giggle.

'Come on.' She took his hand and led him along the path to the door. 'This'll do. You'd better not come in, I don't want to wake my father.'

'I'm not leaving without a kiss,' Jake said, taking her in his arms. 'Not tonight.'

Light flooded over them and the door was snatched open.

'Where the hell have you been?' Jack Warner demanded. The young couple quickly separated. Mandy could detect the faint slur in her father's words that told he had been drinking.

'Get your backside in here, young lady. Your mother's been worried sick about you.'

'I just…it was such a nice afternoon when I finished work that I thought…'

'I don't care what you thought,' Warner snapped. 'Inside.' He glared at Jake. 'And you can piss right off, mister.'

'Dad,' Mandy pleaded.

'I said inside!' He grabbed her by the wrist and pulled her towards the door.

'Hey! There's no need for that.' Jake stepped up to intervene.

'It's all right, Jake,'' Mandy turned to face him. 'I'll see you tomorrow.' The door slammed behind her.

'You won't be seeing anybody tomorrow!' her father yelled.

Jake stood outside the door, a worried frown on his face. He could hear raised voices inside but felt helpless to do anything about it. The light flicked off, plunging him into darkness. He stared miserably at the door, wanting to protect his girl but not willing to cross the line between father and daughter. He sat down on the steps in the dark and waited. Maybe he couldn't intervene, but he wasn't going anywhere until things settled down inside.

'What is your problem, Dad?' Mandy fought back her angry tears. 'Who do you think you're pulling around?'

'You listen to me, my girl!'

'I'm not *your girl*, not any more. Especially when you behave like this. I've finished school now, dad, I'm working full time. I could leave home if I wanted to,' she threatened.

'You can't stop me,' Mandy retorted.

'What's going on?' Pam Warner had been roused by the raised voices and she came into the kitchen, blinking owlishly in the light.

'Your daughter has been out having a good time with that bloody Jake again. I told you we should have nipped that in the bud months ago, but it's too late now. God only knows what the young bastard's been up to with our daughter. Well, you won't be having anymore to do with him, young lady, not if I've got anything to do with it.'

'It's none of your business,' Mandy said hotly. 'Who are you to tell me who I can and can't see?'

'I'm your bloody father, that's who, and it's about time you showed me some respect. You get your arse into your room.'

'I won't. You can't shove me around any more, I'm not your wife, thank God.'

'Mandy!' Pam Warner snapped.

'That's enough out of you, young lady. That's it, do you hear me? From now on there are going to be a whole lot of changes around here, and the first is you're not seeing that young lout any more. Is that clear?' Jack Warner glared at his daughter, his face flushed.

'You can't do that. You haven't got the right,' Mandy shouted. 'I love Jake!'

'That's a load of fucking shit. You wouldn't know what love was.'

'All right, Jack, that's enough. We'll talk about this in the morning.' Pam knew that things were getting out of hand.

'Don't you tell me what to do, woman. I'm still the man of this house, though you'd never know from the little respect I get. Just because you've got a job, just because you're earning a bit of money, don't think you can start ordering me around. You're not taking everything away from me.'

'That's ridiculous. You've had too much to drink.' Pam turned to walk away but he grabbed her by the arm and pulled her back to face him.

'I'll drink as much as I bloody well please. I earn it every day,' he snarled.

'Huh!' she snorted. 'You must be joking.'

'What?' Warner's voice dropped down dangerously low. 'What do you mean by that, woman?'

'Stop it! Stop it, both of you!' Mandy was afraid her father was going to hit her mother. She had never seen him look so angry.

'You keep out of this, you little slut. You're the one who started all the trouble in the first place,' he warned.

'*I* started the trouble? *You're* the one who comes home pissed every day. That's the only trouble in this house.'

Warner slapped her hard across the face.

'Jack!'

The three of them stood in stunned silence for a slow minute. Warner had never struck Amanda in his life.

'Are you all right, Mandy?' Pam reached out to her daughter.

'Leave me alone!' She shrugged her mother's hand aside and stared defiantly at her father.

'You'll never hit me again, you bastard. You're nothing but a lousy drunk.' She turned to face her mother. 'And if you're prepared to take it, you're just as bad.' She gulped back the tears that threatened.

'I'm leaving. Now. Tonight.'

Warner recovered his wits as she closed the door behind her.

'Mandy! Amanda!' he strode to the door and reefed it open. 'Amanda! You walk out tonight, don't expect to come back!'

There was no answer but the sound of two car doors closing as an engine coughed into life.

'Amanda! Amanda, you come back here!' Warner ran out onto the lawn and shouted up the street after the rapidly departing car. The dog across the road started barking and the lights in the house went on.

'Fuck it!' Warner cursed. 'Fuck you!' he muttered, shaking his fist in the air.

He didn't say a word to Pam when he walked back inside.

'You've sunk to a new low.' She turned and walked into the bedroom, closing the door behind her. The lock clicked loudly in the silent house.

Jack stared out into the dark night. It had all gone wrong, everything had gone wrong and he didn't know how to fix it. Maybe it was already too late.

Night enfolded the restless slumber of Paradise, awaiting the golden sunshine of another day.

In his small bedroom, with the lights turned down and the music whispering softly, he planned his next move, the next step towards his ascendancy. He had known from the moment he saw her that she was the one. Pity that her name was Amanda — somehow it just wasn't the name he'd expected. Well, no matter. What difference did a name make? He smiled in the darkness and stroked the hardness between his legs.

CHAPTER 6

He watched her. Followed her. Couldn't remember not knowing her, not watching her, was aware of her during every waking moment. Every line of her beautiful face was burned into his consciousness, etched in fine lines. He knew she felt it too, could sense his presence and his thoughts, was aware of the unspoken communication between them.

He smiled as he followed her, watched her slim body as she strode purposefully along. He knew she shared the mounting anticipation, awaiting the moment they could begin. He wondered how she could remain so calm when every fibre of his being was quivering with excitement.

Dusk was approaching fast as they neared the chosen site. He marvelled at her composure, the strength of her resolve to play her role out to its exact conclusion, the precise minute. His heart skipped a beat. For one instant he feared she wouldn't heed the call, that she would deny him. It didn't occur to him for even an instant that he might be wrong, that she was unaware of him and of his designs.

She half turned her head, as if sensing his anxiety and wishing to reassure him. He quickened his pace, timing his stride to meet her at the correct moment. It was essential that each requirement be met, despite the urgings of his own eagerness. His heightened sense of awareness seemed to slow time as her pace slackened. She was almost at the precise site he had chosen.

'Amanda.'

His voice was hoarse with suppressed excitement.

'What?' Her head whipped around, suddenly aware of his presence on the deserted path. 'You! Stay away from me!'

'Amanda,' he said reproachfully. She didn't have to continue with the game any longer. Their time had come. He shook his head gently, reaching out a tender hand to touch her cheek. 'Everything is as it should be.'

Her eyes widened with fear.

'Don't touch me, don't hurt me, please,' she begged, backing away from him. She turned to run.

His hand reached out quickly, grabbing her thick hair and pulling with all the power of his arm. Amanda was jerked backwards, almost off her feet. She whimpered in pain and terror.

'You shouldn't make me do this to you, Amanda,' he hissed into her beautiful face, his mouth only inches away from hers. 'You can't imagine what I'm going to do for you.'

Amanda's world ground to a halt. The moment

became a slow-motion nightmare while he held her there, only inches from his face. She was so beautiful. His free hand clutched at her shoulder, powerful fingers digging cruelly into the flesh there. The other hand tugged playfully at her long hair. She fought to turn her head away, to block out the paralysing fear.

Street lights flickered on overhead and he looked up, momentarily confused. Being so close to her, feeling her, smelling her was intoxicating after the time when he could only watch and imagine. It threatened to distract him from his purpose. Not yet. Not here. He'd chosen the site with such care. All he had to do now was take her there, away from prying eyes that couldn't possibly understand.

'Come, the moment is at hand,' he whispered gently, his cold eyes locking into hers and holding. She gasped at the sudden sharp tug on her hair as he turned her aside from the path and tried to bustle her into the thick bushes beyond the concrete border.

'No,' she pleaded, thinking, *This can't be happening to me.*

But it was.

Amanda wasn't a stupid girl. She knew reality when it was staring her in the face. This guy was obviously crazy. And she was in deep trouble. Being terrified was not helping.

A car horn blared close behind them and her mind was freed from the numbing grip of terror, galvanising her into action. She drove the blunt heel of her shoe downwards onto his instep with all the strength she could muster. He gasped in pain and surprise, his grasp on her shoulder weakened. Amanda spun within the circle of his arms, ignoring the pain from his hold on her hair. She drove her right knee sharply up into his groin and watched with surprised detachment as he groaned in agony, his hands clutching to protect himself from further assault.

Amanda wasn't finished yet. She swung her handbag up and hit him squarely on the nose. Blood spurted instantly and he cried out in pain, sinking to the ground in agony and confusion. This wasn't supposed to happen. This wasn't how it should have been.

'Amanda!' he moaned.

It spurred her on, reigniting her fury. He wasn't going to get another chance at her. Adrenalin coursed through her veins as she reached for his hair and jerked his head forward and banged it against the concrete. Again. And again. The sounds of it thudding against the hard ground were sickening, but she was beyond caring.

'Hey, what's going on there? Hey!'

A voice penetrated her fear and fury. She looked up, dazed and panting, struggling to focus on her surroundings. A taxi was pulled up at the curb and the driver was out of the car and had come around onto the footpath. He hesitated only a couple of metres away from the two of them.

She stared at his face in confusion, waking from the nightmare. She looked down at the bloodied face beneath her, her mind struggling to breach the depths of terror that encased it in a world of unreality. Slowly she loosed her grip on his hair and his head sank back into the pool of blood on the cement.

Reality hit her. She lurched to her feet and backed away from her would-be attacker, clutching a shaking hand to her mouth. The colour drained from her face and suddenly she was shaking all over as the tide of adrenalin ebbed and pulsed within her. The footpath felt unsteady under her feet.

'Hey, are you all right, lady?' The taxi driver moved quickly towards her, fearing she was going to faint.

Huge brown eyes stared stricken into his face as he put a steadying arm around her shoulders. She pointed a trembling hand at the crumpled figure on the ground and her mouth struggled to form the words, but the sound refused to come out.

'It's okay, lady,' he said gently. 'I'm here now.'

A sob wracked her body, taking her by surprise.

'He…' She raised her hand to the groaning figure on the ground struggling to sit up. 'He attacked me.' She looked up at the taxi driver and shook her head in utter disbelief. 'He attacked me.' She rested her head lightly against his chest and started to cry.

'It's all right now. Don't you cry, you're safe now.' He patted her gently on the shoulder.

'Don't move, you!' he yelled, shaking a warning arm at the bloodied figure on the ground. 'Don't move or I'll smash your fucking head in, you bastard.'

Paul Fletcher ushered the trembling girl into the front seat of his taxi, keeping his eyes firmly on her assailant. He reached in for the reassuring hardness of the iron bar he kept in the cab for safety.

'Are you okay? Nothing broken?' he asked gently, quickly running his eyes over her small frame. She seemed to be physically unharmed. He draped his cardigan around her shoulders. 'You just sit there for a minute, I'll be right back.'

The assailant was struggling to sit up, wiping at his nose with the cloth of his shirt. He regarded Fletcher balefully as he approached.

'This has nothing to do with you.' He sucked in a deep breath and puffed out his chest. 'It was not meant to be this way.'

'I bet it wasn't. Took you by surprise, did she, dickface? Well, you just stay right there and don't try to get up or I'll knock your fucking head off. Got it?' He raised the iron bar menacingly. 'You rotten prick. I'd love to kick you in the guts, but it looks like the little lady fixed you up just fine.' He spat a glob of phlegm into his face. 'Scum.'

He made no move to get up. He wiped at the spit on his face and stared up at the driver, hatred burning in his eyes. He'd pay. He'd make sure he paid.

Fletcher had been in plenty of fights in his time, but even with an iron bar in his hand he didn't like what he saw in the eyes that glared up at him. It gave him the creeps. He glanced over his shoulder towards the taxi where Amanda had slumped down on the seat. He didn't know what to do. He had to look after her, get her to a hospital or the cop station or something, but what about the creep who attacked her? He didn't want to just leave him. Not that he looked like he'd get too far. She'd given him a hell of a beating. His gaze fell speculatively to the iron bar in his hand. Wouldn't take much, just a sharp rap over the back of the head and the bastard wouldn't hurt anybody any more. But he couldn't really do that. Could he? He looked back at the guy on the ground and weighed his choices. Pathetic bastard. Snivelling on the ground, beaten up by the unfortunate kid he'd picked on. Served him right. Looked like he was losing a fair bit of blood.

The moment of indecision passed. He was no thug and the thought of hitting someone over the head didn't appeal to him. No matter what the prick had done. He was just glad the kid was okay. With barely a backward glance he ran around to the driver's side of the taxi and got in. He'd tell the cops where he'd left the guy and they'd pick him up before he got too far. His head was in a spin, as much a victim of shock as the girl on the seat beside him. This sort of shit always happened to somebody else, or at least that's what he'd thought. It didn't even occur to him that he should use his radio to alert the police to the assailant's whereabouts. He tucked the iron bar down the side of his seat as he started the engine.

'You okay?' He asked the kid curled up on the seat beside him. 'Hey?' He lifted her chin and she looked at him with tear-filled eyes. Poor kid. Anger boiled inside him as he hauled the car into gear and slammed the accelerator to the floor, spraying her assailant with gravel from the side of the road as the taxi leapt into motion. Lousy bastards didn't realise how badly they could stuff up a young girl's life. Just for a few thrills. He shook his head in disgust.

Amanda heaved herself up from the seat and slumped in the corner hard up against the door. The cab sped along the familiar road, taking her away from the scene of her nightmare.

'Feeling better?' the cabbie asked.

She didn't feel like answering him. She just wanted to stare straight ahead while he drove.

'You got any cigarettes?' she asked in a small voice, surprised to hear herself talking.

'Sure, just on the seat beside you. Help yourself,' he offered.

She took one and lit it.

'Thanks.'

'No problem.'

'I mean for helping me out back there.'

He looked at her and was rewarded with the ghost of a smile.

'Didn't look like you needed too much help by the time I came along.'

'I was scared,' she said quietly.

The cabbie just nodded.

'Where are you taking me?' Amanda asked after a short silence.

'Cop shop.'

She stiffened on the seat beside him.

'No.'

'What?' He looked at her, incredulous.

'I don't want to go to the police.' She stared straight ahead.

'You have to go to the cops. You can't let bastards

like that run around attacking people. Not everyone's as lucky as you were.'

'Look, I'm feeling okay now and he didn't hurt me, so let's just leave it at that.'

'What do you mean, you're okay? You're a mess, a nervous wreck. You must be in a state of shock or something. You can't just ignore something like that, it don't make sense. That bastard's got to be locked away where he can't hurt anybody else.'

'I don't want to go to the cops. That's all there is to it,' she said firmly.

The cabbie shook his head. 'I just don't understand you kids. I got a daughter, you know. Must be about your age, too. It makes me sick to think that some creep like that guy back there could hurt her, and here you are not doing anything about it. How do you figure that?'

'Look, I've had plenty of bad experiences with cops. I know how they are, I know how they treat somebody who has been assaulted like this. Besides, he didn't really hurt me, just gave me a fright. That's all.'

'Yeah, well, I'm sorry but I'm gonna let the cops know, whether you like it or not.'

Amanda turned away, stared out at the dark night. She knew how her dad would react when he heard about this — he'd probably never let her out of his sight again. But wasn't all of this partly his fault, anyway?

'If you want to go to the cops that's your business, but let me out now. Right here. I don't want anything to do with them,' she stared defiantly at

Fletcher, tried to hide the fear and confusion that bubbled up inside her.

'All right.' Fletcher sighed and shook his head. He was probably doing the wrong thing, but he was a softie at heart and she reminded him of his own daughter. 'Where do you want me to take you?'

'Just take me home,' she stifled the tears that threatened to overwhelm her. 'Home' meant Jake's place now, not the reassuringly familiar house she had shared with her parents. In her dazed state the upheavals of the past few days were almost too much to cope with. She was floundering, confused, frightened.

'Take me to Jake's place.' She needed to feel his strong arms around her, to know that he loved her. She needed some anchor, some basis for reality.

'Okay,' Fletcher shrugged. 'You're the boss. I just hope that bastard doesn't go anywhere before I can do something about him.' He clapped his hand to his forehead. 'What a dumb shit I am.' He reached for his microphone. '421 to base 421 to base, emergency, repeat, emergency.'

'Base — go ahead 421.'

'Got an assault victim in the car — assailant is on the footpath about 300 metres along the Narrowneck strip. He's injured, but they'd better get out there pretty quick.'

'Roger 421 — I'll get back to you.'

He glanced at Amanda. 'I'm gonna tell them where I dropped you off too, they'll need you as a witness.'

Amanda shrugged and stared out the window. She

didn't care, as long as he got her back to Jake's place quickly. Nothing else mattered now.

He lifted his head up and supported himself on his arms, waited for the wave of nausea to pass. Blood dripped slowly onto the cement, he could taste its metallic warmth in the back of his throat.

The bitch. How could she have done that to him? He had been so sure. Slut. She was nothing but an imposter. She'd been toying with him all along. She was just like all the others. But he'd had plans for this one. He thought she was the one, the one who would understand his tortured reality, who would make him a man again.

Betrayed! Whore!

He struggled to his feet, clenching his jaw against the waves of nausea that threatened his balance. The night air steadied him and he found he could stand upright. He shook his head to clear his vision, but that brought bright stabs of agony from his offended skull. The bitch. The rotten fucking bitch.

Swaying slightly, frustrated tears of anger and hurt blurring his vision, he made his way into the small clearing in the bushes. This was where they should have consummated their love, this was to have been the chosen place. Instead she had spurned him. The bitch didn't know what she was missing out on. His hand groped under the bushes for his blade. He always kept his blade nearby, just in case. He pulled the machete from its sheath. Its blade sparkled blue-white in the moonlight; its finely honed sharpness sent a thrill through his body. The avenger. The equaliser. A thick drop of blood fell onto the mirror-like surface, splattering where it hit.

He left it where it fell and stumbled back onto the path. He looked to right and left, scanning for any further signs of interference. The first part of his plan had gone wrong, but he had made allowances, he had more than one ace up his sleeve. He took three quick breaths, willed himself to overcome the deficiencies of the weak vessel that was his body and set off at a trot, quickly reaching the car park and his mother's battered Valiant.

The night was far from over.

'Jake. Jake?' She could hear the note of hysteria in her own voice as she called into the dark interior of the unit. 'Jake!' She stood in the darkened lounge room, fear rooting her to the spot. There were no certainties any longer, she didn't know what she might find. She jumped when the light flicked on in the bedroom.

'Hey, babe.' Jake appeared in the doorway scratching his unruly hair sleepily. 'I crashed after work.'

'Oh, Jake!' She rushed over to him and buried her head in his chest. Sobs welled up in her throat.

'Hey, what's up?' Jake held her away so that he could see her face. 'What's the matter?'

She couldn't answer, overcome with the horror of what had happened now that she had reached the safety of his arms.

'Is it your dad again?' he asked softly. She shook her head.

'No. It's...I was attacked. On the way home,' she sobbed.

'*What*? Attacked? Who attacked you? When? Are you all right?' He took her into the bedroom and sat her on the bed, anger rising in his chest. 'Mandy, are you all right?' He ran his hands over her, his eyes searching for signs of injury. 'Who was it? Where is he?' he demanded.

'It was when I was walking home along Narrowneck. On the path,' she said between sobs.

'I'll kill the bastard.' Jake was on his feet now, flexing and unflexing his hands. 'I'll *kill* the bastard. Did he hurt you?'

'No,' she said. Jake strode to the door of the bedroom. 'Jake?' He turned to face her. 'Don't leave me.'

His anger crumbled. He rushed back to her side and took her in his embrace.

'Oh, baby.' He held her fiercely. 'I couldn't live without you.' He sat and held her until her sobs slowed. Outside the night descended, blotting out the last traces of evening.

'Jake?' Mandy said quietly. 'I love you.'

Jake held her away so that he could see her tear-stained face. He kissed her puffy eyes and gently wiped her damp cheeks with his hand.

'I bet I look a mess,' she smiled.

'Never!' Jake was glad to see her smile. 'Feeling better now?'

'Yes,' she nodded. 'I felt better as soon as I saw you.' It was Jake's turn to smile.

'Will you make love to me, Jake?' She didn't meet his eyes.

'Are you sure?'

'Yes,' she nodded. 'I want you to.'

They lay together afterwards, their bodies touching. The wind had picked up outside and the trees in the street danced in the reflected glow of the streetlight, casting restless shadows on the ceiling.

'Jake?' He felt her body stiffen.

'I've seen him before.' His face, eradicated by shock, had returned to haunt her as she lay there.

'Who?' He was feeling drowsy in the contented afterglow of love.

'The guy who attacked me.'

He jerked up onto his elbow, instantly alert.

'Who was it?'

They were both startled by a loud knock on the door.

'Shit! It must be the police. He said he was going to report to them.'

'Who?'

'The cab driver.'

'What?'

'The guy who rescued me.' She was already out of bed, throwing on one of Jake's flannelette shirts to cover her nakedness. 'Get dressed,' she said. 'I'll get the door.'

She was too terrified to scream when he burst into the room, his face a bloody mask.

'Jake!' her voice was a dry croak in her throat. 'Jake! It's him!'

Jake heard the note of terror in her voice and raced into the lounge room to protect her.

'You bastard!' he hissed, shielding her with his

body. 'You bastard. I'll kill you!' His voice was pure hatred, fury boiling up within him as the bloodied figure advanced into their home.

'You're going to regret coming here!' Jake squared up against him.

The man stood still, making no move towards Jake, his eyes fixed firmly on Amanda.

Jake swung a savage punch at his head, wanting only to hurt this bastard who had attacked his Mandy. His anger caused the blow to go wide, the assailant sidestepping it easily.

'Jake, look out!' Amanda called. 'He's got a knife!'

Jake was too furious to heed her warning. He didn't care if he did have a knife, he wouldn't have cared if he had a gun. This creep was going to pay for what he'd done, he was going to pay for coming here, to their home. He aimed a second punch at his head, putting all his force into the blow. He'd kill him if he had to.

The assailant jerked his head out of the way at the last moment, Jake's own momentum throwing him momentarily off balance. The long gleaming machete seemed to appear from nowhere. Time was suspended as it swung in a slow arc of flashing silver, biting cold and cruel into Jake's wrist.

'No!' he screamed in agony, staring incredulously at the gaping wound from which his hand dangled precariously. *'No!'* He shook his head in utter disbelief. This couldn't be happening. His vision blurring, he turned to face his attacker. The fucker was smiling! Pain and fear fought with Jake's instinct for survival. There was a sound like the ocean pounding

STALKER

in his ears as he watched the nightmare figure advance on his terrified Amanda.

His fury boiled up from deep within, love for Amanda overriding any fears he held for himself. Jake charged at the advancing figure of menace, heedless of the cruel steel blade he wielded.

The man turned catlike, flourishing the blade over his head and sweeping it downwards with murderous intent, marvelling at the ease with which practice became reality, revelling in the power that he controlled as the bitter blade made contact with the flesh and sinew of Jake's neck. He felt a twinge, an instant of regret as he watched the young body crumple, losing all its purpose, its youthful vigour extinguished with each powerful jet of blood that geysered from the gaping wound. His eyes were drawn to Jake's as life departed, and he shuddered. There was no answer there for him.

He struck again, swatting at Jake's head.

'*Jake!*' the scream ripped from Amanda's throat '*Jake!*' She clutched her hands to her face to blot out the horrible vision of his young body, now a bleeding, crumpled carcass. This couldn't be happening. Desperately she pleaded with herself to wake up, prayed for the terrifying nightmare to end, but she couldn't blot out the evil menacing figure who advanced towards her, the crazed stranger who had wrenched Jake's life away from him.

'What do you want from me?' she screamed. 'What do you *want*?'

He was laughing now and the blood from his wounded lip flowed with renewed vigour, coursing down his chin and dribbling over his neck and chest.

'You had your chance, Amanda. I had plans for us.'

'Leave me *alone*!' she screamed. 'Leave me alone.' She wanted to run, to hide away from all that had happened, from this world that had skewed from its axis. She wanted to die, to drop where she stood, and know no more. Her mind groped blindly for escape but found no release.

'Please,' she pleaded, backing away from him. 'Please.'

She tripped and fell heavily to the floor, exposing the nakedness beneath the shirt she had thrown on in her haste to answer the door only a few minutes earlier.

His fevered brain was inflamed by what he saw revealed to him, his earlier purpose returned with renewed strength. He would not give her the opportunity of thwarting him again.

'Oh, God,' she begged. '*Please. Please* don't hurt me.' Paralysed with fear, she searched frantically for some weapon, something to defend herself with, but her eyes only found Jake's face, twisted in the throes of death. Her scream pierced the night.

'Sure is a lot of blood here. She must have given him a hell of a hiding.'

'Yeah, the cabbie reckoned she'd made a real mess of him.'

The two policemen chuckled quietly.

'Pity there aren't more girls who know how to defend themselves. I don't think this guy's going too far tonight, shouldn't be hard to spot.'

'Hey, looks like he's gone into the bushes there.' The younger of the two pointed to a gap in the bushes marked by bright splashes of blood.

'Makes the job easier. You go in first, Quinny, I'll be right behind you.' He smiled at the younger officer. 'One of the advantages of rank.'

'Sure, Piercey,' Quinn laughed. 'Everyone knows you're a coward.'

'That's Senior Constable Pierce to you, son,' Pierce replied. 'You junior officers get more uppity every year!'

'Sure, Steve,' Quinn replied. They had been together since Mick Quinn's graduation from the academy six months earlier and had become friends as well as partners.

'Come on, let's flush this bastard out of the bushes. Be careful, he could be armed.'

They went in through the opening together, alert to any sounds or movements.

'Nothing,' Quinn shrugged. 'Looks like he's gone.'

'See any signs of departure through another exit?'

'Nope. Besides, there's so much blood in here that we'd be able to see if he'd gone out any other way. The branches are too close together for him not to have left some sign.'

'I guess you're right. Hey, what about over here?' Pierce pointed to an area where thick blood was spattered over some low branches. 'There's something under here!' he called to Quinn. 'I don't know what it is.' He reached under and brought out a sodden mass of red.

'Must have been his hankie,' Quinn commented.

'Yeah,' Pierce grimaced. 'Now I got blood all over me.' He wiped his hands on the grass.

'I wonder what little surprises he had in store for that girl? I don't think he was planning a picnic,' Quinn said.

The radio in the car crackled to life.

'71 come in please, car 71, come in.'

'That's us,' Steve Pierce said, scrambling out through the bushes, still wiping his hands on the sides of his trousers.

'Yeah, 71 here. What's up?'

'You'd better get down to Woodroffe and Cronin Ave in Main Beach, block of flats on the corner. We've had reports of a disturbance in unit twenty-three, fourth floor. Sounds like you'd better go right over.'

'On our way,' Pierce said. 'Come on Quinny, the city needs us.' The powerful engine roared into life and he turned on the lights and the siren.

'Any excuse.' Quinn rolled his eyes and then held on as Pierce indulged in some high-speed driving manoeuvres.

'There it is, on the other side of the road. Across the median strip.' He pointed.

'No problems,' Pierce smiled, reefing on the patrol car's handbrake and sliding over the strip, bringing the car to an expert halt against the gutter on the far side of the road.

'Drama queen,' Quinn accused. Pierce raised one bushy eyebrow and twirled his moustache.

'Best driver to go through the driving school,' he

bragged. 'Should have taken it up professionally.'

'Who would have protected the good law-abiding citizens without you?' Quinn jibed at him.

There was a bloody handprint on the door to Unit 23, smeared where someone had attempted to remove it. The two young police officers sobered instantly. Pierce drew his gun and motioned for Quinn to do the same. They took up positions on either side of the door, flattened against the wall.

'Police! Open up in there!' Pierce called loudly.

No response.

'Open it or we break it in,' he warned. 'Okay, Mick?' They eyed each other for an instant. 'One, two, three! He threw himself at the door, the doorjamb splintering under his solid weight. He spun through the doorway and flattened himself against the wall inside.

'Oh, Jesus,' he groaned. 'Jesus *Christ*. Mick, get *in* here!'

Pierce's eyes were hard and cold as they swept the dishevelled room. The walls were coated in bright blood.

'Jesus Christ, man, looks like that sicko bastard has struck again.'

The stench of fresh blood hung thick in the air.

'Steve.' Quinn pointed haltingly to one of the lounge chairs, its cream fabric dyed crimson. One arm dangled over the side of it.

'Okay, Mick, take it easy now,' said Pierce, trying to make his voice as steady as he could. 'We'll just go over nice and slow. Don't you move one muscle, motherfucker, I'll blow your damn head off,' he warned in a tight voice. He followed his trembling gun around to the front of the lounge chair.

'Jesus Christ!'

The body was slumped in the chair, a gaping bloody mess where the head should have been. Pierce vomited where he stood.

'Jesus, Mick, get someone down here. Fast.' He retched again and stumbled to the balcony, gulping in the fresh air.

Quinn searched desperately for the phone, not willing to use the radio in the patrol car. He didn't want to leave his partner alone in the unit. He quickly scanned the small lounge room, avoiding whatever Steve had seen in the chair. One of them had to be functional, in case the killer was still in here somewhere.

'Must be in the bedroom,' he muttered to himself. 'Should have thought of it before.' He tried to slip into neutral gear, let his mind become detached from his emotions. Still with his gun in hand, he stepped cautiously into the bedroom.

'Oh, my God!' he wailed. 'Oh, my God.' His knees felt weak and he forced himself to swallow the bitter bile that gorged in his throat. 'Pierce!' he shouted. *Jesus Christ.* 'Pierce, it's him again, all right!'

Jake's head stared blankly back at him from its perch between the pillows.

When reinforcements arrived they found the two young officers pale but composed on the landing outside the unit.

'It's in there,' Pierce indicated weakly. 'But there's no fucking way I'm going back in.'

Hughes was on the scene within five minutes, cursing violently when he saw the havoc inside the small unit. His faint hope that the killer wouldn't strike again had proved groundless.

'Looks like he left in a hurry — the body isn't all cut up like the others.'

'Sarge,' a uniform called from the bedroom. 'Take a look at this.' Hughes stepped through the door, ignoring the head perched obscenely between the pillows. The uniformed cop pointed at a crumpled skirt and pair of panties on the floor. 'They're still warm, sarge. Looks like the victim had female company.'

'Fuck!' Who knew what the bastard had in store for the girl? He turned and stalked from the room. 'Don't touch a damned thing,' he roared, 'and get somebody from forensics down here. Pronto.'

'On their way, sir,' Frank Pennington scowled at Hughes's back. Hughes wasn't the only one who had thought of that.

Hughes was sweating badly by the time he reached the bottom of the staircase, the exertion only partly to blame. This case was getting scary, and they weren't any closer to the killer. They could have a full-scale serial killer on their hands. For once he wished this case hadn't fallen on his shoulders.

'Sergeant Hughes!' He was startled by a camera flash, recognised the face of Celia Thompson. 'Is this another murder by the slasher?'

'Get the hell out of my face,' Hughes growled. He turned on the photographer. 'And if you take another picture I'll rip your fucking camera to pieces.' He hurried to his car and left the scene in a screech of rubber.

Celia Thompson watched him leave and hung her head wearily. There must be a better way to earn her living than tailing a stupid, abusive detective like Hughes, but at least it had finally paid off. She'd scored herself another scoop.

It had been a quiet night and Paul Fletcher would be glad when his shift was over. All he wanted to do now was crawl into his warm bed and catch a few hours' sleep before the day got too hot. That was the trouble with this place, it was too damned hot. He lit a cigarette and watched the smoke trail out the window. There were only a few stragglers around by this hour of the morning, the odd holidaymaker trying to make the most of their time and justify the huge accommodation bills they paid for the privilege of staying in the high-rise buildings around Surfers Paradise.

He wondered what had happened to the young girl he had picked up earlier in the night. Probably safe at home, cuddled up to her junior lover. He thought of his own daughter, living with his wife thousands of kilometres away in Melbourne. He hoped Trudy was keeping an eye on her. Maybe he'd give them a call later on, when he was up for the day. He didn't ring them nearly as often as he'd like to. Of course, the fact that he and Trudy were separated had something to do with that.

He'd cruised around for half the night in his

STALKER

mother's Valiant, searching for the only remaining witness. He smiled with satisfaction when he saw him, the only cab on the lonely street. This was almost too easy.

Paul Fletcher must have dozed off, but the noise of the rear door closing snapped him awake. He'd go home after this one. Wouldn't do to go to sleep and give some bum the chance to rip off his night's takings.

'Where to, mister?' He half turned, waiting for the mumbled answer. If the guy was still out this late he was more than likely plastered. 'Hey, where you going?' He turned around fully to see if he could get some sense out of the guy.

'Oh, it's you, is it?'

He was caught completely off guard as his passenger lunged forward, a bright blade flashing in his hand.

'Here's one, Bill,' Melanie giggled. 'See, I told you we'd find one. This is Surfers Paradise, after all. Come on,' she dragged Bill towards the taxi.

'In you go, and don't throw up. We don't want to dirty this nice man's taxi. Isn't that right mister? Mister? God, he must be asleep. Can't blame him I suppose, hey Bill? The bouncers had to help me to wake you so we could get out of the place,' she giggled.

'Yeah, well I got bored watching you dance with that guy,' Bill replied gruffly.

'Oh don't be silly, I was just being friendly.' She kissed him on the cheek. 'Come on Billy boy, don't be jealous.'

Bill smiled despite himself.

'All right. Let's go home, we'll see about who's jealous or not.'

'Ooh. Hey mister, you'd better get us home quick, before Bill goes back to sleep. Mister? Hey!' she shook him by the shoulder. His head lolled back and her hand came away covered with sticky warmth.

'Bill!' she pleaded 'Bill?' She looked dumbfounded at the blood on her hands. 'He's dead!'

Her screams shattered the early morning quiet of the awakening city.

CHAPTER 7

Mervyn Breene groaned and rolled over, cautiously opening one eye. The sun beat in through the open window behind his bed, flooding the bedroom with bright light. He squeezed his eye shut and covered his face with his hand. He felt like shit. Maybe he'd be able to catch a few more hours and wake up feeling human.

No chance. It was too bloody hot. He swung his legs over the side of the bed and sat there, nursing another damned hangover. He cursed Sylvia roundly, cursed his own weakness, his stupidity for even coming to the Coast, for even thinking that they had a chance. The whole trip had been a bloody waste of time.

He wondered vaguely how his buddy Jack Warner was getting on. Seeing him had been the excuse for finally pushing himself to make the trip, but he had barely had any contact with the man. He didn't know what to make of the Jack he'd met a few days ago; he certainly wasn't the Jack Warner

Breene had remembered. The old Jack had always been in control, the master of his own destiny, with a dry wit that took those who didn't know him by surprise. The Jack Warner he'd met the other day could only be described as a loser. A drowning man looking for a life raft.

Poor bastard.

Breene didn't even want to think about the job that had done that to Warner.

Groaning, he struggled up from the bed, winced as his muscles protested and shambled towards the shower. Post-drinking-session remorse threatened to swamp his day, and he could do without the hassle. He pushed Jack, and with more difficulty Sylvia, to the back of his mind and pushed himself into a hot shower, followed by a cold one.

That felt marginally better.

After he had shaved, scrubbed his mouth out and armed himself with a coffee, he felt almost ready to face the day. He stepped out onto the balcony and lit his first cigarette for the day, wincing as the biting smoke assaulted his lungs. At thirty-eight he still had the resilience of youth, his naturally healthy constitution managed to withstand the abuse he inflicted on his body, but he knew there would soon come a time…

Bugger that. Not today, not this morning. He shrugged off the demons of the night before, fought to subdue the melancholy that had settled on him. It was a beautiful day. The sun glinted off the surface of the ocean, turning the foam of the rolling waves so white that it hurt his eyes. The golden sand was bathed in its deceptive strength, gratefully soaked up by the many sun worshippers. Below him the traffic flowed, speeding along the seaside boulevard and winding in and out of the maze of towering unit blocks, most of which boasted an arcade of shops selling overpriced merchandise.

He stretched to his full height, tilting his face back to catch the sun. It was hard not to feel good up here. He took a deep breath of the morning air, tasted the tang of salt from the ocean. He *did* feel good. Why the hell shouldn't he? He walked back inside, into the cool depths of the unit with its smooth pastel-coloured walls hung with prints of multicoloured fishes, but he clung to the buoyant mood of the tourist mecca. Resisting the urge to flick on the TV, he grabbed some change and headed out the door. Moments later he was on the street, smiling as he joined the bustle of tourists. He was here to enjoy himself after all.

It didn't take long to find a table at one of the many eateries offering breakfast in the Cavill Mall, a brightly coloured umbrella offering protection from the glare of the sun. He ordered bacon, eggs and sausages, white toast with butter and a cappucino coffee, thumbing his nose at the best dietary recommendations. He was on holidays. Sighing with satisfaction, he sat back to read the morning paper.

TWO SLAIN IN MADMAN'S RAMPAGE
WOMAN MISSING, FEARED DEAD.
Police hold grave fears for the safety of a woman, kidnapped last night by a madman who claimed the lives

of two men in the Surfers' Paradise/Main Beach area.

It is believed the murders are connected to the grisly slashing murders of two elderly women in their homes last week. Police are baffled, unable to provide a motive for any of the murders.

Detective Sergeant Warren Hughes looked worried last night as he sped from the first murder site, a Main Beach unit. The second murder occurred in the heart of the tourist strip when a taxi driver was slain in his vehicle as he waited for a fare in the early hours of the morning.

He had earlier reported an assault on a woman, believed now to be the woman who is missing. Police responded to his call, but were too late to apprehend the assailant.

Experts fear the murders are the work of a psychopath and are unable to guess at his motives, or predict where he might strike next.

Breene shook his head as he skimmed the article. The police were going to love this, especially the barely veiled criticism of their response time to the initial assault. He stared absently at the passing flow of brightly dressed humanity and couldn't help seeing the irony of the situation. Here they were, holidaying in one of Australia's premier tourist destinations surrounded by sea, sun and all the trappings of relaxation and entertainment, while somewhere out there, concealed behind the beauty and glamour, a terrified woman trembled in the clutches of a demented psychopath who had already killed four people, if he hadn't already made it five.

Breene tried to shrug his thoughts aside, to concentrate on relaxing, but they sat uneasily in his subconscious and spoiled his enjoyment of his cholesterol-choked breakfast. Something about the killer's actions bothered him. Why had he had a second go at the woman? Why not choose another victim? He shook his head. Even here, in Paradise.

'Excuse me.' Breene looked up from his paper, reaching for the last of his coffee. An elderly man was already helping his wife sit down at one of the chairs at Breene's table.

'Well, you have finished,' the man replied in response to Breene's raised eyebrow. 'And there are other people around, you know.' Breene glanced around him, noting at least a couple of tables vacant in the vicinity, if not in quite so good a position. He rose from the table without a word and pushed his chair in.

'I've left some bacon rind there. You might like to finish that off for me as well,' he said, smiling into the face of the old man, and making his way to the counter. Rude old bastard, he thought as he paid for his meal. Gave old people a bad name, expecting the world to step aside for him. Breene smiled as he imagined the tale the man would tell about the rude young man. Probably turn out to be the highlight of the old couple's holiday.

He spent the remainder of the morning just strolling around, enjoying the sunshine and the unhurried pace of the other shoppers. The holiday atmosphere seemed to pervade the air of the place. It was a world away from the bustle of Sydney, uncaring, hostile, everyone going about their business.

And yet somewhere here lurked a killer.

It had been another long night for Warren Hughes, but he knew the day ahead was going to be even worse. He had managed to avoid Bryant so far, but he knew it was only a matter of time. He trudged heavily down the stairs to forensics.

'Ellis on today?' he asked Stafford, the cop on duty behind the desk.

'No, sir. Mitchell and Griffin are the lab men today. Ellis is on days off, and Finch called in sick. Said he'd had some accident.'

Hughes shrugged, uninterested.

'So who did the work on the victims that came in last night?'

'Griffin, sir. Third lab on the left. You should find him in there.'

Hughes didn't bother to thank the constable.

'Griffin? Hughes. What have you got for me?'

Griffin eyed the big man speculatively and lifted his glasses onto his forehead.

'It looks like the same man, Hughes. He must have been in a bit of a hurry this time, which explains why he didn't dismember his victims. Well, the cabbie was a bit exposed, of course, but it looks as if it was the same weapon.'

'So tell me something I don't know.'

Griffin stared at Hughes coolly before he reached for a small plastic sachet.

'We got some hair. Black. Short. And a blood

type, AB negative. Same traces at the site of the attack and in the unit.'

'Thank Christ.' At least they had something now. 'Any way of working out if the hair comes from a Japanese?'

'No, not that I know of. Why?'

'Ah, nothing. Just that one of the witnesses at the first murder thought the guy she had seen was Japanese, but she was as blind as a bat and her husband had fought against them in the war.'

'At a guess, I'd say not.'

'Why?'

'Too tall. The guy who hit that kid last night had to be at least five nine or ten just from the angle of the first blow that severed the jugular. That's a bit taller than your average Japanese, although not impossible.'

'Forget it. Skip the Japanese angle. So we've got a male, five feet nine or ten, with black hair. Anything else you can tell me?'

'He'd have to be pretty strong or practised with a knife to deliver the blow that killed that kid. Particularly upper body strength.'

'Good. Very good. Well done, Griffin, that's more than we've been able to get so far. If you come up with anything else, you let me know straight away.'

'Sure,' Griffin shrugged. 'No problem.'

Hughes was whistling as he left the labs. At least he had something to throw at Bryant now. It was a hell of a lot better than nothing.

The phone was ringing when Breene returned to his unit.

'Hello?'

'Breene? It's Jack.'

Warner's voice was strained and hoarse.

'Jack, what's up?'

'Mandy's been kidnapped.'

'What? Not the...'

'Yes.'

'Christ, Jack, I'm sorry.' What the hell else could he say?

'I've been down at the police station all morning answering questions.'

'Have they got anything?'

'Not fucking much. I'm absolutely stuffed, but I don't really want to go home to Pam, not yet. She was bloody hysterical before I left and I had to call the doctor to sedate her. I got a friend to come and sit with her, but I don't think my presence would be all that welcome at the moment. Do you think...'

'Come around here, Jack. It's not far, is it?'

'No, just around the corner.' He could hear the weariness in his friend's voice and wondered how he was coping.

He was Jack Warner after all. He'd made his name by coping with crises. But then they were always somebody else's crises.

'Listen, I'll come around and pick you up.'

'I'd appreciate that, Merv. I'll wait here for you. You know where it is?'

'Yeah, sure.' He had noticed the cop shop as he drove around — it was the sort of thing he couldn't help but notice, even on holidays.

Warner looked like shit when Breene walked into

the station. The changes he had seen in his friend the other day were even more exaggerated; his shoulders were slumped and his eyes were red-rimmed. He looked like a man who was completely defeated.

'Jack!' he said. Warner straightened when he saw Breene, pulled his shoulders back and took a deep steadying breath.

'Merv,' he nodded briskly. 'Let's get out of here.'

'All right, Jack, do you want to tell me what's going on?' Breene asked after they had driven back to his unit in silence. 'Have they any ideas about Mandy's disappearance at all?'

Warner shook his head. 'Not from what I can work out. I guess that's why they were putting me through the third degree, thinking maybe I'd had something to do with it.'

'What the fuck are you talking about, Jack?'

Warner sighed.

'You got anything to drink? I sure as hell could use something to steady me up a bit.'

'Sure.' Breene collected the almost full whisky bottle and a couple of glasses. Warner obviously had something to get off his chest, and it looked as if it would be thirsty work.

Jack Warner knocked off the first whisky in one hit, blinked his eyes against the burning bite of the liquor and reached out to pour himself another. He was tempted to grab the bottle and upend it, drink as much as he could take and then drink some more, but that was what had got him into this mess in the first place.

And Mandy. He closed his eyes, fought off the

tears that had threatened him from the moment the cops had arrived on his doorstep.

'Well.' He slugged down his second whisky and placed his glass on the table, rejecting the offer of another.

'Let's just start by saying that it is partly my fault.' He waved down Breene's objections. 'I'll tell you why — then you'll believe me.' He filled Breene in on the basics, without going into details. When he had finished, he felt even more like a piece of shit than he had before. 'May I?' He poured himself another generous slug of whisky and sat back in his chair. Breene lit a cigarette and looked steadily at his friend.

'That doesn't say you're to blame, Jack. The guy who's got Mandy is obviously a fruitcake. All the rest of it is just coincidence. And you're not the first father to hit his daughter.'

'Yeah, but you don't know what I've been acting like. You don't know what an arsehole I've been at home, to Pam and to Mandy.'

'Maybe not, but I know some of the reasons behind it.'

Warner stared at him and made no comment.

'Come on, Jack, we both know you were shafted. And people who should have stood up for you, didn't. You weren't shown the loyalty you deserved.'

'Maybe not, but that doesn't excuse my behaviour.'

Breene shrugged.

'I'm not saying it does. But blaming yourself isn't

helping Mandy either. What we've got to work out is how the hell we're going to find her. You're not going to sit around while she's out there, are you?'

'I don't know what the hell I can do.'

'Come off it, Jack, you can do plenty and you know it. Don't give me that bullshit. There must be some reason this nut has chosen Mandy for his target — he's killed four people so far, but he took Mandy away with him. That gives us some hope. And he must have known where she was staying, otherwise how else did he manage to track her down to that kid's unit?'

Warner stared at Breene, suddenly feeling a flicker of hope for his daughter's life. He'd been expecting the police to come in all morning and say they had found her, hacked into pieces; he had been preparing himself for the crushing devastation. And now Breene was giving him hope. Fear bore down on him, twisted in his guts like a serpent, the pain of it a physical weight in his chest. She might still be alive, she just might. And in the hands of a raving lunatic who had already killed four people.

He wasn't grateful to Breene for kindling that slim hope.

'So what do we do?'

'We have to find the link between Mandy and her kidnapper. We have to uncover that connection, find out when their paths crossed.'

'You mean we've got to find the needle in the haystack.'

Both men's expressions were grim. Mandy's future could depend on them, could depend on their actions over the next few hours, or days. If she had that long.

Warren Hughes was more worried about his own future right at that moment. He was seated in Bryant's office, awaiting the arrival of Bryant and the mayor, Tex Ellicott. Tex — he wondered how the mayor had arrived at his name, thought it was strangely incongruous for such a little man.

He turned his mind to the facts he had about the killer so far — a vague description of the assailant, his hair colour, approximate height and build. It wasn't a great deal, he would have liked a whole lot more to present to them, but he wasn't Superman.

The missing girl could prove to be the link in this case, and Hughes was directing some attention towards that area, but it was early days yet. It was interesting that her father was a private investigator — not a very good one, but maybe he'd ruffled a few feathers in his time on the coast, or even in his years on the force in New South Wales. Maybe he had something to hide?

Hughes had managed to pull a few strings and have Warner's file faxed up from down south. The allegations of corruption seemed to have come from out of the blue, but then again maybe Warner had been very clever at covering his tracks. Or had built a ruthless reputation for dealing with squealers. What if a few birds had come home to roost, or he had links with organised crime that had gone sour? It was certainly worth looking into.

Then again, how was that connected with the initial murders?

Hughes mulled over his thoughts, struggled to create a link somewhere, but it wasn't long before his thoughts turned to the promotion that would be his when he had cracked the case. Sure, he had benefited from friends in high places thus far in his career, but he had a burning desire to prove himself, to show his detractors that he was worthy of his position, and then some.

Warren Hughes was cut out for better things. He knew it.

'Hughes!'

He jumped when Bryant entered the room, jerked from his dreams of ambition. He scrambled to his feet, flicking his hair out of his eyes as he turned to face the two men who entered the room.

'Mayor Ellicott, this is Detective Sergeant Hughes. He's heading up the investigation.'

Ellicott eyed Hughes coolly, inclined his head briefly.

'Hughes.'

'Sir.' He could feel the flush creeping up his neck under the mayor's scrutiny, had to stop himself from fidgeting with his clothes.

'All right, gentlemen.' Ellicott's gaze moved past Hughes, dismissing him. 'We've got ourselves a serious problem here.' He walked behind Bryant's desk to gaze out on the street. 'And I want to know exactly what you're doing about it.' His head snapped around, his beady eyes boring into Hughes. 'Well?'

'We've, ah…we've managed to get a description, sir,' Hughes gulped, thrust his chin out at the implied criticism. 'We managed to get some hair from the scene, and a blood type.' The mayor only raised his eyebrows.

'We believe,' he cleared his throat, 'we believe the assailant to be male, about five feet ten with a well built upper torso. There is a possibility that he is of Japanese extraction, but we've got nothing definite on that.'

'I see. And is that all? That's all you've been able to come up with after a week of investigations, with the murder of four of my constituents? Don't you think the residents of the Gold Coast have a right to expect more than that from the police force? They're quaking in their boots, man, they don't know where this madman is going to strike next, and you're congratulating yourself because you've got some vague description? It's hardly thrilling detective work, is it, sergeant?'

Hughes bit back his rage. Who the fuck did this bastard think he was? So what if he was the mayor? He had no right to talk down to Warren Hughes. The thought galled him, burned in his gut like acid.

'Tex, I don't think you understand what we're dealing with here.' Bryant spoke quietly, but his displeasure was obvious. 'This man's a loose cannon, an indiscriminate killer, a fucking psycho…'

'It's you who doesn't understand what we're dealing with, Arthur. This is a major scare. This sort of thing could ruin the reputation of the Coast, ruin our potential for earning tourist dollars for years to come. It could be worth millions. And it's not going to look good on the records of either of you gentlemen,' snapped Ellicott.

'I am investigating another possibility, sir, but it's

only tentative at the moment so I didn't want to waste your precious time.' Hughes wasn't prepared to take that sort of shit from anybody.

'Oh? And perhaps you'd like to share it with us?'

That did it. He wasn't about to take any more goading.

'There may be some links with organised crime.' Both men turned to look at him.

'Go on,' Ellicott was interested now.

'Well sir, like I said it's only a tentative investigation so far, but the missing girl's father, Jack Warner, he's a PI. But that's not the link.' He looked at both men, playing his trump card for all it was worth. 'Warner was a senior sergeant with the NSW force, spent twenty years on the job in Sydney until they caught up with him for corruption. There was a hint that he was dealing with some pretty heavy underworld figures, maybe even the Yakuza in its early days in the country. Of course, they never could prove it, but Warner strikes me as a man who could cover his tracks pretty well. From what I can work out, he resigned soon after and came straight up here, bought a nice canal-front home and set up as a PI. Except he's hardly had any work, and apparently he's a bit of a drinker. I'm wondering where his money comes from. Maybe he's merely moved his operations up north?'

Ellicott and Bryant were silent, considering the possibilities of Hughes's suggestions. It would certainly smell a lot better for Ellicott if the crime wave had originated down south.

'What about the first two murders?' Bryant asked.

'Throw us off the scent,' Hughes shrugged.

'Interesting. Very interesting. Keep with it, Hughes, good work.' Ellicott turned to Bryant. 'Seems I may have underestimated your man, Hughes.' Bryant turned towards Hughes with a new respect.

'Yes. Good work, Warren. Go to it, man.'

'Yes, sir.' Hughes strode from the office, his head held high. He'd shown the bastards. The thing was that the more he thought about it the more likely his scenario seemed. Maybe he'd stumbled onto the answer. A hunch. Yeah, a hunch. Why not? Detective's intuition. It all suddenly made perfect sense to Warren Hughes.

CHAPTER 8

Breene and Warner soon exhausted the leads Warner could supply on his daughter's recent activities. Once they had contacted the people she worked with, he was at a loss.

'That's all I know,' he mumbled.

Breene shrugged.

'I guess most fathers aren't too aware of the movements of their teenage daughters.'

'Yeah, maybe,' Warner sighed.

'Pam should be able to help us. Reckon she'll be up to it?'

'I hope so.' Warner was dreading the thought of facing her. She had been a mess when he left that morning, but he couldn't put off facing her forever. He squared his shoulders and met Breene's gaze. 'Let's go and see.'

Pam Warner was waiting at the door when the car pulled into the garage, her agitation obvious.

'Jack!' She ran to him as he climbed out of the car. 'Oh, Jack, what are we going to do?'

Warner was surprised that she should run to him for comfort. He still blamed himself, no matter what Breene said, and he had prepared himself for anger and accusations when he returned home. He held onto Pam, couldn't remember the last time they'd made contact, real contact. It steadied him, underlined the purpose that Breene had awakened when he stirred hope in Jack Warner's gut.

'We're going to do our best to find our little girl, that's what we're going to do. Come on.' He guided his wife into the house, feeling more like a man than he had in a long time.

But the circumstances were far from favourable.

'All right Pam, we need you to help us out here,' Breene said gently. He met Warner's gaze, both men trying to ignore their feelings of desperation, trying not to convey the sense of urgency they felt to the distraught Pam Warner. She was barely coherent, even after Jack had persuaded her to take another of the tranquillisers the doctor had left for her. Warner wondered if they were a help or a hindrance.

'I know this is tough, Pam. I know you're desperately frightened for Mandy, but you've got to try to think for us. We need to know everything you can tell us about her — her movements, friends, anything she might have done in the past couple of weeks, places she went to. It's our only chance of finding her.'

'I'm sorry, I just can't. Everytime I think of Mandy I just…my poor little baby. God, why did it have to be her? Why Mandy?' She buried her head in her hands. 'And what that animal did to Jake. My poor little girl!' she sobbed brokenly. The entire day had been like a nightmare, a never-ending nightmare. Ever since the phone call late last night — had it only been last night? It seemed like a lifetime ago. Every hour, every minute that ticked by Pam felt the pain, the fear that gnawed at her stomach, threatened to unhinge her mind. Everything had gone wrong, everything. And now this.

'Jack,' she pleaded. He tightened his arm around her shoulders.

'I know, I know,' he soothed her, but he couldn't penetrate the misery, couldn't touch the depths of her despair, not while he struggled against his own fears, tried to suppress the images that kept flashing into his own mind. Their hope was slim, maybe too bloody slim.

'Give her a break, Breene, ease up on the pressure. It's our little girl, you know,' he snapped, anger surging up in him. 'Jesus Christ, you don't know how it feels, how it hurts you way down deep.'

'I'm trying to help, Jack. I know you're hurting, I know you're bloody terrified, but that doesn't change the facts,' Breene said evenly. 'We're trying to give Mandy a chance.'

'I'm sorry.' Warner looked away, couldn't meet Breene's eyes. 'You're right.' He took a deep breath to steady himself.

'Come on Pam, you've got to try. For Mandy's sake.'

They were all startled by the sound of loud knocking on the front door.

Warren Hughes hadn't wasted any time after his conversation with Bryant and the mayor. He drove straight to Warner's house, sure that he'd cracked his first major lead, that if he could break Warner he'd find the answers he was looking for. Promotion dangled invitingly, just out of his grasp.

'I'll get it,' Breene volunteered, acutely aware of the terror that rooted the Warners to their chair.

'Yes?'

'Detective Sergeant Hughes.' He shoved his badge at Breene. 'I'd like to speak to Jack Warner.'

Breene's heart sank.

'What's it about, sergeant? Is it their daughter? Have you found her?'

Hughes glared at him.

'I said I wanted to speak to Jack Warner.'

'Look, they're both very upset. I'm a good friend of theirs and I thought that if it's going to be a blow to them, I should prepare them.'

'We haven't found their daughter. I wish to ask Mr Warner some questions,' Hughes said curtly. 'Now, if you don't mind?'

'All right, wait there.' Breene closed the screen-door and turned his back on Hughes. What the hell was he after?

'Jack, there's a Detective Hughes at the door.'

The Warners clutched at each other.

'Is it?'

'No, he says he wants to ask you a few questions.'

'All right,' Warner shrugged. 'Stay with Pam, will you, Merv?'

'Sure,' Breene nodded. He sat on the lounge beside her, kept his ears pricked to listen to the conversation at the door.

'What the...you must be joking!' he heard Warner yell. 'You can't be serious!'

Breene was at the door in an instant.

'What's going on?'

'He wants to take me in for questioning!' Warner said incredulously. 'He thinks Mandy's kidnapping has got something to do with me.'

'What the hell is this all about, sergeant?' asked Breene. 'You've got to be joking if you think Jack Warner had anything to do with his daughter's disappearance. Either that or you're an idiot.'

'I'm not joking, and unless you're Mr Warner's legal representative I'd suggest you keep your opinions to yourself,' Hughes barked.

'Have you a warrant, sergeant? Is Mr Warner under arrest?'

'Keep out of this, I'm, warning you...'

Breene whipped his badge out and stuck it under Hughes's nose.

'Detective Senior Sergeant Breene, Sydney Central CIB.' Hughes's eyes widened. 'Now, just what the fuck are you going on about, Hughes?'

Hughes stiffened, drew himself up.

'I wish to question Mr Warner about certain criminal activities that have come to light concerning his past. I believe they have a strong bearing on this case.'

Warner deflated visibly, and any strengthening of purpose he might have felt vanished. The past, he couldn't escape it.

'You listen to me, sergeant. If you happen to be referring to those bullshit corruption charges you'll find that the case was dropped. This is a load of crap,

Hughes, you're wasting valuable time when you should be out looking for Amanda Warner.' Breene was furious with the fat detective.

'I'm not prepared to say anything further at this stage. I ask you once again, Mr Warner, to accompany me down to the police station for questioning, and I remind you, sir, that you have no jurisdiction in this matter and I would appreciate it if you'd keep your opinions to yourself,' Hughes bristled.

'You're making a big mistake, sergeant, a big mistake. I'm warning you...'

'It's all right, Merv, I'll go down to the station with him.'

'This is bullshit, Jack. You don't have to go down with him unless he's got a warrant. You don't have a warrant, do you Hughes?'

'No, sir. It would be to Mr Warner's advantage if I didn't have to get one, and it would save time.'

'I said I'll go.'

Breene stared at Warner, helpless rage burning inside him. He had stood by once while his friend took the fall, and now it was happening again.

'I'll just go and talk to my wife,' Warner said tonelessly, numbed, the flicker of hope extinguished, the blame his.

'You listen to me, Hughes,' Breene stepped up to the detective and dropped his voice. 'Those corruption charges were a load of shit. Jack Warner doesn't need this now, and I don't know why you're pursuing such a ridiculous course of action when his daughter's life is on the line. Don't you realise the urgency of this matter?'

'I believe I'm pursuing his daughter's kidnapping to the best of my ability right at this moment, and you're attempting to obstruct me in the course of my duty,' said Hughes evenly. 'That's what I believe. And need I remind you again, you are way out of your jurisdiction.'

'I'll bust your arse for this, Hughes,' Breene hissed. 'I'll make sure of it.'

'All right, Sergeant, I'm ready.' Warner stood passively in the doorway. 'You can take me in now.'

'Jack, I'll come with you.'

'I'd rather you stayed with Pam. She's pretty upset and I can't do anything more for her.'

Breene couldn't meet the look of utter despair in Warner's eyes. He was too consumed with rage.

'All right,' he nodded. He glared at Hughes, but made no further comment. He wouldn't let his friend down this time.

Celia Thompson frowned as she scanned the article. It contained the police description of the man they were looking for, but the whole story just didn't have enough beef for her liking. It certainly wasn't front-page material, and that was where she wanted to keep this story — right on the front page, where it belonged. She needed something sensational, some new development that would keep things rolling right along.

So what was she supposed to do? Go out and commit another murder? She laughed. She hadn't quite sunk that low to get her stories, not yet anyway, though she hadn't been far from it before this one emerged. She had been lucky to get the tip-off about the dismembered dog, that had really spiced things up. She was briefly curious about the caller who had tipped her off, but she had learned not to look a gift horse in the mouth. People had all sorts of reasons for giving journalists tips when it was to their advantage. She sat back in her chair and chewed her pencil, a habit from the old days when they'd actually used the damned things. She poked her tongue out at the computer screen. Bloody computers.

Her mind wandered, tossing up various possibilities for the story. Who the hell was this psycho bastard anyway? She couldn't help being curious. What did make him tick, what motivated him? What was he thinking right now?

Now, that might just work. A psychological profile of the murderer, an attempt to outguess him. It had been done before. That would keep the interest going, add more body to the description the police had issued. And it might be fun, trying to get inside the head of a psychopath. She shivered at the thought of it. Why not? Who was to know that she'd made the story up herself? She could always cite the confidentiality clause, protecting the identity of the expert opinion. Besides, what harm could it do?

Inspired, she attacked the keyboard, the words flying from her fingertips. This was going to keep her name right on the front page. She'd make sure of it.

Pam Warner had composed herself a bit after Jack left.

'Do you really think she could still be alive, Merv?' she asked shakily. 'Oh, God, that sounds so awful. My poor little girl. Why did it have to be her? If only she hadn't moved out of home, maybe none of this would have happened, if only Jack…' She stopped mid-sentence. 'But none of that's doing Mandy any good now, is it? All the "if onlys" in the world aren't going to help her now.' She stared out the window, oblivious to the bright afternoon sunshine that spilled across the expanse of green lawn leading down to the waters of the canal. 'She must be so frightened.'

'I know,' Breene murmured, knowing there was no comfort in any words he could offer. 'Do you think you can help me find her, Pam? I need to work out how she came into contact with this guy. Do you think you can manage that?'

She took a deep breath and looked at Breene.

'I'll try.'

'Good. First of all I'll need to talk to her friends — she must have had at least one close girlfriend, someone she'd confide in?'

Pam put her hand to her mouth, her face crumbling into despair. 'Bronwyn. God, I'd forgotten all about her. She doesn't even know Mandy's missing. She'll be so upset — I hadn't thought to get in touch with her. Thank God they haven't released Jake's name in the papers yet. I just hadn't thought.' She started sobbing, covering her face with her hands as the veil of numbness was ripped apart by another wave of painful reality.

Breene sat in silence and offered her a handkerchief when she had controlled the worst of her sobbing.

'I'm sorry,' she apologised.

'No need to apologise, Pam. I know it's a tough time

for you.' He lit a cigarette and waited for her to get herself together. 'Can I get you a drink?'

'No, thanks. My head feels so numb I can barely even think straight, and the worst part about it is that it just isn't helping. All I can think about is Mandy and poor Jake, and all the while that animal's out there somewhere. I can't even protect her. You know, you spend all your life as a parent worrying about your kid, watching over every little scratch, worrying if she's late home from school, and what her future will be. And then something like this happens. I just feel so damned helpless, Merv, so damned helpless, and it isn't fair. If I could just see her again, just once more.' The tears started again, running down her face. She didn't even bother to wipe them away.

'Do you think you can find her, Merv?' Her dark eyes were pleading.

'I'll find her,' he said. He hoped he sounded reassuring, he had to push his own misgivings aside so he could provide some comfort. 'Do you think you can get me that girl's address?'

'Bronwyn? Yes, of course. I'll just go and see if I can find it.' She got up from the armchair and Breene could hear her riffling through some papers out in the kitchen. 'You probably won't find her at home, not yet anyway,' she called as she searched. 'She'd be out working if I remember correctly, some office assistant job she's picked up until she starts at university next year. She's quite a bright girl, you know, been friends with Mandy ever since we moved up here. Bronwyn used to come around here all the time until she and Mandy left school.' Pam's stream of chatter stopped abruptly and when the silence lengthened Breene went to look for her.

He found her staring blankly out the kitchen window with big tears rolling down her cheeks.

'Pam?'

She turned and buried her head in his chest. He held her while she sobbed brokenly.

'I just can't understand why everything's gone so wrong,' she said quietly when the worst of it had passed. She stepped back and looked at Breene as if sizing him up.

'Jack's changed, you know,' she said after a pause. 'He's not the man he used to be.' Breene wasn't sure he wanted to hear this, but the woman obviously needed someone to talk to and he didn't see anyone else volunteering.

'He got so bitter after we came up here, having to start over as a private detective, wasting all his experience on cases he could barely tolerate. He told me he felt dirty, felt as if he was filth at the end of each day. Of course he could have stayed in Sydney once the corruption charges were dropped, but he just didn't trust anybody any more. Even people he thought were his friends didn't stand by him when things got tough. To a man like Jack Warner friends and loyalty mean everything. It was how he judged his own worth.' She dropped her eyes and studied the tiles on the floor.

'He tried to fight it, he was determined to make a new life up here for us and get a fresh start. He thought he'd eventually build up to better cases once he'd made a reputation for himself. He was so desperate to get away from everything that had happened in Sydney, to put it all behind him and forget about it, but he couldn't do it, Merv.'

She looked at him, her eyes searching his for understanding. She found it — Breene had known Jack Warner for a long time, knew the pain it had caused him when he'd been investigated on corruption charges.

'It was like a light went out in his life, Merv. He fought and he fought, he tried so bloody hard, but it wasn't the same and he couldn't make it the same. Jack just couldn't admit it. He'd get up for work and he'd be like a stranger to me, smiling, polite, but sort of distant, you know? Like he used to be before a football match, tense, preoccupied. He used to ring me every lunchtime when we first came up here, as if he was checking that I was still here. As if he couldn't trust anything any more.' She paused, staring out the window and folding her arms. When she spoke again her voice was without emotion.

'He started to drink of a night, and I mean drink heavily. Every night. And then it would start. Yelling, abuse, sometimes for hours on end until he'd drunk himself into a stupor. I hated seeing him like that. I was frightened.' She was silent for a moment and then looked sharply up at Breene, angry at herself for betraying her husband. 'I love that man. He's a good man and he deserved better. I know he's had a rough time and I'm willing to make concessions for it. I'll see him through, because I know he'll get through it. He's a fighter, a strong bastard. I hate the police for what they did to him. They never had a better, more dedicated officer and what did they do? They shit on him, that's what.' She bit her lip to stem the flow of emotion.

'Mandy couldn't understand it. She started getting frightened of him, especially when he was drunk. He just didn't seem capable of controlling himself and she thought he was going to hurt me. She couldn't understand why he'd changed. Of course, Jack was too proud to ever breathe a word about the corruption charges to his little girl and he forbade me to do so. God, I hated to see them grow apart. The fights they used to have — she's just like him, you know. She'd stand up to him and argue right back. It's been like a bloody nightmare living in this place.' She ran her hand over her eyes.

'The night it all came to a head Amanda had been out and she came home a bit late. Jack was waiting for her and started in on her as soon as she walked through the door. They had a horrible row and Jack said some really cruel things to her. Poor Amanda. She loves her father, at least she used to. But she just lost all her respect for him after he started drinking. He hit her that night. That was something he'd never done before, and I guess it was the last straw. She must have had it planned, I don't know. She just walked right out the door into the night and came back the next day with Jake to pick up her clothes. She told me where she was going to stay, but she didn't want her father to know.' She slumped into a chair at the breakfast table.

'Jack vowed to stop drinking that night, but it was too damned late. Mandy had already moved out, and he couldn't forgive himself for what he did. It was only two nights later that it happened.' Tears formed in her eyes and threatened to spill down her cheeks. She sniffed them back defiantly.

'Breene, you have to find my daughter. For all our sakes. I don't know what will happen to us if you don't.'

'I'll do whatever I can,' he said quietly.

An uncomfortable silence grew between them, punctuated by Pam's sniffles. Though Breene had been friends with Jack for a long time, he had rarely had the occasion for conversation with Pam. Jack Warner wasn't the sort of bloke who talked to his mates about his family life, and that had been just fine by Breene. He cringed inwardly at this exposure of his friend's weaknesses; he would have felt the same way if he had walked in and found Jack and Pam making love. As a friend, he felt that it was none of his business.

The fact that he was now looking for Amanda Warner changed all that.

'How about a coffee?' Pam offered.

'Sounds good to me,' Breene smiled. Pam smiled back and the awkward moment passed. He was relieved that she seemed to have herself more under control, that she'd got a grip on herself now she had partly unburdened herself.

'Is there anything else you can tell me that might help?' he asked.

'I'm afraid Mandy and I weren't sharing intimacies by the time she left home. She was angry at me for putting up with Jack's behaviour and our relationship had deteriorated too. We used to be good friends, you know,' she said sadly.

Breene nodded his understanding.

'I can't help but feel that this sort of thing doesn't come out of the blue. Did she have any old boyfriends, somebody from school with a crush on her, maybe somebody that seemed just a little bit odd?'

She shook her head, searching her memory for something that might help, anything at all.

'No, I can't think of one. As far as I know she hadn't had much to do with boys before Jake. I don't know Merv, I just don't know. Maybe you'd be better off asking Bronwyn, because Mandy never really spoke to me about boys. She never really spoke to me about anything, not once she started to grow up. I guess maybe I didn't let her, I was too caught up with my own worries to even notice that she was growing up.'

She studied her fingernails, angrily shaking the tears away. 'I never realised how badly things were falling apart.' She looked at Breene. 'I guess our perfect little family isn't so perfect any more,' she said, her voice bitter.

Breene studied his coffee, avoiding the look of pain in her eyes.

CHAPTER 9

The description in the afternoon paper didn't bother him. It could refer to anybody. The Japanese angle was amusing, and so, at first, was the attempt to profile him.

...possibly well accepted amongst his peers, quietly spoken, even remote. A typical 'boy next door'. However, he would have difficulty maintaining a relationship with the opposite sex and may have suffered some humiliations at the hands of one or more females toward whom he has directed his attentions. The choice of his initial victims, two elderly women, could be the most telling clue in establishing his identity. He feels a deep-seated sexual desire for older women, possibly inspired by the death of his mother during his infancy.

He threw the paper down in anger, slashed at the page with his pocket knife. How *dared* they. What gave them the right to make such foul suggestions about his motives? What gave them the right to even think they could guess at his intentions? He was beyond their comprehension, his movements pre-ordained at the moment of his birth. Fools! Imposters! The audacity of it was beyond belief.

But he could afford to laugh. He was suddenly taken with the comedy of it all, the ludicrous idea that they could second-guess his motives. He was secure in his position, secure now in his conviction. It had taken him a long time to work it out, years of frustration, but finally it had dawned on him.

His mother had never been touched by a man. He knew that; hadn't she told him often enough over the years while she ranted about the evils of lust and fornication? Over and over, until he knew the very words by heart, every gesture, every nuance of her sermon. And then one day he had realised, he'd discovered the message behind her words, the hidden message that even she hadn't fully understood.

Conceived without human intervention. There was only one conclusion.

And now he had set his feet on the path to his ascendancy, the violent nature of his coming only a reflection of the evil times, a baptism of fire, a baptism of blood. He would not make the mistake of being meek. History had shown the error of that course of action.

His eyes dropped once again to the newspaper article. Celia Thompson. Perhaps he had made a mistake when he rang her. He shook his head. She had made the mistake. He'd have to let her know about that. It wouldn't do to have lies printed about him.

Amanda's friend Bronwyn was short and plump, her freckled face crowned with short brown hair.

'Hi,' she greeted Breene when he knocked on the door. 'Come right in.' Her smile was friendly and showed off a row of even white teeth. Breene returned the smile and thought she was attractive in a fresh, girlish way.

'Have a seat.' She indicated an overstuffed lounge chair covered in a creamy velvet material. Breene perched on the edge of the chair and hoped he wouldn't dirty it. The house was elegantly furnished, the carpet a deep pile in light blue, the walls painted a light shade of apricot. Tasteful modern prints adorned the walls and a couple of healthy-looking ivy plants cascaded over the sides of pots suspended from the ceiling.

'Nice place,' he commented. 'Do you live alone?'

She laughed and shook her head. 'My parents are still at work. They probably won't be home till seven or so.'

Of course she didn't live alone. She was only seventeen. Breene smiled at his mistake. 'Some detective, huh?'

A frown flickered across Bronwyn's features, momentarily dimming her smile. 'Would you like a cup of coffee?' She asked hopefully, as if to avoid discussing the purpose of Breene's visit for as long as possible.

'Love one,' Breene replied. 'Do you mind if I smoke?'

Bronwyn placed an ashtray on the coffee table without comment. A lot of people weren't too keen on having someone smoke in their house these days, but Breene was fairly thick-skinned. He got a sort of perverse pleasure from ignoring the health warnings and other people's disapproval. It added to his sometimes flagging enjoyment of the habit. He lit a cigarette and drew deeply on it.

'Mrs Warner tells me you and Amanda have been friends for some time,' Breene began when they were both seated around the coffee table.

'We've been best friends since she started at my high school,' Bronwyn answered absently, her gaze fixed on her hands. 'I can't believe she's gone.' Her tone was empty and Breene recognised the signs of shock.

'Bronwyn, I know this is hard for you, especially when you've only just found out.' He touched her hand lightly, feeling an urge to comfort her. 'You have to believe I'm doing everything I can. Don't give up hope yet.'

'But this guy's already killed Jake and that taxi driver. What makes you think he hasn't done the same to Mandy?' she demanded, with sudden tears in her eyes.

'I know you're afraid, I'm not saying you shouldn't be. I believe that Mandy is probably still all right because the guy actually wanted her. I'm working on the assumption that he knows her and is infatuated with her, so that gives us a little bit of time.'

'Someone who knows her?' Bronwyn looked shocked by the idea. 'Who?'

'That's what I'm trying to find out. I came here because I thought you'd be the best person to help me.'

Bronwyn was overcome by the thought. 'You think it might be somebody we know? How can that be possible?' She shook her head in stunned disbelief, her eyes searching Breene's face for comprehension. 'The guy's a murderer!'

'It must be hard to understand, and I'm not saying it was a friend of yours. All I'm saying is that I think Amanda has had something to do with this person at some time. An intense boyfriend who was obsessed with her?'

'No way.' Bronwyn shook her head. 'She's hardly even had any boyfriends, and she's been with Jake for over two years. There's no way she would even look at other guys once she fell for him. She was devoted, full on. Before him guys just didn't mean that much to her.'

'What about admirers? Say somebody who liked her but she wasn't open to his advances, did she ever mention anything like that?'

'No.'

'No what, she didn't have any admirers? A pretty girl like Amanda?'

'She was pretty, all right,' Bronwyn said with just a hint of jealousy. 'She just didn't give out any come-ons, didn't pay attention if a guy was trying to put the make on her. She wasn't that sort of girl. I mean, she isn't that sort of girl.' She put her hand to her mouth to cover her dismay. 'God, I hope she's all right,' she added quietly.

'Do you think she might have kept something from you, something she was ashamed of, perhaps?'

'No way. We didn't have any secrets from each other. We're like sisters. I don't know what I'll do if I lose her.' Tears brimmed in her eyes as she looked at Breene. 'Do you mind if I have one of your cigarettes?'

'Sure, go ahead.' Breene offered her one and lit it for her. She held it in shaky fingers and drew tentatively on it.

'Ugh.' She made a face and quickly put the cigarette in the ashtray. 'Sorry' she said, coughing. 'I don't usually smoke them.'

'I could have guessed,' Breene smiled. She caught the look on his face and smiled back.

'Sorry about your smoke, it's all wet now,' she said.

'Don't worry about it.' He sat and allowed her to collect herself before he continued.

'Did Mandy have other friends, maybe some you didn't know about?'

'I don't think so. We were pretty close and spent most of our weekends together, even when she was with Jake.' Bronwyn's voice trailed off into silence and Breene could see that she was struggling to keep her composure. He kept quiet for a few minutes, taking the opportunity to light another cigarette.

'Mrs Warner tells me you're going to university next year,' he said, changing the subject. 'What are you thinking of studying?'

'I'm enrolled in economics.' She made a face. 'I'm not really sure if that's the area I want to go into, but my father says it's a sensible place to start. Trouble is, its hard to decide what to do with the rest of your life when you're only seventeen, you know? It seems like a big decision, and I just don't know if I'm doing the right thing. Anyway, I'll start out with economics. It can't hurt.'

'Sounds like a good move to me,' Breene agreed. For a seventeen-year-old she seemed to have a good head on her shoulders. 'What about Mandy? Was she going to university as well?'

'Yeah, she was going to. She was going to do a science degree specialising in forensics. She wants to be a forensic scientist.' She grimaced. 'She was really worried when she had to move out of home though, she thought it was going to stop her from going to uni. I was only talking to her about it on Wednesday night.' She closed her eyes tight and swallowed. 'I'm sorry, I'm sort of struggling to cope with the news.' Breene felt sorry for her. The facts hadn't even had a chance to sink in yet.

'So she was worried when she had to move?' he prompted, his urgency not allowing for delicacy.

'Yeah. She didn't know how long it was going to be for, she didn't really want to go in the first place, but Mr Warner…' she glanced at Breene. 'He's a friend of yours, isn't he? Mrs Warner said you were old buddies.'

'Yes, he's a friend of mine. But I've heard the stories about how he and Mandy didn't get on. That's the reason she moved out of home, right?'

'Yeah, mostly. It really got to her, you know? She was upset by the whole setup, the fights her parents had, her father's drinking, his problems with the force. They didn't think she knew, but Mandy found out. She was thirteen when they moved up here, and kids aren't as dumb as grownups think. She loves her father, but she hates the way he can't get on with his life. She's worried he'll never get over it, that he'll become an alcoholic or something. I don't know, he seems like a really nice guy to me, but Mandy says he changes once he's got a load of grog inside him.'

Bronwyn sighed. 'It's too bad really. Mandy hated moving out of home against her parents' will. She's pretty straight in a lot of ways, right into families and that. And Jake. She really loves him.' Her expression clouded and the tears rushed to her eyes. 'Oh, I forgot,' she whimpered. She got up and walked to the window. 'God, I hope she's all right.' She didn't say anything for a few moments and Breene could see the tears that slid silently down her face. For a brief moment he shared her pain.

'We were going to go to uni together, you know? We had it all worked out. Go halves in a car, study together, it was going to make things a hell of a lot easier. We were going to get each other through it. Our plans seemed a little shaky over the past few days, but Mandy was determined that it was still going to happen. If anybody could pull it off she could, but if she had to go to work, if her dad wasn't putting her through I could see that money was going to be tight. It just isn't bloody fair.' She started to walk around the room, picking up items and studying them absently before replacing them and moving on.

'I get really pissed off at Mr Warner. He's having a bad impact on her life, not just his own. It's okay for him, that's his decision, but Mandy hasn't even had a chance yet. Now she might never get one.' She turned to Breene. 'Do you think that's fair, Mr Breene? Do you?'

'No, I don't think it's fair, Bronwyn. Please, call me Merv.' He didn't like her calling him Mr Breene. It made him feel old.

'Sure.' Her face relaxed into a smile again, and that made Breene feel better. She had a face that was meant for smiling.

'I remember the day we went over to Bond Uni, that's where we planned to go. Nothing but the best for us.' The tears started to spill onto her cheeks again, but she ignored them. 'Mandy was so excited. We wagged school to go there, and she spent some of her money to hire us a stretch limo. God, she's crazy,' she said with a laugh. 'You should have seen her running around the place, finding little spots where we could have lunch together, quiet tree-shaded areas to study in. She's the best friend I could ever hope for.'

Breene glanced at his watch. It was already seven o'clock. He had to get moving.

'Listen, Bronwyn, I don't mean to cut you off but I have to go.'

'Oh.'

'Your parents aren't home yet. Is there somewhere I can drop you?' He didn't want to leave her alone, knew it was going to hit her like a bomb once he left.

'No, I'll be all right.' She tried to smile but couldn't quite manage it. 'It's just that I'm so worried about Mandy. I don't know what to do.'

'I know Pam Warner would appreciate some company and she'd be the first one to know if they find Mandy. Maybe I could drop you around there and the two of you could talk for a while.'

'Maybe,' she said uncertainly.

'Look, you'd be doing me a favour. Jack's down…Jack's not there at the moment and he sort of expects me to keep an eye on Pam for him.' She had insisted that he get a start, that finding Mandy was more important than babysitting her. 'It would take a load off my mind. What do you say?'

'Okay,' Bronwyn smiled. 'Why not? It beats sitting around this place brooding by myself. The two of us can brood together.'

'Great. Let's roll. I've got things to do.'

Breene frowned once he had dropped her off at the Warners' house. His investigations so far had netted him nothing, only given him a better picture of Mandy the girl and loaded him down with the problems of the Warner family. It had always been his rule during his police career not to carry around excess mental baggage when he was working on a case.

He had blown that one right out of the water this time. People. They sure complicated a man's life.

He sighed, frustrated and tired. What now? He pointed his car in the direction of Surfers, planning

STALKER

to pay a visit to Mandy's work address. Maybe he'd be able to jog somebody's memory down there, pick up something. Anything would do. He wondered how Jack was getting on, anger stirring with the thought of that idiot detective Hughes.

Jack Warner was furious by the time he arrived home. Fucking Hughes had questioned him for the better part of four hours, round and round, implying that he had something to do with his own daughter's kidnapping, for Christ's sake. He had treated Warner as if he was some underworld figure, suggested he had 'extensive connections' with organised crime in Sydney. No matter what he said, Warner hadn't been able to convince him otherwise. The man was a fool.

Pam was sitting up in the lounge with Bronwyn when he walked in, and he was relieved to see the two of them talking quietly, comforting each other. He kept his fury to himself, not wanting to burden her with any more problems than she already had.

'Jack, what was it all about?' She looked up inquisitively.

'It was nothing, he was just trying to trace Mandy's movements, see if there was something I'd forgotten earlier,' Warner lied. 'Listen, I'm pretty wound up. Do you mind if I take a walk or something? I've got a lot of thinking to do.'

She reached up and took his hand.

'Is there anything I can do, Jack?'

'No' he shook his head, shrugged in frustration. 'What about Merv, do you know what he's up to?'

'No. He dropped Bronwyn off and said he had things to follow up on. Jack, do you think he's got a chance of finding her?'

'If anyone can, Merv will. He's a damned good detective. Don't you worry, honey, I'm sure he'll give it his best shot.' He couldn't deny the hope in his wife's eyes, even if he did feel dead inside, any hope he may have had extinguished by the anguish of the past few hours. To think that Hughes was actually laying the blame on him for his own daughter's disappearance. And the thought that precious time was being wasted while Hughes chased such ludicrous leads...

'Are you all right, Jack?' Pam asked anxiously.

'Sure, I'm okay. I'll just be a little while, all right?'

Two young shop assistants were leaning on the counter of the empty jeans store when he entered. They gave him a cursory glance, saw nothing to interest them and returned to their conversation.

'Excuse me, ladies,' Breene flashed them a smile. 'I'd like to have a word with you.'

'Oh?' The taller of the two arched her eyebrows. 'What about?'

'Amanda Warner.'

Her eyes widened.

'What about her?'

'You do realise she's been kidnapped.'

'Yeah.' Some of the studied coolness vanished from her young face. 'They told me when I came on.'

Breene glanced at the other girl.

'Do you know Mandy?'

'No.' She shook her head. 'I'm new here.'

'Well, if you wouldn't mind, I'd like to have a word with your friend here in private.'

She looked at the taller girl. 'It's all right, just go and tidy up the jeans stacks or something,' she said.

'What's your name?' Breene asked when the other girl had walked away.

'Louise.'

'Good, Louise. Mine's Breene. Merv Breene,' he flashed his badge at her and smiled. Her gaze remained frosty.

'Okay, Louise. Just one or two things you might be able to help me with. Mandy worked last night, right?'

'Yeah. I was here with her.' There was just a hint of a lip quiver, which she quickly covered.

'It was pretty awful what happened to her.'

'Yes.' She shook her head and looked down at the counter.

'Were you friends?'

'Not friends. We got along all right.'

'Okay, Louise. I don't want to frighten you, but did you know that Mandy was attacked after she left work here? We think the assailant may have followed her out to Narrowneck and tried to grab her.'

'You're kidding.' Her eyes widened, all pretence of coolness gone. 'From here? Do you think there's any danger? Do you think he's still around?'

'No, I don't think so. I believe he was specifically after Mandy.'

'Oh.' She relaxed visibly.

'So I'm wondering whether you saw anybody in here last night who may have acted suspiciously, maybe paid particular attention to Mandy, hung around for a long time without buying anything. Did you see anyone like that?'

'You think he was in the shop?' She clutched at her shirt front with a manicured hand. 'In here last night?'

'It's a possibility, Louise. I'm just checking out the possibilities.'

She swallowed.

'No, I can't remember anybody like that.' She frowned, concentrating. 'No, I really can't.'

'Nothing unusual happened? Nothing at all?'

'Nothing. I'm just blown away to think that he may have been in here at all. It gives me the creeps just thinking about it.' She shuddered, delicately flicking her long blonde hair from side to side. She stared at Breene, eyes tragically wide. Breene was amused by the performance, wondered if it was for his benefit or if she was just a natural actress.

'All right, Louise, that's all I wanted to know. Now it is possible that you'll remember something once I've left, something odd, anything at all. If you do, call me on this number. Okay?'

'Sure. Sure, I'll call you, Mr?'

'Breene. Remember, anything at all, no matter how small or insignificant. You could really be helping Mandy out.'

She returned his smile this time, watched as he walked out of the shop.

A murderer in the shop. How *creepy*.

Breene left the shop feeling helpless and frustrated. It had been a very long day and all his efforts thus far had proved fruitless. He hadn't helped Amanda Warner, she was still out there somewhere, alone and frightened. God only knew what sort of torture the sick bastard had already put her through. Maybe she'd be better off dead.

He stared gloomily at the gaudy lights of the shopfronts, the slow-moving shoppers gazing at displays of items they would never really need. He avoided looking at the couples, hand-in-hand couples, laughing together, sharing an icecream.

Jesus, he couldn't escape it. The thought was there, lurking in the back of his consciousness, unavoidable, waiting for him to succumb. Sylvia. Anger and despair seemed like physical presences in the car with him, the small cabin empty and reeking of loneliness.

He drove around aimlessly, not much caring where he was headed. The dark night washed over him, intensified the hollow ache in the pit of his stomach. It was bloody ridiculous, crazy that he should allow himself to feel like this, but he couldn't stop it. He wondered if anybody would notice if he dropped off the face of the earth. What difference did the man called Mervyn Breene really make? Did anybody's heart beat faster just knowing he was alive?

He parked on a deserted strip of coastline, killed the engine, extinguished the lights and sat there, alone with the night. The booming crash of the waves obliterated any sense he had of himself.

He stepped quietly from the car, closed and locked the door behind him and merged quietly with the darkness. He slipped his shoes off and left them beside the front wheel and walked down towards the waves, the sand cool and dry between his toes.

What the fuck did it really matter anyway?

He came to a halt on the edge of the wet sand, sensed rather than saw the pounding strength of the waves as they threw themselves at the shore and rushed towards him in a torrent of ever-diminishing white foam until their fury was spent and they were sucked back into the turmoil of the ocean.

Breene sank down into the wet sand. The breeze whipped spray into his face, wetting his hair and his shirt. He reached for a cigarette but thought better of it, preferring to remain anonymous in the night.

Mervyn Breene. Thirty-eight years of age. Balding, out of shape, smoked too many cigarettes and drank too much.

He didn't know how long he sat there, consumed not so much by bitterness as emptiness. Not self-pity, just nothingness. He wondered how long he had felt this way, avoided the realisation that his life counted for nothing, struggled desperately against the final defeat?

And for Amanda Warner that defeat loomed close, before she had even begun the fight, before she'd had the chance to try her wings to see if she could soar above the rest.

Breene shook his head and laughed quietly, reached into his shirt for a cigarette and turned his back on the surging ocean to light it. He walked back up the beach and reached his car without a backward glance. He was in for the long haul, no matter how shitty were the blows life had to deal him. He wasn't about to bloody well quit, not by a long shot.

Breene turned on all the lights in the unit when he returned, flicked the TV on and turned the volume up. He'd had more than enough silence and brooding for one night. It was time to get back to business.

CHAPTER 10

Breene scanned the opening story of the evening paper and wondered where this Celia Thompson had obtained her information. Maybe she had other information, unsubstantiated hints that she couldn't put in the paper. It was certainly worth a try.

'*Gold Coast Herald*,' said the voice.

'Detective Senior Sergeant Mervyn Breene. I want to speak to Celia Thompson.'

'I'm sorry, sir, she's long finished for the day. It is twenty to nine.'

'Look, I realise how late it is, but it really is most important that I get to talk to her. It's pertaining to the murders, I need some information from her.'

'Well, I don't know…'

'That girl is still out there somewhere in the hands of a lunatic. I must talk to Celia Thompson.'

'All right. I can connect you to her home number.'

'Thank you.' He sighed, tapped a cigarette from his pack and lit it.

'Hello?' A sleepy female voice answered.

'Celia Thompson? My name's Breene, I'm with the police.'

'Oh?' she sat up in bed, shaking sleep from her mind. She had a long-standing distrust of the police and it paid to be alert when talking to them.

'I was wondering if you could help me.'

No comment.

'I've seen your article in this afternoon's paper. Very interesting. Who was your source?'

'I'm sorry, that's privileged information.'

'Oh come on, I just want to talk to the guy, see if he can give me anything else. We're really stuck on this one and time could be running out for Amanda Warner.'

'No chance.'

'That's not very helpful of you, Miss Thompson.'

'Ms. Look officer, I'm tired, I've had a long day, so if that's...'

'All right.' Breene bit back his anger. 'Look, all I really want is some help. Anything at all you've heard, hints, unsubstantiated rumour, gossip — I don't give a shit. I'm pretty desperate on this one. I've got to find that girl.'

'What about Sergeant Hughes? What did you say your name was?' She was starting to get suspicious.

Breene drew a deep breath.

'Look, Hughes is an idiot. He's following ridiculous leads that are going nowhere. All I care about is finding that girl. Is there anything you can tell me? Anything at all?'

'So you're not too keen on Sergeant Hughes,

hey?' She couldn't keep the smile from her face. 'Are you suggesting he's incompetent?' She could already see a story forming — 'Police divided by internal squabbling.' It would add more fuel to the fire if the public thought the police were wasting time with internal bickering while this madman plotted his next murder.

'Ms Thompson, I'll be honest with you. I'm not with the Queensland police. I'm not working with Hughes, I'm actually a friend of the Warners.'

'Cop?'

'Sydney CIB. My only concern is for Amanda.'

'Go on,' she said. This was getting even more interesting.

'I...don't necessarily agree with the direction Hughes is taking.'

'Which is?'

'I'd rather not go into it.'

'So why should I help you?'

'Because of Amanda. Because another human being is out there in the clutches of a fucking lunatic, probably terrified half to death. Because you'd like to think you'd get all the help you could if you were in the same boat.'

'Okay, okay, don't get your knickers in a twist. I'll tell you what I know, but I want something in return.'

'Go on.'

'If and when you find the girl, I want the inside running on Hughes. If he's fucking up, I want to know about it. It's an old score I want to settle.'

Breene took the time to light another cigarette,

wondered how far he could go without involving Jack Warner's name.

'I might be able to help you out.'

'And the inside story on how you managed to get to Amanda before the police did.'

'Jesus, you're not greedy, are you?'

'It's a dog-eat-dog world, Mr…?'

'Breene.'

'All right, Mr Breene. Here's what I know.'

Breene listened intently, scribbling a few notes while she laid out the details. She wasn't telling him anything that hadn't been in the papers, but then again he hadn't been looking at the story from a professional point of view before. It helped to have it sketched out, and she didn't throw in any bullshit. Just the facts. She skipped the part about the tip-off — there was no need for him to know that.

'And that's all?'

'It's everything I know.'

'If you think of anything else, let me know.'

She scribbled his number down.

'And the other?'

'I'll keep in touch. I've got to find her first.' He hung up.

Celia Thompson stared at the receiver. Interesting.

Breene went over everything she had told him, filing it away with the rest of the information he'd heard that day — from Jack, Pam, Bronwyn, Louise. Maybe there was a link somewhere, something he'd missed, something that would occur to him at a later stage. So far it was just a jumble of information clogging his brain.

He turned off the lights and the TV, opened the door to let the night in. The crashing of the waves filled the unit and he lay down on the floor, concentrating on the sound until he became a part of it, carried on the foaming crash and roar.

He roused himself at 12.15 and headed for the shower, turning the water on hard and cold so that it needled into his skin and drove the sleep from his bones. He was surprised to hear the phone, hurried dripping to answer it in the hope that it might have been Sylvia.

'Yeah, Breene here,' he said, puffing slightly.

'Mr Breene? It's Louise, you know, from the jeans shop.'

'Yeah, sure.' He tried to hide his disappointment. It had been a stupid hope in the first place. 'What can I do for you, Louise?'

'I don't mean to bother you, and I'm sorry that it's so late, but you said to ring you if I remembered anything.'

'Yes, go on.' Breene tried to keep the impatience from his voice.

'Well, I've been thinking about what you said earlier and, well, it's probably nothing, but I just remembered this guy I saw a couple of times. Not actually in the shop, but sort of staring in the window.'

'So tell me about it,' Breene said, a brief flicker of hope flaring.

'I only saw him a couple of times, but he sort of didn't really look like one of our usual customers, you know what I mean? He looked kind of creepy.'

Breene sighed quietly.

'Go on.'

'Well, he was sort of big, you know, like solid and that, with this bushy black beard. He must work around here somewhere, I guess.'

'Why? What makes you say that?'

'I don't know. I guess because of the way he dressed.'

'Which was?'

'You know, tie, long-sleeved shirt with the arms rolled up. He had, like really hairy arms. I remember that, because I hate hairy arms, you know. Anyway, that's what he looked like.'

'And you say you saw him a couple of times? How many?'

'Two, maybe three.'

'Same day?'

'No, not on the same day. Maybe twice, two days in a row.'

'And he just stared?'

'Yeah, he just sort of stood there and stared in. He could have been looking for Mandy.'

'All right, Louise, thanks for calling.'

'Do you think it's him? He was creepy-looking. Nasty eyes.'

'Who knows? It could be a help.' Breene doubted it, but he needed a break, needed it badly, and he'd learned from experience not to disregard anything. 'If you remember anything else, you let me know.'

'Okay, I will. Bye.'

He could imagine Louise relaying the story to her friends, the tale growing larger with each telling, and he smiled. Everyone was an amateur detective.

Creepy-looking. That could mean anything.

He went back to the bathroom, prepared himself with meticulous care, shaving with a new blade and savouring the thrill of its sharpness against his skin. He splashed on generous amounts of aftershave and his face tingled with the heat of it on his newly aroused skin. Happy with his grooming, he stepped naked onto the balcony into the embrace of the cool night air, filling his lungs with great gusts of its salt-tinged freshness. Now he felt prepared. The thrill of the chase tingled in his veins, the challenge of beating this sicko bastard. The stakes were high, more personal than he would have liked, but maybe that would give him that extra edge. God knows he needed it. He tried to clear his mind, open himself to whatever he may discover, divorce himself from the emotions that had plagued his few days in Surfers.

He was almost successful, managed to extinguish his anguish over Sylvia until it was little more than a pulsing glow in his subconscious. That would have to do for the time being, until he'd had a chance to deal with her properly.

Breene left his unit a short while later, dressed in a casual cotton shirt, crisply ironed, and a pair of cotton trousers. He hoped he looked like one of the late-night holiday revellers, though personally he suspected that he had grown a bit old for it. He set off at a brisk pace, heading towards Narrowneck and the Main Beach area.

Traces of bloodstains on the footpath under the

street lights alerted him to the fact that he was in the area of the first attack. He stopped and took a bit of a breather, facing across the road towards the ocean. Behind him the footpath was lined with ti-tree scrub and mangroves, concealing the clearing Warner had told him about. He scrabbled around in the darkness, searching for the opening and cursing himself for forgetting to bring a flashlight. He relied instead on the wavering flame of his cigarette lighter, lighting a cigarette at the same time. No point in letting the gas go to waste altogether.

Finding a small gap in the bushes, he pushed through to the clearing beyond. The space was no bigger than two metres wide by a metre long, but it looked as if it saw a bit of use. The undergrowth was flattened, and old beer and spirit bottles were scattered around in the bushes, with faded cigarette packets and old butts. Probably used by kids having a drink while their parents thought they were at the movies, and for young-lovers' rendezvous. Not a very romantic place to discover the pleasures of sex, but he didn't remember his early sexual exploits as terribly romantic anyway.

His cigarette lighter wasn't of much use to him, unless he wanted to go down on his hands and knees and search every inch of the place. The thought didn't appeal to him, and his lighter fluid probably wouldn't last the distance. He settled for a cursory look around. The police would have been through the place and they would have picked up anything obvious.

He tried to get a bit of a feel for the man he was

seeking; he'd obviously been in this clearing before at some time. He wondered what had been going through his head — had he planned to kidnap Warner's daughter or was Mandy just a random target? What did a person who was capable of committing such grisly murders think about?

Breene shook his head. He had no idea, no insight into the functioning of such a mind. The thought of the killer actually being in this space made his flesh crawl; who knew what he might have got up to in here? He pushed his way back out to the footpath, the empty road and the booming surf a stark contrast to the claustrophobic closeness of the gap in the bushes.

He walked slowly towards Main Beach, his thoughts troubled by his attempt to get inside the head of his opponent. He had little comprehension of what that mind was like, or what it might be capable of.

Cautiously he approached the small unit block where Mandy and her boyfriend had lived. It was a small block, obviously built some years before most of its more affluent neighbours. Small and squat, built of cream-coloured bricks, it looked decidedly shabby surrounded by multi-storeyed modern holiday apartment blocks with their distinctively shaped balconies and huge expanses of glass.

Breene kept a sharp lookout for police cars or hidden surveillance units in the vicinity, working on the angle that the perpetrator might return to the scene of the crime. Seeing nothing out of the ordinary, he made his way across the unfenced lawn and slipped quickly inside the heavy wooden door. He entered a stark cement stairwell, hedged in by more of the same pale bricks with an iron railing running up one side of the stairs. There were no elaborate security measures here, not even an intercom system.

He reached the third storey landing without incident, ducked under the crime scene tape cordoning the unit off and stood outside the door, panting quietly from the exertion of mounting the stairs. Cursing his lack of physical fitness, he leaned an ear against the door, hoping to detect sounds of movement from within. This was the tricky part — the last thing he wanted was to run into any cops, although he was carrying his badge to provide for that unfortunate circumstance. Explanations could be tiresome and he'd rather avoid trying to deal with the complications, his involvement in the case being decidedly delicate. Things could get a bit touchy, especially if Hughes became involved.

He breathed a sigh of relief when he detected no noise inside — not that he imagined the interior of the unit would provide a pleasant setting for an evening of TV. He tried the handle. The unit was locked, of course; nobody was that dumb. The lock looked simple enough, but locks weren't exactly his forte and he fumbled nervously with a couple of paper clips, the scratching noise loud in his ears. If there were any cops inside the unit they'd definitely be alerted by his amateurish attempts at lock-picking.

Several anxious moments later the lock gave and the door swung back silently. Breene stepped quickly inside, checking the empty hallway before he closed the door quietly behind him.

It had been a hot day, and the unit had obviously been closed up. The heavy, stale air had a stench he recognised instantly, the smell of sudden death, of a body suddenly bereft of all control of its organs, mixed with the rancid stench of dried blood. It swept over him in the close, dark unit and he fought a wave of nausea and panic, making a conscious effort to remain calm and resist the urge to get the hell out of there. Years of training and experience came to his aid. He closed his eyes and put his mind into a kind of emotional neutral, blocking out the horror and loathing, putting aside the human issues. They wouldn't help him isolate any scraps of information that might be of use in finding Jack Warner's daughter. That was the job he had to do.

He moved cautiously around the unit, sensing rather than seeing obstacles in his way. He checked that all the blinds were pulled before he risked taking out his lighter and sparking an orange flame. He lit another cigarette and drew deeply on the bitter smoke, its familiarity steadying his nerves. Locating a table lamp on the floor in the lounge area he flicked it on, risking light for the sake of speed. He didn't intend to stay around any longer than was absolutely necessary.

The unit was a shambles. The armchair directly to his left was smeared with dark clotted blood, concentrated thickly on the frayed fibres of the headrest. The body shadow, drawn around Jake's corpse before it was removed, indicated the reason for the blood. He had to avoid stepping in large patches of the congealed black mess as he quickly scanned the room, its walls spattered by the bizarre patterns that marked the extinguishing of Jake's life. Breene shuddered involuntarily at the thought of the vision that had greeted the cops who found this mess, and fought to regain his neutrality.

Amanda Warner had seen it happen.

He searched the room as thoroughly as he could in the five minutes he had allotted himself for the task, his senses alert to any hint of a police patrol. His expert eyes absorbed the setup of the unit as he tried to picture the scene that had unfolded the previous night. The small lounge area was sparsely furnished, a mismatched sofa beside the armchair, a small TV set toppled from its milk crate stand. Magazines were strewn on the floor beside an overturned coffee table, one of its legs hanging at an awkward angle.

Christ. Bare accommodation; it could be any young kids' first home. It didn't seem right that it should be Jake's last. No matter how many times he visited a crime scene like this, he'd never get over the fragility of human life, the illusion of permanency so easily shattered.

He locked the thought away. There wasn't the time for it.

The way he figured it, the murderer had been after Amanda, had probably followed her after she'd beaten him off the first time. He shook his head. That didn't fit. She'd been driven home in a taxi, apparently leaving the attacker lying on the footpath.

Maybe there were two separate attackers, with no connection. Seemed unlikely. The guy must have known her address.

For some reason that thought chilled him. A psycho of some sort, as his crimes suggested, who knew Amanda Warner's address. How? A friend? If so, she wouldn't have beaten him off on the footpath.

Breene shook his head. Now was not the time to be making guesses, clouding his judgment with half-formed theories. He moved into the small bedroom and glanced quickly behind the curtain to check the cars in the street outside. There had to be some sort of surveillance on the unit, even just a regular drive-by, but there was no sign of any movement below.

He flicked on the light, taking in the small room at a glance. The bed was unmade, the bedclothes an untidy heap on the floor at the bottom. His attention was immediately drawn to the one pillow sitting neatly at the head of the bed, surrounded by a small round body shadow. He didn't have to be Einstein to work out what had caused the bloodstain. Sick bastard — what the hell did anyone gain from stunts like that? He moved on, keen to escape the unit, the growing concern of discovery only part of the reason. A pair of women's jeans, a blouse and a crumpled pair of track pants lay on the floor. The blouse was spattered with blood. One door of the wardrobe hung ajar. Pulling it open, he noted the neatly ironed clothes, the shoes lined up in the bottom. Someone was a fastidious housekeeper, which meant that the clothes on the floor could only have been dropped there on the night of the murder. The young couple obviously hadn't been expecting company.

The wardrobe was the only piece of furniture in the room, so he pulled open the remaining doors and scanned the contents. Nothing. He may as well clear out, there was obviously nothing here for him to find. He'd just extinguished the bedroom light and was moving towards the bathroom when he heard the rattle of a key in the lock.

'Shit!' he cursed, searching frantically for a place to conceal himself. Ducking back into the bedroom he pulled aside the curtains and threw open the floor-length window, hoping to step onto a balcony. To his dismay he found that the balcony only extended the length of the unit's living area. That was definitely a problem, but he had to move now. He could hear voices in the lounge room behind him.

Lunging into space he caught at the bottom railing of the small cement square that was the balcony and hung suspended above the three-storey drop to the ground. He hated heights.

'Hey, did you leave this bedroom window open? I'm sure it was closed last time we checked,' a voice called only feet from where Breene hung. 'Shit, do you think somebody has been in here?'

Breene searched for a line of escape, cursing his own stupidity. He didn't trust his hold on the cold metal and he didn't have a great deal of time to consider his options before one of the cops took a look outside. It was the only logical place to look.

He considered clambering up onto the balcony for an instant, until he heard the latch on the sliding door flick open. There was only one other thing to do. Working up a bit of a swing with his suspended body, he closed his eyes and let go.

He thudded hard onto the balcony below, cracking himself under the chin with his knee. Blood rushed instantly into his mouth and he fought to retain control of his whirling senses. He struggled painfully into an upright position and winced as his ankle buckled under him. He was definitely too old for this. He steadied himself on the door handle for a moment, giving it a hopeful tug. Much to his surprise the door slid open. He quickly stepped inside and closed it behind him.

There was a light on in the lounge room, and Breene thanked his lucky stars. The last thing he wanted now was to stumble around in the dark and alert the occupants. He stepped quietly through the kitchen and came to a halt in the doorway. The television set was on, the sound turned down to virtually nothing. There was no sign of anybody in the room, so he headed quickly for the door, thinking that whoever lived here had just ducked out to the toilet or something.

He pulled up short when he saw a pair of feet sticking out from the end of the lounge. Now he was for it. How could he explain his being here? He moved forward slowly, not even daring to breathe. A woman's head was turned away from him towards the TV set and he pulled back a bit, planning his next move. He might as well have saved himself the trouble of escaping from the unit upstairs; it wouldn't take the cops long to get down here once the woman screamed.

'Uh, lady,' he whispered softly 'don't be alarmed.' No reaction.

'Lady?' She didn't stir. Breene couldn't believe his luck — she must have dozed off in front of the TV. He moved quickly to the door, pausing to ease the lock back with as little noise as possible. Still no movement from the lounge. A horrible thought struck him and he stood and watched her for a minute, just to make sure she was breathing. He smiled with relief when her chest rose and fell. It wasn't as if a murder happened every five minutes in this place. He closed the door quietly behind him and let out a sigh of relief. That had been a close call.

'Excuse me, sir?'

Breene froze. 'Shh,' he put his finger to his lips as he turned to face the young policeman. 'She's just gone to sleep,' he whispered, indicating the door with his thumb. 'First time since last night.'

'Oh, I see, sir,' the cop nodded. 'I guess she must have been pretty shaken up by it?'

'She sure was. Who wouldn't be? God.' He shook his head. 'I never thought that sort of thing would happen here, not in Surfers.'

'That's usually the way, sir. You always think it couldn't happen to you. You just never know. Is the lady going to be alone tonight, sir?'

'Oh no, I'm just popping out for some cigarettes,' he smiled ruefully and shrugged. 'Bad habit.'

'Tell me about it,' the cop smiled.

'Think she'll be all right? I'll only be five minutes,' Breene asked, allowing a trace of concern to creep into his voice.

'Don't you worry about that sir, we'll be around for a while. We'll keep an eye on her.' He winked.

'Thanks, officer.' He didn't have to fake his look of relief. 'I appreciate it.'

He wondered if the cops would notice when he didn't return. He'd better move fast, just in case. By the time he'd reached the bottom of the staircase his ankle was already throbbing painfully.

Celia Thompson was alert to the sound of the phone — in her line of work she couldn't afford not to be. She surfaced from the depths of slumber, snatching the receiver up as she hauled herself into sitting position and flicked her lamp on.

'Thompson.'

There was a pause at the other end.

'Hello?'

'Celia Thompson?' The words were slow, mechanical.

'Who is this?'

There was another long pause. This was starting to spook her.

'You've got it all wrong, Celia.' The voice sounded as if it was coming out of a void, slow and lifeless, the words precise.

'What? Who's calling? What have I got all wrong?'

'You should not guess at my motives. You can only fail.'

She clutched her hand to her mouth.

'What do you mean?'

'The article. Very naughty. I will not be happy if you do it again.' The line went dead.

Celia Thompson leapt out of bed and switched the bedroom light on, chasing away the shadows created by her small lamp. Who the hell had that been? How the hell had he found her number? She jumped back into bed and pulled the covers up around her protectively. Maybe it hadn't been such a good idea to cook up that profile after all.

It was an hour before she began to calm down properly, leaving the light on as she drifted into an uneasy sleep.

By the next morning she'd decided that it was probably just some crank trying to scare her. She'd made more than her share of enemies over the years.

CHAPTER 11

The shrilling of the telephone jarred him from a deep sleep.

'Yeah?' He muttered thickly.

'Merv? It's Pam Warner.' He was instantly awake.

'Pam. What's up? Is it Amanda?' He asked anxiously.

'No, no it's not Mandy. It's Jack — he's had a heart attack.'

'What? When?'

'During the night. He's in the hospital right now, the Gold Coast hospital at Southport. He asked me to call you.'

'Is he all right?'

'The doctors say he's stable. That's all they'll tell me. He keeps asking for you, Merv, can you come over and see him? It would be a big load off his mind if you could talk to him.'

'Sure, of course I'll come, Pam. Are you all right?'

'Yes,' she faltered. 'Yes, I'm all right. I guess I have to be.'

'Keep your chin up, Pam. I'll be over as soon as I've got myself ready. Okay?'

'Okay. Thanks, Merv.'

Breene sat and stared out the window for a moment. Pam Warner sounded as if she was about to come apart at the seams. He wondered how she was going to cope by herself, without even Jack to look after her. Shit, and he thought he had problems. Still, it wasn't his responsibility. He had more important things to do, namely finding their daughter. Unless…He shook his head. He wasn't going to start playing social worker to the Warner family. He couldn't even sort out his own problems.

He struggled out of bed, wincing when his foot touched the ground. He sure wasn't getting any younger.

Half an hour later Breene edged the Fiat into the hospital parking space, the front suspension protesting at the tight turning angle. Bloody hospitals never had enough parking. It had taken him fifteen minutes to find this space and he was going to make the Fiat fit in, whether it liked it or not.

He put his foot gingerly to the ground. It was supported by tight strapping which eased the pain somewhat and allowed him to take weight on it, but the best pace he could manage was a slow limp as he made his way back to the hospital. This holiday had definitely taken a turn for the worse.

Pam Warner met him outside the coronary care unit. She had black circles under her eyes and looked as if she hadn't slept for a week, but she still managed a smile when she saw Breene. He had to admire the woman's courage.

'How is he?' Breene asked.

'He seems all right,' she shrugged. 'I mean, how can you tell with these things?'

'What happened?'

She shook her head.

'He was all worked up when he got home last night, but he wouldn't tell me why. You know how Jack is. Maybe I'm partly to blame — I knew there was something wrong, but I guess I was too worried about Mandy to take any notice. Anyway, he went out for a walk and didn't come back for hours. When he did things weren't any better, he looked as if he had the weight of the world on his shoulders. When I tried to talk to him about it we got into an argument. That's pretty much the way things have been at our house, even before…all of this,' she said quietly, swallowing to restrain the tears that seemed ever ready to swamp her. 'So I went to bed and he stayed up. I could hear him pacing around the place muttering and cursing, and I guess he was drinking as well. I heard him groaning at about three or so, found him out on the lounge. He looked bloody awful.' Breene placed a comforting arm around her shoulders.

'I thought I was going to lose him too, Merv. What would I do then?' she whispered.

Breene avoided her eyes. He didn't have any comfort to offer the woman, didn't know what to say to her. Pam closed her eyes, struggled to stay calm. She knew that if she gave in now she might never surface again, and she was alarmed by how comforting that thought was.

'Is it all right to go and see him?'

'Yes.' Pam regained her composure, searching in her bag for a tissue. 'The doctor says we shouldn't tire him out, but Jack was so insistent on seeing you that he agreed for the sake of keeping him calm. You know what Jack can be like.'

'Yeah, I know.' They shared a brief smile.

'Well, I guess I'll go in then. You coming?'

'No, I've been in and out all morning. I don't think I'm doing him much good, not the way I am. I think I'll go and get a cup of coffee.'

'Okay,' Breene winked. 'And stop worrying.' It was a lame comment, but what the hell else was he supposed to say?

'Sure.' Pam nodded.

Jack Warner did look bloody awful, his face a yellowy-grey colour against the stark white of the hospital linen. He was propped up on a stack of pillows and hooked up to several leads with an IV going into one arm and oxygen tubing connected under his nose.

'Mr Warner,' the sister said, 'you've got a visitor.' Warner opened his eyes. 'Now don't overdo it,' she cautioned before leaving them alone.

Warner growled at her retreating back.

'Don't overdo it,' he mimicked.

'How are you doing, Jack?' Breene asked, uncomfortable with sickness and hospitals.

'Who gives a damn about how I'm doing? The doctor said it was only a minor heart attack, stress induced. Well, of *course* I'm fucking well stressed. What are you doing about finding my little girl?'

'Take it easy, Jack,' Breene said nervously, afraid Warner would have another attack right in front of him.

'Don't you start with that bullshit, Breene, how can I take it easy? Every time I close my eyes it's gnawing at me, tearing me apart inside. I hope to Christ you're doing something about finding her, because that fucking imbecile Hughes sure isn't. He thinks I've got something to do with it, that I'm involved in bloody organised crime and somebody is paying me back. He's tried to come in here twice already this morning, but they wouldn't let him in. I'll tear his bloody head off if he sticks it in here. Now tell me what you've got!'

Breene shrugged and told him everything. He could hardly avoid it.

When he had finished speaking, Warner said, 'And that's it? Nothing more concrete?' He sank back into his pillows, a look of despair on his face. 'It's hopeless, isn't it, Merv? She hasn't got a chance.' He turned away from Breene, fighting to keep the tears back.

'You know, I went for a walk last night after I got back from the cop shop. I did a lot of thinking, about the last three years, about my time on the force and how it all ended, and I wondered what the fucking point was. I've really stuffed up, Merv, I've thrown away the last three years, made them a misery for myself and my family, and for what? It's all a load of bullshit, Merv, none of it means anything. I realised the only thing that's really important to me is my family.' He turned back to face Breene.

'I've got to make it up to them, Merv. I came that close to bumping myself off last night, felt so damned sorry for myself. I've been feeling sorry for myself for the past three bloody years.' The effort of restraining his emotions was almost too much, but he clenched his teeth and went on. 'Now I need you to do me a favour, Merv. I can't bloody well do it myself, God knows I would if I could. You've got to find her, Merv, you've got to find Mandy. I have to have the chance to make it up to her.' He looked away, his breathing ragged. 'You've got to give me the chance,' he said quietly.

Breene sat in silence, waited until his friend had regained some control.

'I'll do my best, Jack. You can count on that.' He reached for Warner's hand, held it awkwardly for a brief moment.

'I know,' Warner nodded, unable to face him. 'I know you will.'

Breene was relieved not to run into Pam before he left the hospital. He didn't know if he could face her.

It was hot outside as Breene joined the stream of traffic going from Southport towards Surfers. The sun sparkled on the wide blue expanse of the Broadwater to his left, the sails atop the Mirage Resort blinding in their whiteness. Breene eyed the flotilla of yachts and pleasure craft tied up at the marina as he fiddled with his air conditioning and tried to get it working. He gave up with a resigned sigh and rolled the window down. It sure was beautiful up here. For some.

His expression turned grim as he followed the road back into the heart of Surfers Paradise, where it was swallowed by the dense cluster of high-rise towers, concrete and glass. Somewhere out there he would find his quarry. He just prayed it would be soon enough.

But what was his next move?

Amanda Warner woke to horror in a cold, cruel darkness. The nightmare continued. She couldn't move, her limbs bound tight within the confines of her tiny prison. She gagged for air, feared for horrified seconds that she was going to suffocate. She dragged in a frantic breath through her nostrils, her mouth bound immobile with thick layers of tape.

Where was she? What day was it? Where was her tormentor?

Waves of nausea and revulsion swept over her as memories crashed in on her in her tiny prison. She wished she had died. With Jake.

The weight of her grief dragged her down, sucked her in until she was a crumpled knot of misery without hope of life or love or happiness. All that had changed when he had forced himself into their lives. Into *her* life. 'They' didn't exist any more.

She slowly became aware of a faint scraping sound. It seemed a thousand miles away, barely discernible in the gloom of her prison.

Michael Finch scowled heavily when he saw Peter

Ellis. The two men's dislike for each other bordered on loathing. Ellis watched intently as Finch entered the little-used pathology lab, kept in store for times of tragedy when the body count was too high for the other two labs to handle.

He went straight to the stainless steel dissecting table and searched through the array of instruments laid out neatly in the shallow drawers beneath. Some of his own precious instruments were missing. Maybe he'd left them here the last time he'd used the room.

His eye caught sight of the body drawer sitting slightly ajar. That just would not do. He strode over to it and jammed it closed.

He was smiling when he exited the lab, whistling a nameless tune.

Amanda Warner held her breath, clamped her eyes shut. There was no more sound. There was no more light. Her senses were numb. The air was stifling, stale. She gave herself up to the void of darkness and knew no more, her consciousness merging gratefully with the blackness that surrounded her.

Breene stalked within the confines of the unit, the remnants of a hamburger growing cold on the coffee table. He was angry now, angry and frustrated. Jack Warner. *Bloody* Jack Warner. Why couldn't he handle his own problems? If it wasn't for him the girl probably wouldn't ever have left home. Why did he feel as if he owed the bastard anyway? *Did* he owe him?

He knew the answer before he had asked the

question. Jack Warner had been a better friend to him than anyone. They had been through a hell of a lot together and he had always known he could depend on Jack if he needed anything. It was this business about Sylvia that was getting him down. He was losing his perspective.

He was running out of time.

Sylvia. It triggered his memory, reminded him of his earlier intention.

'Hello Sylvia, it's Merv.'

'Hello,' she said cautiously. She was surprised to hear from him, even though she'd hoped it was him every time the phone rang over the past day or so.

'Listen, I was wondering if you could do me a favour?'

'Oh?' She noted the urgency in his voice, wondered what the hell he'd involved himself in now.

'That old friend of mine who lives up here, Jack Warner? His daughter's been kidnapped. You must have heard about it?'

'Not the one in the papers? Oh, I'm so sorry.'

'Yeah. It's a bad business, all right. Look, what I was calling about is, well, Jack's had a heart attack. He's laid up in hospital right now, and his wife's on her own. To tell you the truth I'm worried about her. She's holding together pretty well so far, but I don't want her to have to spend too much time on her own. Do you think you could help her out?'

'Well, sure, if you think I'd be of any use to the poor woman.'

'I'm sure you would,' Breene smiled. She'd be bloody perfect. 'Look, even if you could just drop in and see her, stay for a while. I've got too many other things on my mind.'

'Merv…' she paused. 'You're not getting yourself into any danger, are you? You're not going after this guy?'

Breene snorted.

'Somebody's got to help that poor kid out.'

'But wouldn't it be better left to the police?' She knew the question was useless before it was out of her mouth.

'Look, I don't want to go into it. I owe Jack Warner in a big way, and the least I can do is try to put the poor bastard's mind at ease. It's something I've got to do, okay?'

She frowned, unable to quiet the fear that clutched at her.

'Be careful, Merv,' she said quietly.

'Of course,' Breene smiled. 'And thanks.'

That was a load off his mind. He knew he could trust Sylvia to help out when there was somebody in distress. He lit a cigarette, turned his focus back to Amanda's captor. Who *was* the bastard? What was his story, where did he fit in? He ran over the facts he knew so far, forced himself to concentrate. There must be a link somewhere, there had to be. He was convinced that Amanda Warner had seen this guy somewhere, had at least run into him prior to her abduction. And somebody had to hold that vital piece of information, must have seen her. Christ, he was going crazy, his mind was chock-a-block with shit, not just the facts of the case but Jack, his plea from the hospital bed, and Pam, and Sylvia.

It was too much, there were too many things to cloud his judgment. He had to get the fuck out of this unit before the hopelessness of the situation overwhelmed him. He forced himself to switch off, stop thinking for a while and let his brain file everything away before he overloaded it.

He put his swimming trunks on and escaped from his unit to the beach. His ankle was still troubling him a little, but it wasn't as bad as he'd first thought and a good bash in the surf made him feel a hundred times better. He abandoned himself to the waves, revelling in their power as he was picked up and propelled towards the shore, his weight and his problems irrelevant to the force of the water. It was a hell of a lot cleaner than Bondi Beach, but now he heard they were putting sewage outfall pipes into the waterways here too. Bloody idiots. They'd be sorry. Shit in the water definitely didn't rate as a tourist attraction.

He struggled from the water tired but exhilarated and cast himself down on his towel. The early afternoon sun felt good on his back as he caught his breath, wet hair trickling salt water into his eyes. After a few minutes, when he felt sufficiently recovered, Breene sat up and surveyed the beach around him. The high rise unit blocks were already casting shadows over the sand, forcing the dedicated sun worshippers to huddle into the gaps of sunshine in between or to move down closer to the waterline. There were still a few around, shapely young women, their bodies turned golden brown by long hours in the sun each day. He wondered what they would look like in five years or so.

Nearer to the waterline, a constant stream of people passed. Joggers, power walkers, people out for a leisurely stroll, walking dogs, holding hands. It was like a tourist bureau ad. 'Come to sunny Queensland with its golden beaches.' Breene smiled to himself. Sunny Queensland, all right. Night life, twenty-four-hour shopping, beautiful people. Murders and kidnapping. Psychopaths on the loose.

It was time he got back to work.

Celia Thompson had all but put the late-night phone call out of her mind. She sat scratching her head, tried to think of an angle she hadn't used, something, anything to get more mileage from the story, to keep her name on the front page. She'd struggled to make copy for the evening edition, and even then the editor had threatened to relegate it to the third page if something better came in.

'Package for you, Celia.'

'Thanks.' She barely looked up, took the small package and put it on her desk. What the hell was she going to do next? She was reluctant to let this one go, even for a day. Besides, that poor kid was still out there somewhere, wasn't she? Imagine how she must be feeling. Maybe…nah, that wasn't her style, and it meant putting herself in a position that she sincerely hoped never to experience.

She threw her pencil down in frustration, her eyes wandering to the package. What the hell could that be? Certainly not documents. She reached for it, her curiosity aroused. Whoever had sent it sure had taken some trouble with the packaging. She cracked the tape with her letter opener, her curiosity increasing with each successive layer of protective paper.

She frowned, held the small vial of red-coloured liquid up to the light. Ink? She searched around inside the package, found a note in the bottom.

'A gift to you, from Amanda. Just a small reminder.'

'Jesus!' She could feel the colour drain from her face. Amanda Warner's blood. The vial was still warm. She put it back in the box, covered it with several layers of paper.

'Hey, Celia, what's up?' Elliot McCoy was suddenly standing over her desk, displaying his usual curiosity. 'You look as if you've seen a ghost.'

'It's nothing.' She managed a smile. 'Just…' her gaze strayed to the small box. 'It's nothing.'

'Suit yourself,' McCoy shrugged. 'You want some coffee?'

'Sure, thanks.' She needed one.

The unit was warm inside when Breene returned, the bright afternoon sun spilling across the carpet. He made himself a coffee and took it onto the balcony, lighting a cigarette as he settled into a deckchair. Surfers Paradise was spread out before his eyes. To his right the sea crashed and foamed and to his left the sun glinted off the Nerang River. It looked like a great place for a holiday. He wished he was having one.

He was tired, worn out from lack of sleep and too much thinking. A nap would be nice, just twenty minutes with his eyes closed out here in the sun, lulled by the sounds of the ocean. He scowled when the phone rang, unfolded himself from the chair and went to answer it. He couldn't really afford the time for a nap anyway.

'Breene?'

'Speaking.'

'It's Celia Thompson. I think we should meet.'

'When?'

'Now. Twenty minutes — I'll meet you at Costa Dora, it's an Italian restaurant in Orchid Avenue.'

'How will I know you?'

'I'll be sitting at one of the sidewalk tables. I'm wearing a sleeveless blouse, and I've got red hair. You can't miss me.'

'I'll be there,' Breene promised. He could name no reason other than instinct, or maybe it was desperation, for the hope that surged within him. This could be the break he'd been waiting for.

CHAPTER 12

Warren Hughes suffered few moments of doubt. He had always believed in his own ability, believed he was destined to have good luck. And that was usually the way things had worked out.

But he couldn't help having some misgivings about the disappearance of Amanda Warner. Somewhere in the back of his mind was a vague worry that he might not be on the right track. But he *had* to be right. It all fitted, the theory was tight. Retribution against Warner for doing the wrong thing, trying to bring him to heel by holding his daughter. Hughes was certain she was in no danger, not at the moment, and that Warner wouldn't be so stupid as to endanger her life. Whoever he was dealing with obviously meant business. They had demonstrated it only too well.

Of course, both murders on the night Amanda was kidnapped had been absolutely necessary — Jake and the taxi driver had seen the assailant, they had to be eliminated. He dismissed vague misgivings about the attack on Amanda Warner before she had reached home; this was obviously an attempt to avoid complications. He figured that Warner had already been given the warning when the two old ladies were killed. Very gangland, that, especially the dismemberment. And the severing of the young kid's head.

Come to think of it, there must have been some connection between Warner and the two old ladies. He didn't know what, but it must be there. That would explain away the apparently random nature of their slayings.

But what the hell would two old ladies have to do with organised crime? Parcel drops, maybe? Small cogs in the big wheel, dispensable cogs, but sufficient to serve as a warning to Warner? He obviously hadn't taken the warning seriously enough. Yeah. That all fitted. Warren Hughes sat back and smiled. There was no serial killer, there wouldn't be any more slayings on the Gold Coast. He was sure of it. So long as Warner came to heel. His daughter was the trump card.

Hughes cursed Jack Warner. He was a cunning bastard, hard as nails. He hadn't cracked, not even after hours of questioning, but then again he couldn't have got as far as he had if he was an easy mark. And then pulling this heart attack stunt.

Well, Hughes could wait. Bryant had eased the pressure, especially after Hughes had reassured him that he had Warner by the balls, that it was only a matter of time. Even the papers had pulled back, resorting to the psychological profile ploy.

Yes, Jack Warner was the key to this whole thing, he knew it, and he'd get him one way or the other. Even if he was hiding away in hospital under the protection of his doctor. Maybe that link could do with investigating. Who could tell how wide the net of Jack Warner's operations spread? Hughes knew he had a lot of ground to cover, he'd have to be plenty smart to expose the operation, but he was equal to the task.

So where to next? That neighbour, Molly Kurts, for one thing. She might be able to tell him if anything unusual had occurred next door — regular visitors, sudden trips away. Jesus, this could turn out to be a regular mafia operation, even Yakuza. He wouldn't be surprised.

Maybe he'd take a stroll down to forensics first, have a chat with Peter Ellis about the gangland style of the ritual slayings. He hadn't seen Ellis for a couple of days, but he must be back on duty today. Hughes was looking forward to the visit. Maybe he and Ellis really could be friends.

Hughes puffed out his chest, sucked his stomach in. A diet wouldn't hurt, he mused. He wanted to look good for the papers and for TV. After all, he was going to be a certified hero.

Breene recognised Celia Thompson immediately. When she had said red hair, she had really meant red. It stood out a mile.

'Ms Thompson?'

'Yes. You're Breene?'

'That's me,' he smiled. 'May I?'

'Please.' She indicated a chair. 'And it's Celia.' She extended her hand.

'Merv.' He shook hands briefly, took in her emerald-green eyes, her unblemished alabaster skin at a glance. Not bad.

'You've got something on Amanda Warner?' He didn't really have time for pleasantries.

'Yes.' She flushed under Breene's steady gaze. 'I...this arrived for me at the office, by personal delivery, about forty minutes ago.' She handed the package across to Breene, relieved to get it off her hands.

'Shit,' Breene said, holding up the vial. 'It's blood all right, it's already separating.' He put it back in the box. 'You say it was delivered personally? Anybody get a look at who delivered it?'

'Yeah, I already checked that out. The girl on the desk said it was some kind of courier.'

'A courier? What sort of a courier? Nothing more specific?'

'Nope.' She shook her head. 'She just said the guy was in a white shirt and he was driving a small white hatchback. Private contractor, maybe?'

'Christ, a courier. She didn't see any logos, the delivery guy didn't have anything on his shirt? No signature required?' This could be the bastard's first slip.

'Nothing.'

'We've got to be able to trace this courier somehow. What about the phone book?'

'Have you any idea how many courier services there are? Not to mention the number of private contractors, even places that do their own deliveries.'

'Shit, we have to be able to track this somehow. This could be the first real break, a link to this fucking wacko.' Blood. Amanda's blood? Who could tell? The very thought of it chilled him, his mind struggled with its significance. Did this mean that the maniac had already killed her, that he was sitting back mocking them all, setting up his next victim? It couldn't. He *couldn't* have killed her, not now. Not yet. All right, Breene, think, man, think. A courier. There had to be a quicker way to find out who it was than ringing every single courier service, tracking through their deliveries for the day. This was a warning, of that he was sure. But it gave him a chance.

'Why the hell did he send it to you?'

'To warn me,' Celia Thompson shrugged. 'He didn't like my article in yesterday afternoon's paper, the psychological profile. I got a phone call from him last night.'

'What? He called you? Did you tell the police?'

'No. I figured it was just some crank. To tell you the truth, I'd put it completely out of my mind until this package arrived.'

'So why tell me? Why not go to the cops?'

'Like you said, Hughes is an idiot. I figured I'd show it to you first, see what you could make of it.'

Breene nodded, stared absently into the distance. He turned the facts over and over in his mind, certain he was missing something vital.

'This courier is the key. But who the fuck is it? How can we find him quickly?'

'I don't know. I have no idea.'

'White shirt?'

'Yeah, and a white car. Hatch, she thought.'

'But no writing on the side? No insignias?'

'Not that she could see.'

'Shit.' He rapped the table in his agitation. What sort of courier?

'A medical courier.' He snapped his fingers. 'They would carry blood around all the time. It wouldn't even be out of the ordinary.' He smiled in triumph. That had to be it.

'That narrows it down, all right,' she agreed. 'But it still means a lot of checking. I could do it, I suppose…'

'Hold on,' Breene stopped her. 'Let's think about this for a moment. 'Who'd use a medical courier? I mean, not everyone just sends blood around the place, do they?'

'Doctors?'

'Yeah, and hospitals, and pathology labs, forensic labs. Even the cops…'

'Forensics!' She jolted forward in her chair. 'The guy who gave me the tip-off about the dog, you know, the one that got dismembered? He said he was from a forensics lab, said he thought the public should know. Hey, maybe that's how that bastard got my number last night. I thought the voice was vaguely familiar, even though he was obviously trying to disguise it. Maybe it's the same man!'

'Jesus, this could be it, it could be our man.' Breene was gripped with excitement. 'And there's only one forensics lab they'd take something like that to when they want it hushed up. The police forensics lab. Do you know where the closest one is?'

'Sure, there's one attached to the station at Surfers.'

'Right. I'd better get straight onto it.' He got up from the table. 'Thanks. Thanks a hell of a lot.' He leaned down and kissed her on the forehead. 'And maybe you'd better get that blood over to the police, tell them about the phone call.'

She watched him as he turned and ran along the street, his long legs eating up the distance between her and the corner. Definitely interesting. She finished her coffee and stood up, straightening her trousers. Not a bad day's work, she smiled, even if she hadn't come up with a front-page story. Not yet, anyway.

'Stafford, Forensics,' the bored voice answered.

'Hello, Stafford. My name's Breene, Detective Senior Sergeant. Look, we haven't run across each other yet, but they've just assigned me to the Amanda Warner case with Detective Sergeant Hughes. I need a bit of information.'

'Yes, sir?' He swallowed it without a hitch. Breene had counted on it.

'All right, now they tell me that dog, the one that was dismembered, was brought in to you?'

Stafford checked back through his log.

'That's correct.'

'Good. I wanted to check up on those findings — can you give me the names of the forensics guys who were on that day?'

'That would be Ellis and Finch. Uh, Peter and Michael.'

'Right. Either of them working today?'

'Ellis is, but Finch went home with a headache this morning. Apparently he had an accident or something, called in sick the last two days. I don't know why he bothered to show up today either.'

'Oh.' An accident? Or maybe he'd been at the wrong end of a beating, say from Amanda Warner?

'Listen, I'm on the road at the moment. Maybe you could give me Finch's address and I could go and see him before I get back to the station. It would save me time later.'

'Sure thing, hold on a moment.' Breene waited impatiently, anxiety churning in his gut.

'Here it is.' He rattled off an address in Southport.

'Thanks, Stafford. Appreciate that.'

'No worries, sir. Breene, wasn't it?'

'You got it.' Breene was about to hang up when a thought occurred to him. 'By the way, has either of these guys got black hair and a beard?'

'Yes. Finch. Why do you…' the phone was already buzzing in his ear. Stafford shrugged and went back to his crossword.

Breene bit back his impatience as he fumbled with the door lock — the bloody thing always stuck when he was in a hurry. He looked at the address for Finch and reached for the street directory, a renewed sense of urgency burning in his gut. He'd made a connection and experience told him that such things were rarely coincidental.

He gunned the engine of the little Fiat and shot out

of the carpark, headed up the road and pointed his nose in the direction of Southport. There was traffic everywhere and he sweated on the slow-moving cars.

'Come on, fuck you,' he cursed, feeling the pressure of every second. Unable to contain his impatience any longer, he pushed the nose of the Fiat in front of a slow-moving Mercedes, forcing the bigger car to brake sharply. Breene ignored the blare of the horn as he floored the accelerator and weaved in and out of the heavy afternoon traffic, his driving skills honed by years of dealing with traffic snarls in Sydney. Amanda Warner's plight loomed large in his mind and he didn't care about anything else, including his own safety.

'Ellis,' Hughes called down the corridor at the retreating back of the scientist. 'Pete, wait!' He hurried to catch him up. 'Hi!' He reached him, put a friendly hand on his shoulder. 'How's it going?'

'I w-w-was j-j-just about to l-l-leave.'

'Well I'm glad I caught you. I just wanted to ask you a few questions about the murders?'

'Oh?' Ellis's eyes narrowed. 'Wh-what can I h-h-help you with?'

'Well, I've been doing some thinking.' Hughes looked around, not happy to be standing in the middle of the corridor. 'Is there somewhere we can sit down? Or maybe you'd like to go and have a beer? There are a couple of things I want to bounce off you, see what you think.'

'N-n-no, th-thanks. My m-m-mother's exp-expecting me at h-h-home.'

'So that's who you live with, hey?' Hughes clapped him on the shoulder, pleased by the news.

'Th-th-that's right,' Ellis replied coldly. Hughes didn't notice.

'Well, let's just step into this lab here.' He steered Ellis into the empty lab and flicked the light on.

'Okay, wh-wh-what can I help you with?' Hughes hid his smile of satisfaction. His theory was already proving correct — the more familiar he became with Ellis, the less noticeable his stuttering became.

'Like I said, I've been doing some thinking.' He folded his arms and leaned casually against the wall of body drawers. 'These murders, would you say they had the hallmarks of gangland slayings? I mean the dismemberments, the apparent disregard for the victims — would you say that was consistent with your knowledge of underworld hits? Say by the mafia, for conversation's sake.'

Ellis shrugged.

'I s-suppose. Are you sugg-suggesting that these m-murders may be g-gangland 'hits'?'

'That's the way it's starting to look to me.'

'In-interesting. L-l-listen, let's g-get out of the l-l-labs, go out into the s-sunshine? What do you s-say? I g-get sort of s-s-sick of being in h-here all day.'

'Sure,' Hughes beamed. 'I can understand that.' He slapped one of the drawers and laughed. 'I guess they don't make great company.' He laughed at his own joke, thrilled by Ellis' suggestion. For him that had been a bloody speech. Things were progressing more quickly than he'd thought they would.

'Oh, Sergeant Hughes,' Stafford called, seeing him emerge from the lab with Ellis. 'They were looking for you. Apparently a reporter from the *Herald* is upstairs with something concerning the Amanda Warner case. And by the way, I gave that guy who's working with you Finch's address. He said he wanted to check something out?'

'What guy?' Hughes demanded. 'There isn't anybody working with me, I'm heading this investigation alone.'

'Well he said he was working with you — Detective Senior Sergeant Breene.'

'What?' Hughes face went red with anger.

'Breene, sir.'

'Jesus Christ, the meddling bastard. He's with the New South Wales force. What's that address? I'll put a stop to this.' He was halfway up the stairs before he remembered Ellis.

'Listen, Pete.'

'He's gone, sir,' Stafford called.

'Oh.'

Peter Ellis was relieved to escape the presence of Hughes. The man was getting far too personal for his liking.

Breene drove past the old weatherboard cottage slowly. It had definitely seen better years and was badly in need of a coat of paint, as well as some pretty major renovations, from the look of it. He caught a glimpse of a shed at the rear of the block, overgrown with ivy and brambles. He'd take a look inside that, even if he had to force Finch to let him. For an instant he wished he had the support of the police — this could easily turn out to be dangerous.

He brought the Fiat to a halt a few houses down the street. He wished he'd brought a gun.

Michael Finch lived alone in the same house he'd grown up in. He felt safe there, sheltered by the memories of his childhood. He was startled by the sounds of footsteps on the front porch, followed by a loud rapping on the door. Frowning, he went to answer it. Michael Finch did not like to be disturbed.

Breene was tense, chafing with impatience as he waited for an answer to his knock. He had to restrain himself from knocking again, from butting the door with his shoulder and bursting into the house. The links to Finch remained tenuous, fragile: a hint that the tip-off had come from forensics, a vague description from Louise, the late-night phone call to Celia Thompson and now the blood. Nothing concrete, nothing definite, but it was the best lead he'd had so far.

'Yes?' Breene turned sharply at the sound of the voice. He hadn't even heard footsteps approaching.

'Uh, hello,' he fitted a smile to his face, his mouth suddenly dry. Michael Finch was solid, all right — he looked more like a wrestler than a scientist. 'My name's Mervyn Breene. Detective Senior Sergeant. I was wondering if I could have a word with you concerning the Amanda Warner disappearance, particularly in relation to the other murders. And the dismembered dog, of course.'

'Oh? What about them?' Finch was definitely

nervous, and Breene detected a slight flaring of his nostrils when he mentioned the dog.

'Do you think I could come inside?'

'Well,' he hesitated, his eyes furtively scanning Breene's face for an instant. 'I suppose so. I am rather busy…'

Breene pushed past him into the dim hallway of the house.

'Stafford tells me you had to leave work this morning, and that you've been off work for the past couple of days. He said you'd been involved in an accident?' Breene turned quickly to catch his reaction.

'Well yes, I…it's nothing really, just a bit of a knee strain and a banged elbow. I…fell over in the bath.'

Breene couldn't detect any signs of injury on Finch's face, but then again his beard would have covered any recent wound.

'Nice place.' He took in the clutter of furniture, the light from the windows struggling to penetrate the gloom through heavy drapes.

Finch frowned uncertainly. He didn't like having anyone inside his house, inside his own world. It was his escape from life, his sanctuary.

'I was talking to Celia Thompson this morning.' No reaction, but the man was decidedly nervous. 'She was telling me that the tip-off about the dog's body came from the forensic labs.'

'Really?' Finch's eyes narrowed briefly.

'Yes. Did you work on the dog?'

'No.' There was the briefest of pauses. 'No, it

must have been the other scientist, Ellis.' He swallowed nervously. He wasn't a very good liar.

'And what about the other victims? Have you had anything to do with them?' Breene noticed the thick wooden door that led off the dining area, a padlock hanging ajar.

'Yes, I…' He followed Breene's gaze and flushed. 'Look, all of this is documented at the labs. I don't see the need for you to come here, to my home. Maybe you should leave.'

Breene ignored him, swallowed his own fear. This guy Finch was strange, really strange, and he was sure he had something to hide.

'What do you make of those murders, those two old ladies butchered in their own houses?' He watched Finch as he edged his way towards the door. What the hell was the padlock for? And why was Finch so nervous, so keen to get him out of the house? There was only one reason Breene could think of. He sized Finch up, wished he conformed more with the general mould of scientist.

'It was terrible. Horrible.' Finch remembered only too well. They had brought them into the labs in bags and it had been part of his job to piece them back together, work out which limbs belonged to which body. Not his sort of work at all. He grimaced in distaste.

'And then the other two, that young boy and the cabbie. Reckon it was the same person?'

Finch's eyes narrowed.

'What the hell are all these questions about? They're mighty strange, if you ask me. Do you have a point?' He put his huge hands on his hips and glared at Breene.

Breene turned and walked away from him, keeping his tone casual.

'Well, like I said, I heard there'd been a few problems down at the labs.' He grabbed for the handle of the door, turning the knob and thrusting it open.

'*No!*' Finch let out an enraged bellow, surprisingly agile as he covered the distance between himself and Breene. He pinned him against the doorframe, eyes bulging in his flushed face. 'You can't go in there,' he hissed.

Breene squinted in pain, tried to free himself from the powerful grip without success.

'Got something to hide, Finch?' He grunted, staring the other man down. 'What's in the room that you don't want me to see?'

Finch glared at him, his chest heaving with anger. 'That's none of your damned business.'

'I think differently.' Breene growled, 'I think it's very much my business.'

Finch suffered an instant of hesitation and Breene struggled to break his hold. The bigger man was too strong, slammed him against the door frame and encircled his neck with one meaty hand.

'I know what you've done. It's all over, Finch, all over for you. The police are already on their way,' he gasped. He allowed himself to go slack, relaxed against the stranglehold. Finch's eyes narrowed briefly, his mind in turmoil. What did he know?

It was the opportunity Breene had been waiting for. He slammed his knee upwards into Finch's groin and followed up with a solid elbow to Finch's jaw. Finch staggered back in pain but Breene kept after him, hitting him with an uppercut that snapped the larger man's head back, his eyes glazing over. Breene locked his hands together and sledgehammered them down across Finch's neck and he went down.

'Amanda? Mandy?' He burst into the dark room, punching furiously at the light switch. 'Amanda?' His yell trailed off as he surveyed the horror of the room. 'Jesus.'

He was surrounded by the corpses of several animals, their bodies sliced down the middle, the vital organs removed. Dried flesh and fur clung to the skeletons of the hapless victims — dogs, cats, rabbits, mice. Breene gagged, the rancid air of the room suffocatingly thick. What the...did Finch plan on adding a human corpse to the gruesome display?

He ran back out to the living room where a dazed Michael Finch was beginning to recover.

'Where is she?' Breene dropped onto the floor beside him, his forearm crushing into his windpipe. 'Tell me where she is, you sick bastard, before I kill you!' He pressed down until Finch's eyes bulged and the big man struggled for breath. 'Where the fuck have you got her?'

'I don't know...' he gasped.

Breene increased the pressure. Finch flailed helplessly with his arms.

'Tell me where she is, you rotten son of a bitch!' he growled.

Finch's gaze drifted and lost its focus. He was

going to lose it again. Breene eased off, seizing him by the shoulders and shaking him.

Finch struggled to make a sound.

'I don...I don't know what you're talking about.'

Breene slammed his head into the floor. Hard.

'Liar! You fucking liar. Where is she?' He bellowed. 'Tell me where she is!'

He saw the terror in Finch's eyes and it spurred him on.

'How does it feel, you sick bastard?'

Finch lost control of his bladder before blacking out. Breene shook him in fury, could easily have crushed the life out of him, but he hauled himself back from the brink of murder. He had more important things on his mind.

'Amanda?' The urgency returned afresh, the anxiety of it stabbing him in the gut. 'Amanda?' He left Finch where he lay and began a desperate search of the house, turning it upside down in his haste to find her. 'Amanda?'

He was panting from his exertions by the time he reached the rear door. Where was she? His eyes drifted to the dilapidated shed in the back yard and he set off towards it at a run.

The wooden door was dried and cracked, but it wheeled open easily on well oiled hinges. Breene plunged into the dark interior, searched frantically for a light of some kind.

'Amanda?' He called hoarsely. There was a scuffling sound towards the rear of the shed. 'Mandy?' He couldn't see a damned thing. He lunged forward but his progress was abruptly halted by a soft, yielding obstacle that clung to him, smothering his head in its cloying mustiness. He struggled to free himself from its grasp, flailing with his arms until it toppled with a crash and left him free and panting. This was bloody ridiculous. He fumbled in his pocket and pulled his lighter out, striking a tiny orange glow that barely penetrated the gloom.

He searched for fuel, something to kindle a brighter blaze and his eyes fell to the coat rack, a grey dustcoat sprawled on the floor where it had fallen. He snatched it up, ripped one sleeve from it and wrapped it around a metal hanger. The dry material caught instantly.

He held his makeshift torch aloft, the guttering light illuminating a long narrow bench lined with glass jars containing grotesque specimens, grey in their preserving fluid.

'Amanda?' His voice was horse in the rarified atmosphere. There was scratching from the rear and he stumbled in the direction of the sound, picking his way between boxes and barrels that cluttered the floor. His torch illuminated a dim figure in the back corner.

Michael Finch's rage built quickly as his senses returned. His house was in chaos, his secrets discovered. Who was the intruder? Where was he now? He heard the shouting from the shed.

'Amanda?' Breene yelled, moved towards the figure emitting a pale glow in the torchlight. His senses recoiled in horror as he came nearer. Inside a tall glass case suspended in fluid was the body of a large dog, completely denuded of fur. Its eyes trailed obscenely from their sockets.

'Jesus!' he cursed weakly, bile gorging in his throat.

He was taken completely by surprise as the dark form of Michael Finch barrelled into him, knocking him sideways into the wall. The flaming torch flew from his hand and landed in a box, its tinder-dry contents welcoming the flames. Finch was too furious to notice. He lunged after Breene, narrowly missing him as he scrambled out of the bigger man's way. He crashed heavily into the glass display case and it toppled over expelling its gruesome contents, a pool of preserving alcohol quickly spreading across the floor.

Breene picked up a metal barrel and hurled it in Finch's direction, his eyes scanning the rest of the shed for any signs of life amongst the piles of junk.

Finch lumbered towards him, bellowing his rage. His precious belongings, the result of years of careful collection and painstaking labour, had been exposed, his secret experimentation revealed before its time, and this was the man responsible. He caught Breene a glancing blow across the shoulder, sent him sprawling across a wooden crate that splintered under the strain of his weight. Breene rolled aside and came up into a crouch, awaiting the next murderous onslaught.

Finch had lost him in the smoke that swirled around his head, the tears smarting in his eyes. Breene seized the opportunity and charged the bigger man, his shoulder catching him in the centre of a soft stomach. He heard the wind whoosh from Finch's lungs as he propelled him into the solid bench, glass specimen containers crashing to the floor. Finch went down coughing and gasping for air as the pool of alcohol met the flames and erupted into a wall of blinding flame.

'Amanda!' Breene quickly scanned the brightly lit shed. There was no sign of life, no traces of recent disturbance other than the havoc he had wrought himself.

Warren Hughes arrived at Finch's house, furious at the thought of this Breene character who had the hide to pass himself off as Hughes's partner in the investigation. He was in for a shitload of trouble, he was going to learn that nobody fucked with Warren Hughes.

He saw the eruption of flame from the shed out the back of the property and set off towards it at a run. This Breene was a damned cowboy.

Breene stumbled from the shed, the smoke biting painfully into his lungs. He could hear Michael Finch coughing inside, his gasps weakening as the shed was consumed by the fury of the flames. Shit. He was going to have to go back in there and rescue the sick bastard, pull him out of the flames that he deserved. He still didn't know where Amanda was and he wasn't about to let Finch slip away without telling him.

'Breene!' He turned sharply at the sound and was confronted by Warren Hughes. Christ! Just what he bloody well needed.

'In there,' he pointed. 'He's in there.'

'Who?'

'The kidnapper, you fucking idiot. Amanda Warner's kidnapper.'

Hughes stood and stared stupidly. He wasn't going to charge into that blaze. Breene sighed wearily and glared at the fat man before he turned and trotted into the smoke. Finch had managed to crawl most of the way out himself and it was only a matter of pulling him the rest of the distance to the outside. He growled weakly and attempted to lunge at Breene, but Breene easily overpowered him.

'Where's Amanda?' He grabbed a handful of Finch's hair and pulled. 'Where is she?'

Finch stared up at him.

'I don't know.'

Breene let his head drop onto the cement. Finch had something to hide, and he sure as hell was a sick bastard, but for the first time Breene wondered if he was the right sick bastard. Maybe he really didn't know where Amanda was. He cursed silently.

Where the fuck did that leave him now?

He glanced up at Hughes.

'Here, you take over. Arrest the bastard.'

'What? What the hell are you talking about, Breene?'

'Just take a look inside his house, you'll find out.'

Hughes stared in confusion, looking from Breene to the man crawling weakly on the ground. He recognised him as one of the forensic scientists.

'Hey, Breene, get your arse back here!' He shouted as Breene started back along the driveway at the side of the house. 'I'm not finished with you!'

Breene didn't even bother to reply. He didn't have the time to hang around. If Michael Finch was the man he couldn't do any harm for a while, but Breene still had to find Amanda. He couldn't shake the gnawing doubt growing in his mind that he'd jumped the gun and pinned the wrong man. It wasn't the first time he'd stuffed up, but it could prove costly for the girl whose life depended on him.

Not to mention his future as a cop.

CHAPTER 13

'Hey, it's all right, everything's going to be all right.' His voice was soft and gentle as he brushed the trailing hair from her cheek. She smiled at him, reassured by his words, but his hand was so cold. She couldn't understand why it should be so cold. And then his head blossomed into a red cloud.

Amanda Warner awoke from the nightmare with a jerk. She tried to reach out for Jake's reassuring warmth, but she couldn't move her hands. Panic welled inside her. What was happening? She couldn't move. She was cold, so cold. Memory flooded back and threatened to overwhelm her. A hot wave of nausea brought bile gorging up her throat, and dread filled her.

She retreated into a tiny corner of her mind, a corner where she was a little girl cowering against the horrors of the night. Except this time she knew the demon was real. She'd seen him, she's smelt his foul breath. He'd touched her. Amanda whimpered and tried to curl into a protective ball but there was no room to move. It was as if she had already been buried, entombed in a cold world of steel, locked away from everything she had ever known. She tried to shut images of Jake out of her mind. Jake and home and safety and sunlight and happiness.

Because all that had changed. She couldn't think of Jake without seeing his crumpled form spurting blood over the walls of the unit, the unit that had been their home for a brief moment in time. There was no comfort for her. The rest of the world had vanished, replaced by this nightmare reality. This was all that existed. The cold and the damp, the numbness in her back and the raw ache in her wrists and ankles that flared into hot pain every time she tried to move.

She wondered how long it would be before he came back. The demon. The bastard. The fucking bastard. Scalding, boiling water wouldn't wash away the filth and disgust, the horrible ache of self-loathing she felt because he had touched her. She retched violently and bile rushed hotly up her throat, halted by the stifling gag that bound her mouth. She had to swallow it back down to save herself from choking. But she wanted to die. Oh God! She wanted to die. The thought beckoned her, caressed her with its promise of gentle release from the world that had gone so horribly wrong in such a short time.

Hot tears gushed down her cheeks. Why couldn't she just die?

'Jake? Jake, come and get me,' pleaded her agonised mind. She strained against the taut ropes that bound her, her ankles and wrists connected by a rope that ran between them. Oblivious to the pain, she fought with the desperation of growing insanity, enjoyed the sensation of the sawing ropes, revelled in the gush of warm blood that spurted down her hands.

Finally spent she felt the release of unconsciousness rushing to take her in its embrace. 'Please God, please don't let me wake up,' she pleaded silently before she succumbed to the darkness.

She walked in a field of grass, the sun warm on her face, caressed by a gentle whisper of breeze. A spring of happiness welled inside her, happiness that knew no bounds. She was free and she had all day to walk in the field, to pick the daisies, to listen to the chuckling of the stream that she knew flowed just beyond the next hill. She found herself laughing along with it, running to join it, to bathe her feet in its soothing coolness. As she neared the top of the rise she heard the gentle melody of a song, knew it was Jake before she saw him.

She stopped when she reached the crest and gazed on the scene below her. The stream ran into a bend and widened into a small, clear pool. An ancient willow spread its boughs over the water, its leaves ruffled by the gentle breeze. Jake was sitting with his back to the tree, his feet trailing in the water. He turned, sensing her presence, and she could see the smile that lit up his beautiful face.

Amanda was puzzled by the feeling of sadness that suddenly swept over her as she began to walk slowly down the hill towards him. The sun still shone and the water chuckled merrily. The earth beneath her feet smelled rich and the grass cushioned her footfalls.

A faintly rancid reek assailed her nostrils and then was gone, but it triggered a growing sense of disquiet in her. She looked to Jake, but he hadn't seemed to notice. His face smiled back at her, and then he turned to scoop a handful of the water into his mouth.

The ground grew boggy beneath her feet and she could feel the mud seething below the surface, taking on a life of its own.

'Jake?' She called timidly, but he didn't seem to hear. She started to run towards him, her disquiet turning to panic. She had to reach him, then everything would be all right. 'Jake!' she called again, and still he didn't hear her. She wasn't getting any closer to him, he remained distant, oblivious to her calls. She wondered if he was aware of her presence at all.

'Jake, look at me,' she called, a note of panic in her voice. 'Jake?' He was further away now, not coming closer. She couldn't understand it. She tried to run faster, but she was slipping in the mud and the grass seemed to clutch at her ankles, slowing her progress. 'Jake!' she cried. 'Jake, help me, I'm falling.'

Now he turned and saw her. Now she'd be saved. He threw back his head and laughed. And laughed. His laughter swelled in him and sent tremors through the ground that buffeted her as she tried to reach him.

'Stop it, stop it! I'm falling!' she called frantically. 'Help me!'

She couldn't see his face any more, only his mouth, his white teeth huge, his red tongue convulsed with a life of its own. Now the redness spread and his teeth weren't white anymore. The crimson line of his lips erupted and blood gushed out, so much blood.

'Jake!' She screamed. 'Jake! Don't do this to me!'

The flesh melted and peeled back off his head and still he laughed. His empty eye sockets bored into her face and she was unable to tear her gaze from the blackness of those holes. The ground erupted before her feet and crimson gushed in front of her, underneath her. She couldn't see Jake any more, only crimson, a sea of red, coming to sweep her away. It roared like the ocean, and above it all she could hear Jake's maniacal laughter.

'Jake,' she sobbed. 'I thought you loved me!'

His laughter became the roar, its pitch rising higher and higher with the sea of blood.

Amanda lurched back into consciousness, her heart labouring in her chest. Her skin was slick with perspiration, or maybe it was blood. Jake's high-pitched laughter seemed to echo inside her head, jangling her raw nerves.

Peter Ellis had brooded all afternoon in his room, oblivious to the presence of his mother in the house. She no longer existed, not as his mother.

Now the house was silent, the sound of the back door banging and his mother's retreating footsteps echoing in his mind long after she'd departed.

He had to get down to the labs, had known they

weren't safe all along, but still he'd chosen to take the risk. It heightened his sense of power, sneering quietly at the people who worked with him as he withheld his secret from them. How he hated the pity in their eyes, the patronising looks, the way they treated him as if he was a harmless idiot.

Didn't they realise with whom they were dealing?

He bottled the surge of anger and smiled. Soon they would know. Soon everyone would know.

It would be a pity not to have her close, not to have her within touching distance as he went about his work, but then he realised that the time for work had passed. Work. He snorted in derision. It was all part of the veneer, part of the game he had played for so long.

The thought of Warren Hughes sent him scrambling for his keys, searching frantically through his mother's drawers for the spare key to her dilapidated Valiant. Hughes was coming too close, prying where he wasn't welcome, trying to worm his way into Ellis's affections. He knew it, detested the way the man smiled at him, called him Pete. But soon would come a time to deal with Warren Hughes. Very soon.

He found the key and smiled at this small triumph over his mother, who always hid the key as a safeguard against theft, and against his driving it. He hated the bloody thing anyway, preferred the freedom of his motorbike, but he was driven by necessity.

He carefully primed the accelerator three times, pulled the choke out half an inch, no more, and crossed his fingers as he turned the key in the ignition. The engine coughed but refused to fire. With a mounting sense of urgency he went through the ritual once more, pushing the choke in just a little this time. The engine sputtered and caught, but died again before he could tease it into life.

'Damn!' he cursed, hitting the steering wheel with his open fist. 'Start, bugger you.' He needed to get to the labs. His anxiety levels were rising, he never should have left her so long. He remembered that both Finch and Hughes had been in there today, anybody could enter and find her. Luckily he was on call tonight.

The fear that had tugged at his mind erupted — he remembered that somebody had closed the drawer tight. She wouldn't have any air.

The engine fired and roared into life.

'Oh, dear God,' he pleaded, 'let me be in time.'

The irony of his statement struck him and he laughed, the sound escaping involuntarily before he brought himself under control, concentrated on keeping the sputtering engine of the old car alive while he eased it down the driveway and onto the road. He coaxed it along, just a bit more and then it was right, running smoothly, its powerful engine surging beneath the bonnet.

Ellis planted his foot and the car leapt ahead. He needed speed tonight, but the gods were on his side. He was sure of that much. His foot was impatient on the accelerator, his eyes flicking constantly to the speedometer. The seconds seemed to lengthen, every tick of the clock an agony to him.

He drove slowly through the back gates to the parking lot, not wishing to draw attention to himself. He'd often wondered why they didn't post a guard at the rear entrance to the station — maybe they figured nobody would want to break in to a police station.

His heart was pounding loudly in his ears as he slipped the key into the lock. Had he made it in time? He sighed with relief when he found the laboratories in darkness, the stark corridor eerily silent. He tried to control his breathing, to still the wild hammering of his heartbeats as he stalked along the corridor towards the extra lab, the one they kept aside for emergencies. He had seen Finch go in there earlier in the day.

He went straight to the body drawers, hardly daring to breathe. Which one was it? His hand trembled as he reached for the handle and tugged, the drawer sliding out silently on well oiled rollers. He gasped when he saw her, relief flowed over him. Amanda Warner was beautiful, even now.

Amanda stared at him, her eyes wide with fear.

Ellis smiled.

'It's n-n-not s-s-safe here any m-m-more, we-we-we'll have to g-g-go somewhere e-else. Somewhere else.' He nodded, unable to take his eyes away from her beauty for a long moment.

Amanda Warner closed her eyes and turned her head away, a large tear sliding silently down her cheek. She wished she had died before he came back for her.

Ellis rolled the trolley up next to the drawer and

slid Amanda across onto it, his eyes fixed on her face.

'S-s-sorry, I'll h-have to c-c-cover you up now.'

She was grateful when the sheet was placed over her, grateful she wouldn't have to look at his hated face any more. Ellis knew how to get a body out easily — he enjoyed helping the funeral directors as they took the corpses for their penultimate trip. It was a little easier to manoeuvre a body when it was dead, but he managed to get Amanda into the boot of the Valiant without too much trouble.

'I h-h-hope I d-didn't h-h-hurt you,' he said before he slammed the boot lid down, shutting out the light.

Amanda Warner began to shiver uncontrollably, seized by panic. From one tomb to another.

When would the nightmare end? The tears rolled freely down her cheeks. She couldn't stop them any more.

CHAPTER 14

Breene headed for the Warner household, desperate to glean more information, in need of some time to get his thoughts together. He hoped Pam would be home, glanced at his watch. Five o'clock already, the time seemed to slip through his fingers. He knew it wouldn't be the same for Amanda Warner, knew that each minute must drag like an eternity. He cursed the realisation that she would probably have to endure another long, black night in the clutches of the killer and swore to do his ultimate to cut that night short for her.

Sylvia answered his knock at the door.

'Hi!' He couldn't restrain his relief at seeing her face, didn't want to. He pulled her to him and held her close, enjoyed the sensation of just having her near him.

'How are you?' She was taken aback by his greeting, but didn't object.

He grinned widely in response, better for seeing her.

'Any luck?'

'No,' he frowned, his worries only briefly cast aside. 'How's Pam?'

'She seems to be holding up — she's doing better than I could. We've just been getting to know each other, trying to keep her mind off Mandy.'

'Yeah.' He was about to put an end to that. 'What about Jack?'

'Holding his own, apparently. He wanted to check himself out against the doctor's advice, but they managed to talk him into staying for at least another night.'

'Good. If he got out, all he'd be wanting to do would be help me and I can't spare the time to be worrying about a man with a bad heart. Look, I need to see Pam. Think she's up to it?'

'Yeah,' Sylvia shrugged. 'Besides, I already told her I'd stay with her tonight. If it wasn't for her worries about Mandy, and Jack, I think we'd be enjoying ourselves.'

Breene smiled. Sylvia could charm anybody, particularly him, but that was going to have to wait until later. He followed her into the living area.

'Hi, Pam,' he smiled, hoped to allay the fear his visit was sure to inspire. Pam got up from the lounge, the question speaking loudly in the careworn lines of her face.

'No,' he shook his head. 'But I'm getting closer.' She looked awful, her eyes rimmed with dark circles, but she took the news in silence.

'I need some more help from you. Do you feel up to a few more questions? I'd like to go over what

I've learned so far, see if you can add anything to it.'

'Sure.' Her voice was hoarse. 'I'll do whatever I can.'

'Good. Hey Sylvia, would you mind making me a coffee? I sure could use one.'

'Okay,' she scowled good-naturedly. 'But just this once.' Breene winced, remembering the gulf that had grown between them.

'All right, Pam, I'm just going to talk off the top of my head, go over everything that has been said to me over the past day or so. It's probably going to be painful, but I just need to get things clear in my head. If anything occurs to you while I'm talking, you just jump right in, all right?'

'Sure,' Pam nodded. 'I can do that.'

Breene ran through everything he had done over the past twenty-four hours or so, and Pam Warner did not interrupt. Frustrated, he described the forensics leads, omitting the vial of blood that had been sent to Celia Thompson.

'Amanda went to the forensic labs one day last week. At least she planned to and left home early so she could see through before she started work. I heard her on the phone arranging the visit.' Pam said woodenly, her voice drained of emotion.

'You're sure?' Breene sat forward in his chair. 'The police forensic labs?'

'I guess so,' Pam shrugged.

Breene got up from his chair and began pacing the room. Maybe he'd been wrong about Finch, maybe he had been lying and knew of Amanda's whereabouts all along. But where did he have her? He shook his head. The man had been terrified.

Breene was sure he'd have given something away, some hint. What about the other man on duty that day? Ellis? He frowned, wondered if he could pull off the same trick with the constable at the desk, but he doubted it.

Maybe he was barking up the wrong tree altogether, wasting his energies on a lead up a blind alley. Unfortunately, he didn't have much else to go on. He was going to have to pursue this angle.

Both he and the two women jumped at the loud rapping on the door. Breene strode to answer it and was confronted by a very angry Warren Hughes.

'Listen to me, Breene. I don't know what the fuck you're up to, but you'd better get your butt down to the station. Either you've got something on this Finch character or you're in deep trouble. They only just managed to put that shed out before the flames spread to the main house, so everything that was in there is gone and Michael Finch is hopping mad about police brutality. Despite what we found inside we can't charge him with a damned thing, and I want to know exactly what is going on.'

'Okay,' Breene shrugged.

'What?'

'Okay, I'll come down to the station.' He was keen to get another crack at Michael Finch.

'All right, Breene.' Hughes paced in front of him in the small interviewing room. 'You'd better do some explaining and you'd better do it pretty damned fast. I've got Superintendent Arthur Bryant on his way in, and believe me he is far from happy.'

Breene stared at Hughes, took the time to take out a cigarette and light it.

'So you haven't been able to get anything out of Finch?'

'What do you mean? The man doesn't know a damned thing. It's as much as I can do to stop him from pressing charges. God knows why I'm even bothering, except for the good name of the force. The press is hot enough on this story as it is without this sort of shit coming out.'

'You obviously haven't been asking him the right questions,' Breene said evenly.

'What? You've got to be fucking kidding, you idiot. Questions about what? I can't believe you're going on with this charade, Breene, and I'm going to get your buddy Warner whether you like it or not.'

'That, friend, is a crock of shit.' Breene worked hard to restrain his anger. 'You're wasting your time on that angle, and you're wasting Amanda Warner's time — that's damned precious.'

'Listen to me, Breene.' Hughes came close, wagging his finger in Breene's face. 'I am on top of this case, I know what's going on. Your little smoke screen is not going to pull the wool over my eyes.'

'No, you listen to me, Hughes. You say your superintendent is on the way? Well, we can wait until he comes in before I go and talk to this Finch character if you like, because I'm sure he'll be prepared to listen to what I say. Or we can do it now, and you can present Bryant with the answers when he fronts. I couldn't give a shit, I'm only in it for one thing. Amanda Warner's safety.'

Hughes hesitated, bit back his retort. What if this smart arse was right, what if he wasn't on the right track? He'd hate to have Bryant find out via Breene, hate to see his hard toil wasted.

'All right, Breene.' He walked away, made a show of studying his watch. 'I don't believe this bullshit of yours, not for a second, but I'll give you ten minutes. That's all.'

'Good.' Breene nodded. 'That's all I'll need.' He hoped.

Michael Finch glowered at Breene, his face swollen and scratched, his clothes dishevelled.

'What the hell's he doing here?' he snarled at Hughes.

'You shut up, Finch, you're not here to ask questions,' Breene snapped. He shot a warning glance at Hughes.

'All right, we know you haven't got her at your home, Finch. I'm asking you again, where is she?'

'I don't know what you're talking about.'

'I think you do. Amanda Warner, Finch. You killed her boyfriend in their unit, cut his head right off. You remember that, don't you? And those two old ladies, you remember cutting them up don't you? Very nicely dissected, I hear. Very…professional, I believe the word is. And of course the dog, well, we've seen where your passion lies in that area. It was only a matter of time before you advanced to people, wasn't it Finch?'

'That's not true! I've had nothing to do with any of those murders!' There was an edge of fear in his voice. 'I'd never kill anybody, couldn't kill anybody.' Were they going to pin the murders on him? Could they?

'Look, those animals, they're just my hobby. It's my…my way of insulating myself against the job I have to do, my way of keeping my perspective. It separates us from them, don't you see? They're the same inside, they've got bodies just like ours, same organs, skin, teeth, hair, but we're different. It's my way of dealing with death, of knowing that there's something invisible that sets us apart. Can't you understand that? I couldn't kill a human,' he pleaded. 'I couldn't take a life.'

'Is that why you haven't killed Amanda yet? What exactly have you got in mind for her, Finch? A pretty young girl like that, much better than you could ever expect to find. It must have been like seeing a ray of sunshine when you saw her.'

'It wasn't, I haven't…I don't know what you're talking about.'

Hughes watched with growing impatience. This was going nowhere. It was obvious the man knew nothing, despite his gruesome hobby. Breene was desperate, trying to cover up for his mate Jack Warner. He was probably in on it, too.

'All right, Breene,' he said.

'I'm not finished yet.' Breene turned on him angrily, silenced him with the force of his stare. He whipped back around to face Finch.

'You're lying to me.' His voice was low and menacing. 'You're lying to me, Finch. You do know Amanda Warner. You have seen her.'

'I haven't,' he quailed, cowering back in his chair.

'She was in the labs last week. I know she was. That's when you saw her. That's when you were overcome, couldn't take your eyes off her. You even followed her to work. Now where the fuck have you got her?' Breene strode towards him, grabbed him by the shirt front. 'You're going to tell me, you bastard, or I'll rip it out of your throat.'

'Breene!' Hughes barked.

Breene ignored him, kept his grip on Finch's shirt. 'Where is she?'

'I did see her,' Finch squeaked. 'I did see her, I didn't know that was the girl you were talking about. She was here, down in the labs one day last week. It was the day…' He recalled the incident, what he'd been doing before he barrelled into them. 'She was with Ellis, he was showing her around,' he sobbed. 'But I don't know where she is, I never would have touched her.'

Breene let him go, pushed him back into the chair. He knew Finch was telling the truth, that he didn't have Amanda Warner. But what about this Ellis character?

'This has gone far enough.' Hughes confronted Breene. 'If that's all you've got on him, your ten minutes are up.'

'You heard the man, Hughes. She was here, she was in the labs last week. Ellis …'

'It's bullshit, Breene, complete bullshit. Now, get your arse outside.' Breene shot a glance at Finch, sobbing quietly in the chair before he turned and stalked from the room.

'All right, Breene, I don't know what your game is but you've pushed it too far.'

'Listen Hughes, for Christ's sake. She was in the forensic labs and there's evidence that her disappearance is linked to somebody with forensic knowledge. Celia Thompson...'

'Celia Thompson!' Hughes exploded. 'That journalistic prostitute? She'd do anything for a story. She was in here earlier with some concocted bullshit about a vial of blood and I sent her packing. If you were sucked in by her bullshit...'

'It's not bullshit!' Breene was angry now. 'Can't you see, Hughes? This Ellis...'

'It's all fucking crap. I wouldn't be surprised if you and Thompson weren't in this together, hadn't cooked the whole bloody thing up!' Hughes shouted. 'You haven't got a damned leg to stand on, Breene, and this story is about as likely as...'

'Hughes!' Arthur Bryant stood in the doorway. 'Just exactly what is going on here?'

'Sir.' Hughes spun around to face him. 'This is Breene, the cop from Sydney.'

Bryant's steely gaze focussed on Breene.

'Breene,' he nodded coldly. 'What the hell have you got to say for yourself?'

'Sir, I...'

'He hasn't got a damned thing to say for himself. He's trying to manipulate us, he's...'

'I asked Breene, sergeant.'

'Sir.' Breene had to pick his words carefully. 'I believe I'm onto something in the Amanda Warner disappearance. I've got some evidence that there is a connection between the forensics people in your lab and the kidnapper. I'm very interested in seeing Amanda Warner home safe.'

'He's a friend of Jack Warner's,' Hughes cut in.

'What's this evidence you're talking about?' demanded Bryant.

Breene told him about the tip-offs, Louise's description of the man, the fact that Amanda had visited the labs and finally about the threatening phone call, followed by the vial of blood.

'It's Celia Thompson, sir, the journo I told you about at the press conference, the one who broke the dog story and ran the psychological profile,' he said. 'You know how some of these journos will do anything for a story and she seems to be worst than most.'

'So this is why you attacked that man, destroyed his property?' said Bryant.

'Okay, so I was wrong. Shit, I'm in a hell of a hurry to find Amanda and the guy was acting very suspiciously. After I saw those animal carcasses I just sort of went berserk.'

'And what now? You don't believe it was Finch?'

'No, sir, but I'd like to check the other man out. Peter Ellis. He was also on duty that day, showed Amanda around the labs. It's got to at least be worth following up.'

'I disagree,' Hughes said. 'This so-called forensic lead has already proved useless, and I can vouch personally for Peter Ellis. I've had a lot to do with him in the course of the past week or so and I'd be willing to swear that he hasn't got anything to do with this case.'

Bryant turned to face Hughes.

'And what about the vial of blood?'

'We've had it analysed. It's O positive, the most common type there is. Sure, it matches Amanda Warner's type, but it also matches Thompson herself. I just don't think we've got the resources to be following up on it, sir, and to tell you the truth I think it's crap. Thompson has either cooked it up herself, or she's done it in collusion with Breene.

'Let's face it,' Hughes continued, 'Breene is an old mate of Warner's. He was apparently vocal in his defence of Warner while he was being investigated and I'd be willing to bet he might even have been involved in the same ring. What else explains his presence on the Coast at this opportune time? It's a smokescreen, bullshit to throw us off the scent. I'm willing to bet we're even closer than we realise, that this is a desperate bid to lure us away from the truth. Breene even visited Warner in hospital yesterday morning — the doctor only allowed it because Warner kept insisting.'

'This is absolute bullshit!' Breene was enraged. 'Jack Warner was cleared of all charges, he was damned well set up. If this sort of crap is what passes for detective work in this state, then I'm glad I am up here, because without me Mandy hasn't got a chance. Are you really buying this?' he shouted at Bryant. 'For Christ's sake, it's a goddamned fairy story!'

'That is enough out of you, Breene,' Bryant said, tight-lipped. He was not used to being spoken to in such a manner. 'You are already in hot water.' He turned to Hughes. 'I'm going to go and have a word with Finch. You keep Detective Breene here under wraps, see if you can't get him to cool down a bit. He doesn't seem to be familiar with our code of practice up here.'

'Yes sir,' Hughes's mouth curled into a tight grin. 'I'll do my best.'

Bryant marched from the room without another glance at Breene. He was vaguely troubled by what the man had said, his mind tugged by doubt. It did seem highly unlikely that one of their own forensic men could be involved in the case, especially when Hughes had been working closely with him; not impossible, but unlikely. Hughes's story, on the other hand, made some sense. If Warner really was involved in organised crime, if Breene was his associate, what better way to sow confusion, to make the cops look like idiots, then have them chasing around in their backyard while they cleared their trail? After all, there had been no further crimes since the girl's disappearance.

Bryant sighed. He sincerely hoped that Hughes was correct, that he was close to uncovering a major crime ring on the Gold Coast as well as providing the explanation for the bizarre murders. They'd all come up smelling like roses.

Bryant trusted his own judgment, even if he was dubious about that of Warren Hughes. He wouldn't decide what to do with Breene until after he had spoken to Finch.

Arthur Bryant wasn't the only man with doubts

about Warren Hughes on his mind. Peter Ellis, much relieved now he had secreted Amanda Warner where nobody would find her, turned his attention to the overweight, overbearing detective. Just exactly what were his intentions towards Ellis? Why the overt interest, the personal questions? What exactly did the man know? Was it possible that he was the nemesis that Ellis dreaded, the embodiment of his fear of personal failure?

Peter Ellis could not fail, could not afford to fail. The salvation of the world rested heavily on his shoulders, the burden growing ever heavier as his thirtieth birthday approached. Was it possible that Warren Hughes represented his foe, his sworn enemy, the embodiment of everything Ellis opposed? That his mission was to thwart Ellis's claim to his heritage?

He pushed his jigsaw puzzle to one side, heedless of the pieces that dropped to the floor. His time was fast approaching, he should have expected the enemy, should have known he could not claim the throne without a challenge. He smiled quietly, a plan quickly forming in his mind.

He would soon know whether Warren Hughes represented the enemy. He swept the remainder of the jigsaw onto the floor and studied the broken pattern, each piece an entity unto itself, so easily scattered, so delicate as a whole.

CHAPTER 15

Bryant quickly ascertained that Michael Finch had nothing to do with the disappearance of Amanda Warner. His hobbies might have been strange, and he was a man with obvious problems, but he didn't know anything about Amanda Warner. Bryant was prepared to go along with Hughes for a while longer, though he dreaded the thought of another murder. Breene? Well, his theories were even less likely now. It would be most unusual to have two disturbed scientists working in their laboratories, the chances not worth thinking about, though he'd make sure Hughes checked it out. Bryant pursed his lips. Now, what to do with the rogue cop?

The tension was fairly crackling in the small interviewing room when he re-entered, Hughes and Breene eyeing each other across the space that separated them like a couple of gladiators ready for the kill.

'Hughes!' said Bryant. The man was obviously relieved to see him. 'I've decided that the good detective here is going to leave us.'

'What the hell is that supposed to mean?' Breene was on his feet, his face flushing.

'It means, Mr Breene, that I want you out of this state,' Bryant informed him crisply. 'I've just spent a good ten minutes convincing Michael Finch that it would not be to his advantage to press charges, considering what we found in his house. But I am sure I could make him change his mind.'

'You can't seriously mean that you accept Hughes's story that Jack Warner is involved in organised crime? That's worse than ridiculous, it's leaving the fate of that young girl in the hands of a deranged lunatic. Don't you even care about that?' Breene was outraged as he tried to hold his temper in check, tried to make Bryant see sense.

'I have had no communication from down south to indicate that Jack Warner was not, or is not involved in organised crime,' said Bryant evenly. 'My information is that the charges were dropped, that there was no evidence to indict the man on. That is all.'

'But he was offered his job back, with no loss of rank! The man was innocent of any wrongdoing, he was the victim of a set up. He's the most decent cop I ever knew.'

'Yes, well, be that as it may,' Bryant raised his eyebrows, 'I think we can handle it from here on in without your assistance. Hughes, see that someone looks into this Ellis character.'

'Yes sir, I'll deal with it personally.' Tomorrow, or the next day, he thought.

'But what about the girl? Her life is in danger, the

longer she's out there the less chance she has. Can't you get that through your thick heads?'

'That will be all, thank you, Breene,' said Bryant coldly. 'Hughes, see that Mr Breene leaves the state, help him across the border. And post a patrol car there tonight, just in case his impatience urges him back over. I want him pulled in the moment he tries to put a foot across the border.'

'Yes, sir,' Hughes smirked. 'Come with me, Breene.'

Breene pulled away from his outstretched hand.

'Don't touch me, you fat bastard! I'll risk adding assaulting an officer to the charges,' he warned. Hughes decided against touching him.

Breene's fury boiled over once he was in his own car. Fucking Hughes. The man was obviously a moron, a hopeless plodder who had already risen above his level of competence. He'd have trouble writing a legible traffic ticket.

And Amanda Warner's fate rested in his loose grip! Well, not if Mervyn Breene could do anything about it. He'd give her up for dead first, and he wasn't prepared to do that. Not while the faintest of hopes glimmered. But time was running out fast, and here he was being stuffed around by an incompetent idiot.

He wished he had never become involved in the damned case, wished he didn't know or care about Amanda's fate. But he did know, and it was far too late not to care. Breene was in this one up to his eyeballs and he couldn't rest until he'd found her. Dead or alive.

He glanced in his rear view mirror. The cop car

was conspicuously close and Breene could imagine Hughes's fat face contorted by a grin. But this wasn't a game. He would dearly love to knock a few holes in Hughes, could almost imagine the satisfaction of wiping that smile off his face. That wouldn't help Amanda, but it sure would make him feel a hell of a lot better. He snatched a cigarette from his packet and lit it, directing his attention back to the traffic in front of him. He could still feel the presence of the unmarked cop car behind him, and it burned away at his gut. The bastard.

Just short of the point at Kirra Beach Hughes hit the siren and motioned gleefully for Breene to pull over. Clamping down on his anger, Breene pulled the Fiat over to the side of the road and waited in his car. He watched in his side mirror as Hughes made his way to the car, his shirt hanging out of his trousers. His fury mounted as Hughes made a show of inspecting the car, bending to check the tyres and shaking his head as he stood up. He rapped on the window. Breene rolled it down, keeping his eyes to the front.

'What?' He said through gritted teeth.

'Got your license there, Merv? You were speeding, friend. And this car is definitely not roadworthy.' Breene turned his head slowly to face Hughes. The fat cop's face was not improved by the smile he was wearing. He kept his eyes on Hughes as he slipped the Fiat into first, gunned the engine and dropped the clutch.

Hughes's smile was quickly replaced by a look of astonished anger. He shouted at Breene's rapidly departing vehicle and then turned and ran back to his car as fast as his bulk would allow. Breene let some of the anger flow out of him as he watched him in his rear view mirror. He'd gladly pay any fine for the satisfaction of having seen the look on Hughes' face.

Hughes was behind him again just before he crossed the border into Tweed Heads, but now Breene was largely untroubled by his presence. The unmarked cop car stayed with him until he reached the Kingscliffe turnoff. Breene blew his horn and waved as Hughes pulled over to the side of the road. Breene wondered if they would really put a patrol car on the border, whether he could risk driving back in tonight under the cover of darkness.

It was already 9 pm as he drove the little car along the twisting coastal road, the darkness of the night matching his mood. He pulled the Fiat over to the side of the road just after the bridge over Cabarita Creek and got out. He needed to work some of the agitation from his muscles, get rid of some of the aggro. He could just make out the faint glow on the horizon where Surfers would be. He sighed and lit a cigarette. What the fuck was he going to do now? Going back was impossible, at least for the next few hours. Hughes probably figured he would be able to crack Warner in that time, get answers out of him that Breene knew he didn't have.

Cops. He spat into the darkness. There were times when he was ashamed to be associated with them, when he'd rather tell a casual acquaintance that he was anything but a cop. His job consumed his life with details that he'd rather not know about, things he would rather not see. Breene flicked his cigarette at the water and climbed back into the car. Old questions about law and justice resurfaced, questions that had stirred uneasily in his gut after Jack was shafted but had receded as he was reabsorbed into life as a cop. A cop was an outsider, a loner away from his comrades and for a long time that had suited Breene just fine. Now, for the first time, he really wondered whether he needed his job any more, whether he wanted it any more.

Or whether he wanted something totally different. The seed of Sylvia's suggestion had taken root somewhere deep inside, he was surprised to find that he was considering it.

Then again, what the hell else had he come up here for if not to get her back, whatever the cost? Okay, so the gloves were off. He did want her, he did need her. If nothing else, the search for Amanda Warner had cut through the layers of insulating bullshit, cut through to his core. Maybe he wouldn't discover the real heart of his need until he had found her, and until then everything else was just idle chat in his head. His future lay at the end of the search, whatever it might be.

He climbed back into the car and flicked the radio on. He was getting too deeply into his own bullshit and there were more important things to think about.

Like where to go now, what to do, how best to get past the patrol car waiting at the border. First of all, he'd have to ditch his car. The make and numberplate were enough to make him immediately recognisable. He patted the dash ruefully, regretted the necessity of getting rid of something that had been a constant in his shifting life. Where was he going to pick up another one? He'd need a car, there was nothing more certain. But he had bugger-all money, and stealing one was hardly his style.

Damn it. He realised he would have to stop somewhere overnight, throw away valuable hours while he waited for the next day to start so he could find a used car yard and make a swap. There was nothing else he could do, not tonight. Hughes. Fucking Hughes. His knuckles tightened on the wheel, churning rage inside him. Amanda Warner was abandoned to another night and Breene felt as if he was the only man on her side. Fat lot of good he was doing her by driving away from her and into the darkness beyond his headlights.

He spun the facts through his head again and again, searched the recesses of his mind for fragments that might have escaped him, and still the only concrete lead he could come up with was the forensic lead. Ellis. Peter Ellis. He had a name, he could get an address, but for tonight he couldn't get near the bastard courtesy of Warren Hughes and his ridiculous notions.

He reached the small coastal town of Nambucca Heads at about 9.40, scanned quickly through the already deserted streets until he found a car yard, and then a motel. He extracted his emergency bottle of whisky from the boot and settled into the bare motel accommodation, not bothering to kick his shoes off before he lay on the bed and turned the TV on. Then he picked up the phone.

'Sylvia?'

'Merv?' She sounded sleepy, as if the call had woken her. 'Where are you?'

'You wouldn't believe me if I told you.' He sighed. 'Look, the cops decided I was in cahoots with Jack Warner in some sort of organised crime setup. They've advised me to leave the state or be arrested, so for the time being I've taken their advice. I'm at a motel in Nambucca Heads.'

'I can't believe it,' Sylvia said. 'Pam told me there was something like this going on, but it just seems too ridiculous. I mean, who's looking for Mandy?'

'Don't talk about it, it only makes me angry. Listen, do me a favour. In the morning, ring the police forensic labs and get an address on a Peter Ellis for me.'

'How?'

'I don't know, you'll think of something. I have to have that address, and I don't want the cops to know that I'm back on the trial. Can you do that for me?'

'Sure, I'll try.'

'Okay. I'm glad you're there with Pam. It makes me feel better.'

'Just be careful, Merv. This guy is dangerous.'

'Yeah, I know. Listen, I wanted to tell you…I'm thinking about what you said. After all this…'

There was a long pause at the other end of the line.

'Okay, I'll call you in the morning,' he sighed. 'Bye.'

'Goodnight, Merv.'

He hung up and poured himself a shot of whisky, downing it in one go. He hadn't realised how exhausted he was, the exertions of the past few days finally telling on him. He was asleep before he finished his second glass.

Peter Ellis paced restlessly within the confines of his bedroom, the lamp casting a dim light over the poster-covered walls.

'Peter, are you still up?' His mother called from outside the door. He ignored her, hoped she would go away.

'Peter?' He heard her shuffling towards his door and then knock gently on it.

'Go to bed,' he called angrily, 'I'm doing some work.' She shuffled away. 'Stupid old woman,' he muttered angrily, his face twisting into a snarl. 'Leave me alone.'

He snatched up the headphones from his stereo and pushed the power button on. The soothing sounds of Pink Floyd whispered seductively in his ears. That was better. He turned up the volume to drown out the growing noises inside his head.

He was still awake when the tape ended, lying on his bed in the darkness. He groaned in frustration and then ripped the earphones out of the stereo in a burst of sudden rage. Sleep had eluded him again; he hadn't slept properly since the first time he'd seen her. And now she lay within his reach. A short journey through the dark night from him. He reached down to stroke his swelling penis as thoughts of her filled his head. She was so beautiful. So pure. The perfect choice to join him at the masthead, their destinies entwined.

His biggest challenge awaited him, he was fully aware of that, not yet aware of how he was to achieve his purpose. But he had been set one final task, one further step to temper his will for what was to come, a link in the chain of events that had begun with his explosive actions on that first night. He smiled, remembering the strength he had been given, the pure truth of his purpose guiding his hand when the flesh might have faltered.

The task of eliminating Warren Hughes presented a challenge, perhaps his greatest yet, for truly had he realised that there must be a force to oppose his ascension. Yea, verily was it so, written in a hand as yet invisible to his eyes.

He climbed from his bed and dressed quickly in light green cotton pants and an open-necked shirt in a soft shade of pink, his choice dictated by a will that knew all, saw all. It would be pleasing to Warren Hughes.

Warren Hughes's working day had ended in frustration only an hour earlier, his attempt to get in to question Jack Warner thwarted by an over-zealous resident. He would get in there soon, they couldn't shelter him forever. Until then, the whole case had ground to a halt, the resourcefulness of his foe surprising but not altogether unexpected. That damned Breene — if the prick showed his head in the state again, Hughes would take delight in throwing the book at him. He wondered just how deep the corruption ran in New South Wales, how much power they exerted. His mouth set in a grim line, his moustache bristling. They wouldn't beat Warren Hughes.

He wondered vaguely where they really did have Amanda Warner, whether she was safe. Warner would have to crack soon; surely he wouldn't let whoever it was hold his daughter for too long. The man had to have some sort of soul. Maybe…he was startled by the loud ringing of the phone. Frowning, he looked at his watch. 10 pm. This had better be good.

'Hello?'

'H-h-hello, S-s-ergeant H-h-hughes?'

'Yes. Ellis? Pete, is that you?'

'Y-y-yeah. I'm s-s-sorry about r-ringing so l-late, but I c-couldn't sleep. I th-thought maybe we c-could go and h-have a d-drink, have a chat about the c-case?'

'Sure,' Hughes smiled. 'That sounds great to me. Where would you like to meet?'

'W-well, I'm n-not sure. I don't dr-dr-drink very often. S-s-somewhere q-quiet? I really n-n-need to relax.'

'Hm. Somewhere quiet. Hey, what about coming around to my place? I've got a few beers in the fridge and I could heat up a pizza or something. Then we wouldn't have to worry about being disturbed.'

'S-s-sure, okay I g-g-guess.'

Hughes gave Ellis his address.

'See you in about ten minutes then?

'Ok-okay. B-b-bye.'

Perfect. Peter Ellis smiled as he replaced the

receiver. Just the right place for a showdown, without prying eyes that wouldn't understand the necessity of his actions.

Hughes scanned his lounge room, filled with the clutter of a bachelor living alone and not expecting company. For a brief moment he saw the emptiness of his existence, but the reflection passed quickly as he hurried to conceal some of the mess, put away his old socks and throw out at least some of the rubbish. He took off his crumpled shirt, stained from a long day's work, and selected a fresh white one from the wardrobe. He was glad his mother insisted on doing his washing for him, and his ironing — who else was going to do it? He combed his hair and inspected his grin in the mirror, quickly rubbing over his teeth with his finger before splashing on some little-used after shave. He dismissed any qualms he had about the extent of his preparations to see Ellis. He just didn't have company very often.

When he was ready, he went to sit on the lounge, nervous butterflies fluttering in his stomach as he waited, half-dreading the possibility that Ellis may not show. Five minutes later he heard the spluttering of a motorbike out the front and hurried to the window to check. Ellis climbed from his bike and removed his black helmet, swung his bag over his shoulder and walked up the path. Hughes opened the door to greet him.

'Hiya Pete, come on in.' He flashed Ellis a broad grin and stepped aside to let him pass. Ellis returned his smile, concealing his distaste at the sour smell of the man.

'The lounge room is just through there,' Hughes waved his arm, ushering Ellis through to the small, cluttered room. 'Want a beer?'

'Yeah, s-s-sure.'

Hughes found him standing awkwardly in the lounge area as he came in to present the beers with a flourish. Ellis looking young, boyish, his pale shirt only accentuating his pale skin. It made him look vulnerable, fragile.

'Here, come and take a seat, Pete,' he said gently, patting the lounge beside him. There was nowhere else to sit. Ellis smiled awkwardly as he came over to sit beside Hughes, perching himself on the edge of the lounge.

'Get this into you,' said Hughes, shoving the can of beer into his hand, slapping him roughly on the back. 'It'll do you good.' He dropped his hand to the lounge but let it stay close to Ellis, his pulse quickening at their proximity.

'So, what did you want to talk about?' He found it difficult to keep his eyes from straying to Ellis's face, struggled to keep his voice normal.

'Well I ... n-nothing, really.' He turned his blue-eyed gaze on Hughes. 'I g-guess I just wanted to be here.'

Hughes was surprised by his forwardness, delighted to discover that he was barely stuttering. Perhaps there was another explanation for it. Suppressed desire? Hughes knew all about that.

'Well.' He gulped his beer, spilling some of it down his chin. 'I'm glad.'

Ellis held his gaze, allowed his hand to brush

lightly over Hughes's fingers. Hughes's eyes widened, but he didn't pull his hand away, didn't resist as Ellis leaned towards him, his lips inviting. He shivered at the sensation of the kiss, closed his eyes and opened himself up to its warmth.

Ellis put his beer on the floor and reached into his bag, resting against his leg. He pulled out his machete and put his right arm around Hughes' considerable girth, slowly brought it back until it just touched his shirt. He ripped the blade around, slicing Warren Hughes below the ribcage from back to front. Hughes's eyes shot open in pain but Ellis only smiled as he guided his blade up under his heart, piercing the organ with a sharp upward thrust.

Warren Hughes barely had time to grunt, stared in horrified fascination as his lifeblood poured down the front of his fresh white shirt. His eyes drifted briefly to Ellis's face, to those ice-cold blue eyes, before they lost focus.

Ellis smiled in triumph.

It had been easier than he'd expected.

'It's 6.30, sir,' a voice announced. Breene groaned and rolled over, cautiously opening one eye. The whisky bottle was on the bedside table, its level down by only a couple of inches. His drinking last night had been for purely medicinal purposes.

'Sir,' the voice called again, its owner knocking lightly on the door. 'Your breakfast.'

'Oh right,' Breene grunted. 'Thanks.'

Bacon and eggs and fried tomato were just what

the doctor had ordered. Breene sat back with his coffee and turned on the morning breakfast show. His cigarette packet was empty which, he decided, was a good thing. He had been smoking too much lately. He had to make his plan of attack for the day.

His first job was to ditch the Fiat. Hughes or one of his underlings might be set up waiting for his return, and the Fiat would be a dead giveaway. He found a lot that sold cheap cars and a Volkswagon fastback caught his eye. He had a half-formed plan growing in the back of his mind and it would suit his needs perfectly.

The purchase took much longer than he would have liked, the salesman hedging about taking a straight swap from him. When reasoning failed he showed the man his badge and the deal was struck. A badge could do a lot of things for a man.

A sense of urgency was growing in Breene as he searched for a clothing shop that would suit his needs. He settled for a surf shop selling the latest in trendy brand-name clothes and emerged ten minutes later dressed in an oversized black T-shirt with a colourful emblem blazed on the back, a pair of baggy light blue cotton pants with a string-pull waist and fluorescent blue peaked cap. He slung a shapeless haversack over his shoulder and he was ready.

Refreshed and ready to re-engage, Breene folded himself into the old VW and turned the key. The engine roared into life and he chuckled quietly. Hardly inconspicuous, but that suited him perfectly.

He was out on the open highway when the creeping feeling of uneasiness caught up with him. It was more than forty-eight hours since Amanda Warner had been kidnapped. Anything could have happened to her in that time, especially if her kidnapper was as crazy as Breene guessed he was. Breene might still have time, but that wouldn't last forever. The killer had already killed four people to get to her, and his plans for Amanda definitely wouldn't follow the pattern of a traditional love story. A deranged mind was a volatile and formidable weapon. Breene increased the pressure on his foot on the accelerator and the Volkswagon surged ahead. He prayed it was up to the trip, for Amanda Warner's sake.

CHAPTER 16

She couldn't raise Breene, so Celia Thompson had been trying Hughes's number all morning — either he was a big talker or his phone was off the hook. She'd heard a whisper that they'd taken someone into the station in relation to the killings, but nobody down there would confirm anything for her. Lousy bastards. So she'd planned to talk to Hughes, offer him an olive branch. She'd get off his back if he gave her a break. It was a standard tactic in her repertoire.

She sighed, her pencil chewed into a sodden mess as she sat and stared at her idle computer. You'd think the bloody things could write the stories for her if they were so damned smart. Maybe she'd waste the time to go around there, get out of this damned office. There was nothing worse than hearing the furious clattering of other people's keyboards when you were stuck for a story.

A quick phone call provided her with Hughes's home address, not a hard thing to find out when you knew how. She picked up her bag, mumbled over her shoulder about going out and headed for the door.

It was, of course, a beautiful day. She wound the window down and let the air flow through, not caring if it tied her long hair in knots, turned her radio up loud and sang terrible accompaniment all the way to Hughes's Palm Beach home.

She was surprised to find that the address led her to the beachside of the highway, the ocean visible only 50 metres away. Very flash address for a cop, but then she remembered his father had left him quite a bit of money. He had been a politician of some renown years before, and had obviously done all right for himself.

She pulled up, not bothering to lock the car. It didn't seem necessary, not on such a beautiful day. The salt air carried to her nostrils and she threw back her hair in the gentle breeze.

On closer inspection the house was in a state of gradual decay, maintenance obviously a low priority on Hughes's list. There was no answer to her knock, so Celia decided to take a look around. She was naturally inquisitive, and the temptation of walking around Hughes' empty house was more than she could resist. One never knew what little snippets of information one might pick up.

The large windows at the front of the house were protected by heavy shutters, inpenetrable to the eye, but there was a high rounded window on the other side. She searched for something to stand on, found an old wooden slatted chair and pulled it over, keen to get a glimpse inside somebody else's personal life.

It was something that had always fascinated her.

The sight that greeted her would dampen her natural curiosity for some time to come. Warren Hughes was sprawled on the floor, really sprawled. He hadn't died well.

Constables Jackson and Elliot were the first police on the scene, and after they saw Celia Thompson neither was too keen to break the door down. Although they had been none too fond of Hughes, it was disturbing to see a fellow cop meeting such a gruesome death, an end that every cop feared. At least it looked as if he'd gone quickly.

'Hey, Elliot, come in here,' Barry Jackson called from the bedroom. 'Looks as if Hughes was expecting company.' He held up half a dozen gay porno magazines and a package of unopened condoms, his mouth set in a grim line. The discoveries made his death somehow more poignant, the fact that the fantasies he had struggled to subdue in his life were exposed at the scene of his lonely death.

Celia Thompson was in a hurry to get away after giving her statement. It was already 11.44 and she would have to do some very quick work to make the early issue of the evening edition.

Mervyn Breene cursed the thick traffic on the Gold Coast Highway. The tourist population swelled as the Christmas season approached and Breene was impatient with the slow-moving cars. He'd rung Sylvia and she'd told him Ellis's address — he didn't wait to hear how she'd managed it. The trip from Nambucca had seemed eternal as he was caught first behind one truck and then another on the twisting coastal road. By the time he reached the Gold Coast he had had enough of slow-moving traffic. Bloody holidaymakers. He allowed himself a fleeting grin when he remembered that he was a tourist here too. At least he had been.

He pumped his foot to the floor and slipped the little car into a gap that opened up in front of him. Another gap opened to his right and he powered into it, ignoring the angry horn blast from behind. He continued up the highway, the high-revving VW making a throaty roar as he manoeuvred it from one gap to the next. Maybe it wasn't getting him to his destination any faster, but at least he had a focus, something that quelled the wave of anxiety and kept it at a manageable level. Almost.

The traffic light he approached was already orange and turned red as he entered the intersection. He gave the accelerator an extra jab, spurring the car forward. He noticed the looming figure of the Traffic Patrol car an instant before the blue light flashed.

'Fuck!' He threw his hands up in exasperation. 'Just what I bloody well needed.' He pulled over to the side of the road and reached for a cigarette. His hands trembled as he lit it.

'Morning, sir. Did you realise you ran a red light back there?' The cop leaned in on Breene's door, an artificial smile on his face.

'Must have been distracted by the traffic,' Breene muttered.

'May I see your licence, sir?'

Breene dug around in the glove box and pulled

out his tattered licence. He didn't look at the cop as he handed it to him. Now all he needed was for Hughes to have circulated his name to the traffic cops and he was in deep shit. Amanda Warner could ill afford the time.

He watched in his rear view mirror as the lone cop did his paperwork in the car behind him. Why didn't he turn the damned flashing light off? It must have been one of the rules the traffic police followed under the heading 'How to infuriate traffic offenders while booking them'. Making them wait for as long a time as possible would have been the next rule down the list. Breene sat and stewed in silence, gnawing at his fingernails. He'd given that habit up years ago. This search was proving very unsettling to his mental wellbeing.

'Here you go, sir,' the cop leant in and gave him the fine. 'That's payable within twenty-one days, unless you would like to have the matter dealt with by a court of law.' Breene could have punched the shit-eating grin off his face. 'Have a nice day, Mr… Breene' he read the name off the licence before handing it back.

'Yeah. Thanks,' Breene stuffed the licence and the fine into his glovebox. He started up the car and accelerated away from the stationary cop car, resisting the urgent impulse to speed. The fucker would probably pull him over again. With a huge effort of will he restrained his eager foot.

The cop stood with his hands on his hips and shook his head as the VW accelerated noisily up the highway. The name Breene tugged at the edges of his consciousness, vaguely disturbing and familiar. He was sure he had heard it somewhere.

The Ellis household looked deserted when Breene arrived. His knock wasn't answered and he couldn't see any movement behind the security screens that guarded the windows. He ran around to the back of the house in search of somebody. He needed to know where Peter Ellis was.

'Hello, anybody home?' he called. There was no sign of life. Keyed up to the point of explosion, Breene couldn't contain his frustration. He didn't even know if he was any closer to finding Amanda, didn't know if he was searching in the right direction. Where the hell did he go from here?

He had to find this Ellis bastard, would only need about five minutes with him, that would be enough for Breene to know. Those five minutes were proving to be more elusive than he'd imagined.

He looked into the dim interior of the old garage, saw the ancient Valiant crouched there as if waiting. Since there was obviously nobody about he figured he might as well take a bit of a look around.

At first glance the old car looked as if it hadn't moved in a long time, until Breene noticed the fresh mud on the wheels. Interesting. He bent down to take a look, scraped some of the thick clay mixture from the rubber. Not more than a day or two old. Breene shrugged. He would have bet the old girl didn't even move any more, but obviously he was wrong.

He walked further into the dim recesses of the garage, not sure what he was searching for. The space was cramped at the rear of the car — obviously the garage was not intended to accommodate such a large vehicle, or at least not with the accumulation of junk that was piled behind it. He stood and surveyed the collection of junk, disused and discarded. It looked like it was ready for the dump to him, but then again one man's trash…

He leant on the boot of the Valiant and felt it give. A piece of bright red material was wedged under the lock, preventing it from closing properly. Breene tugged at the lid and it came up with a loud creaking noise — it could do with some oil. He glanced inside, was surprised to see a stark white cotton sheet crumpled in the bottom of the boot space. Its clean surface was marred by a few rust-coloured stains. There was something about it that struck Breene as odd, something that wasn't quite right. Frowning, he reached in to take the sheet out for a closer inspection. His hand brushed a small black piece of plastic, maybe a button.

'Peter? Peter is that you?' Shit. He shoved the piece of material and the plastic disk in his pocket and closed the boot lid slowly, wincing at the high-pitched creaking it made.

'Peter?'

'Mrs Ellis?' he called quietly.

'Who's there?' He heard the panic in her voice. 'Who is it?'

'Mrs Ellis, there's no cause for alarm.' He emerged slowly from the dim interior of the garage.

'Help!' Mrs Ellis shrieked. 'Help me!'

'Mrs Ellis,' Breene backed away from the tiny

woman, hands raised in a placating gesture. 'Please, please, I don't mean you any harm.'

'Who are you?' She hissed. 'What were you doing in there?'

'I'm sorry, I apologise. I was looking for your son.' He needed to calm the woman down. He was never going to get any information out of her when she was like this.

'Peter? Do you know Peter?' He saw the moment of hesitation as doubt flickered in her eyes.

'Not exactly, I was just…'

'Well, what do you want from him? What are you doing here? Who are you? I'll call the police!'

'Wait, wait, Mrs Ellis. There's no need to call the police.' It was the last thing he needed and pulling out his own badge would only compound the problem if Hughes discovered his visit. 'I only wanted to ask Peter a few questions, that's all.'

'Well, he's not here.' She backed towards the door, obviously terrified.

'Mrs Ellis, I'm not going to hurt you,' he pleaded. 'I just need to know where your son is.'

'You stay away from me!' she warned. 'If you take one step closer, I'll scream!' She fumbled in her purse for her key.

Breene sighed. This wasn't getting him anywhere.

'I think Peter may be in trouble, Mrs Ellis. I think he may need help.'

'Help?' She stopped and stared at Breene. 'My Peter?' She eyed him suspiciously. 'What makes you think my boy needs help? And who are you to be giving it to him?'

'Has Peter been acting strangely lately, especially during the past week or so?' He tried to press his advantage while her guard was down.

'Strangely? There's nothing strange about my boy. Nothing at all,' she snapped. 'He's just been tired, worn out because they make him work all those late hours down at the laboratories. He's very delicate, you know, very delicate. They expect too much from him.'

'Is he at work now, Mrs Ellis?'

'Why do you want to know? What business is it of yours?'

'I need to know where Peter is,' Breene said firmly. 'I'd like you to tell me.'

'I don't know where he is,' she wavered, her eyes seeking Breene's as if looking for help. 'I don't know where he is.'

'Have you seen him today? This morning?' He couldn't keep the urgency from his voice. 'I have to find him.'

She looked away and the brief instant of contact was severed.

'I don't know and I wouldn't tell you if I did,' she said haughtily. Her head whipped around to face Breene, her eyes suddenly full of suspicion and anger. Breene was amazed by the transformation of her features.

'What were you doing in my garage?' Her voice rose. 'What right do you have to trespass on my property? Help!' She screeched. 'Help me! I'm being attacked!'

'Mrs Ellis,' Breene pleaded.

'Help!'

'I must find your son.'

'Police! Call the police! Help! Help!'

A head poked up over the fence from the property next door.

'What's going on there?' the elderly man thundered. 'What do you think you're up to, young man?' He demanded.

'Sir, I'm merely trying…'

'He tried to grab me!' Mrs Ellis shrieked. 'He's trying to assault me!'

'That's not true. I'm looking for her son.' He turned at the sudden loud banging of the rear door of the Ellis household. Mrs Ellis had escaped inside.

'Now see here, you young ruffian, you wait there until the police arrive. We'll let them sort this out!' he shouted menacingly at Breene.

'I'm calling the police now!' Mrs Ellis screamed from inside.

'I've already called them,' another woman's voice called from the neighbour's house.

'Christ,' Breene cursed. Before long the whole neighbourhood would be out. He turned and trotted back along the driveway, climbed into his car and sped away. He felt like a damned fool.

And he was no closer to finding Peter Ellis. Where was the bastard? Did he have Amanda Warner?

'Fuck it!' He cursed, anger replacing his humiliation. That rotten old bitch. She knew more than she was letting on, of that he was positive. He punched the dashboard in frustration.

Celia Thompsom completed her story in record time, the adrenalin pumping through her veins. She didn't need the facts, not the whos and hows, not when she had seen the victim. A description of the scene in the lounge room of Hughes's cluttered house was enough for several paragraphs, that and some speculation that the slasher, as she liked to call him, might have been motivated by some sexual identity problems. She had lucked out overhearing the two young constables discussing the discovery of homosexual pornography in Hughes' bedroom. It was the only advantage she had derived from being first on the spot, a witness to the gruesome discovery.

'C'mon Celia, we're holding up production waiting for you. It's supposed to be on the stands in an hour and a half.'

'It's ready,' she called, glancing over the final paragraph.

Experts speculate that the slasher may be experiencing a particularly difficult 'coming out', that his maladaptive personality has been overloaded by the realisation that he is a homosexual.

'Take it.' She spun her chair around and got up from her desk, smiling with grim satisfaction. She preferred to come upon her news in a less shocking manner, but she couldn't afford to be too fussy. 'Thank you, Sergeant Hughes, I knew you'd help me with my story.' Gallows humour. She'd developed a pretty thick hide over the years.

She decided against lunch. She didn't really feel

like eating her usual steak sandwich, not today.

The phone on her desk rang and she snatched it up.

'Thompson.'

'Celia, it's Merv Breene.'

'Breene, where the hell were you? I've been trying to ring you all morning.'

'Yeah, well, it's a long story. Suffice it to say that Sergeant Hughes took a particularly strong dislike to me last evening.'

'Not half as strong as the dislike somebody else took to him.'

'What?'

'He's dead. Murdered in his own house. Provided me with my front-page story for the evening edition.'

'Dead? Jesus, do they think it was the same killer?'

'It sure looked like it to me. He was, well, everywhere. I saw it.' She didn't feel like going into details. Now that the heat of creating the story was cooling she was beginning to feel decidedly unwell. Maybe it was the onset of delayed shock.

'Shit.' Breene pondered the significance of this latest killing. Why Hughes? Why now? Did it indicate that the killer had finished with Amanda, that he was moving on?

'So listen.' Celia Thompson recovered, remembering her reason for wanting Breene earlier. 'What about this guy they pulled in yesterday evening? You know anything about that?'

'I had something to do with it, but it didn't result in anything. Unless…did it look as if Hughes' house had been broken into?'

'Uh-uh. It looked as if he'd been expecting company.' She told Breene about the magazines and condoms beside the bed and he frowned, puzzled. What the hell could this new development mean, how did he explain it?

'What were you going to suggest?' She wasn't about to let anything slip by her.

'I was just thinking.' Breene paused.

'Thinking what, Breene? Come on, don't hold out on me, man.'

'The man they took in last night for questioning. I was wondering if he might not have taken exception and slipped around to pay Hughes a visit last night.' Was it possible that Finch was responsible after all? It would be too damned obvious, surely the cops would have been onto that angle as soon as the body was discovered. The killer had been too clever by half to make such a stupid stumble now.

'What was his story?'

Breene hesitated, then decided to tell her what he knew. He had few allies, would probably have even fewer if the police discovered he was back in the state now, especially if they were still swallowing Hughes's organised crime scenario. Bryant had been prepared to go along with it last night, and Hughes's death could only confirm his suggestion that they were getting too close. Christ, he couldn't count on any police support, or information, for that matter. He was even more alone than he had been to start with, maybe even a suspect in Hughes's murder.

'You think they would have pulled him in for questioning again this morning?' Thompson asked.

'They'd have to, surely.'

'Yeah, you're right. Listen, let me check it out and I'll get back to you. Where are you?'

'I'm at a phone booth in Palm Beach. Look, I have to head over to the Warners' house for a while, though I probably should make my visit as brief as possible. If you don't catch me there, I'll contact you.'

'Okay, gotcha.'

'Hold on, could you also find out if a Peter Ellis turned up for work at the forensic labs today? And if he was on call last night?'

'Sure, no problem.'

Breene hung up and sighed. Warren Hughes dead. It wasn't any great loss to the police force of Queensland, not from what he'd seen of the man's performances, but it certainly raised the stakes in the search for the killer. It also made his presence in the state a whole lot more dangerous, from a professional point of view. He lit another cigarette, his lungs tight from continual abuse. Breene ignored them, confined fears of lung cancer to the back of his mind along with the constant gnawing of anxiety in his gut. However significant the murder of Warren Hughes, he was certain it wasn't a good sign for Amanda Warner.

Peter Ellis had decided to put in an appearance at work. He had enjoyed killing Warren Hughes, had derived a greater sense of his own power as he watched the lifeblood drain from the body of his opponent. He was invincible, the enemy was no match for him. He had despatched his nemesis with consummate ease.

Obviosly they had underestimated him. His smile grew broader. Or maybe they had nothing to match his burgeoning power. It seemed only fitting, for what power could match him as events rushed to their conclusion?

He had taken more than his usual pleasure in his job today, especially after they brought the body in for his examination. What fun he'd had with Warren.

There was one thing that bothered him, though. Several times that day he'd heard it, a sound just on the edge of his consciousness, a half-whisper that had caused him to look around quickly, certain somebody had spoken just nearby. The first few times he had shrugged it off, flushed with his victory, but as the morning turned to afternoon, and particularly after he had finished with Hughes, the noises had become more troublesome. Snatches of conversation seemed to hang in the air around him, voices, their words becoming clearer when he tried to focus on them.

What he heard was decidedly unfriendly. Peter Ellis threw down his scalpel, asked his assistant to clean up the mess and stalked from the laboratory. He was gripped by fury, a helpless rage seeping into every pore of his being.

The enemy wasn't finished with him yet. Somehow, it had seeped inside to challenge him at the last. The voices he heard were coming from inside his own head.

He washed his hands viciously, scrubbed at them with scalding water until they were red and chafed. He would *not* be defeated. He could not. But he knew the time to move was now, knew he must claim his throne and take his queen with him.

He ground his teeth in anger when he realised that the way was yet to be revealed. How much longer must his suffering endure, the interminable wait? The way must be revealed; if not, by nightfall he would have to take matters into his own hands. Fate and destiny had guided his actions thus far, perhaps now was the time to take control of his own actions.

CHAPTER 17

Jack Warner was waiting at the door when Breene arrived at the Warner household.

'Jack, when did you get home?'

'Any news?' He ignored Breene's question. 'Are you any closer to finding my little girl?'

'Not for certain, Jack.' Breene met Warner's angry glare. 'I'm still working on it.'

'Christ,' Warner muttered and walked away into the house. Breene followed him.

'Is Sylvia still around?'

'No, she left about an hour ago. She wanted to go home to freshen up. Said she'd come back later this evening to see how Pam was getting on.'

Breene was disappointed by the news that she had left. He'd planned on seeing her when he arrived.

'So how is Pam getting on?'

Warner slumped into a lounge chair.

'We got into an argument about ten minutes after Sylvia left. She's in the bedroom.' He didn't even look up.

'So, is your heart all right? They gave you a clean bill of health?'

Warner shrugged.

'I think they let me go because I was driving them mad. They figured I'd be better off closer to the action than cooped up in that fucking place.'

'But you're still supposed to take it easy, right?'

'Fuck off, Breene. I'll do what I like.'

Breene left him sitting there with his bitterness and anger. He was better off talking to Pam.

'Pam?' The bedroom was dark, all the curtains drawn to keep the daylight out. He could make out a small form lying beneath the bed covers. 'Pam?'

'What?' Her voice was hoarse and weak, muffled by the bedclothes and her own misery.

'I need your help.' He stood and waited for her reaction, suppressed his own feelings of discomfort. He didn't usually talk to his friend's wives in their bedrooms, especially when they were in bed, but circumstances rendered the usual conventions null and void.

The bedclothes lifted and she looked at Breene through the gloom.

'You want my help?' Her voice sounded strained. She'd obviously been doing a lot of crying.

'Yes.' Breene got down onto the floor, squatted on his haunches so his face was level with hers. 'I need some more help to find your daughter.'

'Where's Jack?'

'He's out in the lounge room. He's pretty angry.'

'I know,' Pam sniffed. 'He's been like that ever since he walked through the door. I wish he'd never come home.' She sobbed deep down in her chest and winced with pain. 'I haven't done anything but cry since he got back. When Sylvia was here it didn't seem so bad, at least we could talk, share things, but now I feel so alone. I miss Mandy, I want her to come home.'

'I know, Pam. I want to help you, believe me. I'm working as hard as I can on this thing, I'm doing my best.' He needed her to believe that. 'I really think I'm getting close. Listen, how about if you get up out of there and we'll go out and talk with Jack? He's not really angry, not with you anyway. He needs you like you need him. You're a great team, you and Jack. You've pulled each other through some real tough times and I know you won't let each other down now.' He felt like a bloody counsellor.

'If the two of you could sit down and talk together, try to work on this, I'm sure you'll be able to come up with something more that's going to help me find Amanda,' he urged.

'I don't know.' She sounded as if she was about to cry again.

'Well, I do. You're all she's got on her side. You can't let her down, not without giving it your best shot. Come on, she needs you. Jack needs you.'

She sat up in the bed and pushed the bedclothes away.

'Okay,' she sniffed. 'You're right. I'm not doing Mandy any good lying around here.'

'That's the way,' Breene smiled. 'I'll leave you in privacy for a moment while I talk to Jack.'

'Jack?' Warner didn't look up as Breene walked back into the lounge room. He hadn't moved from his earlier position.

'Jack!' His eyes turned slowly in Breene's direction. 'What?'

'Look mate, it's not me you're angry with. It's not your wife you're angry with. It's that fucker who's got your daughter. It's no good getting shitty with me, because I'm telling you that I'm on your side, I'm the only one you've got in there swinging for you and your daughter. Now, I need your help. I'm having a tough time — you know how tough it can be in this sort of case, and you know how it often only takes one little lead to break it. We're going to find that fucking lead, you, me and Pam. And we're going to sit here until we do. Right?'

Warner didn't reply.

'Right, Jack? For your daughter's sake if nothing else. We're all she's fucking well got!'

'All right,' Warner sighed heavily. 'All right. You're right. Damn you.' He looked at Breene, the ghost of a smile on his lips. 'Let's do it.'

Pam Warner entered the room. She looked tired, her eyes were puffy and red, but her chin was tilted with determination. She glared defiantly at Jack, as if challenging him to say something.

He didn't say a word. He got out of his chair and walked towards her, caught her in an awkward embrace.

Breene looked out the window and lit a cigarette. Pity he couldn't do the same job on his own relationship.

'Jesus,' Warner muttered thickly. 'I could use a drink.'

'All right then. Let's see what we can come up with.' The three of them were seated around the dining-room table, Jack taking charge. Breene allowed himself a smile. That was more like the Jack Warner he knew. 'Breene, what have you been doing so far?'

Breene recounted every step he'd taken, making sure to fill in every detail, examining everything he said in case he had missed something. There must be an answer in there somewhere, something tucked away whose significance he hadn't realised. Pam and Jack listened intently, stopping him occasionally to ask a question, to clarify some minor detail.

'So this Ellis guy is the only thing you haven't been able to follow up on?'

'Yeah, like I said I had to hotfoot it out of there before the boys in blue arrived. That was the last thing I needed, especially now I've heard about Hughes.'

'Jesus, I don't like the sounds of his being killed. He's a damned cop.' Warner frowned, then over-rode his anxiety. 'So what do you make of him? This Ellis, I mean?'

'I just don't know. Part of me is sure it's him, but that's only because I haven't got anything else. The forensic stuff looked good, even better when I went to Finch's house with all that weird shit there. I was certain he was the man and I was plenty damned frightened, but look how that turned out. Maybe the other stuff was from a crank, an old enemy of Celia

Thompson's. Maybe Hughes was right on that one. I'll tell you what, though, Mrs Ellis sure is a queer old bird.'

'And if it's not Ellis?'

'I'll just have to keep looking,' Breene said grimly. The two men eyed each other across the table. They both knew this was the last roll of the dice, if Ellis wasn't the man the case was hopeless.

'I'm just waiting to hear back from this Thompson woman. Maybe they've already got Finch and pinned the murders on him, although I don't think he's the man. Still,' Breene shrugged, 'we could be lucky.'

'And if we're not? What are you going to do then?'

'I'll go back and try to catch Ellis at home, although if he's cool enough to go to work it must almost exclude him. Christ.' Breene rested his forehead against his hands. The whole bloody thing seemed hopeless. 'There just has to be something we're all missing.'

'Yes, but what?' Pam Warner wrung her hands together. 'All this time my poor Mandy's out there, God only knows where, frightened, hungry and I don't like to think what else and there's not a damned thing I can do about it.' She looked away, fighting tears. 'I don't know if I can take it any more. Even if they'd find a…something.' She started to sob. Warner took her hand and held it firmly.

'All right, let's go back to the Ellis woman again. Why did she get so upset? Is she just some sort of loony tune, was it because you were on her property, or was it more than that? I mean, you couldn't calm the old bird down and you say she got jumpy when you started talking about her son. Maybe this lead of yours isn't so hopeless after all. Maybe she's got something to hide out in that garage of hers?'

'I don't know, Jack,' said Breene. 'Maybe she was a bit potty, I was too busy trying to calm her down to think about it. She certainly became hysterical pretty quickly after I mentioned Peter's name. As for the shed, well, there was plenty of junk out there. It left barely enough room for the old Valiant.' He frowned and put his hand into his pocket.

'Look, I got this out of the lock in the boot. It was wedged in there, stopped the boot from closing properly.' He laid the tattered piece of grease-stained red cloth on the table. 'Look familiar?'

Warner shrugged. 'Could be anything.'

Pam picked it up from the table and examined it.

'Doesn't look like hers. It's a piece of flannelette I think, maybe from a man's shirt.'

'Oh, and this.' Breene produced the black plastic object. 'Looks like a button, but it hasn't got a hole in it.'

'Give me a look at that!' Pam Warner snapped, reaching for it and taking it from Breene's grasp.

'Oh, my God!' She clamped her hand over her mouth. 'It's Mandy's. It's one of her earrings, those dreadful old black things she was always glueing back together.'

'I remember them.' Warner took it from her hand. 'Christ, there's even old glue on the back of it!'

Breene nearly knocked the table over in his haste

to get up. It was all he needed, a definite connection between Ellis and Amanda, proof that he was the one. He raced for the door before either of the Warners had the time to react.

'Wait!' Jack yelled. 'I'm coming with you.'

'Like hell you are.' Breene was already halfway out the door.

'You bastard!' Warner shouted after him. 'Wait for me, it's my little girl!' He ran out onto the lawn but Breene already had the VW started and pulled away from the curb as Warner ran towards him.

'You bastard!' Warner shook his fist in the air. 'You bastard!'

'Sorry, Jack,' Breene said, watching him in the rear view mirror. 'I can't afford to risk it.' He had enough to worry about without the fear that Warner was going to have another heart attack. He turned the corner and sped away, cursing the distance, cursing his stupidity.

She had to be alive. She had to.

'Hold on, Mandy. I'm coming!'

Peter Ellis was furious by the time he reached home, the speed of his bike unable to outrun the noises growing in his head. He knew this was the most serious challenge he had yet faced, the final onslaught from his foe. He slammed through the back door, his mother cowering back into the corner of the kitchen. She knew better than to approach him in such a mood.

The paper was laid out on the table in the dining room and the headline caught his eye.

SLASH KILLER STRIKES AGAIN
COP SLAIN IN HIS OWN HOME

He skimmed the article, his anger somewhat mollified by his memory of the previous evening, his memory of how easily he had been victorious on that occasion.

Until he read the final paragraph.

He gripped his head in his hands, buffeted by the sudden crashing of sound, a roar like an angry crowd.

He stumbled to his bedroom and shut the door firmly behind him as he struggled with the noises, his eyes squeezed shut, his face slick with perspiration as he clamped down on them, brought them under his control and pushed them back, away from their position of menace.

He would not be defeated.

Peter Ellis quickly stripped out of his clothes, discarded the layers of being that made him into the pathetic creature that lived and breathed, stumbled from one day to the next in an endless chain of insignificance.

He stared at his reflection in the mirror, barely recognising himself. The promise of what was to come burned in his eyes and distanced him from this present reality. Reality. He laughed, a hollow mocking sound. Was this reality, this body that served him poorly, subjected him to the cruelty of its weakness? But it was necessary for him to suffer, for his essence to be hampered by such an incapable vessel, open to the harsh judgments of others. To be laughed at. Mocked. Scorned, his true meaning translated into gibberish by the force of his message. He longed to break free, to have his essence bear its own rich fruit, unhampered by the many who clamoured to override his voice.

'Peter?' his mother called. 'Peter, are you all right?'

He snorted. His mother. She was fortunate to have been chosen to bear the flesh that was his prison. He ignored her aged voice and shut out the vision of her stooped form as she shuffled painfully around the small house. Old before her time, unaware of the price her body had paid to nurture his ravaging spirit.

'Peter?' She tapped on his door and then turned the handle. The door started to inch its way open.

'Out!' He snarled. 'Get out, old woman!' He lunged towards the door. It snapped to with a bang as his startled mother jumped back in fright. Her boy wasn't well and she ached to help him, sick to the stomach with fear for his future. She knew only too well the torment that her own mind could create, had created all those years ago. It was a torment that dogged her still, but one that had become bearable with the passage of time. She wrung her hands, helpless to come to the aid of her son. She remembered all too well the feeling of betrayal as the police had taken her away from home when she was only a young woman, had never forgiven her parents for allowing that to happen to her. Or for the years spent inside a nightmare that they called a hospital.

No. She would not cause her son to suffer as she had, would not allow a similar invasion into his life.

He would conquer his illness, just as she had, and when Peter was well, when he managed to conquer this threat to his very soul, she wanted them to be friends. As they had been before.

Pangs of guilty memory threatened to fight their way to the surface of her consciousness, memories of a relationship that exceeded the bonds of love between a mother and her son, but she pushed them down into the dark recesses of her mind. She hurried out to the kitchen to put the kettle on.

Peter eyed the machete in his hands, unaware that he had picked it up in his flight to close his mother outside his tiny realm. She did not have the right to invade his sanctuary. His chest was heaving from the exertion of restraining his essence. It was so close to the surface. He couldn't allow her to see that, couldn't allow anybody to suspect the truth. He turned the machete over in his hands and looked speculatively at the door. Maybe it would be better if she was out of the way, unable to interfere with his plans. She was old and stupid, but it was just possible that she would be able to sense his purpose. He was the fruit of her loins. She must have known, her inadequate mind must have some grasp of his purpose. Ellis trusted nobody, could afford to trust nobody. Was she too much of a danger to him? Could she thwart his destiny, thrust a dagger into the heart of his ultimate release? He still had this one task to complete, still had to drive this body to one final act of fulfilment to achieve the rich bounty that awaited him. Could she hinder that?

It would require only a simple act to eradicate that

fear, to ensure his destiny. What was she to him? Little more than a package that had nurtured his body. To his spirit she was nothing, without consequence.

For several moments June Ellis's life hung in the balance as she shuffled around the small kitchen preparing their dinner. Her arthritis would have allowed no defence against her able-bodied son. Unaware, she poured boiling water onto tea leaves, muttering to herself in her concern for her son's future. If only he'd had a father, a real father. She could never tell him he was the product of a lustful coupling inside a state mental institution.

He reached for the doorknob, his chest heaving. She was a small price to pay, her blood a minor contribution to the sacrifices that would have to be made. But that blood was tainted. He caught his hand as it started to pull the door open, drawing it back to his will. Such slips of control would not be tolerated. He raised the sharp-bladed machete and brought it down. The top joints of two fingers from the left hand fell to the floor, wriggled spasmodically for a few moments and stopped. Soon, very soon he would have no use for his body whatsoever. Until then he would have to keep it under very tight rein, would have to exert considerable force to ensure it was capable of achieving the purpose his raging essence demanded. He put the bloodied stubs of his fingers into his mouth and sucked hungrily at the hot fluid, unwilling to deprive the weak vessel of the nourishment.

He smiled, his saliva stained pink. His spirit was

crouched within the body, ready to uncoil. He must find it release. Quickly. Carefully, he packed his instruments into the pure white linen scarf he had bought for this very purpose.

'Fuck!' He cursed in rage when he saw the bright red blotches of blood from his severed fingers, then quickly decided they were acceptable. The blood was of this body, a sign of its imminent demise, a proper seal to place on the tools that would expedite his release. He threw back his head and laughed, felt the power that swelled inside. His spirit was ready to explode into the world, to tear asunder the confines of his pathetic body and stand alone for all the world to behold.

He felt the first premonitions of fear. What if he could not control the raging spirit inside this body? Would it not then cease to be him?

The confines of this mind could not grasp such a concept. He sought only release.

Unguided, Peter Ellis decided to take matters into his own hands. His thirst for blood had to be sated. And Celia Thompson was the perfect vessel to provide that satisfaction. He hurried from his room, brushed aside the frail figure of his mother, his fingers leaving a bloody imprint on her cardigan. Fleeing through the back door, he emitted a high-pitched howl of joy and ran for the shed.

'Peter! Peter!' June Ellis stood on the steps watching her son flee. Something was wrong. Dreadfully wrong. Where had all that blood come from? What could she do? She clutched her hand to her mouth in horror as his trailbike roared into life. He slewed out of the shed, his back tyre digging a deep black trench in the green lawn. She had to shield her eyes from the terrible look on his face. His high-pitched scream rose over the noise of the engine as he disappeared from sight past the corner of the house.

June Ellis collapsed in the doorway, her distress too great for weeping.

Celia Thompson frowned when Jack Warner told her that Breene had already left, his tone hinting at the promise of another story to be told. She shrugged. She hadn't learned anything new for him anyway, and for once she was not interested by the scent of another story. She just felt tired and sick. Maybe she would make it an early day, pack up her handbag and go home to bed. God knows she'd earned it.

Her spirits rose as she left the office. The afternoon sun still had some warmth at 4.30 pm. She couldn't remember the last time she had finished the day with any part of the afternoon left. It felt good, an unexpected treat. Maybe that was exactly what she needed.

Celia was smiling by the time she got into her car, planning what she would do with the time. She was mildly irritated by the sound of the motorbike that roared into noisy life as she pulled away from the kerb, but shrugged it off. She wasn't going to let anything spoil this perfect afternoon.

The traffic was slow but it flowed smoothly as she drove along the Broadwater, heading away from the busy heart of Southport towards Labrador. She smiled as she looked over the wide expanse of impossibly blue water, a breeze rustling through the boats tied at mooring and providing the sailboarders with the fuel necessary for their craft. It lifted her spirits. She realised that she rarely noticed the views that accompanied her on her drive home and took special delight in them today. She made a mental note to take the time to appreciate her surroundings more often. She so rarely had the time to relax.

Celia Thompson was vaguely troubled by the presence of the motorbike when she made the right turn off the Gold Coast Highway heading for Marine Parade, felt that it had been with her since she'd left work. But that was ridiculous, she was getting paranoid. It roared past as she made the turn into the driveway of her unit block and she smiled at her foolishness. She opened the garage and put the car away, remembering only as she locked the door that she needed milk.

What the hell, she shrugged. She might as well walk to the shop. It was only half a block away.

Peter Ellis watched carefully as she walked away from her garage, saw her turn and head back up the street. The noises in his head had receded, seemed much more manageable now that he had decided on a course of action. He strolled back along the footpath until he reached her block, paused with his hands on his hips to stare up at the four-storeyed dwelling. Which one was hers? Making a show of nonchalance, he walked up the driveway, noted the number on her garage door. Unit one. Good. It was on the ground floor, making his job that much easier. He smiled broadly, jammed his hands in his pockets and turned to see if his actions had been noted. There wasn't a person in sight.

He trotted quickly around the side of the building and pushed through a high wooden gate, gaining direct access to Celia Thompson's little courtyard. Too easy.

Celia decided she may as well treat herself properly, use this time to pamper herself a little. She took her time selecting a couple of chocolate bars and a container of chilled iced coffee. She meandered over the magazine rack, completely dismissing any thoughts of buying a newspaper. She'd had enough of them, for today at least. She finally settled for a copy of *Who Weekly*. Maybe she'd read it in the bath — now that sounded like a good idea. A long hot soak to ease the tension away. She might even take herself out for dinner later.

She took her time walking home, watched as a pair of pelicans swooped low over the water and came in for a landing, their webbed feet planing the water like skis, wings spread wide to slow their speed. She sighed happily. This was the life. She should finish early more often.

Her small courtyard and garden were sadly neglected, not that she usually had the time to notice. She'd have to do something about it, a few nice plants…she smiled to herself. She'd change the world today if she could, but tomorrow? She shrugged. Who knew what she'd even think tomorrow?

She reached for the door handle, searching in her

pocket for her key, and frowned when the door slid back. She must have forgotten to lock the bloody thing again. She pulled the curtain back, checked that her stereo and TV were still there. Lucky it was a safe neighbourhood.

Celia Thompson inspected her naked body in the full-length mirror in her bedroom while the bath filled with hot water and puffs of white bubbles. Not bad for thirty-three, even if the tits were starting to sag a little. She lifted them with her hands — maybe a bit of a tuck there, when she had the time. Her long bare legs showed no sign of cellulite, thank God, but she would have preferred a few less freckles. Butt still stood up nice and firm. Not bad, she shrugged. She tugged at the red thatch of pubic hair and laughed, ran naked into the bathroom and switched the taps off. She sank into the steaming heat, bubbles tickling her as she lowered her body down. Ah. That felt just great. She closed her eyes and lay back.

Peter Ellis watched her from inside the wardrobe, felt himself stiffening as his eyes drank in her nakedness, watched the performance that he alone could see. He reached down and rubbed his swelling crotch.

And the voices returned, their sound an angry buzz, a confusion of shouting and static. He shook his head to clear them, frowned as he concentrated and tried to distinguish what was being said. He couldn't make it out, couldn't understand the message. His hand dropped away from his penis and the noise receded. Perhaps now he understood.

He stepped from the cupboard, heard the sounds

as she lowered herself into the bathtub, lusted for another sight of her naked body. He edged quietly closer to the bathroom and the foot of the bath became visible, her painted toenails drifting enticingly above the sea of bubbles. Then a pale, freckled knee, the swell of a breast.

He pulled back panting, the machete dangling loosely in his grasp, clenched his eyes tightly against the assault of noise that hammered at his consciousness. He had to subdue them, had to consume their strength with his own, could not afford the division they created. He felt suddenly weak, his arm trembling, his fingers loosing their grip on the blade.

God! he pleaded. And the whispering voice of a woman came to his aid, soft and gentle, yet it overrode the orgy of noise that rose to consume it.

He recognised her instantly. His Queen. The soft voice that had murmured in his sleep for so long finally revealed to him in his waking hours. He smiled, confident now, and stepped back towards the bathroom door. The hand that clutched the machete was filled with a renewed vigour, the blade eager to taste the blood of Celia Thompson. He wondered idly how the bubbles would look in a nice shade of red.

Celia Thompson screamed when she saw him advancing, the cruel blade of the machete in his hand, his face fixed in a queer grin. She cowered down in the water, sought the protection of the thin veil of bubbles and knew her time had come. She squeezed her eyes shut, waited for the bite of cold steel.

Peter Ellis recoiled in sudden agony as the bubbles became a blazing, intense white veil that was torn asunder to reveal her there before him. His Queen. Clad in the purest of white cloth, the beauty of her face blinding. An inferno blazed mightily behind her, its might threatening to engulf her fragile purity.

He shuddered with fear, the pain of it clutching deep down in his bowel. He struggled to turn his eyes away but her love held him firmly. He was entering his realm, his own realm, the vision of what was to come a gift from her to him, a gift to strengthen his purpose. She hovered on the very brink of peril and only he could save her. A tear spilled silently onto her cheek, seeming to grow as it slid down. It dropped onto the cloth at her breast and he watched in dismay as the white turned to red, the blotch on the pure cloth spreading, growing into a stain above her heart.

And then he became aware of them, sensed rather than saw their lurking malice. They who would wrest his rightful majesty from him before he was able to come into his full power. She alone stood against them, buffeted by the strength of the chant that echoed their evil purpose. Red eyes reflected the growing might of their fire, their forms a black shadowy menace just outside the ring of red light.

The noise of their hissing, scalding chant grew louder, pounded into his skull, threatening to shatter the frail human brain into a million pieces, scattering the bright promise of his essence to the mercies of the waiting cosmos. He turned away, eyes clamped shut, fists clenched in agony, but the vision remained. What was she trying to tell him?

And then he knew. The image of her was extinguished as the curtain fell again. The chant evaporated, its menace crumbling into dust. He knew with crystal clarity: the key to his kingdom was within his reach. He held out a shaking hand and studied it, a bemused smile on his face.

The girl's form contained the essence of his Queen, just as this body held his own essence as its prisoner. The cleansing and release would be achieved with blood. His blood. Her blood. It was that simple. He turned and fled the bathroom, stumbled from the unit and ran out into the gathering dusk. His transformation was in peril, greater peril than he had realised. He must prepare for his release now. Nothing else mattered.

Celia Thompson heard his departure but couldn't open her eyes, couldn't trust the evidence of her senses. She wondered if she had passed out, if she'd failed to feel the blow that had ended her life, and had passed over. She certainly felt as if she was floating.

She opened one eye, then the other. It was still her bathroom all right, and she was still in the bath. Reprieved. Saved by who knows what fate. She lay back, started to tremble and then to shake, her stomach expelling its contents in the bath once, twice and then again. Jesus. Jesus God. Tears flowed unbidden down her cheeks and she was wracked by huge, convulsive sobs.

That was how her neighbour found her half an hour later, after he'd worked up the courage to enter her unit in response to her scream. It was one story Celia Thompson was never going to write.

CHAPTER 18

Amanda Warner hovered between the worlds of waking and unconsciousness, the nightmare reality of her existence blurring the lines so that the two were indistinguishable. She didn't know how long she had lain there on the cold concrete floor, unable to move, unable to open her mouth, to feel, to think, to be. Time was irrelevant, marked only by his presence or his absence. She would have cried if any tears would come, but her body didn't have the fluid to spare.

Surely the end must come soon, release from the torture of her existence. In her lucid moments she realised that she must die, that her body could not sustain her without nourishment. She willed herself to seek the comfort of death's embrace, but even that was denied her.

So she lay in a limbo between terror and emptiness and hoped she would be gone before he returned.

The rhythmic thudding of an engine nearby

ended that hope. She closed her eyes at the sound of the heavy metal door scraping on the concrete floor as he heaved it open. She sank gratefully into the void that rushed to consume her consciousness.

He had to battle to control his laboured breathing as his ever-strengthening essence threatened to overwhelm his body. He frowned with the effort of it, perspiration beading on his forehead. Just a little while longer, but he must not hurry the preparation. Already he had lost some hours, wasted in the pursuit of Celia Thompson. None of that mattered, not any more. He concentrated, focused on his one true purpose. He couldn't afford another lapse. Time and concentration were vital to his transition, it was vital that this final step was undertaken with the due ceremony it demanded.

He approached the inert form on the ground and his face was softened by a smile. *Soon, my love.* He crouched down beside her, his eyes straying guiltily down to the tops of her legs, to the smooth milky perfection marred by the thatch of dark hair.

'*No!*' They were back, the force of their sudden return crashing around his head and making him whimper. He clutched his hands to his ears and stood, closing his eyes with the effort of focusing.

His purpose was higher than this, above the demands of this base vessel that carried his spirit. He quailed briefly, buffeted by the doubts that pierced his mind like arrows, that tore at the logic of his true purpose. He was not of this body. He had to cast all doubts aside, to rid himself of the weakening lure of false promise and misdirected purpose.

Amanda opened her eyes and saw him standing above her. Terror returned with renewed force, sucked at the precious stores of her own remaining sanity and engulfed them. What further horrors would she be forced to endure at the hands of this monster?

He became aware of her gaze, looked down and saw the terror in her eyes and for an instant Peter Ellis tasted her fear.

'No-n-n-no...n-n-no...i-i-i-it's al-al-all...' The voices crashed in his ears, laughing, mocking. He feared they would consume him, extinguish his being in a moment of weakness, and knew it was the opportunity they awaited. He could not allow it, would not forfeit his inheritance from the cosmos.

'*No!*' His voice boomed loud and strong. 'You will not deny my purpose.' He cast his gaze at Amanda Warner, laughing with the strength of his mastery. 'Soon, my Queen, soon you will share in the rich heritage that only I can offer to you. You lie and quail with fear, yet verily I say to thee that I am the salvation! I am the light!'

Turning, he strode from her. The preparations must begin, the time was now. There was much to do.

Amanda Warner could find no escape from the terror that consumed her mind. Was there no end to her torment?

Breene was burning with anger as he forced the VW around the tight corner that led into Nobby Parade. He was going to find Peter Ellis, even if he had to beat his whereabouts out of his crazy mother. Evening was already descending and he would not allow Amanda to spend another night of terror in the clutches of her evil son.

'Mrs Ellis!' He banged loudly on the door. 'Mrs Ellis, open up!' There was no response, but Breene knew she was inside. 'Open up!' He shouted. 'Or I'll break your fucking door down!' He delivered a solid blow to the door to prove his intent.

'I'll call the police!' Her voice came muffled through the door. 'I'll call them straight away!' she threatened.

'Call them' Breene shouted. 'And while you're at it tell them your son is the murderer they've been after.' He didn't care who was listening, wouldn't have cared if the whole neighbourhood was listening from behind drawn curtains. Nothing mattered.

The door opened slowly, only the security screen separating them.

'You let me in,' Breene growled. 'I want to know where your bastard son is.'

'Now see here,' Mrs Ellis was stunned by Breene's ferocity. 'My Peter is *not* a murderer.'

'He is a damned murderer, and you know it. I'm trying to prevent him from killing anyone else, and if you stop me you'll pay for it dearly.'

'Oh, dear.' She hesitated, her hand clutching at her throat as an internal debate raged inside her head. Who was this man? What did he know about Peter?

'I think you'd better come in.' She unlocked the security door distractedly. Breene was puzzled by the sudden change that came over her.

'Do you know where Peter is?' he demanded, following her into the dim interior of the house.

'What? Peter — oh, not exactly.' Peter. Her poor Peter. She knew he needed help, knew she had failed him miserably.

'Please, Mrs Ellis, I must find Peter. I think he needs help. He's in a great deal of trouble.' His impatience chafed at him, but he sensed her confusion. He needed to tread carefully if he was going to get anything out of her.

She led Breene into the dim interior of the lounge room where she indicated that he should sit on the ancient sofa, covered in blue woollen material with ornately carved wooden armrests. The springs protested as he sank into the sagging cushion.

'I won't be a minute,' Mrs Ellis said, rubbing her hands together nervously before disappearing into the interior of the house.

Breene leaned forward in the chair, uncomfortable in the dark, cold room. What the hell was she up to? He didn't have much bloody time, didn't have the patience to wait for her to play some trick on him. Maybe she was calling the police? He strained his ears for any sounds while he scanned the bare walls, unadorned by photographs or pictures but for the print of the Sacred Heart of Jesus that hung above the ancient HMV television. Venetians over the window were tightly closed, as if to keep the outside world separate from the sparse interior. The whole place gave him the creeps.

Mrs Ellis returned several long minutes later and placed a cup of tea on the edge of his chair before darting quickly away as if frightened he would touch her. She perched herself nervously on the edge of an armchair, the only other piece of furniture in the room. Her glance settled on him briefly before skittering around the room from one object to another. She reminded Breene of a sparrow on the lawn, ready to take off at the slightest hint of danger.

'I don't get many visitors.' Her voice trembled with fear as she fought back her terror of this man.

'What was it you wanted to ask me about Peter?' Her voice sounded strange to her own ears. 'What trouble is he in?'

'Does Peter live here, Mrs Ellis?'

'Sometimes,' she said after a pause. Breene caught her furtive glance.

'Is he home at the moment, Mrs Ellis?'

'No,' she said quickly, clutching her hand to her throat. 'He…had to duck out for something.' The colour drained from her already pale cheeks and she stared fixedly into her cup of tea.

'Was he all right when he left?'

Her head whipped around, her stare focusing sharply on Breene.

'What do you mean, was he all right?' What did he know?

'Mentally. Did he seem all right mentally?' He kept his voice steady and stared directly into her eyes. She held his stare for a moment, defiance struggling to the surface.

'Of course he was all right mentally. What do you mean by that? There's nothing wrong with my Peter.' She looked quickly away from Breene's steady gaze. 'Nothing,' she repeated falteringly.

'He's very bright, my boy, Peter. He works at the police forensic labs, you know. They want him to start studying to be a doctor next year. They invited him.' The words came out fast, tripping over one another in their haste. Her head was up, a flush of pride in her cheeks.

'He's a murderer, Mrs Ellis. I must find him. He is in a great deal of trouble.' It was as much as Breene could do to restrain himself from shouting at her, grabbing her by the shoulders and shaking her. Something told him it wouldn't get him anywhere, he had to play it her way. She was as mad as her son was, maybe even as dangerous in her own way.

'Why do you keep insisting my boy is in trouble? And all this business about murder. Not my Peter, not my boy. You just don't know him, he couldn't do any such thing.' She spoke mildly, as if Breene had told her Peter was walking his dog.

'Well, if that's the case I'll know when I find him. The sooner you tell me, the quicker we can prove his innocence.' Breene watched her face, amazed by the rapid play of emotions that flickered through her eyes.

'But you won't believe him,' she said shrilly, jumping to her feet and upsetting her cup of tea. 'Who are you really?' Her eyes narrowed as she stared at him. 'I know. I've met your type before. They sent you, didn't they? How much are they paying you?' She strode up and down in front of him, wringing her hands in a state of acute agitation. 'How dare you come to my house now, after all these years. You can't have him. He's my son. I've worked hard to raise him by myself without any help from the likes of you. And now you come around here pretending to be his friend, pretending you want to help him. I know what you're really after. Well, you can't have it!' she screamed, pushing her face at Breene, spittle flying. 'I won't let you. I should never have listened in the first place!'

Breene pulled back into his chair, sure the woman was going to attack him. Where was the frail little thing who'd answered the door?

Mrs Ellis stormed around the room, muttering agitatedly to herself, her face twisted into a mask of agony. Some sort of debate raged inside her and he watched in fascination as she cursed and jabbered, casting venomous looks in his direction, her hands gesticulating wildly.

Obviously the woman was insane, probably had been for years. She was hiding from the world, and she'd drawn her son into the same frightening insanity. He'd probably never had a chance.

But maybe Amanda Warner still did.

'Mrs Ellis!' Breene rose abruptly to his feet. 'Get a hold on yourself!'

She shrunk away from him as if he had struck her.

'Leave me alone!' she shrieked.

They were both startled by a loud crash from the back of the house. For an instant their eyes met, Breene's purposeful and angry, hers terrified and clouded with insanity. Then she turned and fled from the room, evading Breene's outstretched hands.

'Peter! Peter!' she screamed, running towards the back of the house 'Get out! They're here, they've discovered us!' She cast a terrified look over her shoulder and then burst through a doorway on her left, trying to close the door behind her.

Breene forced it open with some difficulty, remembering with surprise the incredible strength that came with extreme psychiatric disturbance.

'No!' she shrieked, tears coursing down her cheeks. 'No, I've paid my dues.'

She turned to face the room. It was empty. Peter wasn't there. She stopped in complete confusion, her chest heaving from exertion. A mottled tabby looked up and miaowed.

'Huh!' She turned to Breene in triumph. 'He's escaped. You can't hurt him now, he's escaped.'

Breene looked out the window at the empty expanse of tin roofing below him. A smashed picture frame on the floor told him the cat had been responsible for the noise. He ignored Mrs Ellis, lost in her gloating over some imagined triumph. What was the cat licking at? He walked over, shooing it away from the dark patch of red on the worn grey carpet, and recoiled in revulsion when he realised what the cat had found. The top joints of two pale fingers lay shrivelled where they had fallen when Peter Ellis severed them.

Mrs Ellis made a strangled noise in the back of her throat, the colour draining rapidly from her cheeks. Breene caught her before she hit the floor.

It was five long minutes before she stirred. Breene rapidly fanned her cheeks and shook her frail body.

'Mrs Ellis? Mrs Ellis, you must wake up. We haven't got any time to lose.'

She coughed as she sat up, immediately recoiling from the physical contact with Breene.

'What have you done to my son?' she sobbed weakly. She held her head in one shaking hand. 'My poor Peter,' she whispered.

'Mrs Ellis, I have to get to your son before he can do any more damage. You have to tell me where he is.'

'More damage? More damage — what are you talking about?'

'Murder, Mrs Ellis. He's murdered five people, two of them old women like yourself. I already told you.'

'Oh my God. No, it can't be, not my Peter. Not my son. He couldn't, he…' her voice trailed off into nothing. What if it had been her? She could recall the nights she'd lain awake, terrified of what he might do. Her poor, poor boy. Where had she failed him?

'Listen.' Breene shook her, forced her to meet his eyes. 'He's got a girl somewhere, a young girl who hasn't even had a chance at life yet. I must stop him, I have to stop him. I know he isn't well, I know he's disturbed, but I have to save that girl.'

'You're lying,' she insisted stubbornly. 'Who are you? You want to take him away from me, don't you? That's why you're really here, telling me all these lies. My God, can't you people ever let me forget the mistakes of my past? Must I always be subject to your cruel testing? I've done my time, I did my penance, as you well know. Why do you insist on pursuing me? Haven't I already been punished enough?'

'Stop it!' Breene shouted. 'Stop it now. I haven't

got the damned time for your crap. If I'm too late to save that girl I'll come back for you, Mrs Ellis. Then you'll see who I really am.' He felt at risk of losing control himself. He had to get the information out of this crazy old woman, and he didn't seem to be winning. 'That girl's innocent, Mrs Ellis, she has nothing to do with whatever torment your son is going through. I must save her,' he pleaded.

'Innocent? Innocent?' she snorted with derision. 'Who is the slut? What's she doing with my boy? He doesn't know about girls. I wouldn't let him know about girls. He loves his mummy. What does he want with girls? Dirty little sluts. They only want to take him away from me. No, I won't have it. Not in my house, not under my roof!'

'Mrs Ellis.' Breene grabbed the front of her blouse and pulled her face close to his. 'I want to know where your son is. I want to know where he is *now*. If you don't tell me you will be an accessory to murder and I will see to it personally that you are put away for a very long time. I don't think you'd like that very much, Mrs Ellis. They don't take too kindly to crazy old ladies in jail.'

'Keep away from me!' she shrieked. 'Don't you dare touch me!'

'I mean what I say, Mrs Ellis. I have run out of sympathy and patience with you. You will tell me where your son is.' He let her go and she scrambled to her feet, stepped away from him with her mouth working agitatedly, her eyes wide with fear. Breene could almost see the wheels turning in her head as she weighed up her options.

She started to sob brokenly.

'Peter must have cut those fingers off, Mrs Ellis. He's out of control. Tell me where he is!' Breene demanded, panicked by a desperate sense of urgency that raged beyond his control. 'Where is he?'

'Oh, Peter!' Mrs Ellis cried, locked in her own misery.

'You must know where he is, Mrs Ellis.' Breene was oblivious to her distress. 'You said he told you everything. Where is he? Where would he go to hide, to get away? You have to know!' He could almost have hit her, beat the truth out of her. He had to get to Amanda. Now.

'Tell me where he is,' he growled at the sobbing woman. 'You're not helping him by not telling me, you're not doing him any favours. He's already killed five people, that's bad enough. Do you want him to kill another, a young, innocent girl?' His eyes bored into hers, transmitting the fury that was building inside him. 'Your hands will be tainted with her blood. You say your son is not responsible? *You* are. If this girl dies you may as well have killed her yourself as far as the law is concerned. Think about that Mrs Ellis. *You'll* be charged with murder. Do you think that's going to help your precious son?'

The threat hit its mark. She wasn't that crazy.

'All right, all right.' She turned away, wished this stranger out of her presence. She'd left it too late for her boy. She should have done something before, she should have saved him.

'I'm not sure where he is.' She threw her head back defiantly, hanging onto the tatters of the world she had built for herself and Peter. 'I can only guess. He hasn't got any friends. We have no relatives, not since my parents died. It was the only place he was ever really happy, out on their farm in the Currumbin Valley. It was called Kurrajong. There was a shed there, I don't know where. He used to go out there on his motorbike sometimes. It's the only place I know where he could go to hide.' Her voice faltered. She felt like she'd betrayed him, even now. She lifted her head and stared haughtily at Breene. 'I still refuse to believe that Peter has done the things you say he has.'

'You're not a well woman, Mrs Ellis. I doubt your son ever had much of a chance living here,' Breene said, his voice full of contempt for the woman. He reached for the phone and punched in the number for the Surfers Paradise Police.

'Hello? This is Mervyn Breene. I want to speak to the officer in charge of the murder investigation now that Hughes is dead. I know where Amanda Warner is.' He waited impatiently, the silence broken by the sounds of June Ellis's sobbing.

'Breene, this is Arthur Bryant. Just what exactly is going on? You're in big trouble, man.'

'Shut up, Bryant. I know where Amanda Warner is. Still interested? Meet me at 17 Nobby Parade, Miami.' He hung up with Bryant spluttering in his ear.

'I don't know how far gone Peter is, Mrs Ellis. I don't carry a gun and I may have a chance of stopping him without anyone getting hurt too badly. If I go now it'll give me a chance, a few minutes before the police get there. I did that for your son Mrs Ellis. I know he's not well. Do me the favour of telling the police where I've gone.'

She stared at Breene, stony-faced.

He turned and walked out of the house, anger and fear churning in his gut.

'Please!' Mrs Ellis came running out of the house as he climbed into the car. 'Don't hurt my baby? He's all I've got.' She burst into fresh tears.

Breene nodded once and shut the door. If Amanda Warner was still alive he was going to save her. No matter what. He owed Mrs Ellis nothing.

CHAPTER 19

Currumbin Valley — he didn't know the way, had to snatch his street directory up and search for the address as he powered back towards the highway. Shit, it was further than he would have liked, the minutes now seemed vital. His anxiety was tinged with desperation. Amanda Warner had to be alive. After all this time, after all his effort, she *had* to be alive.

Breene was beginning to realise how important this search had become to him. The truth was he didn't know how he'd cope if he was too late. It would be too much of a personal failure. Long-suppressed emotions had resurfaced during the past seventy-two hours and life coursed through his veins once more after too long a period of hibernation. His future depended on finding this girl he had hardly met. He urged the little car forward, thrusting it into gaps that opened in front of him.

His patience was at breaking point. The sea of uncaring humanity around him, all the little self-contained units in their self-contained transports going to their own little worlds. He felt like ramming his car into them. They didn't care whether Amanda Warner lived or died. They didn't even know she existed. The whole drama that had played itself out over the past few days, the murders, Amanda's kidnap, Peter Ellis's growing insanity meant nothing to them.

Breene shook his head and fumbled in his pocket for a cigarette. This really was getting to him. Philosophy definitely was not his strong suit and when it came to living in a self-contained little world, he'd written the book. But finding this kid alive was all he wanted to do. Nothing else mattered. He just wanted to find her before Ellis could do whatever he had planned for her.

The thought of Peter Ellis renewed the stab of urgency that was gathering in his chest. He had screwed himself up so tight that it hurt. He ached for release. His emotions were barely suppressed, bottled but threatening to burst out and overwhelm him. She had to be alive. He closed his eyes against a startlingly vivid image of her bloodied body stretched out on a concrete floor with Peter Ellis looming over her.

The VW had edged up to 120 kilometres per hour under the urging of his anxious foot and he eased up as he came to the turn-off for the valley. He braked hard going around the corner, fighting the body roll to maintain enough speed to cut off the car in the lane he was merging into. He ignored the blaring of the driver's horn. He was almost there now. He didn't care about anything else.

It was already dusk and he had to slow down once he'd passed the battered sign proclaiming 'Kurrajong' to watch for signs of the track that would lead him to the shed Mrs Ellis had told him about. He squinted in the failing light, sweated on finding the entrance. It had to be here.

He flicked the lights on, switched them up to high beam as he scanned the road side. There. A faint track was just visible, a couple of wheel ruts in the springy grass quickly disappearing between the trees and on up the hill. Breene slewed the VW off the road, his wheels losing purchase in the gravel before he reefed the little car back under control. He accelerated along the rutted track, the VW bouncing wildly on the uneven surface. It was meant to be attacked at a more sedate pace, but he didn't have the time.

He was sweating freely as he gripped the wheel, his eyes scanning the trees ahead for some sign of the shed. Where the hell was it? It was obviously some time since it had been in general use. Maybe it was some time since it had been used at all. He pushed on, jaw clenched in determination. This was the right track, it *had* to be the right track.

His headlights picked up the irregular shape as he rounded a twisting corner, the dull gleam reflected back against the dark shapes of the trees. His foot dropped off the accelerator and the car lurched to a halt. There was no sign of life, no sign of movement. If there was anybody in the shed to hear, he had announced his arrival loud and clear. He killed the engine and turned the lights off, stepping out into dead silence. The night was already thick amongst the trees.

What if Ellis wasn't even here? What if he had Amanda stashed away somewhere else, somewhere his mother didn't know about? What if it was too late? He prayed that his noisy approach wouldn't panic an already psychotic Peter Ellis and force his hand. But what choice did he have?

He approached the shed warily. He was unarmed, had no means of defending himself except his own skill. That wouldn't be enough, especially if Ellis was armed. If he had a gun it would mean a very quick end to any imagined confrontation between the two of them. He threaded his way between the trees, trying to keep something between himself and any possible line of fire, struggling to steady his breathing so he would be alert to any other sounds. There were none. The night was eerily silent.

The shed shone faintly in the gloom. It was larger than he had first thought, probably about the size of a double garage. It was obviously some part of the older farm, long since disused and forgotten. He had to run the last half-dozen metres across open ground — if Ellis could see him now would be the perfect time to pick him off.

He came up against the rear wall of the shed, his blood thudding in his ears, fighting to still his breathing. Still no sound, still nothing. Where the fuck were they? Why wasn't there any noise? Was he already too late? He pressed his ear against the cold metal of the shed, strained to detect the slightest noise.

Maybe there was something, a faint hiss, the crack of a twig. He tensed, scanned the ground around his feet for a weapon of some sort. It was suicidal to go charging in there completely unarmed. He found a stick, part of a stout branch and clutched it in his hand. It was better than nothing. He wondered briefly about the wisdom of his decision to come by himself instead of waiting for the cops. But then he'd probably still be waiting, or arguing with Bryant.

Right now he was far from help. He could only hope that the cops wouldn't tarry when Mrs Ellis told them the story. If she told them.

Breene cursed. There where too many damned ifs for his liking. He'd done this by himself so far. Now he had to see it through to its conclusion.

He slipped quietly around the corner, expecting Ellis to spring out at him at any moment and trap him like a fly in a spider's web. He must be aware of Breene's presence, yet still he had made no move. Breene was tense with coiled energy, awaiting the move, almost welcoming it. Anything would have been better than this silent waiting while the minutes ticked by.

Another thought occurred to him. Maybe Ellis was too intent on another task to have heeded Breene's arrival. It was all the push he needed to make his final assault on the dark shed. He located the door, made of corrugated iron on a heavy frame. It remained basically intact, secured by a slide bolt that had been left open. It was too late now for any last-minute nerves.

Steeling himself, Breene leant against the door and

felt it give slightly to his push. He thrust against it and barged his way into the shed, the metal door scraping loudly on the concrete floor. He threw himself against the wall and quickly scanned his immediate environment for movement. Nothing. The only sound was that of his own laboured breathing and his blood pounding in his ears. If he got out of this, he'd have to give up cigarettes.

The interior of the shed was musty and stifling, in contrast to the cool night outside. The rancid stench of wild animals was overpowering — obviously the shed offered them some entry. Breene started at the sound of light-footed scurrying nearby and sprang aside, his branch at the ready. He sighed with relief when he realised it was only a small creature, probably a mouse or a rat. He grimaced in the darkness at the thought of what else he might find in here.

The thought brought him up short. There were still no obvious signs of movement, no sign that anyone had been near the place recently. Yet some kind of sixth sense alerted him to the presence of something in the shed. He paused to listen, stilled his breathing and strained his eyes to scan his immediate surroundings. He could make out the dim shapes of objects around him, any one of which could hide sinister intent. This was bloody useless. He reached into his pocket and took out his lighter, abandoning caution. He may as well see what was to be seen as stumble around in the darkness waiting for a surprise attack.

'Come on, you bastard,' he growled. His voice didn't sound nearly as intimidating as he would have liked. A small orange flame flared at the end of his lighter and he swung it in a quick arc, searching frantically for a sudden rush of violence, the sweep of a gleaming knife. Still nothing.

'Coward,' he muttered to himself. His eyes fell upon a tarp-covered mound directly to his left. He nudged it with his foot, heard the heavy scrape of iron on the floor. He bent down quickly and tore a strip from the rotting tarp, wrapping it around the end of his club and setting a flame to it. It caught slowly, the flame gradually building until it cast a reasonable light around him. Breene felt vulnerable to attack from any side, had to resist the constant temptation to turn and guard his back.

He stepped cautiously around the tarp, his light illuminating a rotting pile of hay, scraps of old machinery, a couple of old tractor tyres. He swung quickly at the gleam of eyes and swiped at the head of an old rocking horse, its mouth gaping where the metal bit had rotted through the wood. He had to force himself to keep moving, alert to every sound and whisper, his own breathing hoarse in his ears.

'Amanda?' He called softly. 'Amanda Warner?' He collided with the rusting hulk of a plough, sent a heavy wooden beam clattering to the floor. He jumped back, ready. Still nothing.

'Shit.'

The sweep of his torch revealed a space that had been cleared in the clutter. The dust had been stirred where piles of junk had been moved to either side. It was the first sign of recent occupancy. Breene's pulse quickened. He strained his eyes, searching for anything out of the usual. There. A glimmer of white cloth in the flickering glow of his torch, partly hidden behind a low tarpaulin covered mound. He reached in to retrieve it, his arm brushing the tarp.

It was warm. He pulled back quickly, ran his eyes over the tarp, saw the rust-coloured spots on it. Blood.

'Shit.' He breathed softly, raised his club over his head as he bent to tug back the tarp, not knowing who, or what, to expect. He jerked the tarp back with a quick movement, jumping back ready to defend himself.

He stopped and drew a shuddering breath, his heart sinking at the sight revealed in the weak light from his torch. The inert form of a young girl lay trussed up, hands and feet tied together behind her back. Cruelly tight ropes dug into the tender flesh of the wrists, coated in black, dried blood. He reached gingerly for the bloodstained sack that covered her head, readying himself to witness the cruel ending to his search. He cringed inwardly, crushed by defeat. He was too late.

He gently pulled back one corner of the sack. A blood-soaked gag was pulled tightly across her mouth, her lips were cracked and colourless. The torch cast a faint orange glow over her features, but Breene knew it was only a trick of the light. Pale freckles stood out on her nose.

And then she opened her eyes.

She was alive. It was Amanda Warner and she was alive. He couldn't believe his good fortune. His spirits soared within him. She was alive.

'Amanda?' Her eyes struggled to focus, saw a face wreathed in a blinding light smiling down at her.

'Amanda, it's all over. I've come to take you home.'

Her eyes focused suddenly on Breene and she frowned, her dazed mind struggling to comprehend his presence. Was this the end? She felt weak, her body was wracked with pain. Who was this stranger staring down at her? What was this new trick that was being played on her tortured soul? For a brief instant she allowed hope to enter her mind, allowed herself to believe that somehow the nightmare might have an end, but then her glance flicked over Breene's shoulder and crushed the briefly blossoming flame of hope that sprang unbidden into her heart. This was just one more trick. Her nightmare had returned.

Breene didn't feel a thing as the handle of the machete whistled down and cracked him across the back of the neck.

Peter Ellis watched him sprawl senseless to the floor. The sound of his laughter chilled Amanda Warner to the very marrow of her bones. She clamped her eyes shut to block out the sight of him.

Ellis dropped to his knees beside her.

'My Queen.' He took her face fiercely between his hands. 'My Queen, thou wouldst betray me?' He frowned, sought some answer from her. 'Don't you k-know what I c-c-can do for you?' He quailed, feared her loss. Why did she not understand?

'*No!*' He roared. 'I will not tolerate this!' He leapt to his feet. 'I do not understand.'

He grabbed the inert figure of Breene, dragged him away from Amanda into the centre of the floor. The noises started in his head, a tumult of furious sound that matched his agitation, matched his confusion. What new test was being set for him now, on the very brink of his time? He sensed the vague and shadowy hand that stretched to snatch his ascendancy away from him, threatened the very essence of his being.

He was a fool to think that his trials were nearing an end. He stared at the face of the man on the floor. This was his adversary. This was the man who threatened to take his Queen. But how had he known?

Fear clutched at his vitals. This man *knew*. Knew because he sensed it, in the same way that Ellis himself sensed it. This was his final trial, the defeat of this man who reached out now to claim supremacy. Was there no end to the testing? Ellis closed his eyes, summoned up the strength that bound this body to his will, quailed at a suggestion that he might fail.

He could not fail. Not now.

But he must hurry. Time was running short, he felt it. He searched for the answer, strove for anxious moments to bring it to the surface against the clamour that fought to subdue him.

And it came to him. Whispered in the gentle voice that had come to guide him, silencing the other voices with its gentle strength. He leapt to his feet, the gleam of triumph in his eyes. He would succeed. He knew it.

CHAPTER 20

Constables Pierce and Quinn had resumed work after two days of intensive crisis counselling. Neither of them felt one hundred per cent, but they'd agreed with the police counsellor when he'd suggested that they had to 'get back on the horse', so to speak.

'What do you make of the Amanda Warner case?' Pierce asked tentatively when they had left the station. 'Did you hear the word on it?'

'Only that Hughes was handling it.' Quinn pursed his lips. 'Now that he's out of the picture, Bryant himself has taken over. They're working on some theory that it's a mob warning, or a payback. Whatever way you look at it, it doesn't sound too good for the girl. Especially after this long.'

'Yeah, I guess you're right,' Pierce sighed. 'It seems odd that Bryant has stepped in, though. I guess that if Hughes was right, then the stakes are high. Not that he ever struck me as…you know…' he shrugged. 'Not real bright.'

'Yeah, I know what you mean. This theory of his…'

'Car 71,' the radio crackled into life. 'Car 71 come in, please.'

Pierce gripped the wheel tightly as Quinn responded.

'Yeah, 71 here.'

'Car 71, proceed to number 17, that is one seven Nobby Parade Miami, Inspector Bryant requires backup.'

'Affirmative.' They looked at each other across the wide front seat. Pierce nodded briefly and Quinn flashed him a tight smile. If Bryant needed backup, it could mean only one thing. It had to do with the Amanda Warner disappearance.

'I guess you'll need to use the siren.'

'You bet,' Pierce grinned.

Bryant was already waiting out the front when the patrol car rolled up.

'Kill the siren,' he signalled agitatedly. 'You bloody cowboys.'

'They said you needed backup, sir, we wanted to get here as soon as we could.'

Bryant scowled, but Pierce only shrugged. What was he supposed to do?

'All right, I'll tell you what's going on. There's some smartarse getting around sticking his nose in the Warner disappearance, an old police mate of the father's. I've already run him out of the state once, now he's called me and arranged to meet me here. I'm expecting trouble from the bastard — Hughes came down on him hard before, so he could be out for revenge. I want you two guys to back me up. Got it?'

'Sure,' Quinn nodded.

'No problems,' Pierce agreed. 'Should I go around the back in case he tries to make a break for it?'

'No, I want you both at the front with me. This guy's none too smart and I figure he'll go for a frontal attack, if anything.' Bryant seemed nervous.

'Are you all right, sir?' Pierce asked.

'Of course I'm all right,' Bryant barked. 'You just never know with some of these guys. This Breene's a bit on the edge, that's all. I don't know what he's got cooked up for me.' He didn't mention that Breene had said he knew the whereabouts of Amanda Warner. He planned to arrest him, take him into the station. Then he'd find out where Amanda Warner was. In his own way. He was looking forward to having Breene under his control again. The smartarse should never have set foot back in this state.

'Open up in there!' he ordered, banging loudly on the door. 'Police.'

The light flicked on over their heads. Bryant shifted nervously. It was a long time since he'd been on active duty, instead of being stuck behind a desk.

'Watch this guy,' he warned, stepping closer to Pierce and Quinn as the door opened.

The woman who answered definitely did not look threatening. She wrung her hands pitifully and her eyes were redrimmed. She'd obviously been crying. Bryant stepped towards her and she cringed.

'Where's Breene?' He demanded.

'Don't hurt my boy,' she whimpered.

'What?'

'Don't hurt my boy.'

'I'm looking for a Mervyn Breene. He rang and told me to meet him here. Now, where is he?' Bryant tried to look over her shoulder into the dark interior of the house. 'Is he inside?'

'No.' She shook her head miserably. 'He went to get my Peter. He said he'd done terrible things.'

'Oh?' Bryant looked at the woman. 'So Breene's not here?'

'No, he's after my son. I'm so afraid he'll hurt him.'

'Did he threaten you, ma'am?'

'He shook me.' She started to sob. 'I was so frightened. And now he's after my boy.'

'Why is he after your boy?' Pierce asked, the obvious question. Bryant glared at him.

'He said he'd done terrible things. Said he had a girl and he was going to harm her. I know it isn't true, not my boy, not my Peter.'

'Where did he go?' Bryant snapped. He wasn't going to let this one go by. Maybe Breene was onto something.

'To my father's old farm. In the Currumbin Valley — it's called Kurrajong,' she sobbed. 'Please, you won't let him hurt my little boy?'

Bryant had already turned away from the old woman and was heading down the stairs.

'We'll look after things, ma'am,' Mick Quinn assured her before following after Bryant.

'Right, you two had better follow me,' Bryant snapped as he got into his car. 'Shit, I haven't got my light.'

'That's all right, sir, you follow us.' Steve Pierce smiled. Bryant glowered at him. A bit too big for his boots, this one. He'd need watching.

Pierce wasted no time, his tyres peeling rubber as he accelerated away from the curb, his siren already screaming.

'Hey Steve, you reckon it could be Amanda Warner, you reckon this Breene's onto her?'

'I don't know.' Their eyes met briefly.

He spurred the car on, a sudden sense of urgency outstripping the pleasure he usually took in the thrill of speed. Both men had paid a personal price in the Amanda Warner case, and finding her alive and safe would go a long way towards laying some ghosts to rest.

The air was tense in the patrol car. Neither man spoke.

Peter Ellis had been thrown by the appearance of Mervyn Breene. At first. Now he recognised him for what he was, the embodiment of the voices that taunted him from inside his head, the physical presence of the forces that rose to oppose him and strip him of his ultimate victory. He smiled in the darkness. He would not be opposed. He could feel the strength of the force that grew within him, snarled at the disembodied snatch of conversation that rumbled just below his level of hearing. Soon he would be free of their interference, their constant taunts and criticisms, their ability to sap his strength, to plant seeds of doubt in his head. They would remain behind, trapped within this body as he now was.

He would be out of their reach. Unattainable.

He frowned impatiently, continued his search in the darkened bushland. His urgency gnawed at him. He trembled to contain himself within this body, but the arrival of his nemesis had forced his hand. Any miscalculations now could have catastrophic effects.

He swooped with lightning speed at the noise to his right, plucked the rabbit from the ground and snapped its neck with one deft movement. Pleased, he added it to the string of rabbits suspended from his waist. It reminded him of his days living out here on the farm, the days before…he banished the memories that threatened him. He had been a fool then, unaware of his destiny. He couldn't afford to focus on anything but his purpose, could not afford the weakness of emotion.

He turned around, shutting himself off from all that had gone before. His preparation had been painful, but necessary.

Now he was ready.

Breene's head throbbed, a sound like the rushing of the ocean roared in his ears. He winced and tried to sit up, but he couldn't move. Where was he? What the hell was going on? He opened his eyes, struggled to focus his fogged brain on his present predicament. Bright stars swam in the darkness in front of him and his head throbbed all the way down to the back of his neck. Jesus, somebody had given him one hell of a whack. He rode a wave of nausea, his stomach threatening to expel its contents. He swallowed hard and clenched his teeth on the wad of cloth that was wedged tightly in his mouth. He sucked air in through his nostrils.

Amanda.

He winced in pain.

He'd found her. He remembered that much, the joy of seeing her alive, of knowing his search had not been in vain. So where was she now?

Slowly, his vision cleared. The corrugated roof of the shed above danced with an orange glow. Fire! Had his makeshift torch set fire to the building? Ellis must have hit him and left him to burn, taking Amanda with him. He turned his head to the right, wincing at the pain in his neck. Several small piles of wood burned on the concrete floor, the flames greedily consuming the timber. Rolling his head to the other side, he saw several more small fires. His arms were anchored by thin ropes secured to wooden poles on either side of the shed. His feet must have been similarly attached, though he couldn't see them.

He was stretched out on the concrete floor surrounded by a ring of fires.

Like a sacrifice.

Desperation brought renewed strength to his aching body. Amanda Warner was the reason he was here. Where the fuck had that mad bastard taken her now? In the condition she was in he knew she couldn't last much longer. Breene struggled against the ropes that held him, felt them burn as they dug into the flesh of his wrists. He rode the pain, held on to it to focus his mind. He had to get out of this. He'd come so far, he was so close. He wouldn't be denied now. She wouldn't lose her life while Mervyn Breene still had strength in his body.

He struggled to gain a purchase on the knots that bound his wrists, fought with numb fingers to make some impression on them, but it was futile. He could not gain a grip on the thin rope. Perspiration ran into his eyes and his breath came in ragged bursts from the exertion. He wasn't in good shape. His head throbbed and nausea gorged in his throat. Exhausted, he lay back on the cold concrete.

Cursing his weakness, Breene struggled to retain consciousness. He tried to steady his breathing, squeezed his eyes shut tightly and concentrated on clearing his head. He was not going to pass out again. He had to find a way out of this. God, where was Amanda now? Where were the cops? He clung to the pain that throbbed in his neck and the burning of his wrists.

Steeling himself for another effort, Breene forced his numb fingers to take a grip on the rope. He locked his fingers painfully around the twine and slowly pulled his head up again, biting hard on the cloth of the gag until he tasted his own blood in the back of his throat. His feet were anchored to the uncovered bulk of an ancient tractor. His chest was laid bare where the front of his shirt had been torn out.

Why had Ellis left him here like this? Why not finish the job?

He saw her form slumped in the chair at the same moment as the shrieking of the door announced that Peter Ellis had returned. His head fell back to the concrete with a thud. Ellis hadn't taken Amanda anywhere. The game was still on, and Breene was as helpless a participant as she was.

Ellis's head loomed into Breene's swimming vision, a faint smile on his blurred face. Breene watched as Ellis moved to his feet, muttering to himself as he dropped the twisted rabbit's bodies, one by one.

He stood and surveyed his handiwork, nodding in satisfaction at what he saw. His head was all but silent, the voices receding to little more than a murmur. He knew what had to be done now. He was above their recriminations. Now they huddled in fear of him. He had the power. He was the master. His gloating gaze swept over Breene. He stepped towards him and plucked the gag from his mouth. He was well prepared to face him now.

'So, you dare to thwart me?'

Breene's eyes stared back at him, unsettling him, throwing his focus out.

'I know of your purpose, evil one. You would rob me of what is mine, you have long planted the seed of doubt in my mind with your constant whisperings.' He shook his head. 'Such is my lot, to endure and to overcome. But you choose your hour poorly — my time is at hand.'

Breene returned his gaze steadily. The guy was obviously crazy.

'Listen, it's not too late for you, Ellis.'

Ellis hissed at the use of his name.

'It's not too late, you can still let the girl go. You obviously need help, they'll understand that. Just let the girl go.'

'Be quiet, foul emissary of darkness. Give up my Queen, you say? Give to you the mainstay of my power, the embodiment of my Queen, the one true voice that has long striven against your evil intent? You judge me incorrectly!' He strode up and down within the ring of fire, his glare malevolent. 'I will not give her up, not now, not at your urging.'

'You're speaking nonsense,' Breene said evenly. 'She isn't your Queen, I don't know what you're talking about. Her name is Amanda Warner. She is the girl you kidnapped the same night you murdered her boyfriend and that taxi driver. Any other shit you've got in your head is a figment of your imagination. The cops will be here any minute, your mother will tell them where I am. She knows.' He saw the hesitation, the moment of doubt flicker behind Ellis' eyes. His mouth worked furiously.

'Liar!' he shouted. His mother. He knew he should have disposed of her when he'd had the chance. Foolish indecision, the weakness of this body that trammelled his own pure spirit within. What had been the use of the first two sacrifices, if not to prepare him for the sacrifice of the woman he called mother? Traitor. Whore. He whimpered, retreated into his pain, quailed at his own weakness. He was not worthy.

'No!' he shouted. He would not give in. His gaze met Breene's and he laughed, a high-pitched utterance lacking any semblance of control. 'Fool. Still, even now, you attempt to overthrow me with doubt, to supplant yourself on the throne that waits in preparation for me. Behold, my Queen is ready, awaiting my ascension even now. You have left your time too late.'

'Look at her,' Breene hissed. 'Your Queen? She's nearly dead. She can barely hold her head up. She has no part in this, she doesn't have a role to play. It's just you and me, and you know it.' Breene was desperate, playing for time, anything to delay Ellis's intent. Surely the police must arrive at any moment.

'Enough! I will brook no further insolence. I have you in my power now. Your time is done.' He hastily replaced the gag, shoving the ball of material tightly into Breene's mouth. Breene thrashed his head from side to side, aggravating the injury to his neck. He strained at the cords that bound him until the blood rushed to his head and his vision swam. Ellis sprang away from him, intimidated by the fury in his eyes.

'You c-c-c-can't h-h-h-hurt me n-n-now.' Ellis turned away from Breene, had to avoid his glare. He was in danger even now, had to proceed with absolute caution. He must not underestimate the power of his adversary, he had to control his own powers, re-establish his focus.

A shudder ran through his body. He closed his eyes, consciously calling up the soothing gentle voice of his Queen.

'Soon my love, soon,' he crooned. He opened his eyes, rested his gaze on the pale face of Amanda Warner. His expression softened, his breathing steadied. Soon.

He moved up beside Breene, avoiding his glare. He produced the viciously gleaming blade of the machete, held it up so that the orange light of the fires was mirrored in its perfect sheen. Smiling, he brought the point of the blade down so that it rested on Breene's exposed sternum. He had only to exert the slightest pressure and a pinpoint of blood appeared. Breene shivered, searched for some light of sanity in Ellis' eyes and found none. So this was how it all ended. He felt the bite of the cruel blade as Ellis traced a line from his sternum to his navel, clenched his eyes against the agony as he waited for the cold bite to reach down to the vitality of his organs. Regret cascaded through him. His life had meant so little now that he had reached the bitter end. His only hope was that by stalling Ellis he would enable Amanda to be saved. Not that he'd ever know about it.

He sensed rather than felt Ellis moving away from him. Jerking his head up he looked down at the blood that pooled around his navel, slowly building until it trickled over his sides onto the floor. Relief mingled with fear, overriding any sensations of pain for the time being. He watched Ellis as he approached the chair in which Amanda was slumped. What the hell was he up to now? Breene's brow furrowed with the effort of holding himself upright. His wrists throbbed fiercely where the rope cut into them.

Ellis reached under the chair and pulled out his white cloth-bound bundle. He shivered with anticipation. Just a little while longer. The correct ritual was essential, the presence of another sacrifice only made his transition more assured. The symmetry of events had aligned themselves in the correct order, ultimately confirming for Ellis that his coming had been predestined.

His hard gaze softened for a moment as he regarded Amanda. He reached out a tender hand to stroke her face, but his arm was shaken by a sudden convulsion. He frowned. His powers would soon outgrow the confines of this weak vessel. He must not hesitate.

Quickly unwrapping the array of surgical instruments, he grasped the fine handle of a scalpel and snatched up the first of the rabbit bodies, making a large incision in the fur-covered neck. Dark blood dribbled from the wound and he laughed. Blood. The vehicle of his liberation. Taking another rabbit, he repeated his actions, smearing a hand full of the still-warm fluid on his chest before he stood with both carcasses suspended by their rear legs so that a trail of blood dripped onto the floor. He made his way slowly around the inside of the circle of fires, muttering fiercely to himself while he traced a thin line of blood on the floor. Retracing his steps he seized the limp bodies of another two rabbits.

When the circle was complete he shivered in ecstasy. His teeth chattered and his limbs trembled with suppressed excitement. He strode towards Amanda and stood over her, swaying and chanting. Breene watched in horrified fascination as Ellis picked up the last of the rabbit bodies, this time slicing it down the middle and digging inside until with a triumphant growl he withdrew the heart. Sinking to his knees, Ellis rubbed the heart over his own chest, as if anointing himself. He did likewise to Amanda, exposing her pale chest and marking it with dark red smears of blood. He bowed his head and closed his eyes, summoning his strength for the final act, the culmination. He knew it would require all he could give.

Breene needed no further proof that Peter Ellis was totally insane. He pulled desperately against the ropes that held him, stretching him wide open to the savage blade that lay by Ellis's side. Terror wormed its way into his gut. He was completely at the mercy of a raving lunatic. He bit down on his gag, fought against the fog that dimmed his senses. He was on his own, but he wasn't about to let this fucking loon finish him off without a good fight. He wasn't going to take Mervyn Breene out without a whimper.

He decided that fighting against the ropes wasn't doing him much good, not in the time he had left. He searched desperately for something, anything that might help him, something he could reach, a weapon. Anything. There was nothing. He looked back to Ellis, wondered how much time he had before the madman decided he was prepared. His eyes strayed upwards to Amanda. How was he going to save her now, when he couldn't even save himself?

He was startled to see her eyes open. She stared in confusion at Peter Ellis, head bowed and on his knees only a few feet away from her. She lifted her head to look about her, frowned as she struggled to comprehend what was happening, what further twist her nightmare was about to take.

It was then that Breene noticed that she wasn't tied to the chair. The ropes that had bound her wrists and ankles had been removed. She was free to move, free to save him. Hardly daring to hope, Breene tried frantically to attract her dazed attention, to draw her gaze towards him, away from the swaying, chanting form of Ellis. How much longer could they have?

He began flapping his wrist up and down, fluttering his fingers in the hope that the movement would catch her eye. He prayed that the faint flapping sound of his hand against the concrete would not attract Ellis's attention.

Too late. He held his breath as Ellis moved, picked himself up from the floor as if in a trance. Now it was all over surely. His eyes followed as Ellis bent to collect his surgical instruments, spread them out on the blood-spattered white linen. Still he chanted and swayed, his eyes closed, his face in a state of ecstasy as he communed with unheard voices.

'Come on, Amanda,' Breene pleaded silently. 'Come on.'

She'd seen him. She frowned as her eyes travelled up his body, hesitated when she saw the pool of blood around his navel. Gritting his teeth against the gag Breene jerked his hips into the air.

'Come on, for Christ's sake, look at me!'

Their eyes met, briefly. Hope drained from Breene. Her gaze was vague and unfocused. The ordeal had been too much for her mind to deal with. What was fucking Ellis doing now? Still chanting over his instruments. How much longer could it take? Anger rose, blotting out his despair. Why didn't he just bloody well get it over with, why not finish it? He could take it, he'd be prepared, if only the bastard would stop fucking around. Crazy bastard.

He glanced back at Amanda. Her eyes were locked onto his, her gaze focused and full of terror.

Christ, he had no time to waste. He scanned the floor for the club he had carried in with him, located it just to her left where it had fallen when Ellis hit him. His eyes darted back to her face, saw that she followed him, that she understood. Still terror rooted her to the spot, froze her in the chair. She quailed, her eyes raking Breene's face with the agony of her fear.

Breene hardened himself against his sympathy for her. They didn't have the time for the luxury of that emotion. He glared sternly at her, tried to give her strength through the force of his own will. If she didn't move they were both fucked.

Falteringly, she rose from the chair, grimacing in pain as blood rushed to her circulation-starved ankles. She stumbled as she bent to pick up the pine branch and Breene's hope almost died in him, certain that she would not have the strength to reach Ellis, let alone put him out of action.

Ellis's moans were increasing in volume. His chest heaved as he sucked in great lungfuls of air, drew himself up for this final act of rending, for the dissolution of this mortal form that bound him. His eyes snapped open and he roared with murderous intent as he lunged towards Breene armed with a wickedly curved surgical blade.

In that instant Amanda Warner sprang forward, emitting her own high-pitched scream. She struck Ellis with all her might, rage erupting as she sought atonement for the evils he had imposed on her. The club caught him above the right ear, sent him sprawling onto the ground. He struggled to regain his feet but she struck him again, catching him across the top of his forehead. Ellis pitched backwards, his head thudding onto the hard concrete of the floor and lay motionless.

Amanda Warner sank to the ground beside him, her already depleted reserves drained by the fury of her attack. A low-pitched keening sound rose in her throat.

She had bought him precious moments, but Breene knew it was up to him now. Desperately seizing his opportunity, he pulled frantically at his bindings. Still unable to gain any purchase, he turned his wrist over, concentrating on rubbing the rope on the coarse cement. It was his only chance.

Working furiously, he ignored the burning ache in his wrists, the chafing rawness where his elbow rubbed on the hard ground in time with his wrist. Rivulets of sweat ran burning into his eyes and his neck throbbed as he strained to manoeuvre the knot into the correct position. Slowly, ever so slowly it was giving.

Too slowly.

Ellis was starting to groan, regaining consciousness.

Too late, Breene cursed. Too fucking late. Tears of anger and frustration built up in his eyes. He didn't deserve to die at the hands of a madman like Ellis. Amanda Warner didn't deserve to die like this. Was this all he'd lived and striven for?

Ellis started to whimper. Breene whipped his head around to look in his direction, to curse him before his life was wrenched from his body. Amanda Warner was on her knees, her eyes darting from Ellis's still inert form to Breene's.

Please, Breene pleaded silently. Don't give up on me now. He looked steadily into her eyes, tried to instil some reality into her. Ellis began to rise. Blood streaked down his forehead from the blow Amanda had dealt him and he wiped it out of his eyes, searching frantically for his weapon.

Fear overcame Amanda Warner's inertia and she scrambled for the machete, reaching it only seconds before Ellis. She clawed her way desperately towards Breene holding the machete outstretched.

'*Do not betray me now!*' Ellis roared, lunging at her and catching her by the ankle.

'*No!*' She screamed falling forward, her eyes filled with terror. Somehow she retained her purpose. As she fell she aimed the machete at the rope that held Breene's left hand, striking it a solid blow with the force of her body weight behind it.

Breene felt the give, pulled hard on the still connected rope as the spectre of Ellis' demented, blood-streaked visage flew towards him.

'I *will not be denied! You do not have the right!*' He grappled for the blade, clawing and punching at Amanda as he fought for control.

With one final heave the rope parted. Breene's left

hand was free, the severed rope flapping from his wrist.

Ellis pushed Amanda Warner over backwards, the machete gleaming in his hand. He howled in triumph, his malicious bloodstained glare falling onto Breene's face.

'I will not be denied,' he gasped. 'I am the master. My hour is at hand.' Lurching, he staggered towards Breene, ignoring the blood that dripped into his eyes, the throbbing of his head. What was pain to him? What was this body to him but a pathetic vessel, a shroud for his glory?

He sank to his knees beside Breene, intent on his victory. His face wore a smile of gloating victory. Wearily, he raised the machete above his head.

'There!' Quinn spotted the gap in the bushes. Pierce reefed on the handbrake, sliding the rear end of the patrol car in a sharp semicircle and bringing the nose around until it pointed up the narrow track. He accelerated, the powerful V8 engine throbbing as the car churned up the loose ground beneath the wheels. He killed the siren and the flashing light as he forced the car onwards, coming to a sliding halt behind the VW that blocked the path.

'Out!' he shouted to his partner. 'Let's go!' Together they sprinted up the path, guns drawn, faces grim with determination. The lights of Bryant's vehicle illuminated their footsteps as he slid to a halt behind them.

'Wait!' He called. Neither man heeded him.

Breene's fist struck the back of Ellis's elbow, sending the machete flying in a graceful arc through the air. It landed with a dull clang on the concrete floor.

Ellis howled in fury, scrambling to retrieve it. Breene caught him by the back of his hair before he had a chance to get away, jerking him backwards. He aimed a savage punch at the back of his head, driving it home with all the force he could muster with his left hand. Ellis turned on him in rage, his weakness forgotten as he faced his adversary.

He would not be deprived of his purpose. For too long he had been a helpless victim to the voices that haunted and mocked him. Now in his moment of triumph those voices were embodied, his nemesis had made one final bid to pull him from his throne. He would not tolerate it. He was the master. Ignoring the machete he propelled his own fist down into the face of the still-bound creature, grunting in satisfaction when the head snapped back into the concrete. He dug his fingers fiercely into Breene's neck, digging with all his strength to grip the windpipe and throttle the air from his mortal body, to silence his malevolent opposition forever. Breene pushed desperately upwards with his free hand, catching Ellis under the chin and thrusting upwards. Ellis struggled to turn his head, losing his grip for an instant. Breene's fingers gouged upwards, clawing at the blood-slippery face, searching for some purchase. He sunk his fingers into Ellis's eye socket, gouging with all his strength.

Ellis screamed his fury. He let go of Breene's windpipe and pulled away, then smashed a two-fisted drive into the face below him. He was rewarded by the sound of crunching bone as Breene's nose disintegrated. Blood gushed from the mangled nostrils.

Ellis's gloating victory cry filled the shed. He pulled away from Breene, his purpose reawakened by the sight of so much blood. Angling a vicious kick into the side of his head he raced to retrieve his machete, eager to complete his mission. There must be no further interruptions. He could drive this body only so far. Already he sensed its imminent failure.

He raced back towards the inert form on the ground, gurgling and spluttering in its own blood. The sight of the blood inflamed him. His release! His key to the realisation of his own rich reward.

Breene could only watch through a mist of pain and fear as Ellis raised the machete. The descent seemed slow, almost graceful. Now that his fate was sealed he felt a peculiar detachment, almost a willingness to let go of his life. There was no sudden replay of pictures, no rapid flashback, only a keen sense of remorse when he thought of Sylvia, of the time he'd wasted that could have been spent with her. An overwhelming wave of sadness washed over him.

'Stop! Police!'

The words echoed absurdly in his head. They were followed by the deafening roar of gunfire as two distinct shots rang out. The machete flew from Ellis's hand as bullets thunked into the flesh of his forearm. He muttered a strangled cry of fury, lurched to his feet oblivious to the pain of his shattered arm.

'Halt! Stay right where you are!' Pierce shouted.

'Don't move another inch!' He took aim at the quickly-moving figure of Ellis, prepared to blow his head apart if he had to.

A bellow of rage from behind took both the cops by surprise as Bryant burst into the shed, tumbling into Pierce and throwing his aim off. His shot echoed loudly in the small shed, the bullet grazing Peter Ellis's temple before thudding into the wall beside him. He dived to the floor, scrambling on hands and knees for the opening in the wall that he'd used as a child.

'Stop!' Quinn regained his balance first, charged around the piles of junk that obscured his sight and squeezed off another shot as Peter Ellis scrambled out into the darkness of the night. 'He's out, Steve!' he called to his partner.

Pierce ran out into the black night, searching frantically for his quarry. He set off in the direction of the wild crashing in the bushes. Ellis already had a good start on him, and he was in familiar territory. A motorbike engine roared into life ahead of him and quickly accelerated away.

Pierce dropped to his knee and squeezed off four shots in the direction of the sound.

The motorbike continued, the sound of its engine rapidly departing as Peter Ellis made good his escape.

CHAPTER 21

Breene woke in the grip of panic, his eyes focusing dimly on the white ceiling above him. Where was he? Where was Ellis? He jolted upright, wincing at the tearing pain in his stomach, and stared around him. The diffused light from a curtained window revealed a hospital room, and he sank back gratefully into soft pillows.

Ellis was gone, that much he remembered, vanished into the dark night to trouble the peaceful quiet of the Currumbin Valley. And Amanda Warner?

'Hello?' He called. 'Hello? Anybody here?'

A head poked around his door.

'Shh! It's only five in the morning. You'll wake everybody up.'

'Where am I?'

'You're in hospital. They brought you in last night.'

'What about Amanda? Amanda Warner — do you know anything about her? Is she okay?'

'As far as I know she's doing fine. Which is more than you'll be if you wake any of my other patients. Now shut up and lie back down.' She retreated from the door.

'Nurse,' Breene called.

'Sister,' she corrected as she came back in. 'What is it now?'

'What's all this about?' He held up the hand with the IV line attached to it.

'You had an operation last night when you came in. Didn't they tell you?' she asked, puzzled.

'Tell me what? I don't even remember coming in.'

'They had to take you to theatre to reduce that nose of yours. It was a real mess, from what I hear. While you were in there they sutured your stomach as well. X-rays of your head showed that there was no fracture, but you've got a pretty nasty bump on the back of your neck. The IV is standard procedure after an anaesthetic, but they'll probably take it out as soon as you've had breakfast. Now, is that all?'

'Just one more thing,' Breene halted her.

'Yes?' She sighed.

'Thanks for being so nice.'

Her face broke into a smile.

'Long night,' she shrugged.

'Know the feeling.' Breene tried to smile back, but it came out as more of a grimace when pain shot up his battered nose. 'Ouch.'

'Don't smile,' the sister said sweetly.

Breene sank back into the pillows and winced at the pain in his neck. Amanda was safe. For the moment that was all that mattered. He'd done his bit.

Peter Ellis was a Queensland police problem now. He tried to turn on his side and drift back to sleep but he couldn't get comfortable, found that he was aching all over. Bloody hospital beds. He drifted into an uneasy sleep.

'Breakfast, sir,' a voice called.

Breene groaned and struggled into a sitting position. His head throbbed dully and his nose was stuffy and uncomfortable. This definitely was not his idea of fun.

'Morning, Mr Breene,' a cherry male voice greeted. 'How are we this morning?'

'Just bloody great,' Breene growled.

'Beautiful day outside,' said the man, pulling the curtains back to reveal an expanse of carefully tended green lawn bathed in sunlight.

'What are you, a doctor?'

'Nah, not me. I'm one of the nurses. Well, sister, actually,' he said with an embarrassed smile. 'But you can call me Danny.'

'Danny, hey? Well Dan, what can you do for me? I feel like a shithouse. My neck's aching, my nose feels like it's full of cotton wool and I'm bloody uncomfortable.'

'I see you're recovering, then? Basically, your nose *is* full of cotton wool. I'll be taking that out soon. As for being uncomfortable, if you sit forward I'll fix your pillows a bit, and I'll get you something for pain.'

'That sounds mighty fine, Danny. What is it

they've given me for breakfast here?' Breene sat forward while Danny rearranged his pillows and took the cover off the plate on his breakfast tray. 'Hey, this looks all right. Bacon and eggs, a croissant. Coffee, toast — what sort of hospital is this?'

'Private hospital, sir. Nothing but the best in this place. Just lean back and see how that is.'

'Breene sank back into the pillows.

'Much better. Good work, Dan. Thanks son.'

'No worries. Need anything, just give me a buzz.'

Now that was more like it. Breene almost felt human again. Surprisingly, he was ravenous. Then again, he hadn't eaten since lunch yesterday. Was it only yesterday? Seemed like bloody ages ago.

He'd polished off all his breakfast and was just finishing his coffee while watching the breakfast shows on TV when a horrible thought occurred to him.

'Hey, Danny,' he called as he saw the nurse hurrying past in the corridor.

'Problem?'

'I was wondering. Who's paying for all of this?'

His face creased into a grin.

'Don't worry. Mr Warner's picking up the tab. Told us to make sure you were well looked after.'

Breene sank back into his pillows with a smile on his face.

He must have drifted off again, because the next thing he knew Jack Warner's voice was filling his room.

'Merv, you look bloody awful,' he greeted him. He was all smiles and looked a hell of a lot better than he had the last time Breene saw him.

'Thanks a lot Jack. You're looking disgustingly healthy.'

'And feeling it, my boy, and feeling it. It's great to be alive.' He puffed his chest out.

'Glad someone thinks so.'

'Cut it out, Merv,' Warner said, his tone suddenly sharp.

'Joking, Jack.'

'Yeah. Listen.' His expression sobered. 'That was bloody good work you did, Breene. Bloody good.' He walked to the window and stared out in silence.

Breene started to feel uncomfortable.

'Jack…'

Warner held up a hand to silence him. When he turned around his eyes were moist.

'I've got something to say to you, Merv, and I don't want you to interrupt.' He looked away, studying the pattern on the curtains.

'I never realised how important my family was to me. All that time, all those years, I took them for granted. When Amanda went missing…' his voice shook and he sniffed fiercely. 'When she went missing I realised how much they mean to me. How much I love my daughter. And my wife. They mean more to me than anything, more than some stupid fucking job where nobody ever really gave a damn anyway. And when I thought I might never see her again…' he hung his head and made a show of studying his fingernails. 'It was more painful than anything that's ever happened to me.' Tears glistened on his eyelashes when he looked at Breene. He made no attempt to brush them away.

'You gave me another chance, Merv. And I'll never forget it. It's the greatest gift anyone could have given me. Another chance.' He turned away and when he spoke again his voice was even and calm.

'I'm going to forget all that shit about the force. It's all behind me now, I want to start my life again. I realised that I'm not a cop anymore, Merv, and I don't want to be. Now I'm a dad. And a husband.' His voice had grown husky.

'I've got you to thank for that too.'

Breene had to clear his own throat before he spoke.

'How's Amanda?'

Warner turned to face him.

'I won't lie to you, Merv. Physically, the doctors say she'll be fine. Her major problem was dehydration and shock. Psychologically, well, they don't know. She's been through a hell of a lot.' His face grew grim. 'We'll probably never know exactly what that bastard did to her, how she's suffered...' he bit off his words and took a deep breath.

'They say that with time and understanding, and a lot of love, she should pull through it. We're going to do our best to give her that. She's decided to come back home.'

'That's good, Jack. I'm glad for you.'

Warner drew himself up and forced a grin onto his face.

'And how about you? Looks like you got yourself pretty well busted up.'

'Yeah, well. It only hurts when I smile.'

Warner shrugged.

'So don't smile.'

Breene laughed.

'Thanks for the advice.'

'Didn't turn out to be much of a holiday.'

'It isn't over yet. Besides, I felt sort of guilty having a break when I hadn't worked for it. Now I reckon I've earned one.'

'Amen to that, Merv. Amen to that. Any plans?'

'Oh, I might have a thing or two up my sleeve.'

'By the way,' Warner frowned. 'I'm not sure I should be telling you this — I've been sworn to silence, but we had a guest at our house last night.' He studied Breene in silence for a moment.

'And?' Breene wasn't in the mood for games.

'Well, she was pretty shook up when she saw you last night. I think she's serious about you, Merv. I think you should know.'

'Sylvia?' He'd tried to block her out of his head for the past day or so, never quite succeeding.

'Yes,' Warner nodded.

'She stayed at your place last night?'

'Yeah. She wanted to stay here, but they wouldn't let her. Besides, she needed somebody to talk to. She and Pam seem to have built up quite a friendship over the past couple of days. They were up half the night chattering away like a couple of schoolgirls.' He smiled fondly. 'She seems like a hell of a nice lady, Merv.'

'Yeah. She is,' Breene sighed heavily. 'Maybe too nice for the likes of me.'

'I don't know about that. Maybe you sell yourself

short.' Warner held Breene's gaze. 'You're a hell of a nice bloke, Merv, one who cares about his friends. That says a lot in my book.'

It was Breene who looked away first, embarrassed by his friend's candour.

'You've changed, Jack,' he said quietly.

'Yes. Something like this makes you realise what really matters, cuts through the bullshit. I've spent too much time worrying about the bullshit, Merv, missing out on the important stuff. It's about time I changed, smelt the flowers, that sort of shit.' He laughed. 'It's going to be quite a change. I feel like I'm starting again, and it's a bloody good feeling. A clean slate.'

Breene turned to look at his friend. He was impressed.

'It wouldn't do you any harm, either. A bloke your age needs to start gathering a bit of moss.'

'Maybe you're right,' he nodded.

'I usually am.' They both laughed and the awkward moment passed.

'Listen, Mandy would like to see you when you're feeling up to it.'

'Really? Is she up to it? Wouldn't I frighten her, sort of remind her of the whole thing?'

'It happened, Merv. The whole thing did happen. The doc says it might be the best thing for her, to be reminded of the positive side, to be reminded that she wasn't alone, even though she felt like it. You saved her life, Merv; if it hadn't been for you, that madman would have finished her off by now. I think it's important for her to know that you were in there swinging for her all along.'

'Okay.' Breene took a deep breath. 'I'll go around and see her later this morning. Once they've taken this out of my arm.' He held up the IV line and frowned. 'Never did like these damned things. You reckon I could get air in the line?'

Warner laughed.

'Jesus, after all you've been through you're worried about getting knocked off in a hospital? I figure that's the least of your problems.'

Breene laughed too. It did seem to pale in comparison.

Later that morning, after a shower and what he could manage of a shave, Breene hesitated outside the door of Amanda Warner's room. He couldn't understand his nervousness and put it down to the fact that the last time he had seen her they'd both been in pretty uncomfortable circumstances. A brief image of Peter Ellis poised above him with a machete in his hand flashed through his mind and caused him to shudder.

He could only imagine what sort of images Amanda might be haunted by.

He knocked softly and put his head around the door. Pam Warner was reading at the side of her daughter's bed and Breene smiled. She was one mother who wouldn't let her kid out of her sight for some time to come.

'Hello, Merv.' Her smile was warm and the look of gratitude in her eyes spoke volumes. Breen shuffled uncomfortably. He wasn't used to being a hero.

'Mandy,' Pam shook her daughter gently. 'You have a visitor.'

She woke quickly, terror pounding in her stomach until she saw her mother, realised the nightmare had ended. She couldn't believe it was over, that she was safe. She squeezed her mother's hand and managed a hesitant smile. So much had happened, so many things had changed that she wondered if she would ever really feel safe again. And she knew he was still out there somewhere. Her gaze followed the direction of her mother's and she turned to Breene.

'Hi,' Mervyn Breene smiled sheepishly, his nose swaddled in plaster and bandages, his face bruised.

'Hello,' Amanda said quietly, her steady gaze meeting his. Yes, it had all happened. It had all been real. A tear slid down her cheek and she reached for his hand.

Breene took her hand in his, was surprised by the fiercely protective feelings that overwhelmed him as he looked down at the trusting face of the young girl who lay in the bed, so full of the vigour and fleeting beauty of youth and yet so fragile. There was a bond between them now, a feeling that had taken root during his desperate search, his desperate struggle to save her life. It was something that could never be put into words, but both of them sensed it. He guessed this was a part of what it felt like to be a father, only different. He wondered if he could ever submit himself to the pain of that commitment.

'How are you feeling?' he asked finally, not awkward, but needing to escape his intense feelings.

'All right now,' she smiled, understanding his need. 'What about you?'

'I'll survive.'

'Good.' She began to cry quietly. Breene crouched down beside the bed and wiped the tears gently from her face, ignoring the dampness of his own eyes.

'We're going to be all right now,' he whispered.

'Yes,' she nodded. 'We'll be all right.'

Sylvia was sitting on his bed waiting when he returned to his room. She turned her head at the sound of his entry, her dark eyes clouded by concern.

'Merv.' She came around the bed and into his arms. 'I was so worried about you.'

Breene took her in his embrace and held her tight. 'Jesus God, I need you, woman.' He buried his face in her dark fragrant hair, felt the tears start again and couldn't have cared less.

'Listen.' He held her away from him, his tone earnest. 'Sylvia, I've done a lot of thinking. I love you. I love you too damned much to lose you over something as meaningless as a stupid job. Did you mean what you said, about wanting me if I was prepared to make some sacrifices? Because I know I want you.'

'Oh, Merv,' she hugged him tightly. 'I do want you. I never realised how much.'

'Neither did I.' He felt the hot moisture of her tears through his shirtfront, ignored the discomfort of the stitches in his stomach. 'It's a hell of a way to discover that you love somebody. I'm glad I'll only have to do it once, I don't think I could survive a second time.'

Sylvia held him tight, smiled into his shirtfront.

She could only hope she'd never come so close to losing him again.

By afternoon he couldn't wait to get out of the place, chafing at the restrictions of being a patient. He wanted to breathe the fresh air, sit and drink coffee looking out over the ocean, soak up the atmosphere of relaxed tourism. Warner was right, it hadn't been much of a holiday, but he planned to make the rest of it more than good.

Besides, Sylvia had agreed to spend a whole week with him and he didn't want to waste one moment. He didn't know how long the smooth sailing would last between them — he suspected theirs was what could be termed a 'stormy' relationship, but he wanted to make the most of it while the good feelings lasted. A hospital was not the most conducive setting for romance to flourish, and definitely not the place for what he had in mind.

'It's against my advice,' the doctor insisted.

'I'll take my chances,' Breene told him.

'But you need to rest up more. I'd like to keep you in for further observation for another twenty-four hours.'

'I'll have somebody to look after me.' Breene put his arm around Sylvia. 'And if I have any problems I'll come back in.'

'All right, fair enough,' the doctor shrugged. 'Those sutures will need to come out in about a week. Don't overdo things.'

'I'll do my best, doc.' Breene grinned.

Sylvia picked him up out the front in the VW — Breene already had a soft spot for the ugly car.

Maybe he wouldn't go back to retrieve the Fiat after all. He had probably been due for a new car.

'You're a hero,' Sylvia said drily, handing him a newspaper as he climbed stiffly into the car. He hurt more than he would have liked, but he didn't let on. There was no way he was going to stay in hospital for one minute longer. He lit a cigarette and breathed deeply, exhaling the smoke with a sigh. Sylvia raised an eyebrow but didn't comment.

DRAMATIC RESCUE ON GOLD COAST
MACHETE WIELDING MADMAN FLEES
Kidnap victim Amanda Warner was rescued last night after three days in the clutches of a madman believed responsible for five murders on the Gold Coast in the past ten days.
Police raced to the scene last night after a tip-off from an-as-yet unidentified source. They found Warner in an abandoned shed in secluded bushland. Police were forced to fire at a man wielding a machete after he refused to surrender his weapon.
He was struck by two bullets as he threatened a second victim, Mervyn Breene, 38, a resident of Sydney. The man, described as being extremely disturbed by police, escaped through a hole in the wall of the dilapidated shed and ran off into surrounding bushland, escaping on a motorcycle.
Inspector Arthur Bryant has described the police effort in finding the missing girl as 'nothing short of courageous'.
'It's a tribute to the police force that protects this fine city of ours,' he said in a late-night statement.

> *'Of course, we are making every effort to apprehend the man responsible for the worst spate of murders ever to occur on the Gold Coast and we are optimistic about our chances. Any assistance the public may be able to offer would be appreciated.'*
>
> *He was reluctant to speculate on the presence of the second man at the scene, who was taken to Pindara private hospital with head and abdominal injuries. Both his and Amanda Warner's conditions are described as satisfactory.*

Breene snorted in disgust. Courageous police work. Typical. Left to the police, Amanda Warner would be dead by now. He was surprised to see the story hadn't been written by Celia Thompson — she probably would have given his name a bit more significance, realised that he was the one who had ultimately cracked the case, but what the hell.

Breene's pride was bruised, but then again he didn't really want his name splashed across the paper like a hero. He hadn't done any of it for credit. It was a favour to an old mate, something he'd had to do to save a young life. Breene felt good about it. He liked himself more than he had for a long time, and that was worth it. That and seeing Amanda Warner's smile, hearing the gratitude in Jack Warner's voice. He'd actually made a difference. Given them the opportunity to start over. What they did from here was up to them.

The day was warm and sunny and Breene should have been happy. But a worm of anxiety gnawed at his gut. Peter Ellis was still out there somewhere. He couldn't truly rest until the deranged bastard had been brought to justice. The thought taunted him as he looked across at Sylvia, reaching out to place a hand on her thigh.

He couldn't quite shake the feeling that this whole thing hadn't finished with him yet.

CHAPTER 22

Peter Ellis nursed his wounds in the misery of the dark bushland all through the night. His queen was gone, his preordained destiny ripped from him in the very hour of his fulfilment. He was tortured by the voices that taunted him, the voices he could not escape.

Even her voice, that one sweet voice, could offer him no succour. She had been consumed as he had, and now she was at the mercy of the roaring violence that crashed inside for Ellis's ears alone.

But Peter Ellis was not finished. Not yet. A glimmer of hope existed, a faint chance for his future. But first he had to destroy those who had thwarted him. He stood in the rays of the early morning sunlight, oblivious to the injuries his body had received. His eyes grew dark as he thought of what must be done.

His mother. That base vessel that had spawned him, had betrayed him at the last, delivered him into the hands of his nemesis. But she would pay. He cursed the weakness that had stayed his hand when he'd had the opportunity, scorned the symbolism of the first two sacrifices he'd made. They had counted for nothing, had not sufficed to eradicate the vindictive force of the woman's will.

He would have smiled, but the huge effort required to restrain the voices that threatened to overwhelm him made him whimper with pain. When would he be free of their taunts, free to fly on his own, untroubled by voices that raised a million doubts, that questioned his every thought, ridiculed his every decision?

He found the answer within himself, waiting to be noticed. When he had dealt with his nemesis.

He didn't know his name, didn't know where he was, but Peter Ellis knew he had to find him and destroy him, whatever the cost. It was imperative to his future existence. It would free him from the crippling forces that strove to dominate his spirit.

Slowly, his limbs thawed by the rising sun, he began a ritual of movement, stretching and twisting, controlling his body by the force of his will. His eyes fixed on the points of blood that erupted on his arms, watched as they grew and rolled down. Sobs welled in his chest, unrestrained, unrestrainable. He sensed the heartbeat of the world around him, felt the discord within his own being and knew the two would not beat in harmony. Not now. Not ever. In a flash of insight he knew he would never attain his goal now, never reach the bright promise of his vision. All of that had been taken away.

The one purpose that remained now was to eradicate those who had done the taking.

His jaw locked into a grim line. The voices receded to a level where he could exert some control, push them back until they were a dull yammering in his head. He could overcome the pain.

His fingers sought out the first festering pucker of flesh, examined the oozing warmth that trickled from the wound and searched deeper, probing through the hot flesh, seeking for the invader into his realm. He touched the hard round ball, felt the blinding sear of pain that assaulted his being and allowed it to become a part of him, used its intensity to add to his own strength as his fingers sought for purchase, rolled the invader to the surface and held it up with a gleam of triumph in his eyes.

The second was nestled against shattered splinters of bone. He blinked in surprise, realised his arm was broken and embraced the pain, knitted it to his will. This body was nothing to him. It had only one task to achieve now and his mind was sufficient to push it to the limits, drive it to the conclusion he now sought with all the power of his essence.

He climbed stiff-legged onto his motorbike, kicked the engine into sputtering life and reached for the throttle. His eyes travelled along his arm, furious at its refusal to obey his will. The hand was bent at a curious angle, the truncated fingers unwilling to move as he desired. Sweat beaded on his forehead as he strove to bring the injured limb back under his control. He would tolerate no disobedience, not from this body. Slowly the hand gripped the throttle and twisted, raising the revs of the engine until it screamed its defiance in the shattered silence of the morning. He nodded once, engaged the gears and roared into action.

Peter Ellis knew the bushland well and emerged far from the area patrolled by the police that morning. Their search had been fruitless so far, but they expected to find him sometime that day, holed up and nursing his wounds.

They had totally underestimated the extent of his insanity.

June Ellis gasped in horror when she read the morning paper. Not her boy, not her Peter. Surely it wasn't him. But that man's name, that Mervyn Breene — she knew it was the name of the man who had been in the house yesterday, the violent man who had come searching for Peter.

She got up from the table and cautiously approached Peter's room, inched the door open, expecting him to shout at her.

'Peter? Peter!' She bobbed her head timidly around the door. Maybe he was still asleep.

The bed was empty, the covers rumpled. Clothes were strewn all about the floor and she wrinkled her nose at the smell that assaulted her nostrils. She glanced down, remembering too late the severed digits on the floor.

'Oh, Peter.' The words caught in her throat. 'My poor Peter.' She reached down gingerly and picked them up, popped them into the pocket of her dressing gown. Maybe they could sew them back on. She smiled, patting her pocket. She'd surprise him with them when he got home. He would come home, she knew he would. All she had to do was wait. She set about tidying his room, happy to be doing something for him again. It had been a long time since he had allowed her into his room, but this time she felt sure he wouldn't mind. She was his mother after all, and he had to come home to her because he was hurt. Then everything would be all right.

She was startled by loud knocking on the door. That might be him now...

'Peter?' The smile died on her face as the door swung open. 'Oh.' There was a policeman at the door.

'Mrs Ellis, we're searching for your son. Have you seen him today?' Errol Matthews had been assigned to the case at this late stage to do the 'mopping up', as Arthur Bryant had called it. He didn't share Bryant's confidence, didn't believe they had heard the last of Peter Ellis. Not yet.

'Go away.' June Ellis turned and tried to close the door, but Matthews insinuated his bulk between it and the frame.

'Mrs Ellis, do you realise that your son is wanted in relation to some very serious offences? It would be in your best interests to co-operate fully with the police.'

'It's your fault,' she snarled, whirling around to face him, her face a mask of fury. 'It's all your fault!'

Matthews stepped back, taken off guard by the sudden transformation.

'You leave my boy alone, you hear me? He's been hurt, he needs his mother. Just you leave him alone, do you hear me?' Spittle flew from her lips, striking him in the face.

'Mrs Ellis,' he said sternly. 'Is your son at home? Did he return here last night?'

'No' she snapped. 'You know that quite well, don't you? You know my boy isn't here because you've hurt him. Haven't you? Haven't you hurt my boy, my poor Peter?' She started to sob. 'Why can't you leave him alone?'

'Ma'am, I understand you're upset.' Matthews tried to placate her. 'I know this is a very trying time, but it's imperative that we find your son as quickly as possible.'

'Imperative?' She hissed at him. 'Imperative? So you can shoot him again? So you can hurt him some more? Take me!' She screamed. 'Take me, I'm the one you really want! He doesn't have to pay!' She ripped at the front of her dressing gown, tore the buttons of her nightdress open and bared her sunken white chest. 'Take me now!' she screamed, striking herself in the chest. 'Shoot me!'

Matthews didn't know what to do. The old lady was as crazy as her son.

'Ma'am…' He held up a cautionary hand, backing away from her.

'Shoot me!' she screamed, advancing toward him, her face red and streaked with tears. 'Shoot me, I'm ready now. You don't have to take my boy! Please,' she sobbed. 'Take me now!'

'We don't want you, I don't want to shoot you.' Matthews was out of his element here, had no idea how to deal with the ranting madwoman.

'Liar!' she screamed. 'You liar! You think you can fool me, after all these years? I know, I've hidden, I thought you'd leave me alone, but I can see I was wrong. Don't get at me through my boy, don't take him away. Shoot *me*!'

Matthews had backed off the verandah and into the front yard, but June Ellis followed, her flaccid breasts bared to the bright sunshine. Neighbours had come out into the street at the sounds of commotion and he looked around him, embarrassed. What the hell was he supposed to do now, with this ranting madwoman? He had a lot to do this morning, his mind was filled with the burden of finding Peter Ellis. But one thing was for certain; this woman wasn't going to be of any assistance whatsoever.

'Listen, lady, I have no idea what you are going on about…' He raised his hands in a placating gesture.

'Shoot me!' June Ellis was way beyond reason. 'Shoot me!' She pulled her dressing gown right off, her light cotton nightdress concealing very little as she thrust herself towards him.

Matthews felt helpless, didn't know what to do. He turned and ran to his car, left June Ellis on her lawn screaming after him as he scrambled in. The engine roared to life and he hotfooted it the hell out of there.

'Get someone around to 17 Nobby Parade, Miami,' he barked into the radio. 'It's Peter Ellis's mother, she's out of control and out on the streets. Definitely needs to be sedated and confined if we're going to get anything out of her.'

'Affirmative,' the voice on the other end crackled. The radio operator frowned. Bryant had told him finding Ellis was a priority and every spare unit was out combing the bushland looking for him. June Ellis would just have to wait.

Mervyn Breene was perched at the cocktail bar of Grumpy's restaurant on the wharf at the Southport Spit, oblivious to the view from the window where a flotilla of pleasure craft bobbed on the swell. His eyes were firmly fixed on Sylvia, greedily drinking in her beauty.

'So.' He raised his glass in salute. 'Here's to you.'

Sylvia smiled into his eyes.

'Let's see if we can't make a real holiday out of the next week,' she said, sipping at her drink.

'Amen.' Breene drained his glass and called for another.

'What about food?' Sylvia raised an eyebrow. 'If we don't get something in our stomachs soon, I won't want to eat.'

'Well, we can't have that now, can we? I don't want you getting drunk and making a fool of yourself.'

'I'm sure I'd be under the supervision of an expert if it came to that.' They both laughed.

'I'll take that as a challenge,' Breene said seriously. He pushed his glass away only half finished. 'Waiter, give me a mineral water, please.'

'Well!' Sylvia raised an eyebrow.

'I'll have to look after you,' Breene grinned. 'Besides, I don't need that shit to make me feel better today. I couldn't feel any better.' He ignored the small knot of anxiety that gnawed at his gut, put it down as a hangover from the past few days. He didn't have a care in the world.

'Let's eat.' He got up from the bar, offered Sylvia his hand and helped her down from her chair. He brushed her cheek with a kiss and put his arm around her protectively as he led her to a table by the window. 'Madame.' He swept the chair out gallantly, helped her to sit down.

'What's this, a new man?'

'Maybe,' Breene smiled. 'For the time being at least.'

'I'll make the most of it while it lasts,' Sylvia laughed. 'But don't send the real Merv too far away.'

'Don't worry, I'm right here,' Breene winked. His nose reminded him that he'd had surgery only the night before and he slid carefully into his own chair. The small knot tightened, but he swallowed it with his mineral water and picked up the menu.

'Lobster looks good.'

'Hm,' Sylvia murmured, her eyes never leaving his face. 'So do you.'

Breene flushed under her gaze, felt the quickening current between them as her foot brushed his leg.

'Let's order,' he growled softly. 'I don't want to be here all day. I've got other things in mind.'

'Me, too.' They both laughed and looked up guiltily as the waiter approached. Breene couldn't quite still the thumping of his heart. He felt like a school kid again, and it felt damned good.

June Ellis lay sobbing on her bed, her anger dissipating into a nauseating wave of despair. What had she ever done, why wouldn't they leave her alone? After all these years, all she'd been forced to endure, the fear, the doubt, the constant worry of prying eyes and disapproving glares. She'd made mistakes, initially, before she'd learned not to ignore the cautioning voice that was always with her.

Until yesterday, that was. Her need had been intense, her fears for her son overriding her caution. And this was the price she paid. Her poor Peter. The tears built up again. He'd had to pay for her sins, fallen into the abyss she'd always known lurked in wait for her. This was her punishment.

Her head jerked up at the sound of the back door banging shut. Peter? Despair fled as she peeled herself off the bed, hope rising in her chest.

'Peter?' she called, hurrying out into the dining room, wanting only to see his face. Noises came from the closed bedroom door. 'Peter, is that you?'

'Yes mother, it is me.' She froze in her tracks. That didn't sound like Peter, not her Peter. The cautioning voice hissed in her ears, sent a chill into her heart. She backed away from the door, stricken by an unnamed fear.

The door was jerked open from the inside and he was revealed to her. Her son. Fear erupted in her vitals. She recognised that face, recognised the lines, but not the fire that burned in his eyes. Her gaze took in the bloody crease in the skin at his temple, dropped briefly to the maimed and bloodied arm that hung by his side but was drawn back to his eyes.

'Peter,' she quailed. 'What have they done to you?'

Laughter erupted in his chest, the sound of it crashing in on her like the pounding of the surf. Her heart was stricken in her chest, she felt as if she couldn't breathe.

'It matters not, mother.' He spat the name at her. 'It matters not what they have done to me. It matters not what you have done to me. Vengeance is mine!' He swept his good hand from behind his back, revealed the knife that glittered within his grasp and smiled.

'I've got something for you, mother.'

June Ellis backed away from her son, her tongue stuck fast to the roof of her mouth in her terror. Her eyes searched for her little boy, sought him in the black pits of his eyes and found nothing. She sobbed as she sank to her knees and knew at last that the price she would have to pay was beyond what she had to give. She had lost her only son.

She tasted the bitter depths of her despair, but she wasn't allowed to wallow there. Her boy had mastered at least one skill with exacting precision and her moment of agony was mercifully short. He owed her that much.

When he had finished, Peter Ellis went and had a hot shower and washed away as much of the blood as he could. He went to his bedroom, carefully stepping over the mess in the living room. He wrinkled his nose in disgust. The house stank of her. He dressed carefully in the complete silence, mildly surprised at the vacuum inside his head. He went to the kitchen, boiled the kettle and made himself a cup of tea, settling down to read the morning paper.

The front-page article caught his interest, his smile growing as he read the story. Mervyn Breene. He felt grateful for the guiding hand that dictated his actions. At least that had not failed him.

He finished his cup of tea, took the cup out to the sink and carefully folded the paper. He glanced at the bloody stubs of his fingers with minor irritation and went to get a bandage which he carefully wrapped around them. That was better.

Now he was ready to fulfil the final act. Then his role would be completed. He walked calmly from the house and out into the street, found his motorbike where he had left it so he could surprise his mother. A smile flickered on his lips. He *had* surprised her.

Now it was Mervyn Breene's turn.

CHAPTER 23

It was already much too late for June Ellis by the time Steve Pierce and Michael Quinn arrived at the Ellis household. Quinn re-emerged from the dining area and shook his head.

'Don't go in there, Steve, she's already dead.'

It had been a hell of a week for the two young cops.

'What'll we do now?' Pierce said wearily, his appetite for action well and truly sated.

'I guess we should let Matthews know what's happened.'

'Yeah.'

Mervyn Breene was in no particular hurry to get back to the holiday unit. He and Sylvia enjoyed their seafood lunch, both acutely aware of the sexual tension that built all through the meal. They had tarried over dessert, relishing the sparks that flew between them, feeling the electricity of each tiny gesture, the quickening with each brush of the other's hand.

When they finally left the restaurant and climbed

into the VW each of them was looking forward to the long afternoon together, entwined in a slow lovemaking in their eyrie above the sights and sounds of the Gold Coast. Breene had managed to extinguish his anxiety, for the present at least. Surely the cops could manage to bring Ellis in now. They weren't all as useless as the unfortunate Sergeant Hughes. They couldn't be.

'What's wrong?' Sylvia's hand sought his own across the throbbing vibration of the VW.

'Nothing,' Breene lied.

'Oh, come on, Merv, don't close up on me now.'

'It's just — it's probably nothing.' He looked helplessly at her. 'I can't shake this worry that he's still out there, that he hasn't given up. I guess I won't be happy until I know he's in custody.'

'Or dead,' Sylvia said quietly.

'You too?'

'He almost killed you, Merv. I can't forget that. I'd like to know he was out of the way, where he can't hurt anyone else.'

'Me, too,' Breene sighed.

'You want me to keep driving?' she asked, squeezing his hand. 'We could go along the coast a bit, find a secluded spot?'

'No way,' Breene smiled. 'No sand, not today. We've got the rest of the week for that. I was thinking more along the lines of four-star luxury — a spa bath with bubbles, maybe some champagne, and the entire afternoon to enjoy it.'

'You've got me.' Sylvia chuckled deep in her throat. Breene's pulse quickened.

'I know.'

Sergeant Errol Matthews was more than worried when he heard the news from Pierce and Quinn.

'All right, boys, it's obvious this is far from over yet. Recall all the men from the Currumbin Valley site. Ellis has obviously made it out, and he's armed himself again. Jesus.' He shook his head. Why him, and why now? He was in the unenviable position of having to bottle up an increasingly disturbed serial killer without the benefit of any knowledge of the man. Fuck Warren Hughes. Dead or alive, the man was still a problem. He had to know at least something about the nut, had to gain some inside information on the bastard.

And the only man who really seemed to know what was going on was Mervyn Breene.

'F-f-flowers for M-m-mister Mervyn B-breene.'

The sister looked up from her desk at the pale face of the delivery boy, wisps of black hair escaping from the baseball-style cap that covered his head.

'I'm sorry, Mr Breene was discharged this morning.'

'Oh,' he face fell. 'I was sup...I was sup-supposed to g-g-get these h-h-here this m-morning, b-b-but my bike b-broke down. The b-boss said he'd s-s-sack me if I d-d-didn't get th-th-this right.'

The sister couldn't help feeling sorry for him. He looked so upset, standing there like a little lost boy.

'Listen, I'm not supposed to do this.' She hesitated, frowning as she considered her decision. 'Oh, what the hell, it can't do any harm.' She leaned forward. 'I'll give you his address. I don't want to see you lose your job,' she winked.

Peter Ellis smiled broadly.

'Thank you.'

The sister frowned as she watched him stride back up the corridor, troubled by a vague uneasiness she couldn't place. She shrugged and put it out of her mind. She had a lot of work to do.

Sylvia felt Mervyn Breene's hand tighten on hers before she noticed the two uniformed cops walking towards them as they entered the stark foyer of his unit block.

'Merv?' Breene stared grimly ahead, his jaw clenched. What the hell did they want now?'

'Mr Breene? Uh, I mean, sir...'

'Yes?' His tone was edged in steel.

'Sir, Sergeant Matthews was wondering if he could have a word with you? About Peter Ellis?'

'What about him?'

'He's on the loose, sir.'

Breene stiffened.

'Have you posted guards around Amanda Warner? You'll have to make sure she's safe.'

'I'm not sure, sir.'

'Well do it. Now. Can you call in?'

'I can do it from the car, sir.'

'Well, do it. This guy is insane. He believes he's some kind of saviour and he thinks Amanda Warner is his queen. The first thing he's going to do is try to get back to her.'

'Yes sir' Pierce ran out of the foyer to his patrol car.

'Now then, what's this all about?' Breene turned to the other constable.

'Sir, Sergeant Matthews is in charge of the case now.'

'Matthews? I thought Bryant was taking over?'

'Yes, sir. Well, I guess he thought it would just take a cleaning-up operation this morning. Ellis was wounded, and all available units were in the area searching for him.'

'But he got away,' Breene scowled.

'Yes, sir.'

Breene looked the young constable up and down, his mind in turmoil. Ellis was still in the game, still dangerous and armed. His only possible target was Amanda Warner, Breene knew it. And he was crazy enough to get to her, no matter what protective measures the police might take. Christ, he was going to have to go in again, get back inside the world that Peter Ellis created. Real or not, it was a world he and Amanda Warner had entered.

'What's your name, constable?'

'Quinn sir. Michael Quinn.'

'And what do you think about this Ellis?'

Quinn's boyish face turned hard.

'Sir, my partner and me, we were the first on the scene when Amanda Warner was kidnapped. We saw what he did to that young guy.' He shook his head, still struggling to come to terms with what he'd seen. 'I want to see Peter Ellis put away for a long time, sir. Out of action. I don't particularly care how.'

Breene nodded.

Pierce strode briskly back through the door.

'Sir, I've spoken to Sergeant Matthews and he's agreed to post a twenty-four-hour guard on Amanda Warner, sir. He also asked me to tell you he'd be glad to follow any other suggestions you might have, and that he'd like you to come down to the station. He wanted me to ask you for your help, sir.'

Breene knew he was caught, knew he couldn't walk away now with the fight only half-won. They might be ahead on points, but Ellis had a hell of a knockout punch.

'Sylvia.' He held her briefly, kissed her on the forehead. She froze in his arms. 'Listen.' He leant down and spoke softly to her. 'You know I have to go. I know the man, I know what he's like. I have to help them, I have to know he's out of the way.'

'I know,' she whispered. 'Be careful.'

'I will,' Breene promised. 'I'll be back before you know it. How about if you go upstairs and wait for me? We've got some very important unfinished business to take care of ourselves.'

'Sure.' She managed a faint smile. 'But don't take too long.'

'Okay, men, let's go.' The two young cops followed Breene from the foyer. Sylvia watched them go and shook her head. She knew she'd never have him, not completely.

Celia Thompson woke late in the afternoon and felt better than she had all day. She'd barely even glanced at the morning's paper, envy flickering only briefly. She'd had more than enough of the story, had not

STALKER

liked it when she herself had stepped within its boundaries.

She walked out to the kitchen of her small unit and brewed up a strong coffee, nibbling on a biscuit while she waited for it to cool. So they'd managed to save Amanda Warner. She had never really thought they would do it, but then she remembered her meeting with Mervyn Breene. Now, there was a man who achieved what he set out to do. Typical for the cops to claim all the credit for themselves. She couldn't help wondering what was the real story behind the headlines.

'Where to?' Breene was in a hurry when he reached the station. He was keen to unload what he knew, purge himself of everything he had learned about Peter Ellis. Maybe then he would feel free to pursue his own life, make his own new beginning.

'This way, sir.' Pierce pointed him past the imposing front desk into a warren-like corridor illuminated dully by fluorescent lights. He could hear the clatter of typewriters punctuated by the curses of ill-trained users, the snatches of conversations, feel the pulse of life that beat inside a police station. He wondered whether he would miss it, whether he was considering giving up the job and the life that went with it. Already the threat that Ellis had posed was receding from his life, decisions made under that pressure not so certain now that he was back on top. Or so it seemed.

Sylvia couldn't rest in the airy unit, couldn't allow

herself to relax. A dull throb of resentment pulsed in the back of her neck, tinged with the anxiety of knowing Breene was a step closer to danger now that he'd allowed himself to be dragged back into the search for Peter Ellis. Was this what life with Mervyn Breene was going to be like? Damn him. She was furious at him for leaving her like that, sending her up to the unit to wait for him like some bimbo waiting for her sugar daddy. What did he have that made him so bloody special, anyway?

She shook her head, didn't allow herself to get involved in guessing what the future would hold. You couldn't predict such things, not when you were talking about Mervyn Breene. She looked at her watch, saw that it was still only twenty past three. Knowing she'd never be able to relax alone in his unit, Sylvia decided to go home and get some work done. She'd have to tidy up a few loose ends if she and Breene were to spend the next week together, anyway.

She hastily scribbled Breene a note, leaving him her address. Things might work out a whole lot better if they started off from her place this time, on her own territory. And it would do him good to realise that she wasn't going to wait around at his beck and call.

She slipped out the door but left it unlocked, not sure whether Breene would have a spare key.

Peter Ellis waited patiently in the foyer, his bunch of flowers concealing much of his face. He watched casually as the elevator light indicated the descent of the elevator, his expression calm. He had been possessed by an incredible sense of calm since the removal of his mother. Maybe she had represented his weakness, held him back to this world as tangible evidence of his humanness. He was surprised he hadn't realised it before. He should have removed her long ago.

Sylvia was about to leave the lift car when a young man delivering flowers leapt inside, knocking into her. For a moment their eyes met and she clutched her hand to her throat protectively, threatened by what she saw.

'S-s-sorry, m-m-ma'am'. The doors started to slide closed, but his bandaged hand darted to the control panel, stabbing the 'open doors' button.

'Thank you' Sylvia murmured, stepping quickly from the lift. She could feel his eyes on her back until the doors slid closed behind her.

'Sir, this is Sergeant Matthews.'

'Matthews,' Breene nodded, noting that Matthews was a uniformed cop, not a member of the CIB. Errol Matthews realised Breene was looking at his uniform.

'Breene, I just want to explain that Bryant put me in charge of this thing this morning when it looked as if finding Ellis was only going to be a matter of flushing him out of the bushes. The Inspector went away after that, and things have been in an uproar since the discovery of Ellis's mother. We've barely had the time to organise ourselves, so in the meantime I'm still in charge. I thought you'd be the best man to talk to about catching this Ellis, give us something to go on, something I can hand on to whoever they get to run this investigation now that things have got hot again. I'm dead keen to see this animal brought to justice, sir.'

'Okay, Matthews, I'll tell you what I know. I think the greatest fear you have to concentrate on is surrounding Amanda Warner.' Matthews listened while Breene recounted his experiences with Ellis culminating in the dramatic rescue in which Pierce and Quinn had participated.

'And that's as much as I know.'

The silence in the room was broken by the appearance of Inspector Arthur Bryant in the doorway, dressed in old jeans and a grease-stained shirt. His terry-towelling fishing hat was still perched on top of his head.

'Matthews, I'll take over now.' He marched briskly into the room. 'I've just heard what has occurred since I left — it would seem that my departure was somewhat precipitate.' He turned to face Breene, his expression hard. 'Well, Breene, it looks as if you were right. I'm glad you've decided to help us out this time.'

Breene didn't comment.

'Sir,' a young, fresh-faced constable interrupted. 'There's a phone call.'

'I'm not to be disturbed,' Bryant snapped.

'Sir, it's not for you. It's for Mr Breene. Says his name's Peter Ellis.'

The men in the room froze, their eyes turning to Breene.

Celia Thompson couldn't get Breene on the phone, but he'd given her the address to his unit a couple of days earlier. It was only a short drive from where she lived and she decided she might as well go around and see if she could catch him. The least she could do was leave a note, and who knew. She might get lucky and bump into him. Her interest wasn't wholly in the story he might be able to tell her, either.

She was puffed out by the brisk walk from her car as she entered the foyer and called out as the elevator doors started to slide closed on an elderly couple. The man looked up at her and reached to halt the door's progress, his wife glaring haughtily at Celia. Old bat. Celia smiled her thanks to the man, rolled her eyes when he winked at her. She got off on the twelfth floor, found Breene's door and knocked, waited expectantly for him to open it. Maybe she should have worn her emerald-green top.

She waited impatiently, realised to her disappointment that he wasn't there. Oh well, she'd catch up with him. She reached into her handbag for a notepad and biro, leant against the door while she scribbled her number and 'call me' on the piece of paper. The door rattled against her. Maybe? She tried the doorknob, smiled when it turned in her hand. Nobody left their door open these days, not unless they were supremely confident or extremely stupid. Mervyn Breene hadn't struck her as being stupid.

She stepped quietly into the unit.

'Hello? Anybody here?' She looked cautiously around, remembered the last time she'd gone snooping uninvited and shrugged it off. Ellis must be miles away by now, if the police hadn't already cornered him. Maybe Breene had ducked out to the shop for something and would return shortly. Why not just wait, give him a surprise? She shivered in excitement, closed the door quietly behind her. She'd surprise him all right. She tiptoed across to the lounge, excited by the feeling that there were eyes trained on her, imagined them as Breene's eyes. She quickly took her clothes off and dropped them in a pile behind the lounge before settling herself, clad only in black underwear, onto the long couch.

She caught the movement out of the corner of her eye, managed to sit up and cover her chest with her arms before he was onto her, a long knife flashing in his hand.

Ellis had waited inside, waiting for the return of Mervyn Breene, hating the man who had ripped his destiny from him, had taken everything that he was meant to be. He'd hidden at the first sounds outside, waited nervously when he heard the woman's voice. Who was she? He dared not look, did not wish to expose himself and ruin his chances of taking Breene. Finally, he heard the springs of the lounge creak, knew that he would be concealed from the woman's line of vision.

He padded quickly across the deep pile carpet and was onto her before she'd had a chance to defend herself, had his knife raised before he realised that it was her. The reporter. Celia Thompson. Momentary confusion halted his hand, his mind struggling to comprehend the significance of her being here. They must be in it together. The realisation staggered him. She and Breene were in it together. He had underestimated his enemies from the first, had not realised that he had been at their mercy from the very start. He was crushed by his own folly, his own audacity in believing that he could claim his prize virtually unopposed. Everything else, all the obstacles they had thrown in his way, had been for their amusement alone. They had known his thoughts from the first, had been inside his head from the moment he had tipped off Celia Thompson. Maybe even before.

He had been the instrument of his own downfall.

Tasting the bitter ashes of his defeat afresh, Peter Ellis looked into the terrified eyes of Celia Thompson and laughed. They hadn't counted on this, hadn't counted on his resolve. She was frightened without her protector.

Celia Thompson watched Ellis's eyes grow flat and hard.

'S-s-so, y-y-you p-played me all the w-w-way.' He pulled away from the woman, held his knife between them to ward her off. He must not underestimate her, not any more.

'I don't know what you're talking about,' she gasped. 'Please, I...what do you want?

Ellis laughed.

'W-w-w-want? Wh-what do I w-w-want? Ah, b-b-but you toy with m-me, even n-n-now! You k-know only too w-w-well what it was th-that I desired. That which was r-rightf-f-fully mine!' His eyes bored into hers and he felt the thrill of realisation. She was in his power now.

'Please.' She started to sob, couldn't keep her head together. She fully realised that she was in the clutches of Peter Ellis, that somehow she had plunged herself back into the story.

Ellis laid the blade of the knife against the pale skin of her neck and laughed as he traced it down between her breasts, watching in fascination as a thin red line appeared like magic, quickly growing into an oozing red weal.

Celia Thompson was too terrified to scream as the knife sliced poker-hot into her skin. She couldn't tear her eyes away from his, couldn't comprehend the malice that lurked there as the knife sliced again and again until she felt as if she was on fire. She didn't want to die, was too young to die. She hadn't even started to live, not yet. She felt herself sinking, the distance between them growing larger, his face blurring and losing focus. God, she didn't want to die.

'M-mister B-b-breene, this is P-p-peter Ellis. I kn-know where y-y-you are, b-because I s-saw you with the p-p-police. G-g-guess where I am n-now?'

Breene felt the chill premoniton of fear deep in his vitals. Sylvia. Jesus, he hadn't even considered the possibility.

'Ellis, what the fuck are you doing? What have you done to Sylvia?' he shouted into the phone. The sound of Ellis' laughter made his veins run with ice.

'She's d-d-decided to w-w-wear red f-for w-when you r-r-return.' He gazed across the room at the slumped form of Celia Thompson, her groans indicating that consciousness was returning. Good.

He wanted to play a bit longer, wanted to make her realise that she hadn't won at all, that her victory had been her downfall, just as his false victories had been his downfall.

'If you've hurt one hair of her head I'll rip you apart, you freaky bastard, you sick little creep.'

'Y-y-you'd better, h-h-hurry, Merv, s-s-she can't w-wear this c-c-colour red forever. It's a once-in-a-l-l-lifetime g-gift,' he giggled, revelling in the fear in Breene's voice. 'H-h-how does it f-f-feel to h-h-have the one you l-l-love ripped away from you?' His eyes dropped to the sheet of paper on the bench beside the phone and scanned the message as he listened to Breene splutter. Silly man. He should have known…*Sylvia*? *Love, Sylvia*? He glanced quickly at the slumped body of Celia Thompson. What new trick? He replaced the receiver and ran from the apartment, furious at his latest folly, at the cunning of his adversary. Truly, his nemesis was a worthy opponent, but Peter Ellis was equal to the challenge, would rise above him at the last. Good would always triumph over evil.

Breene slammed the phone into the cradle and ran out of the small office, the police in the room staring after him open-mouthed.

Matthews was the first to react.

'Go with him, for Christ's sake!' he ordered. Pierce and Quinn raced after Breene.

'Come on, come on!' Breene was in a state of panic, not prepared even to speculate on what he might find in the unit once the elevator finally made it to the twelfth floor. The ride seemed to take forever. Pierce and Quinn stood quietly in the rear of the car watching Breene's agony helplessly. They already knew how Ellis operated, knew that anything they might say could only inflame Breene further. He'd see for himself soon enough.

Sylvia rushed to answer the knock at the door, thinking Breene had been able to fast talk his way out of the situation at the police station.

'F-f-flowers for Mervyn Breene.' The delivery boy pushed them at her.

'Oh. Thank you.' She accepted them. 'How did you…' Her scream of terror caught in her throat as Peter Ellis stepped towards her, a wicked-looking knife appearing magically in his hand.

'What do you want?' Her voice was no more than a whisper, strangled with fear. 'Why are you here?'

Peter Ellis smiled, absently ran his thumb down the sharp blade and watched the slow trickle of blood that formed.

'I want M-m-mervyn Br-breene.'

'He…he's not here.' Sylvia backed away from him, eyes wide and searching for some escape and knowing there was none.

'Oh?' Ellis said casually. 'I thought he w-would be. Then ag-again, he w-w-wasn't expecting y-y-you to be h-h-here either, was he?'

'Wh…what do you mean?'

'Y-your note, b-b-back at his u-u-unit.'

Sylvia's mind was racing, searching frantically for some ray of hope, some chance for salvation, but she found no welcoming respite from the terror that towered above her head like a wave waiting to break and crush her under its weight.

'I th-th-think I'll w-wait. You s-s-see, it's very important that I see him.' He smiled. It wasn't a comforting sight for Sylvia.

'Listen,' she gulped, her eyes straying back to the knife in his hand. 'I was just about to go out for a few minutes. You see, I've run out of milk and I wanted a cup of coffee. Would you like to wait here while I'm out? I won't mind.'

'N-no.' He shook his head sadly. 'No, I don't think so.' His unfocused gaze came to rest on her face. Such a pretty face, really. What a shame. 'You w-won't have t-t-time for a coffee.'

'I can have it black,' she blurted nervously, her hand fluttering up to her mouth. She realised she was shaking uncontrollably and quickly folded her arms. 'Wouldn't you like to have one too, while you wait, I mean?'

'No. You see, I've k-k-k-killed my m-m-m-mother.'

Sylvia stifled the gasp that caught in her throat.

'Oh,' she nodded, trying desperately to keep her fear under control, to react normally to him. 'I understand.'

'You d-d-do?' Ellis's eyes snapped into focus, registered Sylvia's face for the first time. Maybe? The storm erupted, crashed in on him with staggering force. They were back, the cruel voices in his head had returned to stab him with their lances of uncertainty. Laughter reverberated in his head, the force of their taunts doubled because he'd believed himself finally free of them.

'*No!*' he shrieked in protest. 'N-n-nooo …' His voice trailed off into a moan of pain. 'I am of no f-f-further use. I am d-d-defeated. Leave me!' He tore at his hair, twisting his head wildly from side to side as if he could shake off the strangling grip of the voices that raged within. 'No,' he sobbed. 'M-m-m-must you haunt me to the last?'

Sylvia watched Ellis wage his internal battle in horrified fascination. She knew she couldn't run, couldn't risk making herself a target for him. Somehow she would have to win his trust, delay the moment of attack. The question was how — how the hell was she supposed to deal with a homicidal maniac? She quailed at the thought that he'd killed his own mother. What chance did she have?

'Peter.'

The voice. Her voice! His head turned in Sylvia's direction.

'Peter,' she said soothingly.

His mouth dropped open in wonder. The crashing in his head ceased and he trembled. It was her voice. And it was coming from this woman's mouth.

'Is it y-y-y-you?' Noises erupted again. The eye of the cyclone had passed. He dropped to his knees, hissing in pain.

'Help me,' he pleaded. 'H-h-help me.'

Sylvia took a tentative step towards him, shuddered at the sight of the knife still firmly in his grasp.

What choice did she have?

Breene burst through the door to the unit, Pierce and Quinn only a pace behind him.

'Sylvia!'

He heard the strangled moan and his heart leaped with unexpected hope. He ran towards the sound and saw the blood-spattered lounge, the slumped body covered in gaping bloody wounds and he sobbed, ran to pick her up, to comfort her.

'Get an ambulance,' he shouted over his shoulder. Even the seconds could be precious. He realised it wasn't Sylvia and his heart lurched with new fear. Where was she? He dropped to his knees beside the inert body of Celia Thompson, scooped her head up in his hands.

'Celia?' He shook her gently, belying the fear that rose to consume him. 'Celia!'

She opened her eyes slowly, her energy draining away from her body with the blood that flowed from her wounds.

'Celia, where is she? Where's Sylvia?' He could barely restrain himself from shouting at her. God, where was she? Celia Thompson's eyes were blank, didn't register the name.

'Celia, you have to help me out here. Where's Sylvia?'

'Sir,' Pierce called out from the phone. 'There's a piece of paper here with a message from a Sylvia. It says she's gone home, gives her address.'

'Jesus Christ!' Fear stabbed him afresh. 'Ellis must have seen it while he was talking to me. Come on!' He charged from the unit, leaving Pierce and Quinn confused in his wake.

'Quinny, you'll have to stay here with her until the ambulance arrives,' Pierce decided. 'I'll go with Breene.'

Sylvia cowered in the corner as Peter Ellis stode up and down the room, his mouth working agitatedly. His mood was swinging wildly from whimpering pathetically to raging anger, shouting back at unseen voices. He kept the knife, clutched it firmly in his hand, caressed it, lunged at her, dangled it loosely by his side. She was almost at her wits' end, didn't know how much longer she could keep him away from her. Her eyes darted furtively towards the door, only metres from where she crouched trying to make herself as small as possible. It might as well have been a hundred miles away. She knew that if she moved he would be on her, watched in her mind as he lunged at her from behind with the knife poised. But she had to do something, couldn't just wait for him to finally turn on her without some sort of fight. She didn't want to die.

'I am bereft,' Peter Ellis sobbed, his voice sounding as if it had been torn from his throat. 'Stripped, robbed, raped and plundered. Burn, burn, burn — I'm going to burn now, spiral downwards to the pit, queens and princes, shattered thrones and all is black.'

Sylvia stifled the sobs that welled in her throat, tried to overcome the fear that numbed her mind, paralysed her limbs. Ellis was getting worse, beyond the reach of any words she might have to offer. Her voice seemed to inflame him now, start him ranting and shouting about queens torn asunder and burning flames. Surely Breene must reach her soon, surely somebody had overheard the insane ranting coming from the room.

But she knew she couldn't rely on anyone else, couldn't wait for salvation. She would have to take matters into her own hands, to make a last desperate bid for life. She refused to go down without a struggle.

Her eyes travelled to the knife in Ellis's hand. Jesus, if only it wasn't a knife. She had always had a terror of knives, could imagine the searing pain as the cold steel sunk into her flesh, the cold terror of a slow and painful death as the knife plunged again and again.

Ellis turned his back on her, confronting some new voice, slashing at the air with vicious sweeps of his weapon.

'And yet all is in vain!' he shouted. 'And I stand already defeated.' His shoulders slumped and his body went limp, the knife dangling loosely by his side.

This was her chance. She had to act now or never. She held back for an instant, clenched her eyes shut and shook with terror at the thought of what she had to do. She had no choice.

Sylvia sprang up from the corner where she cowered and lunged at the stooped form of Peter Ellis, her hand reaching for his knife hand as she cannoned her shoulder into his back. Ellis reacted swiftly, clutched tightly to his knife as he stumbled forward, slipped on the tiles of the kitchen floor and lost balance, seemed certain to fall.

Somehow, miraculously, he managed to stay on his feet, screamed in anger as he swept around and caught Sylvia with a backhanded swipe that sent her sprawling into the cupboards with a heavy thud. She struggled to get up but he was onto her in a flash, startling in his speed.

'You!' He howled in fury. 'And now even you betray me!' He dragged her to her feet and shook her, his face only inches from hers. 'Bereft at the very end!' He pushed her hard up against the wall, raised his knife hand menacingly above her head.

'No,' Sylvia pleaded. 'No, please, not this way.'

Ellis' eyes snapped into focus and she felt the trembling in the arm that held her. Slowly, he loosened his grip, let her slide from his grasp and down onto the floor. He stood above her, panting and bewildered.

'But I do not understand.'

The door burst open behind him and Breene charged into the unit. He had left Steve Pierce far behind calling for backup while he charged up the four flights of stairs to Sylvia's unit, his fear for her far outstripping his body's protests. His panicked glance took in the scene before him, he saw Sylvia slumped on the floor with Ellis above her and he bellowed his anger, roared in pain like a wounded animal. Ellis turned to greet him, his knife hand poised in recognition of his nemesis as Breene hurtled into him. The knife stroke went wide as Breene crushed the wind from his lungs and sent him sprawling onto the floor. Ellis felt the renewed flame of his defeat burning bright inside him, knew this was his last chance to redeem himself, to defeat his nemesis and neutralise the damage his failure would cause. Leaping to his feet he slashed the knife in front of him as Breene made another charge and forced him to swerve to avoid the bitter point of the blade. He swept around in a graceful curve to follow his line of flight and stabbed downwards with his knife. Breene cursed in agony as the sharp blade sliced down his arm, blood erupting immediately from the wound. Working on instinct alone, intent on survival, he ignored the pain and turned the blade aside with his own flesh, jabbing out with his other fist and catching Ellis with a heavy blow to his exposed stomach. He fired off another punch, put all of his desperate strength into the blow and caught Ellis across the right cheek. There was a splintering crack of bone.

Ellis screamed in pain and anger.

'I will not be denied!'

He angled a savage kick at Breene's groin but Breene pulled back, absorbing the full force with his stomach. He doubled over, winded, knew he couldn't afford the time. He threw himself over onto his right shoulder, narrowly avoiding the vicious sweep of Ellis's blade as he hit the floor and rolled, coming up hard against the coffee table that crashed and splintered under his weight. Ellis bore down on him, his bloodied face grim with murderous intent, his entire existence focused on eradicating the force that had robbed him of his heritage. Breene kicked out, sweeping his leg around and catching Ellis below the knee, knocking him off balance. Breene seized his advantage, striking upwards with his left arm at the hand clutching the knife. It spun loose from Ellis's grasp, flew in a slow arc and landed with a thud by the open balcony door. Ellis scrambled after it but Breene lunged for his ankle, brought him crashing down to the floor and tried to climb over the top of him, get to the knife before Ellis recovered.

Ellis was too quick, his insanity driving his body beyond the limits that hampered Breene, who was older, restricted by pain and his unhealed wounds from their previous encounter. Peter Ellis had no such restrictions, his mind driving the vehicle that was his body with reckless force, heedless of its limitations. He grasped the knife inches in front of Breene's outstretched hand and flicked back with his elbow, catching Breene on the bridge of the nose. Stars erupted in Breene's head. He felt as if he'd been hit with a sledgehammer as the neat row of sutures burst asunder and blood cascaded brightly down his face. Dazed, he was unable to counter the downward thrust of the knife as Ellis buried it deep in his left shoulder. Howling in agony, Breene lashed out with his right arm and caught Ellis above the ear. The knife pulled out as Ellis was thrown backward, but the blow did not erase the fierce smile on his face. He had his quarry now. Could feel him weakening.

Breene lunged at him, his fists gouging at Ellis's face, fury mingled with hatred.

'Merv!' He turned at the sound of Sylvia's voice, his heart wrenching in his chest. Ellis smashed him savagely across the neck, sent him thudding heavily onto the hard tiles of the patio.

'*No!*' Breene roared, lashing out but contacting only with air as Ellis pulled his head out of reach.

He kicked Breene hard between the legs, battered his head with his maimed left hand while holding the right poised for the master stroke. The power was his. He took Breene by the hair, crushed him against the iron railings that separated him from the gaping fall that beckoned below and smiled, blood dripping from between his teeth.

'Now taste death,' he spat, drawing back his hand for the final thrust.

A blur of movement in the corner of his eye distracted him at the last moment, snapped his head up in surprise. It was all Mervyn Breene had been waiting for, his last chance for survival. He heaved upwards, felt the tearing heat of pain in his stomach as he wrenched both his legs up, caught the already poised Ellis neatly between the legs and lifted him pitching forward to the low railing, his momentum carrying him over the top. For an instant one maimed hand scrabbled to grasp onto the painted metal and their eyes locked. Ellis smiled briefly and then he was gone, plummeting four storeys to the ground below.

Breene collapsed against the cold metal as Steve Pierce raced to the railing and looked down, saw the limp form of Peter Ellis sprawled awkwardly on the ground below. He wouldn't be going anywhere in a hurry.

'Merv...' Sylvia's sobs filtered down to him through a haze of pain, her face swimming in his vision as she clutched his head to her lap. Breene sighed and managed what he could of a smile before he lapsed into unconsciousness.

EPILOGUE

Breene woke in a sweat, the sun falling across the bed from the tall picture window. He yawned and sat up, dangling his feet over the side of the bed. It looked as if it was going to be another hot summer's day. They had had little relief in the past week from a mini-heat wave, the temperatures consistently above thirty-seven degrees with barely a murmur of breeze even at night.

He got up from the bed and padded over to the window, looked out over the rows of roofs and caught a glimpse of the blue water of the harbour beyond, one of the Opera House sails barely visible. Harbour views. He laughed quietly to himself when he remembered how thrilled Sylvia had been when they purchased the unit. Stretching, he went to the fridge and gulped orange juice straight from the bottle. Sylvia would have scowled at him, but she was already at work. He smiled at the thought of her. Things had never been so good between them.

Funny how a close brush with death could make

you look at your life in an entirely different way. He fingered the purple scar on his abdomen — the doctor told him the scars would fade with time, but he hoped the lesson he'd learned never would.

His thoughts travelled across the distance to Queensland. He wondered how Jack and Pam were getting along, and how Amanda's recovery was progressing. He frowned. She seemed like a nice kid. They shared a bond, he and Mandy, something that couldn't quite be put into words, but it was something special. Breene looked forward to the weekly letters he received from her, though his own stumbling efforts in reply were less than reliable in their timing. Still, he tried, and she didn't seem to mind if more than a couple of weeks elapsed between his own efforts.

Yep, he sighed. Things sure had changed over the past few months, and it had all started with the sudden decision to take a holiday at Surfers Paradise. Some holiday. He bent to fiddle with the air conditioning in the vain hope that it might suddenly decide to kick into life, but gave it up as a bad joke. Bloody air conditioners — he had a bad track record with the machines.

He glanced at the clock on the wall. It was about time he got ready and made his way down to his office, only a couple of blocks' walk from the unit he now shared with Sylvia. He'd kept his promise to leave the force, and Sylvia had compromised and moved back to Sydney with him. Breene had been surprised by the feeling of relief brought by the decision to leave the job after so many years under the protective wing of the force. He had been stagnating, allowing his life to follow a preordained path, dragged along by events. Well, not any more. He was going to live life, to be in control of what happened to him from now on. He'd decided to follow Jack Warner's lead and had applied for a private investigator's license and was starting to pick up a few jobs here and there, enough to chip in his share of the bills. He hoped to branch out in the next few months, but he had time to wait.

The whole experience had changed him more than he cared to admit. He found himself doing things and saying things he would never have allowed to slip out before. He'd even enrolled at university starting with the March semester, much to Sylvia's delight. He didn't know how he'd take to studying after all this time, but he figured it was worth a go.

Psychology. He laughed; never could have imagined himself enrolling in a course in the subject before. He guessed he never really would work out what made people like Peter Ellis tick, but he found himself fascinated just the same. Maybe he'd be able to predict the next time…Jesus. He shook his head, prayed there would never be a next time, not like the Ellis case. He'd grown, sure, but he felt as if it had taken ten years off his life.

And yet he couldn't say things had turned out badly, in fact he was more content with his lot than he could remember being. If only the rites of passage had been a little easier. He shrugged, stared out over the street life that sprawled below him and mused about the directions his life had taken him in. It just didn't pay to become complacent.

Enough of the bullshit. The less he thought about Peter Ellis the better, and the more time that elapsed between the events that had taken place the better he liked it. He still woke sometimes in the grip of a nightmare, though he could never quite place it when he awoke. He knew it had something to do with Ellis.

He frowned at the sound of the door bell. Who the hell was calling on him at this hour, and at home? 'Coming,' he yelled, quickly pulling on a pair of shorts.

'Yes?'

'M–mister B–b–breene?'

Breene froze, clenched his fists at his sides and felt the colour drain from his face.

'I-I-I've g-gota j-job to do.'

'What?' Breene heard his voice echo strangely in his ears, as if from a great distance.

'The a-a-air conditioning?' The guy was looking at him as if he was an idiot.

'Oh yeah, of course.' Breene stepped aside. 'It's right over there.' He pointed to the unit mounted in the wall.

'Are y-y-you all right?' the repair man asked uncertainly.

'Yeah, sure.' Breene ran his hand through his damp hair. 'Just felt a bit crook there for a minute.'

He took a deep breath, would have reached for a cigarette if he still smoked. His nose throbbed as the blood returned to his face and he shook his head.

He guessed some scars would take longer to heal. If they ever did.

'All f-f-fixed, sir,' the repairman declared half an hour later. 'Simple.'

'Great,' Breene smiled, reaching for his wallet. 'Thanks a lot. We need it in this weather.'

He whistled as he stepped out into the heat of the morning, the glare of the footpath bright on his eyes. It was going to be a hot bastard of a day, but what the heck. Breene smiled. It sure beat being dead.

He couldn't help but check the street up and down before he set off towards his office, wary of anything out of the ordinary. Nothing. He set his sunglasses on his face. You could never be too sure. Not any more.